James Anthony Froude

Thomas Carlyle - A History of the First Forty years of his Life-

1795-1835

Vol. I

James Anthony Froude

Thomas Carlyle - A History of the First Forty years of his Life- 1795-1835
Vol. I

ISBN/EAN: 9783337063290

Printed in Europe, USA, Canada, Australia, Japan

Cover: Foto ©Raphael Reischuk / pixelio.de

More available books at **www.hansebooks.com**

THOMAS CARLYLE

A HISTORY OF THE FIRST FORTY
YEARS OF HIS LIFE

1795 1835

BY

JAMES ANTHONY FROUDE, M.A.

FORMERLY FELLOW OF EXETER COLLEGE, OXFORD

IN TWO VOLUMES

VOL. I.

WITH PORTRAITS AND ETCHINGS

NEW EDITION

LONDON

LONGMANS, GREEN, AND CO.

1891

PREFACE.

(*REPRINTED FROM THE FIRST EDITION.*)

—·✿·—

Mr. Carlyle expressed a desire in his will that of him
no biography should be written. I find the same reluctance in his Journal. No one, he said, was likely to
understand a history, the secret of which was unknown
to his closest friends. He hoped that his wishes would
be respected.

Partly to take the place of a biography of himself,
and partly for other reasons, he collected the letters of
his wife—letters which covered the whole period of his
life in London to the date of her death, when his own
active work was finished. He prepared them for publication, adding notes and introductory explanations, as
the last sacred duty which remained to him in the
world. He intended it as a monument to a character
of extreme beauty; while it would tell the public as
much about himself as it could reasonably expect to
learn.

These letters he placed in my hands eleven years ago,
with materials for an Introduction which he was himself unable to complete. He could do no more with it,
he said. He could not make up his mind to direct
positively the publication even of the letters themselves.
He wished them to be published, but he left the decision
to myself; and when I was reluctant to undertake the

sole responsibility, he said that, if I was in doubt when the time came, I might consult his brother John and his friend Mr. Forster.

Had he rested here, my duty would have been clear. The collection of letters, with the Memoir of Mrs. Carlyle which was to form part of the Introduction, would have been considered among us, and would have been either published or suppressed, as we might jointly determine. Mr. Carlyle's remaining papers would have been sealed up after his death, and by me at least no use would have been made of them.

Two years later, however, soon after he had made his will, Carlyle discovered that, whether he wished it or not, a life, or perhaps various lives, of himself would certainly appear when he was gone. When a man has exercised a large influence on the minds of his contemporaries, the world requires to know whether his own actions have corresponded with his teaching, and whether his moral and personal character entitles him to confidence. This is not idle curiosity; it is a legitimate demand. In proportion to a man's greatness is the scrutiny to which his conduct is submitted. Byron, Burns, Scott, Shelley, Rousseau, Voltaire, Goethe, Pope, Swift, are but instances, to which a hundred others might be added, showing that the public will not be satisfied without sifting the history of its men of genius to the last grain of fact which can be ascertained about them. The publicity of their private lives has been, is, and will be, either the reward or the penalty of their intellectual distinction. Carlyle knew that he could not escape. Since a ' Life ' of him there would certainly be, he wished it to be as authentic as possible. Besides the Memoir of Mrs. Carlyle, he had written several others, mainly autobiographical, not distinctly to be printed, but with no fixed purpose that they should not be printed. These, with his journals and the whole of his correspondence, he made over to me, with unfettered discretion to use in any way that I might think good.

In the papers thus in my possession, Carlyle's history, external and spiritual, lay out before me as in a map. By recasting the entire material, by selecting chosen passages out of his own and his wife's letters, by exhibiting the fair and beautiful side of the story only, it would have been easy, without suppressing a single material point, to draw a picture of a faultless character. When the Devil's advocate has said his worst against Carlyle, he leaves a figure still of unblemished integrity, purity, loftiness of purpose, and inflexible resolution to do right, as of a man living consciously under his Maker's eye, and with his thoughts fixed on the account which he would have to render of his talents.

Of a person of whom malice must acknowledge so much as this, the prickly aspects might fairly be passed by in silence ; and if I had studied my own comfort or the pleasure of my immediate readers, I should have produced a portrait as agreeable, and at least as faithful, as those of the favoured saints in the Catholic calendar. But it would have been a portrait without individuality —an ideal, or in other words, an ' idol,' to be worshipped one day and thrown away the next. Least of all men could such idealising be ventured with Carlyle, to whom untruth of any kind was abominable. If he was to be known at all, he chose to be known as he was, with his angularities, his sharp speeches, his special peculiarities,

meritorious or unmeritorious, precisely as they had
actually been. He has himself laid down the conditions under which a biographer must do his work if
he would do it honestly, without the fear of man before
him ; and in dealing with Carlyle's own memory I have
felt myself bound to conform to his own rule. He shall
speak for himself. I extract a passage from his review
of Lockhart's ' Life of Sir Walter Scott.'[1]

' One thing we hear greatly blamed in Mr. Lockhart, that he has been too communicative, indiscreet,
and has recorded much that ought to have lain
suppressed. Persons are mentioned, and circumstances not always of an ornamental sort. It would
appear that there is far less reticence than was looked
for ! Various persons, name and surname, have
" received pain." Nay, the very hero of the biography is rendered unheroic; unornamental facts
of him, and of those he had to do with, being set
forth in plain English : hence " personality," " indis-
cretion," or worse, " sanctities of private life," &c.
How delicate, decent, is English biography, bless its
mealy mouth ! A Damocles' sword of *Respectability*
hangs for ever over the poor English life-writer (as
it does over poor English life in general), and reduces
him to the verge of paralysis. Thus it has been
said, " There are no English lives worth reading,
except those of players, who, by the nature of the
case, have bidden respectability good day." The
English biographer has long felt that if in writing
his biography he wrote down anything that could by

[1] *Miscellanies*, vol. v. p. 221 *sqq.*

possibility offend any man, he had written wrong. The plain consequence was that, properly speaking, no biography whatever could be produced. The poor biographer, having the fear *not* of God before his eyes, was obliged to retire as it were into vacuum, and write in the most melancholy straitened manner, with only vacuum for a result. Vain that he wrote, and that we kept reading volume on volume. There was no biography, but some vague ghost of a biography, white, stainless, without feature or substance ; *vacuum* as we say, and wind and shadow. . . . Of all the praises copiously bestowed on Mr. Lockhart's work there is none in reality so creditable to him as this same censure which has also been pretty copious. It is a censure better than a good many praises. He is found guilty of having said this and that, calculated not to be entirely pleasant to this man and that ; in other words, calculated to give him and the thing he worked in a living set of features, not to leave him vague in the white beatified ghost condition. Several men, as we hear, cry out, " See, there is something written not entirely pleasant to me ! " Good friend, it is pity ; but who can help it ? They that will crowd about bonfires may sometimes very fairly get their beards singed ; it is the price they pay for such illumination ; natural twilight is safe and free to all. For our part we hope all manner of biographies that are written in England will henceforth be written so. If it is fit that they be written otherwise, then it is still fitter that they be not written at all. To produce not things, but the ghosts of things, can never be the duty of man. . . .

The biographer has this problem set before him:
to delineate a likeness of the earthly pilgrimage of a
man. He will compute well what profit is in it, and
what disprofit; under which latter head this of
offending any of his fellow-creatures will surely not
be forgotten. Nay, this may so swell the disprofit
side of his account, that many an enterprise of
biography otherwise promising shall require to be
renounced. But once taken up, the rule before all
rules is to do *it*, not to do the ghost of it. In speaking of the man and men he has to do with, he will of
course keep all his charities about him, but all his
eyes open. Far be it from him to set down aught
untrue; nay, not to abstain from, and leave in
oblivion, much that is true. But having found a
thing or things essential for his subject, and well
computed the for and against, he will in very deed
set down such thing or things, nothing doubting,
having, we may say, the fear of God before his eyes,
and no other fear whatever. Censure the biographer's
prudence; dissent from the computation he made,
or agree with it; be all malice of his, be all falsehood,
nay be all offensive avoidable inaccuracy condemned
and consumed; but know that by this plan only,
executed as was possible, could the biographer hope
to make a biography; and blame him not that he
did what it had been the worst fault not to do.
. . . The other censure of Scott being made unheroic springs from the same stem, and is perhaps
a still more wonderful flower of it. Your true hero
must have no features, but be a white, stainless,
impersonal ghost hero! But connected with this,

there is an hypothesis now current that Mr. Lockhart at heart has a dislike to Scott, and has done his best in an underhand treacherous manner to dis-hero him! Such hypothesis is actually current. He that has ears may hear it now and then—on which astounding hypothesis if a word must be said, it can only be an apology for silence. If Mr. Lockhart is fairly chargeable with any radical defect, if on any side his insight entirely fails him, it seems even to be in this, that Scott is altogether lovely to him, that Scott's greatness spreads out before him on all hands beyond reach of eye, that his very faults become beautiful, and that of his worth there is no measure.'

I will make no comment on this passage further than to say that I have considered the principles here laid down by Carlyle to be strictly obligatory upon myself in dealing with his own remains. The free judgments which he passed on men and things were part of himself, and I have not felt myself at liberty to suppress them. Remarks which could injure any man—and very few such ever fell from Carlyle's lips—I omit, except where indispensable. Remarks which are merely legitimate expressions of opinion I leave for the most part as they stand. As an illustration of his own wishes on this subject, I may mention that I consulted him about a passage in one of Mrs. Carlyle's letters describing an eminent living person. Her judgment was more just than flattering, and I doubted the prudence of printing it. Carlyle merely said, 'It will do him no harm to know what a sensible woman thought of him.'

As to the biography generally, I found that I could not myself write a formal Life of Carlyle within measur-

able compass without taking to pieces his own Memoirs
and the collection of Mrs. Carlyle's letters; and this I
could not think it right to attempt. Mr. Forster and
John Carlyle having both died, the responsibility was
left entirely to myself. A few weeks before Mr. Carlyle's
death, he asked me what I meant to do. I told him
that I proposed to publish the Memoirs as soon as he
was gone—those which form the two volumes of the
'Reminiscences.' Afterwards I said that I would
publish the letters about which I knew him to be most
anxious. He gave his full assent, merely adding that
he trusted everything to me. The Memoirs, he thought,
had better appear immediately on his departure. He
expected that people would then be talking about him,
and that it would be well for them to have something
authentic to guide them.

These points being determined, the remainder of my
task became simplified. Mrs. Carlyle's letters are a
better history of the London life of herself and her
husband than could be written either by me or by anyone.
The connecting narrative is Carlyle's own, and to meddle
with his work would be to spoil it. It was thus left to
me to supply an account of his early life in Scotland,
the greater part of which I had written while he was
alive, and which is contained in the present volumes.
The publication of the letters will follow at no distant
period. Afterwards, if I live to do it, I shall add a
brief account of his last years, when I was in constant
intercourse with him.

It may be said that I shall have thus produced no
'Life,' but only the materials for a 'Life.' That is true.
But I believe that I shall have given, notwithstanding,

a real picture as far as it goes; and an adequate estim-
ate of Carlyle's work in this world is not at present
possible. He was a teacher and a prophet in the Jewish
sense of the word. The prophecies of Isaiah and
Jeremiah have become a part of the permanent spiritual
inheritance of mankind, because events proved that
they had interpreted correctly the signs of their own
times, and their prophecies were fulfilled. Carlyle, like
them, believed that he had a special message to deliver
to the present age. Whether he was correct in that
belief, and whether his message was a true message,
remains to be seen. He has told us that our most
cherished ideas of political liberty, with their kindred
corollaries, are mere illusions, and that the progress
which has seemed to go along with them is a progress
towards anarchy and social dissolution. If he was
wrong, he has misused his powers. The principles of
his teaching are false. He has offered himself as a guide
upon a road of which he had no knowledge; and his own
desire for himself would be the speediest oblivion both
of his person and his works. If, on the other hand, he
has been right; if, like his great predecessors, he has
read truly the tendencies of this modern age of ours,
and his teaching is authenticated by facts, then Carlyle,
too, will take his place among the inspired seers, and
he will shine on, another fixed star in the intellectual
sky.

Time only can show how this will be:

ἁμέραι ἐπίλοιποι μάρτυρες σοφώτατοι

CONTENTS

OF

THE FIRST VOLUME.

— ·❖· —

ILLUSTRATIONS.

ECCLEFECHAN.

LIFE

OF

THOMAS CARLYLE.

CHAPTER I.

THE RIVER Annan, rising above Moffat in Hartfell, descends from the mountains through a valley gradually widening and spreading out, as the fells are left behind, into the rich and well-cultivated district known as Annandale. Picturesque and broken in the upper part of its course, the stream, when it reaches the level country, steals slowly among meadows and undulating wooded hills, till at the end of forty miles it falls into the Solway at Annan town. Annandale, famous always for its pasturage, suffered especially before the union of the kingdoms from border forays, the effects of which were long to be traced in a certain wildness of disposition in the inhabitants. Dumfriesshire, to which it belongs, was sternly Cameronian. Stories of the persecutions survived in the farmhouses as their most treasured historical traditions. Cameronian congregations lingered till the beginning of the present century, when they merged in other bodies of seceders from the established religion.

In its hard fight for spiritual freedom Scotch Pro-
testantism lost respect for kings and nobles, and looked
to Christ rather than to earthly rulers; but before
the Reformation all Scotland was clannish or feudal;
and the Dumfriesshire yeomanry, like the rest, were
organised under great nobles, whose pennon they
followed, whose name they bore, and the remotest
kindred with whom, even to a tenth generation, they
were proud to claim.   Among the families of the
western border the Carlyles were not the least distinguished.   They were originally English, and were
called probably after Carlisle town.   They came to
Annandale with the Bruces in the time of David the
Second.   A Sir John Carlyle was created Lord Carlyle
of Torthorwald in reward for a beating which he had
given the English at Annan.   Michael, the fourth lord,
signed the Association Bond among the Protestant
lords when Queen Mary was sent to Lochleven, being
the only one among them, it was observed, who could
not write his name.   Their work was rough.   They
were rough men themselves, and with the change of
times their importance declined.   The title lapsed, the
estates were dissipated in lawsuits, and by the middle
of the last century nothing remained of the Carlyles
but one or two households in the neighbourhood of
Burnswark who had inherited the name either through
the adoption by their forefathers of the name of their
leader, or by some descent of blood which had trickled
down through younger sons.[1]

---

[1] When Carlyle became famous, a Dumfries antiquary traced his
ancestry with apparent success through ten generations to the first Lord

In one of these families, in a house which his father, who was a mason, had built with his own hands, Thomas Carlyle was born on December 4, 1795. Ecclefechan, where his father lived, is a small market town on the east side of Annandale, six miles inland from the Solway, and about sixteen on the great north road from Carlisle.[1] It consists of a single street, down one side of which, at that time, ran an open brook. The aspect, like that of most Scotch towns, is cold, but clean and orderly, with an air of thrifty comfort. The houses are plain, that in which the Carlyles lived alone having pretensions to originality. In appearance one, it is really double, a central arch dividing it. James Carlyle, Thomas Carlyle's father, occupied one part. His brother, who was his partner in his trade, lived in the other.

Of their ancestors they knew nothing beyond the second generation. Tradition said that they had been long settled as farmers at Burrens, the Roman station at Middlebie (two miles from Ecclefechan). One of them, it was said, had been unjustly hanged on pretext of border cattle-stealing. The case was so cruel that the farm had been given as some compensation to the widow, and the family had continued to possess it till their title was questioned, and they were turned

Torthorwald. There was much laughter about it in the house in Cheyne Row, but Carlyle was inclined to think on the whole that the descent was real.

[1] The usually received etymology of Ecclefechan is that it is the same as Kirkfechan, Church of St. Fechanus, an Irish saint supposed to have come to Annandale in the seventh century; but Fechan is a not unusual termination in Welsh, and means 'small,' as in Llanfairfechan.

out, by the Duke of Queensberry. Whether this story
was true or not, it is certain that James Carlyle's
grandmother lived at Middlebie in extreme poverty,
and that she died in the early part of the last century,
leaving two sons. Thomas, the elder, was a carpenter,
worked for some time at Lancaster, came home afterwards, and saw the Highlanders pass through Ecclefechan in 1745 on their way to England. Leaving his
trade, he settled at a small farm called Brownknowe,
near Burnswark Hill, and, marrying a certain Mary
Gillespie, produced four sons and two daughters. Of
these sons James Carlyle was the second. The household life was in a high degree disorderly. Old Thomas
Carlyle was formed after the border type, more given
to fighting and wild adventure than to patient industry. 'He did not drink,' his grandson says, 'but
he was a fiery man, irascible, indomitable, of the
toughness and springiness of steel. An old market
brawl, called Ecclefechan dog-fight, in which he was
a principal, survives in tradition to this day.'[1]   He
was proud, poor, and discontented, leaving his family
for the most part to shift for themselves. They were
often without food or fuel ; his sons were dressed in
breeks made mostly of leather.

They had to scramble (Carlyle says scraffle) for their very
clothes and food. They knit, they thatched for hire, they
hunted. My father tried all these things almost in boyhood.
Every dale and burngate and clengh of that district he had
traversed seeking hares and the like. He used to talk of
these pilgrimages. Once I remember his gun-flint was tied

[1] This, it should be said, was written sixty years ago.

on with a hatband. He was a real hunter like a wild Indian from necessity. The hare's flesh was food. Hareskins at sixpence each would accumulate into the purchase money of a coat. His hunting years were not useless to him. Misery was early training the rugged boy into a stoic, that one day he might be the assurance of a Scottish man.

'Travelling tinkers,' 'Highland drovers,' and such like were occasional guests at Brownknowe. 'Sandy Macleod, a pensioned soldier who had served under Wolfe, lived in an adjoining cottage, and had stories to tell of his adventures.' Old Thomas Carlyle, notwithstanding his rough, careless ways, was not without cultivation. He studied 'Anson's Voyages,' and in his old age, strange to say, when his sons were growing into young men, he would sit with a neighbour over the fire, reading, much to their scandal, the 'Arabian Nights.' They had become, James Carlyle especially, and his brother through him, serious lads, and they were shocked to see two old men occupied on the edge of the grave with such idle vanities.

Religion had been introduced into the house through another singular figure, John Orr, the schoolmaster of Hoddam, who was also by trade a shoemaker. Schoolmastering in those days fell to persons of clever irregular habits, who took to it from taste partly, and also because other forms of business did not answer with them. Orr was a man of strong pious tendencies, but was given to drink. He would disappear for weeks into pothouses, and then come back to his friends shattered and remorseful. He, too, was a friend and visitor at Brownknowe, teaching the boys by day, sleeping in the room with them at night, and discussing arithmetical problems with their father. From him James Carlyle gained such knowledge as he had, part of it a knowledge of the Bible, which became the guiding principle of his life. The effect was soon visible on a remarkable occasion. While he was still a boy, he and three of his companions had met to play cards. There was some disagreement among them, when James Carlyle said that they were fools and worse for quarrelling over a probably sinful amusement. They threw the cards into the fire, and perhaps no one of the four, certainly not James Carlyle, ever touched a card again. Hitherto he and his brother had gleaned a subsistence on the skirts of settled life. They were now to find an entrance into regular occupation. James Carlyle was born in 1757. In 1773, when he was sixteen, a certain William Brown, a mason from Peebles, came into Annandale, became acquainted with the Carlyles, and married Thomas Carlyle's eldest daughter Fanny. He took her brothers as apprentices, and they became known before long as the most skilful and diligent workmen in the neighbourhood. James, though not the eldest, had the strongest character, and guided the rest. 'They were noted for their brotherly affection and coherence.' They all prospered. They were noted also for their hard sayings, and it must be said also, in their early manhood, for 'hard strikings.' They were warmly liked by those near them; 'by those at a distance they were viewed as something dangerous to meddle with, something not to be meddled with.'

James Carlyle never spoke with pleasure of his young days, regarding them 'as days of folly, perhaps sinful

days;' but it was well known that he was strictly
temperate, pure, abstemious, prudent, and industrious.
Feared he was from his promptness of hand, but never
aggressive, and using his strength only to put down
rudeness and violence. 'On one occasion,' says Carlyle,
'a huge peasant was rudely insulting and defying the
party my father belonged to. The other quailed, and
he bore it till he could bear it no longer, but clutched
his rough adversary by the two flanks, swung him with
ireful force round in the air, hitting his feet against
some open door, and hurled him to a distance, supine,
lamed, vanquished, and utterly humbled. He would
say of such things, "I am wae to think of it" — wae
from repentance. Happy he who has nothing worse to
repent of!'

The apprenticeship over, the brothers began work
on their own account, and with marked success; James
Carlyle taking the lead. He built, as has been already
said, a house for himself, which still stands in the street
of Ecclefechan. His brothers occupied one part of it, he
himself the other; and his father, the old Thomas, life
now wearing out, came in from Brownknowe to live
with them. James, perhaps the others, but James
decisively, became an avowedly religious man. He had
a maternal uncle, one Robert Brand, whose advice and
example influenced him in this matter. Brand was a
'vigorous religionist,' of strict Presbyterian type. From
him James Carlyle received a definite faith, and made
his profession as a 'Burgher,' a seceding sect which
had separated from the Establishment as insufficiently
in earnest for them. They had their humble meeting-house, 'thatched with heath;' and for minister a

certain John Johnstone, from whom Carlyle himself learned afterwards his first Latin; 'the priestliest man,' he says, 'I ever under any ecclesiastical guise was privileged to look upon.'

This peasant union, this little heath-thatched house, this simple evangelist, together constituted properly the 'church' of that district; they were the blessing and the saving of many: on me too their pious heaven-sent influences still rest and live. There was in those days a 'teacher of the people.' He sleeps not far from my father who built his monument in the Ecclefechan churchyard, the Teacher and the Taught. Blessed, I again say, are the dead that die in the Lord.

In 1791, having then a house of his own, James Carlyle married a distant cousin of the same name, Janet Carlyle. They had one son, John, and then she died of fever. Her long fair hair, which had been cut off in her illness, remained as a memorial of her in a drawer, into which the children afterwards looked with wondering awe. Two years after the husband married again Margaret Aitken, 'a woman,' says Carlyle, ' of to me the fairest descent, that of the pious, the just, and the wise.' Her character will unfold itself as the story goes on. Thomas Carlyle was her first child, born December 4, 1795; she lived to see him at the height of his fame, known and honoured wherever the English language was spoken. To her care ' for body and soul' he never ceased to say that ' he owed endless gratitude.' After Thomas came eight others, three sons and five daughters, one of whom, *Janet*, so called after the first wife, died when she was a few months old.

The family was prosperous, as Ecclefechan working life understood prosperity. In one year, his best, James Carlyle made in his business as much as 100*l*. At worst he earned an artisan's substantial wages, and was thrifty and prudent. The children, as they passed out of infancy, ran about barefoot, but were otherwise cleanly clothed, and fed on oatmeal, milk, and potatoes. Our Carlyle learned to read from his mother too early for distinct remembrance; when he was five his father taught him arithmetic, and sent him with the other village boys to school. Like the Carlyles generally he had a violent temper. John, the son of the first marriage, lived usually with his grandfather, but came occasionally to visit his parents. Carlyle's earliest recollection is of throwing his little brown stool at his brother in a mad passion of rage, when he was scarcely more than two years old, breaking a leg of it, and 'feeling for the first time the united pangs of loss and remorse.' The next impression which most affected him was the small round heap under the sheet upon a bed where his little sister lay dead. Death, too, he made acquaintance with in another memorable form. His father's eldest brother John died. 'The day before his funeral, an ill-behaving servant wench lifted the coverlid from off his pale ghastly befilleted head to show it to some crony of hers, unheeding of the child who was alone with them, and to whom the sight gave a new pang of horror.' The grandfather followed next, closing finally his Anson and his 'Arabian Nights.' He had a brother whose adventures had been remarkable. Francis Carlyle, so he was called, had been apprenticed to a shoemaker. He, too, when his time

was out, had gone to England, to Bristol among other
places, where he fell into drink and gambling. He lost
all his money; one morning after an orgie he flung
himself desperately out of bed and broke his leg.
When he recovered he enlisted in a brig of war, distinguished himself by special gallantry in supporting his
captain in a mutiny, and was rewarded with the command of a Solway revenue cutter. After many years of
rough creditable service he retired on half-pay to his
native village of Middlebie. There had been some
family quarrel, and the brothers, though living close to
one another, had held no intercourse. They were both
of them above eighty years of age. The old Thomas
being on his death-bed, the sea captain's heart relented.
He was a grim, broad, fierce-looking man ; 'prototype
of Smollett's Trunnion.' Being too unwieldy to walk,
he was brought into Ecclefechan in a cart, and carried
in a chair up the steep stairs to his dying brother's
room. There he remained some twenty minutes, and
came down again with a face which printed itself in
the little Carlyle's memory. They saw him no more,
and after a brief interval the old generation had
disappeared.

Amidst such scenes our Carlyle struggled through
his early boyhood.

It was not a joyful life (he says) ; what life is ? yet a safe
and quiet one, above most others, or any other I have witnessed, a wholesome one. We were taciturn rather than
talkative, but if little was said that little had generally a
meaning.

More remarkable man than my father I have never met in

my journey through life ; sterling sincerity in thought, word, and deed, most quiet, but capable of blazing into whirlwinds when needful, and such a flash of just insight and brief natural eloquence and emphasis, true to every feature of it as I have never known in any other. Humour of a most grim Scandinavian type he occasionally had ; wit rarely or never—too serious for wit—my excellent mother with perhaps the deeper piety in most senses had also the most sport. No man of my day, or hardly any man, can have had better parents.

The Sunday services in Mr. Johnstone's meeting-house were the events of the week. The congregation were 'Dissenters' of a marked type, some of them coming from as far as Carlisle; another party, and among these at times a little eager boy, known afterwards as Edward Irving, appearing regularly from Annan, 'their streaming plaids in wet weather hanging up to drip.'

A man (Carlyle wrote in 1866) who awoke to the belief that he actually had a soul to be saved or lost was apt to be found among the Dissenting people and to have given up attendance at Kirk. All dissent in Scotland is merely stricter adherence to the National Kirk in all points. Very venerable are those old Seceder clergy to me now when I look back. Most figures of them in my time were hoary old men ; men so like evangelists in modern vesture and 'poor scholars and gentlemen of Christ' I have nowhere met with among Protestant or Papal clergy in any country in the world. . . . That poor temple of my childhood is more sacred to me than the biggest cathedral then extant could have been ; rude, rustic, bare, no temple in the world was more so; but there were sacred lambencies, tongues of authentic flame which kindled what was best in one, what has not yet gone out. Strangely vivid are some twelve or twenty of those old faces whom I used to see every Sunday, whose names, employments or precise dwelling places I never knew, but whose portraits are yet clear to me as in a mirror.

Their heavy-laden, patient, ever attentive faces, fallen solitary most of them, children all away, wife away for ever, or, it might be, wife still there and constant like a shadow and grown very like the old man, the thrifty cleanly poverty of these good people, their well saved coarse old clothes, tailed waistcoats down to mid-thigh—all this I occasionally see as with eyes sixty or sixty-five years off, and hear the very voice of my mother upon it, whom sometimes I would be questioning about these persons of the drama and endeavouring to describe and identify them.

Of one of these worshippers in the Ecclefechan meeting-house, 'tall, straight, very clean always, brown as mahogany, with a beard white as snow,' Carlyle tells the following anecdote:—

Old David Hope [that was his name] lived on a little farm close by Solway shore, a mile or two east of Annan—a wet country with late harvests which are sometimes incredibly difficult to save—ten days continuously pouring, then a day, perhaps two days, of drought, part of them, it may be, of roaring wind; during which the moments are golden for you, and perhaps you had better work all night as presently there will be deluges again. David's stuff, one such morning, was all standing dry, ready to be saved still if he stood to it, which was much his intention. Breakfast, wholesome hasty porridge, was soon over, and next in course came family worship, what they call taking the book, *i.e.* taking your Bibles, psalm and chapter always part of the service.   David was putting on his spectacles when somebody rushed in. 'Such a raging wind risen will drive the stooks (shocks) into the sea if let alone.' 'Wind!' answered David.   Wind canna get ae straw that has been appointed mine. Sit down and let us worship God.'

CHAPTER II.

A.D. 1805.   ÆT. 10.

EDUCATION is a passion in Scotland. It is the pride
of every honourable peasant, if he has a son of any
promise, to give him a chance of rising as a scholar.
As a child Carlyle could not have failed to show that
there was something unusual in him.   The schoolmaster in Ecclefechan gave a good account of his
progress in ' figures.'   The minister reported favourably of his Latin. ' I do not grudge thee thy schooling,
Tom,' his father said to him one day, ' now that thy
uncle Frank owns thee a better arithmetician than
himself.'   It was decided that he should go to Annan
Grammar School, and thence, if he prospered, to the
University, with final outlook to the ministry.

He was a shy thoughtful boy, shrinking generally
from rough companions, but with the hot temper of
his race.   His mother, naturally anxious for him, and
fearing perhaps the family tendency, extracted a
promise before parting with him that he would never
return a blow, and, as might be expected, his first
experiences of school were extremely miserable.   Boys
of genius are never well received by the common
flock, and escape persecution only when they are able
to defend themselves.

' Sartor Resartus ' is generally mythic, but parts

are historical, and among them the account of the
first launch of Teufelsdröckh into the Hinterschlag
Gymnasium. Hinterschlag (smite behind) is Annan.
Thither, leaving home and his mother's side, Carlyle
was taken by his father, being then in his tenth year,
and 'fluttering with boundless hopes,' at Whitsuntide,
1805, to the school which was to be his first step into
a higher life.

Well do I remember (says Teufelsdröckh) the red sunny
Whitsuntide morning when, trotting full of hope by the side
of Father Andreas, I entered the main street of the place
and saw its steeple clock (then striking eight) and Schuld-
thurm (jail) and the aproned or disaproned Burghers moving
in to breakfast ; a little dog, in mad terror, was rushing past,
for some human imps had tied a tin kettle to its tail, fit
emblem of much that awaited myself in that mischievous
den. Alas ! the kind beech rows of Entepfuhl (Ecclefechan)
were hidden in the distance. I was among strangers harshly,
at best indifferently, disposed to me ; the young heart felt
for the first time quite orphaned and alone. . . . My schoolfellows were boys, mostly rude boys, and obeyed the impulse
of rude nature which bids the deer-herd fall upon any stricken
hart, the duck-flock put to death any broken-winged brother
or sister, and on all hands the strong tyrannise over the
weak.

Carlyle retained to the end of his days a painful and
indeed resentful recollection of these school experiences
of his. 'This,' he said of the passage just quoted
from 'Sartor,' 'is true, and not half the truth.'
He had obeyed his mother's injunctions. He had
courage in plenty to resent ill usage, but his promise

was sacred. He was passionate, and often, probably, violent, but fight he would not, and every one who knows English and Scotch life will understand what his fate must have been. One consequence was a near escape from drowning. The boys had all gone to bathe; the lonely child had stolen apart from the rest, where he could escape from being tormented. He found himself in a deep pool which had been dug out for a dock and had been filled with the tide. The mere accident of someone passing at the time saved him. At length he could bear his condition no longer; he turned on the biggest bully in the school and furiously kicked him; a battle followed in which he was beaten; but he left marks of his fists upon his adversary, which were not forgotten. He taught his companions to fear him, if only like Brasidas's mouse. He was persecuted no longer, but he carried away bitter and angry recollections of what he had borne, which were never entirely obliterated.

The teaching which Carlyle received at Annan, he says, 'was limited, and of its kind only moderately good. Latin and French I did get to read with fluency. Latin quantity was left a frightful chaos, and I had to learn it afterwards; some geometry. Algebra, arithmetic tolerably well. Vague outlines of geography I learnt; all the books I could get were also devoured. Greek consisted of the alphabet merely.'

Elsewhere in a note I find the following account of his first teaching and school experience :—

My mother (writes Carlyle, in a series of brief notes upon

his early life) had taught me reading. I never remember when. Tom Donaldson's school at Ecclefechan—a severely-correct kind of man Tom . . . from Edinburgh—went afterwards to Manchester ; I never saw his face again, though I still remember it well as always merry and kind to me, though to the undeserving severe. The school then stood at Hoddam Kirk. Sandie Beattie, subsequently a Burgher minister at Glasgow, I well remember examining me. He reported me complete in English, age then about seven . . . that I must go to Latin or waste my time. Latin accordingly, with what enthusiasm ! But the schoolmaster did not himself know Latin. I gradually got altogether swamped and bewildered under him. Reverend Mr. Johnstone, of Ecclefechan, or rather first his son, home from college, and already teaching a nephew or a cousin, had to take me in hand, and once pulled afloat I made rapid and sure way.

In my tenth year I was sent to the grammar school at Annan. May 26, a bright sunny morning—Whit-Monday—which I still vividly remember, I trotting at my father's side in the way alluded to in 'Sartor.' It was a bright morning, and to me full of moment—of fluttering, boundless hopes, saddened by parting with mother, with home, and which afterwards were cruelly disappointed.

'Sartor' is not to be trusted in details. Greek consisted of the Alphabet mainly. Hebrew is a German entity.[1] Nobody in that region except old Mr. Johnstone could have read a sentence of it to save his life. I did get to read Latin and French with fluency—Latin quantity was left a frightful chaos, and I had to learn it afterwards. Some geometry, algebra, arithmetic thoroughly well, vague outlines of geography, I did learn ; all the books I could get were also devoured. Mythically true is what 'Sartor' says of my

---

[1] Alluding to a German biography in which Carlyle was said to have learnt Hebrew.

schoolfellows, and not half the truth. Unspeakable is the damage and defilement I got out of those coarse unguided tyrannous cubs, especially till I revolted against them and gave stroke for stroke, as my pious mother, in her great love of peace and of my best interests, spiritually chiefly, had imprudently forbidden me to do. One way and another I had never been so wretched as here in that school, and the first two years of my time in it still count among the miserable of my life. Academia ! High School Instructors of Youth ! Oh, ye unspeakable !

Of holidays we hear nothing, though holidays there must have been at Christmas and Midsummer; little also of school friendships or amusements. For the last, in such shape as could have been found in boys of his class in Annan, Carlyle could have had little interest. He speaks warmly of his mathematical teacher, a certain Mr. Morley, from Cumberland, ' whom he loved much, and who taught him well.' He had formed a comradeship with one or two boys of his own age, who were not entirely uncongenial to him ; but only one incident is preserved which was of real moment. In his third school year Carlyle first consciously saw Edward Irving. Irving's family lived in Annan. He had himself been at the school, and had gone thence to the University of Edinburgh. He had distinguished himself there, gained prizes, and was otherwise honourably spoken of. Annan, both town and school, was proud of the brilliant lad that they had produced; and Irving one day looked in upon the class room, the masters out of compliment attending him. ' He was scrupulously dressed, black coat, tight pantaloons, in the fashion of the day, and looked very neat, self-possessed, and

amiable; a flourishing slip of a youth with coal-black
hair, swarthy clear complexion, very straight on his feet,
and, except for the glaring squint, decidedly handsome.'
The boys listened eagerly as he talked in a free airy
way about Edinburgh and its professors. A University
man who has made a name for himself is infinitely
admirable to younger ones; he is not too far above
them to be comprehensible. They know what he has
done, and they hope distantly that they too one day
may do the like. Of course Irving did not distinguish
Carlyle. He walked through the rooms and disappeared.

The Hinterschlag Gymnasium was over soon after,
and Carlyle's future career was now to be decided on.
The Ecclefechan family life was not favourable to displays of precocious genius. Vanity was the last quality
that such a man as James Carlyle would encourage, and
there was a severity in his manner which effectively
repressed any disposition to it.

We had all to complain (Carlyle says) that we dared not
freely love our father. His heart seemed as if walled in.
My mother has owned to me that she could never understand
him, and that her affection and admiration of him were
obstructed. It seemed as if an atmosphere of fear repelled
us from him, me especially. My heart and tongue played
freely with my mother. He had an air of deepest gravity
and even sternness. He had the most entire and open contempt for idle tattle—what he called clatter. Any talk that
had meaning in it he could listen to; what had no meaning
in it, above all what seemed false, he absolutely could not
and would not hear, but abruptly turned from it. Long
may we remember his ' I don't believe thee ;' his tongue-
paralysing cold indifferent ' Heh.'

Besides fear, Carlyle, as he grew older, began to experience a certain awe of his father as of a person of altogether superior qualities.

None of us (he writes) will ever forget that bold glowing style of his, flowing free from the untutored soul, full of metaphor, though he knew not what metaphor was, with all manner of potent words which he appropriated and applied with surprising accuracy—brief, energetic, conveying the most perfect picture, definite, clear, not in ambitious colours, but in full white sunlight. Emphatic I have heard him beyond all men. In anger he had no need of oaths ; his words were like sharp arrows that smote into the very heart.

Such a father may easily have been alarming, and slow to gain his children's confidence. He had silently observed his little Tom, however. The reports from the Annan masters were all favourable, and when the question rose what was to be done with him, he inclined to venture the University. The wise men of Ecclefechan shook their heads. ' Educate a boy,' said one of them, 'and he grows up to despise his ignorant parents.' Others said it was a risk, it was waste of money, there was a large family to be provided for, too much must not be spent upon one, &c. James Carlyle had seen something in his boy's character which showed him that the risk, if risk there was, must be encountered ; and to Edinburgh it was decided that Tom should go and be made a scholar of.

To English ears university life suggests splendid buildings, luxurious rooms, rich endowments as the reward of successful industry ; as students, young men between nineteen and twenty-three with handsome allowances, spending each of them on an average double the largest income which James Carlyle had earned in any year of his life. Universities north of the Tweed had in those days no money prizes to offer, no fellowships and scholarships, nothing at all but an education and a discipline in poverty and self-denial. The lads who went to them were the children, most of them, of parents as poor as Carlyle's father. They knew at what a cost the expense of sending them to college, relatively small as it was, could be afforded; and they went with the fixed purpose of making the very utmost of their time. Five months only of each year they could remain in their classes; for the rest of it they taught pupils themselves, or worked on the farm at home to pay for their own learning.

Each student, as a rule, was the most promising member of the family to which he belonged, and extraordinary confidence was placed in them. They were sent to Edinburgh, Glasgow, or wherever it might be, when they were mere boys of fourteen. They had no one to look after them either on their journey or when they came to the end. They walked from their homes, being unable to pay for coach-hire. They entered their own names at the college. They found their own humble lodgings, and were left entirely to their own capacity for self-conduct. The carriers brought them oatmeal, potatoes, and salt butter from the home farm, with a few eggs occasionally as a luxury. With their thrifty habits they required no other food. In the return cart their linen went back to their mothers to be washed and mended. Poverty protected them from temptations to vicious amusements. They formed their economical friendships; they shared their breakfasts and their thoughts, and had their clubs for conversation or discussion. When term was over they walked home in parties, each district having its little knot belonging to it; and known along the roads as University scholars, they were assured of entertainment on the way.

As a training in self-dependence no better education could have been found in these islands. If the teaching had been as good as the discipline of character, the Scotch universities might have competed with the world. The teaching was the weak part. There were no funds, either in the colleges or with the students, to provide personal instruction as at Oxford and Cambridge. The professors were individually excellent, but they had to teach large classes, and had no leisure to attend particularly to this or that promising pupil. The universities were opportunities to boys who were able to take advantage of them, and that was all.

Such was the life on which Carlyle was now to enter, and such were the circumstances of it. It was the November term 1809. He was to be fourteen on the fourth of the approaching December. Edinburgh is nearly one hundred miles from Ecclefechan. He was to go on foot like the rest, under the guardianship of a boy named 'Tom Smail,' two or three years his senior, who had already been at college, and was held, therefore, to be a sufficient protector.

How strangely vivid (he says in 1866), how remote and wonderful, tinged with the hues of far-off love and sadness,

is that journey to me now after fifty-seven years of time !
My mother and father walking with me in the dark frosty
November morning through the village to set us on our way :
my dear ever loving mother, her tremulous affection, my &c.

'Tom Smail' was a poor companion, very innocent,
very conceited, an indifferent scholar. Carlyle in his
own mind had a small opinion of him. The journey
over the moors was a weary one, the elder lad stalking
on generally ahead, whistling an Irish tune; the
younger 'given up to his bits of reflections in the
silence of the hills.' Twenty miles a day the boys
walked, by Moffat and over Airock Stane. They
reached Edinburgh early one afternoon, got a lodging
in Simon Square, got dinner, and sallied out again
that 'Palinurus Tom' might give the novice a glance
of the great city. The scene so entirely new to him
left an impression on Carlyle which remained distinct
after more than half a century.

The novice mind (he says) was not excessively astonished
all at once, but kept its eyes open and said nothing. What
streets we went through I don't the least recollect, but have
some faint image of St. Giles's High Kirk, and of the Luckeu
booths there with their strange little ins and outs and eager
old women in miniature shops, of combs, shoe-laces, and
trifles ; still fainter image, if any, of the sublime horse statue
in Parliament Square hard by ; directly after which Smail,
audaciously, so I thought, pushed open a door free to all the
world and dragged me in with him to a scene which I have
never forgotten. An immense hall dimly lighted from the
top of the walls, and perhaps with candles burning in it here
and there, all in strange chiaroscuro, and filled with what I

thought exaggeratively a thousand or two of human creatures,
all astir in a boundless buzz of talk, and simmering about in
every direction—some solitary, some in groups.   By degrees
I noticed that some were in wig and black gown, some not,
but in common clothes, all well-dressed ; that here and there
on the sides of the hall were little thrones with enclosures
and steps leading up, red velvet figures sitting in said
thrones, and the black-gowned eagerly speaking to them ;
advocates pleading to judges as I easily understood.   How
they could be heard in such a grinding din was somewhat a
mystery.   Higher up on the walls, stuck there like swallows
in their nests, sate other humbler figures ; these I found
were the sources of certain wildly plangent lamentable kinds
of sounds, or echoes, which from time to time pierced the
universal noise of feet and voices, and rose unintelligibly
above it as in the bitterness of incurable woe : criers of the
court I gradually came to understand.   And this was Themis
in her ' outer house ; ' such a scene of chaotic din and hurly-
burly as I had never figured before.   It seems to me that
there were four times or ten times as many people in that
' outer house ' as there now usually are ; and doubtless there
is something of fact in this, such have been the curtailments
and abatements of law practice in the head courts since then,
and transference of it to county jurisdiction.   Last time I
was in that outer house (some six or seven years ago in
broad daylight) it seemed like a place fallen asleep, fallen
almost dead.

Notable figures, now all vanished utterly, were doubtless
wandering about as part of that continual hurly-burly when
I first set foot in it fifty-seven years ago ; great law lords
this and that, great advocates *alors célèbres*, as Thiers has it.
Cranstoun, Cockburn, Jeffrey, Walter Scott, John Clerk.   To
me at that time they were not even names ; but I have since
occasionally thought of that night and place where probably

they were living substances—some of them in a kind of relation to me afterwards. Time with his *tenses*—what a miraculous entity is he always! The only figure I distinctly recollect and got printed on my brain that night was John Clerk, there veritably hitching about, whose grim strong countenance with its black far-projecting brows, and look of great sagacity, fixed him in my memory.

This scene alone remains recorded of Carlyle's early Edinburgh experience. Of the University he says that he learned little there. In the Latin class he was under Professor Christieson, who 'never noticed him nor could distinguish him from another Mr. Irving Carlyle, an older, bigger boy, with red hair, wild buck teeth, and scorched complexion, and the worst Latinist of his acquaintance.'

In the classical field (he writes elsewhere) I am truly as nothing. Homer I learnt to read in the original with difficulty, after Wolf's broad flash of light thrown into it; Æschylus and Sophocles mainly in translations. Tacitus and Virgil became really interesting to me; Homer and Æschylus above all; Horace egoistical, *leichtfertig*, in sad fact I never cared for; Cicero, after long and various trials, always proved a windy person and a weariness to me ex- tinguished altogether by Middleton's excellent though mis- judging life of him.

It was not much better with philosophy. Dugald Stewart had gone away two years before Carlyle entered. Brown was the new professor, 'an eloquent acute little gentleman, full of enthusiasm about simple suggestions, relative, &c.,' unprofitable utterly to Carlyle, and bewildering and dispiriting, as the autumn winds among withered leaves.

In mathematics only he made real progress. His temperament was impatient of uncertainties. He threw himself with delight into a form of knowledge in which the conclusions were indisputable, where at each step he could plant his foot with confidence. Professor Leslie (Sir John Leslie afterwards) discovered his talent and exerted himself to help him with a zeal of which Carlyle never afterwards ceased to speak with gratitude. That he made progress in mathematics was 'perhaps,' as he says,

due mainly to the accident that Leslie alone of my Professors had some genius in his business, and awoke a certain enthusiasm in me. For several years geometry shone before me as the noblest of all sciences, and I prosecuted it in all my best hours and moods. But far more pregnant inquiries were rising in me, and gradually engrossing me, heart as well as head, so that about 1820 or 1821 I had entirely thrown mathematics aside, and except in one or two brief spurts, more or less of a morbid nature, have never in the least regarded it further.

Yet even in mathematics, on ground with which he was familiar, his shy nature was unfitted for display. He carried off no prizes. He tried only once, and though he was notoriously superior to all his competitors the crowd and noise of the class room prevented him from even attempting to distinguish himself. I have heard him say late in life that his thoughts never came to him in proper form except when he was alone.

'Sartor Resartus,' I have already said, must not be followed too literally as a biographical authority. It is mythic, not historical. Nevertheless, as mythic it may be trusted for the general outlines.

The university where I was educated (says Teufelsdröckh) still stands vivid enough in my remembrance, and I know its name well, which name, however, I from tenderness to existing interests shall in no wise divulge. It is my painful duty to say that out of England and Spain ours was the worst of all hitherto discovered universities. This is indeed a time when right education is, as nearly as may be, impossible ; however in degrees of wrongness there is no limit ; nay, I can conceive a worse system than that of the Nameless itself, as poisoned victual may be worse than absolute hunger. It is written, when the blind lead the blind, both shall fall into the ditch. Wherefore in such circumstances may it not sometimes be safer if both leader and led simply—sit still ? Had you anywhere in Crim Tartary walled in a square enclosure, furnished it with a small ill-chosen library, and then turned loose into it eleven hundred Christian striplings, to tumble about as they listed from three to seven years ; certain persons under the title of professors being stationed at the gates to declare aloud that it was a university and exact considerable admission fees, you had, not indeed in mechanical structure, yet in spirit and result, some imperfect substance of our High Seminary. . . . The professors in the Nameless lived with ease, with safety, by a mere reputation constructed in past times—and then, too, with no great effort—by quite another class of persons ; which reputation, like a strong brisk-going undershot wheel sunk into the general current, bade fair, with only a little annual repainting on their part, to hold long together, and of its own accord assiduously grind for them. Happy that

it was so for the millers! They themselves needed not to
work. Their attempts at working, what they called edu-
cating, now when I look back on it fill me with a certain
mute admiration. . . .

Besides all this we boasted ourselves a rational university,
in the highest degree hostile to mysticism. Thus was the
young vacant mind furnished with much talk about progress
of the species, dark ages, prejudice and the like, so that all
were quickly blown out into a state of windy argumentative-
ness, whereby the better sort had soon to end in sick impotent scepticism; the worser sort explode in finished
self-conceit, and to all spiritual interests become dead. . . .
The hungry young looked up to their spiritual nurses, and
for food were bidden eat the east wind. What vain jargon
of controversial metaphysics, etymology, and mechanical
manipulation falsely named Science was current there, I
indeed learnt better than perhaps the most. Among eleven
hundred Christian youths there will not be wanting some
eleven eager to learn. By collision with such, a certain
warmth, a certain polish was communicated; by instinct and
by happy accident I took less to rioting than to thinking
and reading, which latter also I was free to do. Nay, from
the Chaos of that library I succeeded in fishing up more
books than had been known to the keeper thereof. The
foundation of a literary life was hereby laid. I learned on
my own strength to read fluently in almost all cultivated
languages, on almost all subjects and sciences. A certain
ground-plan of human nature and life began to fashion itself
in me, by additional experiments to be corrected and in-
definitely extended.[1]

The teaching at a university is but half what is
learned there; the other half, and the most important,

---

[1] *Sartor Resartus*, book ii. chap. iii.

is what young men learn from one another. Carlyle's friends at Edinburgh, the eleven out of the eleven hundred, were of his own rank of life, sons of peasants who had their own way to make in life. From their letters, many of which have been preserved, it is clear that they were clever good lads, distinctly superior to ordinary boys of their age, Carlyle himself holding the first place in their narrow circle. Their lives were pure and simple. Nowhere in these letters is there any jesting with vice, or light allusions to it. The boys wrote to one another on the last novel of Scott or poem of Byron, on the 'Edinburgh Review,' on the war, on the fall of Napoleon, occasionally on geometrical problems, sermons, college exercises, and divinity lectures, and again on innocent trifles, with sketches, now and then humorous and bright, of Annandale life as it was seventy years ago. They looked to Carlyle to direct their judgment and advise them in difficulties. He was the prudent one of the party, able, if money matters went wrong, to help them out of his humble savings. He was already noted, too, for power of effective speech—'far too sarcastic for so young a man' was what elder people said of him. One of his correspondents addressed him always as 'Jonathan,' or 'Dean,' or 'Doctor,' as if he was to be a second Swift. Others called him Parson, perhaps from his intended profession. All foretold future greatness to him of one kind or another. They recognised that he was not like other young men, that he was superior to other young men, in character as well as intellect. 'Knowing how you abhor all affectation' is an expression used to him when he was still a mere boy.

His destination was 'the ministry,' and for this, knowing how much his father and mother wished it, he tried to prepare himself. He was already conscious, however, 'that he had not the least enthusiasm for that business, that even grave prohibitory doubts were gradually rising ahead. Formalism was not the pinching point, had there been the preliminary of belief forthcoming.' 'No church or speaking entity whatever,' he admitted, 'can do without formulas, but it must *believe* them first if it would be honest.'

Two letters to Carlyle from one of these early friends may be given here as specimens of the rest. They bring back the Annandale of 1814, and show a faint kind of image of Carlyle himself reflected on the writer's mind. His name was Hill. He was about Carlyle's age, and subscribes himself Peter Pindar.

To Thomas Carlyle.

Castlebank: January 1, 1814.
Wind SW. Weather hazy.

What is the life of man? Is it not to shift from trouble to trouble and from side to side? to button up one cause of vexation and unbutton another? So wrote the celebrated Sterne, so quoted the no less celebrated Jonathan, and so may the poor devil Pindar apply it to himself. You mention some two or three disappointments you have met with lately. For shame, Sir, to be so peevish and splenetic! Your disappointments are 'trifles light as air' when compared with the vexations and disappointments I have experienced. I was vexed and grieved to the very soul and beyond the soul, to go to Galloway and be deprived of the pleasure of—something you know nothing about. I was disappointed on my return at finding *her* in a devil of a bad shy humour. I was

—but why do I talk to *you* about such things? There are joys and sorrows, pleasures and pains, with which a Stoic Platonic humdrum bookworm sort of fellow like you, Sir, intermeddleth not, and consequently can have no idea of. I was disappointed in Bonaparte's escaping to Paris when he ought to have been taken prisoner by the allies at Leipsic. I was disappointed at your not mentioning anything about our old acquaintances at Edinburgh. Last night there was a flag on the mail, and to-night when I expected a Gazette announcing some great victory, the taking of Bayonne or the marching of Wellington to Bourdeaux, I was disappointed that the cause of all the rejoicing was an engagement with the French under the walls of Bayonne, in which we lost upwards of 500 men killed and 3,000 wounded, and drew off the remainder of our army safe from the destroying weapons of the enemy. I was disappointed last Sunday, after I had got my stockings on, to find that there was a hole in the heel of one of them. I read a great many books at Kirk-ton, and was disappointed at finding faults in almost every one of them. I will be disappointed; but what signifies going on at this rate? Unmixed happiness is not the lot of man—

> Of chance and change, oh! let not man complain,
> Else never, never, will he cease to wail.

The weather is dull; I am melancholy. Good night.

P.S.—My dearest Dean,—The weather is quite altered. The wind has veered about to the north. I am in good spirits, am happy.

From the Same.

Castlebank: May 9.

Dear Doctor,—I received yours last night, and a scurrilous, blackguarding, flattering, vexing, pernicked, humorous,

witty, daft letter it is. Shall I answer it piecemeal as a
certain Honourable House does a speech from its Sovereign,
by echoing back each syllable ?   No.   This won't do.   Oh !
how I envy you, Dean, that you can run on in such an off-
hand way, ever varying the scene with wit and mirth, while
honest Peter must hold on in one numskull track to all
eternity pursuing the even tenour of his way, so that one of
Peter's letters is as good as a thousand.

 You seem to take a friendly concern in my *affaires de
cœur*.   By the bye, now, Jonathan, without telling you any
particulars of my situation in these matters, which is scarcely
known to myself, can't I advise *you* to fall in love ?   Grant-
ing as I do that love is attended with sorrows, still, Doctor,
these are amply compensated by the tendency that this
tender passion has to ameliorate the heart, ' provided always,
and be it further enacted,' that, chaste as Don Quixote or
Don Quixote's horse, your heart never breathes a wish that
angels may not register.   Only have care of this, Dean, and
fall in love as soon as you can—you will be the better for it.

 Pages follow of excellent criticism from Peter on
Leyden's poems, on the Duke of Wellington, Miss
Porter, &c.   Carlyle has told him that he was looking
for a subject for an epic poem.   Peter gives him a
tragi-comic description of a wedding at Middlebie, with
the return home in a tempest, which he thinks will
answer; and concludes :—

 Your reflections on the fall of Napoleon bring to my mind
an observation of a friend of mine the other day.   I was repeating these lines in Shakespeare and applying them to Bony—

> But yesterday the word of Cæsar might
> Have stood against the world ; now lies he there,
> And none so poor to do him reverence.

' Ay, very true,' quoth he ; ' the fallow could na be content wi' maist all Europe, and now he's glad o' Elba room.'

Now, Doctor, let me repeat my instructions to you in a few words. Write immediately a very long letter ; write an epic poem as soon as may be. Send me some more ' remarks.' Tell me how you are, how you are spending your time in Edinburgh. Fall in love as soon as you can meet with a proper object. Ever be a friend to Pindar, and thou shalt always find one in the heart subdued, not subduing,

PETER.

In default of writings of his own, scarcely any of which survive out of this early period, such lineaments of Carlyle as appear through these letters are not without instructiveness.

CHAPTER III.

HAVING finished his college course, Carlyle looked
out for pupils to maintain himself. The ministry was
still his formal destination, but several years had still
to elapse before a final resolution would be necessary—
four years if he remained in Edinburgh attending
lectures in the Divinity Hall; six if he preferred
to be a rural Divinity student, presenting himself once
in every twelve months at the University and reading
a discourse. He did not wish to hasten matters, and,
the pupil business being precarious and the mathematical tutorship at Annan falling vacant, Carlyle
offered for it and was elected by competition in 1814.
He never liked teaching. The recommendation of the
place was the sixty or seventy pounds a year of salary,
which relieved his father of further expense upon him,
and enabled him to put by a little money every year,
to be of use in future either to himself or his family.
In other respects the life at Annan was only disagreeable. His tutor's work he did scrupulously well, but
the society of a country town had no interest for him.
He would not visit. He lived alone, shutting himself
up with his books, disliked the business more and more,
and came finally to hate it. Annan, associated as it
was with the odious memories of his schooldays, had

MAINHILL.

indeed but one merit—that he was within reach of his
family, especially of his mother, to whom he was
attached with a real passion.

His father had by this time given up business at
Ecclefechan, and had taken a farm in the neighbourhood. The great north road which runs through the
village rises gradually into an upland treeless grass
country. About two miles distant on the left-hand
side as you go towards Lockerby, there stands, about
three hundred yards in from the road, a solitary low
whitewashed cottage, with a few poor outbuildings
attached to it. This is Mainhill, which was now for
many years to be Carlyle's *home*, where he first learned
German, studied 'Faust' in a dry ditch, and completed
his translation of 'Wilhelm Meister.' The house itself
is, or was when the Carlyles occupied it, of one story, and
consisted of three rooms, a kitchen, a small bedroom,
and a large one connected with the kitchen by a passage. The door opens into a square farmyard, on one
side of which are stables, on the other side opposite
the door the cow byres, on the third a washhouse and
dairy. The situation is high, utterly bleak and swept
by all the winds. Not a tree shelters the premises;
the fences are low, the wind permitting nothing to
grow but stunted thorn. The view alone redeems the
dreariness of the situation. On the left is the great
hill of Burnswark. Broad Annandale stretches in front
down to the Solway, which shines like a long silver
riband; on the right is Hoddam Hill with the Tower
of Repentance on its crest, and the wooded slopes which
mark the line of the river. Beyond towers up Criffel,
and in the far distance Skiddaw, and Saddleback, and

Helvellyn, and the High Cumberland ridges on the track of the Roman wall. Here lived Carlyle's father and mother with their eight children, Carlyle himself spending his holidays with them; the old man and his younger sons cultivating the sour soil and winning a hard-earned living out of their toil, the mother and daughters doing the household work and minding cows and poultry, and taking their turn in the field with the rest in harvest time.

So two years passed away; Carlyle remaining at Annan. Of his own writing during this period there is little preserved, but his correspondence continued, and from his friends' letters glimpses can be gathered of his temper and occupations. He was mainly busy with mathematics, but he was reading incessantly, Hume's Essays among other books. He was looking out into the world, meditating on the fall of Napoleon, on the French Revolution, and thinking much of the suffering in Scotland which followed the close of the war. There were sarcastic sketches, too, of the families with which he was thrown in Annan. Robert Mitchell (an Edinburgh student who had become master of a school at Ruthwell) rallies him on 'having reduced the fair and fat academicians into scorched, singed, and shrivelled hags;' and hinting a warning 'against the temper with respect to this world which we are sometimes apt to entertain,' he suggests that young men like him and his correspondent 'ought to think how many are worse off than they,' 'should be thankful for what they had, and not allow imagination to create unreal distress.'

To another friend, Thomas Murray, author afterwards

of a history of Galloway, Carlyle had complained of his
fate in a light and less bitter spirit. To an epistle
written in this tone Murray replied with a description
of Carlyle's style, which deserves a place if but for the
fulfilment of the prophecy which it contains.

I have had the pleasure of receiving, my dear Carlyle,
your very humorous and friendly letter, a letter remarkable
for vivacity, a Shandean turn of expression, and an affectionate pathos, which indicate a peculiar turn of mind, make
sincerity doubly striking and wit doubly poignant. You
flatter me with saying my letter was good ; but allow me to
observe that among all my elegant and respectable correspondents there is none whose manner of letter-writing I so
much envy as yours. A happy flow of language either for
pathos, description, or humour, and an easy, graceful current
of ideas, appropriate to every subject, characterise your style.
This is not adulation ; I speak what I think. Your letters
will always be a feast to me, a varied and exquisite repast ;
and the time, I hope, will come, but I trust is far distant,
when these our juvenile epistles will be read and probably
applauded by a generation unborn, and that the name of
Carlyle, at least, will be inseparably connected with the
literary history of the nineteenth century. Generous ambition and perseverance will overcome every difficulty, and
our great Johnson says, 'Where much is attempted something is performed.' You will, perhaps, recollect that when
I convoyed you out of town in April, 1814, we were very
sentimental : we said that few knew us, and still fewer took
an interest in us, and that we would slip through the world
inglorious and unknown. But the prospect is altered. We
are probably as well known, and have made as great a figure,
as any of the same standing at college, and we do not know,
but will hope, what twenty years may bring forth.

A letter from you every fortnight shall be answered faithfully, and will be highly delightful; and if we live to be seniors, the letters of the companions of our youth will call to mind our college scenes, endeared to us by many tender associations, and will make us forget that we are poor and old. . . . That you may be always successful and enjoy every happiness that this evanescent world can afford, and that we may meet soon, is, my dear Carlyle, the sincere wish of

Yours most faithfully,
THOMAS MURRAY.

5 Carnegie Street: July 27, 1814.

Murray kept Carlyle's answer to this far-seeing letter.

Thomas Carlyle to Thomas Murray.

August, 1814.

Oh, Tom, what a foolish flattering creature thou art! To talk of future eminence in connection with the literary history of the nineteenth century to such a one as me! Alas! my good lad, when I and all my fancies and reveries and speculations shall have been swept over with the besom of oblivion, the literary history of no century will feel itself the worse. Yet think not, because I talk thus, I am careless of literary fame. No; Heaven knows that ever since I have been able to form a wish, the wish of being known has been the foremost.

Oh, Fortune! thou that givest unto each his portion in this dirty planet, bestow (if it shall please thee) coronets, and crowns, and principalities, and purses, and pudding, and power upon the great and noble and fat ones of the earth. Grant me that, with a heart of independence unyielding to thy favours and unbending to thy frowns, I may attain to literary fame; and though starvation be my lot, I will smile that I have not been born a king.

But alas! my dear Murray, what am I, or what are you, or what is any other poor unfriended stripling in the ranks of learning?

These college companions were worthy and innocent young men; none of them, however, came to any very high position, and Carlyle's career was now about to intersect with the life of a far more famous contemporary who flamed up a few years later into meridian splendour and then disappeared in delirium. Edward Irving was the son of a well-to-do burgess of Annan, by profession a tanner. Irving was five years older than Carlyle; he had preceded him at Annan School; he had gone thence to Edinburgh University, where he had specially distinguished himself, and had been selected afterwards to manage a school at Haddington, where his success as a teacher had been again conspicuous. Among his pupils at Haddington there was one gifted little girl who will be hereafter much heard of in these pages, Jane Baillie Welsh, daughter of a Dr. Welsh whose surgical fame was then great in that part of Scotland, a remarkable man who liked Irving and trusted his only child in his hands. The Haddington adventure had answered so well that Irving, after a year or two, was removed to a larger school at Kirk-caldy, where, though no fault was found with his teaching, he gave less complete satisfaction. A party among his patrons there thought him too severe with the boys, thought him proud, thought him this or that which they did not like. The dissentients re-solved at last to have a second school of their own, to be managed in a different style, and they applied to

the classical and mathematical professors at Edinburgh
to recommend them a master. Professor Christieson
and Professor Leslie, who had noticed Carlyle more
than he was aware of, had decided that he was the
fittest person that they knew of; and in the summer
of 1816 notice of the offered preferment was sent down
to him at Annan.

He had seen Irving's face occasionally in Ecclefechan church, and once afterwards, as has been said,
when Irving, fresh from his college distinctions, had
looked in at Annan school; but they had no personal
acquaintance, nor did Carlyle, while he was a master
there, ever visit the Irving family. Of course, however,
he was no stranger to the reputation of their brilliant
son, with whose fame all Annandale was ringing, and
with whom kind friends had compared him to his own
disadvantage.

I (he says) had heard much of Irving all along, how distinguished in studies, how splendidly successful as a teacher,
how two professors had sent him out to Haddington, and
how his new academy and new methods were illuminating
and astonishing everything there. I don't remember any
malicious envy towards this great Irving of the distance
for his greatness in study and learning. I certainly might
have had a tendency hadn't I struggled against it, and tried
to make it emulation. 'Do the like, do the like under difficulties.'

In the winter of 1815 Carlyle for the first time
personally met Irving, and the beginning of the acquaintance was not promising. He was still pursuing
his Divinity course. Candidates who could not attend

the regular lectures at the University came up once a
year and delivered an address of some kind in the
Divinity Hall. One already—in the first year of his
Annan mastership—he had given in an English sermon
on the text ' Before I was afflicted I went astray,' &c.
He calls it ' a weak flowery sentimental piece,' for
which, however, he had been complimented ' by com-
rades and professors.' His next was a discourse in Latin
on the question whether there was or was not such a
thing as ' Natural Religion.' This, too, he says was
' weak enough.' It is lost, and nothing is left to show
the view which he took about the matter. But here
also he gave satisfaction, and was innocently pleased
with himself. It was on this occasion that he fell in
accidentally with Irving at a friend's rooms in Edinburgh, and there was a trifling skirmish of tongue
between them, where Irving found the laugh turned
against him.

A few months after came Carlyle's appointment to
Kirkcaldy as Irving's *quasi* rival, and perhaps he felt
a little uneasy as to the terms on which they might
stand towards each other. His alarms, however, were
pleasantly dispelled. He was to go to Kirkcaldy in
the summer holidays of 1816 to see the people there
and be seen by them before coming to a final arrangement. Adam Hope, one of the masters in Annan
School, to whom Carlyle was much attached, and whose
portrait he has painted, had just lost his wife. Carlyle
had gone to sit with the old man in his sorrows, and
unexpectedly fell in with Irving there, who had come
on the same errand.

If (he says) I had been in doubts about his reception of me, he quickly and for ever ended them by a friendliness which on wider scenes might have been called chivalrous. At first sight he heartily shook my hand, welcomed me as if I had been a valued old acquaintance, almost a brother, and before my leaving came up to me again and with the frankest tone said, ' You are coming to Kirkcaldy to look about you in a month or two. You know I am there ; my house and all that I can do for you is yours ; two Annandale people must not be strangers in Fife.' The doubting Thomas durst not quite believe all this, so chivalrous was it, but felt pleased and relieved by the fine and sincere tone of it, and thought to himself, ' Well, it would be pretty.'

To Kirkcaldy, then, Carlyle went with hopes so far improved. How Irving kept his word; how warmly he received him ; how he opened his house, his library, his heart to him ; how they walked and talked together on Kirkcaldy Sands on the summer nights, and toured together in holiday time through the Highlands ; how Carlyle found in him a most precious and affectionate companion at the most critical period of his life—all this he has himself described. The reader will find it for himself in the Reminiscences which he has left of the time.

Irving (he says) was four years my senior, the *facile princeps* for success and reputation among the Edinburgh students, famed mathematician, famed teacher, first at Haddington, then here, a flourishing man whom cross fortune was beginning to nibble at. He received me with open arms, and was a brother to me and a friend there and elsewhere afterwards—such friend as I never had again or before in this world, at heart constant till he died.

I am tempted to fill many pages with extracted pictures of the Kirkcaldy life as Carlyle has drawn them. But they can be read in their place, and there is much else to tell; my business is to supply what is left untold, rather than give over again what has been told already.

CHAPTER IV.

A.D. 1817. ÆT. 22.

CORRESPONDENCE with his family had commenced and was regularly continued from the day when Carlyle went first to college. The letters, however, which are preserved begin with his settlement at Kirkcaldy. From this time they are constant, regular, and, from the care with which they have been kept on both sides, are to be numbered in thousands. Father, mother, brothers, sisters, all wrote in their various styles, and all received answers. They were 'a clannish folk' holding tight together, and Carlyle was looked up to as the scholar among them. Of these letters I can give but a few here and there, but they will bring before the eyes the Mainhill farm, and all that was going on there in a sturdy, pious, and honourable Annandale peasant's household. Carlyle had spent his Christmas holidays 1816-17 at home as usual, and had returned to work.

James Carlyle to Thomas Carlyle

Mainhill: February 12, 1817.

Dear Son,—I embrace this opportunity of writing you a few lines with the carrier, as I had nothing to say that was worth postage, having written to you largely the last time. But only I have reason to be thankful that I can still tell you that we are all in good health, blessed be God for all his mercies towards us. Your mother has got your stockings ready now, and I think there are a few pairs of very good ones. Times is very bad here for labourers—work is no brisker and living is high. There have been meetings held by the lairds and farmers to assist them in getting meal. They propose to take all the meal that can be sold in the parish to Ecclefechan, for which they shall have full price, and there they sign another paper telling how much money they will give to reduce the price. The charge is given to James Bell, Mr. Miller, and William Graham to sell it.

Mr. Lawson, our priest, is doing very well, and has given us no more paraphrases ; but seems to please every person that hears him, and indeed he is well attended every day. The sacrament is to be the first Sabbath of March, and he is visiting his people, but has not reached Mainhill. Your mother was very anxious to have the house done before he came, or else she said she would run over the hill and hide herself. Sandy[1] and I got to work soon after you went away, built partitions, and ceiled—a good floor laid—and indeed it is very dry and comfortable at this time, and we are very snug and have no want of the necessaries of life. Our crop is as good as I expected, and our sheep and all our cattle living and doing very well. Your mother thought to have written to you ; but the carrier stopped only two days at home, and she being a very slow writer could not get it done, but she will write next opportunity. I add no more but your mother's compliments, and she sends you half the cheese that she was telling you about. Say in your next how your butter is coming on, and tell us when it is done and we will send you more. Write soon after you receive this, and tell us all your news and how you are coming on. I say no more, but remain,

Dear son, your loving father,

JAMES CARLYLE.

[1] Alexander Carlyle, the second son.

Thomas Carlyle to Mrs. Carlyle (Mainhill).

Kirkcaldy: March 17, 1817.

My dear Mother,—I have been long intending to write you a line or two in order to let you know my state and condition, but having nothing worth writing to communicate I have put it off from time to time. There was little enjoyment for any person at Mainhill when I was there last, but I look forward to the ensuing autumn, when I hope to have the happiness of discussing matters with you as we were wont to do of old. It gives me pleasure to hear that the bairns are at school. There are few things in this world more valuable than knowledge, and youth is the period for acquiring it. With the exception of the religious and moral instruction which I had the happiness of receiving from my parents, and which I humbly trust will not be entirely lost upon me, there is nothing for which I feel more grateful than for the education which they have bestowed upon me. Sandy was getting fond of reading when he went away. I hope he and Aitken[1] will continue their operations now that he is at home. There cannot be imagined a more honest way of employing spare hours.

My way of life in this place is much the same as formerly. The school is doing pretty well, and my health through the winter has been uniformly good. I have little intercourse with the natives here ; yet there is no dryness between us. We are always happy to meet and happy to part ; but their society is not very valuable to me, and my books are friends that never fail me. Sometimes I see the minister and some others of them, with whom I am very well satisfied, and Irving and I are very friendly ; so I am never wearied or at a loss to pass the time.

I had designed this night to write to Aitken about his

[1] John Aitken Carlyle, the third son, afterwards known as John.

books and studies, but I will scarcely have time to say anything. There is a book for him in the box, and I would have sent him the geometry, but it was not to be had in the town. I have sent you a scarf as near the kind as Aitken's very scanty description would allow me to come. I hope it will please you. It is as good as any that the merchant had. A shawl of the same materials would have been warmer, but I had no authority to get it. Perhaps you would like to have a shawl also. If you will tell me what colour you prefer, I will send it you with all the pleasure in the world. I expect to hear from you as soon as you can find leisure. You must be very minute in your account of your domestic affairs. My father once spoke of a threshing machine. If twenty pounds or so will help him, they are quite ready at his service.

I remain, dear mother, your affectionate son,

THOMAS CARLYLE.

Mrs. Carlyle could barely write at this time. She taught herself later in life for the pleasure of communicating with her son, between whom and herself there existed a special and passionate attachment of a quite peculiar kind. She was a severe Calvinist, and watched with the most affectionate anxiety over her children's spiritual welfare, her eldest boy's above all. The hope of her life was to see him a minister—a ' priest ' she would have called it—and she was already alarmed to know that he had no inclination that way.

Mrs. Carlyle to Thomas Carlyle.

Mainhill: June 10, 1817.

Dear Son,—I take this opportunity of writing you a few lines, as you will get it free. I long to have a crack,[1] and

---

[1] Familiar talk.

look forward to August, trusting to see thee once more, but in hope the meantime. Oh, Tom, mind the golden season of youth, and remember your Creator in the days of your youth. Seek God while He may be found. Call upon Him while He is near. We hear that the world by wisdom knew not God. Pray for His presence with you, and His counsel to guide you. Have you got through the Bible yet? If you have, read it again. I hope you will not weary, and may the Lord open your understanding.

I have no news to tell you, but thank God we are all in our ordinary way. I hope you are well. I thought you would have written before now. I received your present and was very proud of it. I called it ' my son's venison.' Do write as soon as this comes to hand and tell us all your news. I am glad you are so contented in your place. We ought all to be thankful for our places in these distressing times, for I dare say they are felt keenly. We send you a small piece of ham and a minding of butter, as I am sure yours is done before now. Tell us about it in your next, and if anything is wanting.

Good night, Tom, for it is a very stormy night, and I must away to the byre to milk.

Now, Tom, be sure to tell me about your chapters. No more from

Your old
MINNIE.

The letters from the other members of the family were sent equally regularly whenever there was an opportunity, and give between them a perfect picture of healthy rustic life at the Mainhill farm—the brothers and sisters down to the lowest all hard at work, the little ones at school, the elders ploughing, reaping, tending cattle, or minding the dairy, and in the intervals reading history, reading Scott's novels, or even trying at geometry, which was then Carlyle's own favourite study. In the summer of 1817 the mother had a severe illness, by which her mind was affected. It was necessary to place her for a few weeks under restraint away from home—a step no doubt just and necessary, but which she never wholly forgave, but resented in her own humorous way to the end of her life. The disorder soon passed off, however, and never returned.

Meanwhile Carlyle was less completely contented with his position at Kirkcaldy than he had let his mother suppose. For one thing he hated school-mastering, and would, or thought he would, have preferred to work with his hands; while except Irving he had scarcely a friend in the place for whom he cared. His occupation shut him out from the best kind of society, which there, as elsewhere, had its exclusive rules. He was received, for Irving's sake, in the family of Mr. Martin, the minister; and was in some degree of intimacy there, liking Martin himself, and to some extent, but not much, his wife and daughters, to one of whom Irving had, perhaps too precipitately, become engaged. There were others also—Mr. Swan, a Kirkcaldy merchant, particularly—of whom he had a grateful remembrance; but it is clear, both from Irving's letters to him and from his own confession, that he was not popular either there or anywhere. Shy and reserved at one moment, at another sarcastically self-asserting, with forces working in him which he did not himself understand, and which still less could be understood by others, he could neither properly accommodate himself to the tone of Scotch provincial drawing-rooms, nor even to the business which he had especially to do. A man of genius can do the lowest work as well as the highest; but genius in the process of developing, combined with an irritable nervous system and a fiercely impatient temperament, was not happily occupied in teaching stupid lads the elements of Latin and arithmetic. Nor were matters mended when the Town Corporation, who were his masters, took upon them, as sometimes happened, to instruct or rebuke him.

Life, however, even under these hard circumstances, was not without its romance. I borrow a passage from the 'Reminiscences':—

The Kirkcaldy population were a pleasant, honest kind of fellow mortals, something of quietly fruitful, of good old Scotch in their works and ways, more vernacular, peaceably fixed and almost genial in their mode of life, than I had been used to in the border home land. Fife generally we liked. Those ancient little burghs and sea villages, with their poor little havens, salt-pans and weather-beaten bits of Cyclopean breakwaters, and rude innocent machineries, are still kindly to me to think of. Kirkcaldy itself had many looms, had Baltic trade, whale fishery, &c., and was a solidly diligent and yet by no means a panting, puffing, or in any way gambling 'Lang Toun.' Its flax-mill machinery, I remember, was turned mainly by wind; and curious blue-painted wheels with oblique vans rose from many roofs for that end. We, I in particular, always rather liked the people, though from the distance chiefly, chagrined and discouraged by the sad trade one had. Some hospitable human fire sides I found,

and these were at intervals a fine little element; but in
general we were but onlookers, the one real society our books
and our few selves. Not even with the bright young ladies
(which was a sad feature) were we generally on speaking
terms. By far the brightest and cleverest, however, an ex-
pupil of Irving's, and genealogically and otherwise, being
poorish and well-bred, rather a kind of alien in the place, I did
at last make some acquaintance with—at Irving's first, I think,
though she rarely came thither—and it might easily have
been more, had she and her aunt and our economics and
other circumstances liked. She was of the fair-complexioned,
softly elegant, softly grave, witty and comely type, and had
a good deal of gracefulness, intelligence, and other talent.
Irving, too, it was sometimes thought, found her very interesting, could the Miss Martin bonds have allowed, which
they never would. To me, who had only known her for a
few months, and who within a twelve or fifteen months saw
the last of her, she continued, for perhaps three years, a
figure hanging more or less in my fancy, on the usual
romantic, or latterly quite elegiac and silent terms, and to
this day there is in me a good will to her, a candid and
gentle pity, if needed at all. She was of the Aberdeenshire
Gordons, Margaret Gordon, born I think in New Bruns-
wick, where her father, probably in some official post, had
died young and poor; her accent was prettily English, and
her voice very fine.

An aunt (widow in Fife, childless with limited resources,
but of frugal cultivated turn; a lean proud elderly dame,
once a Miss Gordon herself; sang Scotch songs beautifully,
and talked shrewd Aberdeenish in accent and otherwise) had
adopted her and brought her hither over seas; and here, as
Irving's ex-pupil, she now, cheery though with dim outlooks,
was. Irving saw her again in Glasgow one summer tour-
ing, &c.; he himself accompanying joyfully—not joining, so

1—2

I understood it, the retinue of suitors or potential suitors;
rather perhaps indicating gently 'No, I must not.' A year
or so after we heard the fair Margaret had married some
rich Mr. Something, who afterwards got into Parliament,
thence out to 'Nova Scotia' (or so) as governor, and I
heard of her no more, except that lately she was still
living childless as the 'dowager lady,' her Mr. Something
having got knighted before dying. Poor Margaret! I saw
her recognisably to me here in her London time, 1840 or so,
twice; once with her maid in Piccadilly promenading—little
altered; a second time that same year, or next, on horseback
both of us, and meeting in the gate of Hyde Park, when her
eyes (but that was all) said to me almost touchingly, yes,
yes, that is you.

Margaret Gordon was the original, so far as there was
an original, of Blumine in 'Sartor Resartus.' Two
letters from her remain among Carlyle's papers, which
show that on both sides their regard for each other had
found expression. Circumstances, however, and the
unpromising appearance of Carlyle's situation and
prospects, forbade an engagement between them, and
acquit the aunt of needless harshness in peremptorily
putting an end to their acquaintance. Miss Gordon
took leave of him as a 'sister' in language of affectionate advice. A single passage may be quoted to
show how the young unknown Kirkcaldy schoolmaster
appeared in the eyes of the young high-born lady who
had thus for a moment crossed his path.

And now, my dear friend, a long long adieu; one advice,
and as a parting one consider, value it. Cultivate the milder
dispositions of your heart. Subdue the more extravagant

visions of the brain. In time your abilities must be known. Among your acquaintance they are already beheld with wonder and delight. By those whose opinion will be valuable, they hereafter will be appreciated. Genius will render you great. May virtue render you beloved! Remove the awful distance between you and ordinary men by kind and gentle manners. Deal gently with their inferiority, and be convinced they will respect you as much and like you more. Why conceal the real goodness that flows in your heart? I have ventured this counsel from an anxiety for your future welfare, and I would enforce it with all the earnestness of the most sincere friendship. Let your light shine before men, and think them not unworthy the trouble. This exercise will prove its own reward. It must be a pleasing thing to live in the affections of others. Again adieu. Pardon the freedom I have used, and when you think of me be it as a kind sister, to whom your happiness will always yield delight, and your griefs sorrow.

Yours, with esteem and regard,

M.

I give you not my address because I dare not promise to see you.

CHAPTER V.

A.D. 1818.   ÆT. 23.

CARLYLE had by this time abandoned the thought of the
'ministry' as his possible future profession—not without a struggle, for both his father's and his mother's
hearts had been set upon it; but the 'grave pro-
hibitive doubts' which had risen in him of their own
accord had been strengthened by Gibbon, whom he
had found in Irving's library and eagerly devoured.
Never at any time had he 'the least inclination' for such
an office, and his father, though deeply disappointed,
was too genuine a man to offer the least remonstrance.[1]
The 'schoolmastering' too, after two years' experience
of it, became intolerable.   His disposition, at once
shy and defiantly proud, had perplexed and displeased

---

[1] 'With me,' he says in a private note, 'it was never much in favour,
though my parents silently much wished it, as I knew well.   Finding I
had objections, my father, with a magnanimity which I admired and
admire, left me frankly to my own guidance in that matter, as did my
mother, perhaps still more lovingly, though not so silently; and the
theological course which could be prosecuted or kept open by appearing
annually, putting down your name, but with some trifling fee, in the
register, and then going your way, was, after perhaps two years of this
languid form, allowed to close itself for good.   I remember yet being on
the street in Argyll Square, Edinburgh, probably in 1817, and come
over from Kirkcaldy with some intent, the languidest possible, still to
put down my name and fee.   The official person, when I rung, was
not at home, and my instant feeling was, "Very good, then, very
good; let this be Finis in the matter," and it really was.'

the Kirkcaldy burghers. Both he and Irving also
fell into unpleasant collisions with them, and neither
of the two was sufficiently docile to submit tamely to
reproof.[1]   An opposition school had been set up which
drew off the pupils, and finally they both concluded
that they had had enough of it—'better die than be
a schoolmaster for one's living'—and would seek some
other means of supporting themselves.   Carlyle had
passed his summer holidays as usual at Mainhill
(1818), where he had perhaps talked over his prospects
with his family.   On his return to Kirkcaldy in
September he wrote to his father explaining his
situation.   He had saved about 90*l.*, on which, with
his thrifty habits, he said that he could support himself in Edinburgh till he could 'fall into some other

---

[1] Carlyle says in the *Reminiscences* that Irving was accused of harshness to the boys.   Kirkcaldy tradition has preserved instances of it,
which sound comical enough at a distance, but were no matter of
laughter to the sufferers.   A correspondent writes to me:—'Irving
has the reputation to this day of being a very hard master.   He
thrashed the boys frequently and unmercifully.   A story in illustration
was told me.   A carpenter, a bit of a character, whose shop was
directly opposite Irving's school, hearing a fearful howling one day,
rushed across, axe in hand, drove up the door, and to Irving's query what
he did there, replied, "I thocht ye were killin' the lad, and cam' over
tae see if ye were needin' help."   Carlyle, on the contrary, I was
assured, never lifted his hand to a scholar.   Still he had perfect command over them.   A look or a word was sufficient to command attention
and obedience.   Nor have I ever heard that this command was attri-
butable to fear.   So far as I can learn, it was entirely due to the respect
which he seems to have obtained from the first.'   There is *some* truth
in these legends of Irving's severity, for Carlyle himself admits it.
But tradition always tends to shape stories and characters into an
artistic completeness which had no real existence.   The authentic
evidence of Irving's essential kindness and affectionate gentleness makes
it impossible to believe that he was ever wantonly or carelessly cruel.

way of doing.' He could perhaps get a few mathematical pupils, and meantime could study for the *bar*. He waited only for his father's approval to send in his resignation. The letter was accompanied by one of his constant presents to his mother, who was again at home, though not yet fully recovered.

John Carlyle to Thomas Carlyle.

Mainhill: September 16, 1818.

Dear Brother,—We received yours, and it told us of your safe arrival at Kirkcaldy. Our mother has grown better every day since you left us. She is as steady as ever she was, has been upon haystacks three or four times, and has been at church every Sabbath since she came home, behaving always very decently. Also she has given over talking and singing, and spends some of her time consulting Ralph Erskine. She sleeps every night, and hinders no person to sleep, but can do with less than the generality of people. In fact we may conclude that she is as wise as could be expected. She has none of the hypocritical mask with which some people clothe their sentiments. One day, having met Agg Byers, she says : 'Weel, Agg, lass, I've never spoken t'ye sin ye stole our coals. I'll gie ye an advice : never steal nae more.'

Alexander Carlyle to Thomas Carlyle.

September 18, 1818.

My dear Brother,—We were glad to hear of your having arrived in safety, though your prospects were not brilliant. My father is at Ecclefechan to-day at a market, but before he went he told me to mention that with regard to his advising you, he was unable to give you any advice. He thought it might be necessary to consult Leslie before you gave up, but you might do what seemed to you good. Had my advice any weight, I would advise you to try the law. You may think you have not money enough to try that, but with what assistance we could make, and your own industry, I think there would be no fear but you would succeed. The box which contained my mother's bonnet came a day or two ago. She is very well pleased with it, though my father thought it too gaudy; but she proposes writing to you herself.

The end was, that when December came Carlyle and Irving 'kicked the schoolmaster functions over,' removed to Edinburgh, and were adrift on the world. Irving had little to fear; he had money, friends, reputation; he had a profession, and was waiting only for 'a call' to enter on his full privileges. Carlyle was far more unfavourably situated. He was poor, unpopular, comparatively unknown, or, if known, known only to be feared and even shunned. In Edinburgh 'from my fellow-creatures,' he says, 'little or nothing but vinegar was my reception when we happened to meet or pass near each other—my own blame mainly, so proud, shy, poor, at once so insignificant-looking and so grim and sorrowful. That in " Sartor " of the worm trodden on and proving a torpedo is not wholly a fable, but did actually befall once or twice, as I still with a kind of small, not ungenial, malice can remember.' He had, however, as was said, nearly a hundred pounds, which he had saved out of his earnings; he had a consciousness of integrity worth more than gold to him. He had thrifty self-denying habits which made him content with the barest necessaries, and he resolutely faced his position. His family, though silently disapproving the

step which he had taken and necessarily anxious about
him, rendered what help they could.   Once more the
Ecclefechan carrier brought up the weekly or monthly
supplies of oatmeal, cakes, butter, and, when needed,
under garments, returning with the dirty linen for
the mother to wash and mend, and occasional presents which were never forgotten ;   while Carlyle,
after a thought of civil engineering, for which his
mathematical training gave him a passing inclination,
sate down seriously, if not very assiduously, to study
law.   Letters to and from Ecclefechan were constant,
the carrier acting as postman.   Selections from them
bring the scene and characters before the reader's eyes.

Sister Mary, then twelve years old, writes :—

I take this opportunity of sending you this scrawl.   I got
the hat you sent with Sandy [brother Alexander], and it fits
very well.   It was far too good ; a worse would have done
very well.   Boys and I are employed this winter in waiting
on the cattle, and are going on very well at present.   I
generally write a copy every night, and read a little in the
'Cottagers of Glenburnie,' or some such like ; and it shall be
my earnest desire never to imitate the abominable slatteries
of Mrs. Maclarty.   The remarks of the author, Mrs. Hamilton, often bring your neat ways in my mind, and I hope to
be benefited by them.   In the mean time, I shall endeavour
to be a good girl, to be kind and obedient to my parents,
and obliging to my brothers and sisters.   You will write me
a long letter when the carrier comes back.

The mother was unwearied in her affectionate solicitude—solicitude for the eternal as well as temporal
interests of her darling child.

Mrs. Carlyle to Thomas Carlyle.

Mainhill: January 3, 1819.

Dear Son,—I received yours in due time, and was glad to hear you were well. I hope you will be healthier, moving about in the city, than in your former way. Health is a valuable privilege; try to improve it, then. The time is short. Another year has commenced. Time is on the wing, and flies swiftly. Seek God with all your heart; and oh, my dear son, cease not to pray for His counsel in all your ways. Fear not the world; you will be provided for as He sees meet for you.

As a sincere friend, whom you are always dear to, I beg you do not neglect reading a part of your Bible daily, and may the Lord open your eyes to see wondrous things out of His law! But it is now two o'clock in the morning, and a bad pen, bad ink, and I as bad at writing. I will drop it, and add no more, but remain

Your loving mother,
PEGGIE CARLYLE.

Carlyle had written a sermon on the salutary effects of 'affliction,' as his first exercise in the Divinity School. He was beginning now, in addition to the problem of living which he had to solve, to learn what affliction meant. He was attacked with dyspepsia, which never wholly left him, and in these early years soon assumed its most torturing form, like 'a rat gnawing at the pit of his stomach.' His disorder working on his natural irritability found escape in expressions which showed, at any rate, that he was attaining a mastery of language. The pain made him furious; and in such a humour the commonest calamities of life became unbearable horrors.

I find living here very high (he wrote soon after he was settled in his lodgings). An hour ago I paid my week's bill, which, though 15s. 2d., was the smallest of the three I have yet discharged. This is an unreasonable sum when I consider the slender accommodation and the paltry, ill-cooked morsel which is my daily pittance. There is also a schoolmaster right overhead, whose noisy brats give me at times no small annoyance. On a given night of the week he also assembles a select number of vocal performers, whose music, as they charitably name it, is now and then so clamorous that I almost wished the throats of these sweet singers full of molten lead, or any other substance that would stop their braying.

But he was not losing heart, and liked so far as he had seen into it, his new profession.

The law (he told his mother) is what I sometimes think I was intended for naturally. I am afraid it takes several hundreds to become an advocate ; but for this I should commence the study of it with great hopes of success. We shall see whether it is possible. One of the first advocates of the day raised himself from being a disconsolate preacher to his present eminence. Therefore I entreat you not to be uneasy about me. I see none of my fellows with whom I am very anxious to change places. Tell the boys not to let their hearts be troubled for me. I am a stubborn dog, and evil fortune shall not break my heart or bend it either, as I hope. I know not how to speak about the washing which you offer so kindly. Surely you thought, five years ago, that this troublesome washing and baking was all over ; and now to recommence ! I can scarcely think of troubling you ; yet the clothes are ill-washed here ; and if the box be going and coming any way, perhaps you can manage it.

While law lectures were being attended, the difficulty was to live. Pupils were a not very effective resource, and of his adventures in this department Carlyle gave ridiculous accounts. In February, 1819, he wrote to his brother :—

About a week ago I briefly dismissed an hour of private teaching. A man in the New Town applied to one Nichol, public teacher of mathematics here, for a person to give instruction in arithmetic, or something of that sort. Nichol spoke of me, and I was in consequence directed to call on the man next morning. I went at the appointed hour, and after waiting for a few minutes, was met by a stout, impudent-looking man with red whiskers, having much the air of an attorney, or some such creature of that sort. As our conversation may give you some insight into these matters, I report the substance of it. 'I am here,' I said, after making a slight bow, which was just perceptibly returned, ' by the request of Mr. Nichol, to speak with you, sir, about a mathematical teacher whom he tells me you want.' 'Aye. What are your terms ? ' ' Two guineas a month for each hour.' ' Two guineas a month ! that is perfectly extravagant.' ' I believe it to be the rate at which every teacher of respectability in Edinburgh officiates, and I *know* it to be the rate below which I never officiate.' 'That will not do for my friend.' ' I am sorry that nothing else will do for me ; ' and I retired with considerable deliberation.

Other attempts were not so unsuccessful ; one, sometimes two, pupils were found ready to pay at the rate required. Dr. Brewster, afterwards Sir David, discovered Carlyle and gave him occasional employment on his Encyclopædia. He was thus able to earn, as

long as the session lasted, about two pounds a week,
and on this he contrived to live without trenching on
his capital. His chief pleasure was his correspondence
with his mother, which never slackened. She had
written to tell him of the death of her sister Mary.
He replies :—

Edinburgh: Monday, March 29, 1819.

My dear Mother,—I am so much obliged to you for the
affectionate concern which you express for me in that brief
letter that I cannot delay to send you a few words by way of
reply. I was affected by the short notice you give me of
Aunt Mary's death, and the short reflection with which you
close it. It is true, my dear mother, 'that we must all soon
follow her,' such is the unalterable and not unpleasing doom
of men. Then it is well for those who, at that awful moment
which is before every one, shall be able to look back with
calmness and forward with hope. But I need not dwell upon
this solemn subject. It is familiar to the thoughts of every
one who has any thought.

I am rather afraid I have not been quite regular in reading
that best of books which you recommended to me. However, last night I was reading upon my favourite Job, and I
hope to do better in time to come. I entreat you to believe
that I am sincerely desirous of being a good man : and
though we may differ in some few unimportant particulars.
yet I firmly trust that the same power which created us with
imperfect faculties will pardon the errors of every one (and
none are without them) who seeks truth and righteousness
with a simple heart.

You need not fear my studying too much. In fact, my
prospects are so unsettled that I do not often sit down to
books with all the zeal I am capable of. You are not to
think I am fretful. I have long accustomed my mind to

look upon the future with a sedate aspect, and at any rate my hopes have never yet failed me. A French author, d'Alembert (one of the few persons who deserve the honourable epithet of honest man), whom I was lately reading, remarks that one who devoted his life to learning ought to carry for his motto, 'Liberty, Truth, Poverty,' for he that fears the latter can never have the former. This should not prevent one from using every honest effort to attain a comfortable situation in life ; it says only that the best is dearly bought by base conduct, and the worst is not worth mourning over. We shall speak of all these matters more fully in summer, for I am meditating just now to come down to stay a while with you, accompanied with a cargo of books, Italian, German, and others. You will give me yonder little room, and you will waken me every morning about five or six o'clock. Then *such* study. I shall delve in the garden, too, and in a word, become not only the wisest but the strongest man in those regions. This is all *claver*, but it pleases one.

My dear mother, yours most affectionately,

Thomas Carlyle.

D'Alembert's name had probably never reached Annandale, and Mrs. Carlyle could not gather from it into what perilous regions her son was travelling —but her quick ear caught something in the tone which frightened her.

Oh, my dear, dear son (she answered at once and eagerly), I would pray for a blessing on your learning. I beg you with all the feeling of an affectionate mother that you would study the Word of God, which He has graciously put in our hands, that it may powerfully reach our hearts, that we may discern it in its true light. God made man after His own image, therefore he behoved to be without any imperfect faculties. Beware, my dear son, of such thoughts ; let them not dwell on your mind. God forbid ! But I dare say you will not care to read this scrawl. Do make religion your great study, Tom ; if you repent it, I will bear the blame for ever.

Carlyle was thinking as much as his mother of religion, but the form in which his thoughts were running was not hers. He was painfully seeing that all things were not wholly as he had been taught to think them; the doubts which had stopped his divinity career were blackening into thunderclouds; and all his reflections were coloured by dyspepsia. ‘I was entirely unknown in Edinburgh circles,’ he says, ‘solitary, eating my own heart, fast losing my health too, a prey to nameless struggles and miseries, which have yet a kind of horror in them to my thoughts, three weeks without any kind of sleep from impossibility to be free of noise.’ In fact he was entering on what he called ‘the three most miserable years of my life.’ He would have been saved from much could he have resolutely thrown himself into his intended profession; but he soon came to hate it, as just then, perhaps, he would have hated anything.

I had thought (he writes in a note somewhere) of attempting to become an advocate. It seemed glorious to me for its independency, and I did read some law books, attend Hume's lectures on Scotch law, and converse with and question various dull people of the practical sort. But it and they and the admired lecturing Hume himself appeared to me mere denizens of the kingdom of dulness, pointing towards nothing but money as wages for all that bogpool of disgust. Hume's lectures once done with, I flung the thing away for ever.

Men who are out of humour with themselves see their own condition reflected in the world outside them, and everything seems amiss because it is not well with themselves. But the state of Scotland and England also was well fitted to feed Carlyle's discontent. The great war had been followed by a collapse. Wages were low, food at famine prices. Tens of thousands of artisans were out of work, their families were starving, and they themselves were growing mutinous. Even at home from his own sternly patient father, who never meddled with politics, he heard things not calculated to reconcile him to existing arrangements.

I have heard my father say (he mentions), with an impressiveness which all his perceptions carried with them, that the lot of a poor man was growing worse, that the world would not, and could not, last as it was, but mighty changes, of which none saw the end, were on the way. In the dear years when the oatmeal was as high as ten shillings a stone, he had noticed the labourers, I have heard him tell, retire each separately to a brook and there drink instead of dining, anxious only to hide it.[1]

These early impressions can be traced through the whole of Carlyle's writings; the conviction was forced upon him that there was something vicious to the bottom in English and Scotch society, and that revolution in some form or other lay visibly ahead. So long as Irving remained in Edinburgh 'the condition of the

---

[1] *Reminiscences,* vol. i. p. 60.

people' question was the constant subject of talk between him and Carlyle. They were both of them ardent, radical, indignant at the injustice which they witnessed, and as yet unconscious of the difficulty of mending it. Irving, however, he had seen little of since they had moved to Edinburgh, and he was left, for the most part, alone with his own thoughts. There had come upon him the trial which in these days awaits every man of high intellectual gifts and noble nature on their first actual acquaintance with human things—the question, far deeper than any mere political one, What is this world then, what is this human life, over which a just God is said to preside, but of whose presence or whose providence so few signs are visible? In happier ages religion silences scepticism if it cannot reply to its difficulties, and postpones the solution of the mystery to another stage of existence. Brought up in a pious family where religion was not talked about or emotionalised, but was accepted as the rule of thought and conduct, himself too instinctively upright, pure of heart, and reverent, Carlyle, like his parents, had accepted the Bible as a direct communication from Heaven. It made known the will of God, and the relation in which man stood to his Maker, as present facts like a law of nature, the truth of it, like the truth of gravitation, which man must act upon or immediately suffer the consequences. But religion, as revealed in the Bible, passes beyond present conduct, penetrates all forms of thought, and takes possession wherever it goes. It claims to control the intellect, to explain the past, and foretell the future. It has entered into poetry and art, and has been the interpreter of history. And thus there had grown round it a body of opinion, on all varieties of subjects, assumed to be authoritative; dogmas which science was contradicting; a history of events which it called infallible, yet which the canons of evidence, by which other histories are tried and tested successfully, declared not to be infallible at all. To the Mainhill household the Westminster Confession was a full and complete account of the position of mankind and of the Being to whom they owed their existence. The Old and New Testament not only contained all spiritual truth necessary for guidance in word and deed, but every fact related in them was literally true. To doubt was not to mistake, but was to commit a sin of the deepest dye, and was a sure sign of a corrupted heart. Carlyle's wide study of modern literature had shown him that much of this had appeared to many of the strongest minds in Europe to be doubtful or even plainly incredible. Young men of genius are the first to feel the growing influences of their time, and on Carlyle they fell in their most painful form. Notwithstanding his pride, he was most modest and self-distrustful. He had been taught that want of faith was sin, yet, like a true Scot, he knew that he would peril his soul if he pretended to believe what his intellect told him was false. If any part of what was called Revelation was mistaken, how could he be assured of the rest? How could he tell that the moral part of it, to which the phenomena which he saw round him were in plain contradiction, was more than a 'devout imagination'? Thus to poverty and dyspepsia there had been added the struggle which is always hardest in the noblest minds, which Job had known, and David, and Solomon, and Æschylus, and Shakespeare, and Goethe. Where are the tokens of His presence? where are the signs of His coming? Is there, in this universe of things, any moral Providence at all? or is it the product of some force of the nature of which we can know nothing save only that 'one event comes alike to all, to the good as to the evil, and there is no difference'?

Commonplace persons, if assailed by such misgivings, thrust them aside, throw themselves into occupation, and leave doubt to settle itself. Carlyle could not. The importunacy of the overwhelming problem forbade him to settle himself either to law or any other business till he had wrestled down the misgivings which had grappled with him. The greatest of us have our weaknesses, and the Margaret Gordon business had perhaps intertwined itself with the spiritual torment. The result of it was that Carlyle was extremely miserable, 'tortured,' as he says, 'by the freaks of an imagination of extraordinary and wild activity.'

He went home, as he had proposed, after the session, but Mainhill was never a less happy home to him than it proved this summer. He could not conceal, perhaps he did not try to conceal, the condition of his mind; and to his family, to whom the truth of their creed was no more a matter of doubt than the presence of the sun in the sky, he must have seemed as if 'possessed.' He could not read; he wandered about the moors like a restless spirit. His mother was in agony about him. He was her darling, her pride, the apple of her eye, and she could not restrain her lamentations and remonstrances. His father, with supreme good judgment, left him to himself.

His tolerance for me, his trust in me (Carlyle says), was great. When I declined going forward into the Church, though his heart was set upon it, he respected my scruples, and patiently let me have my way. When I had peremptorily ceased from being a schoolmaster, though he inwardly disapproved of the step as imprudent and saw me in successive summers lingering beside him in sickness of body and mind, without outlook towards any good, he had the forbearance to say at worst nothing, never once to whisper discontent with me.

A letter from Irving, to whom he had written complaining of his condition and of his friend's silence, was welcome at this dreary period.

Edward Irving to Thomas Carlyle.

Edinburgh: June 4, 1819.

Dear Sir,—My apology for neglecting you so long is that I have been equally negligent of myself. By what fatality I know not, I have been so entirely devoted to idleness or to insignificant employments since you left me, that German, Italian, and every other study, useful or serious, has been relinquished. Perhaps this renewal of our intercourse may be the date of my awakening from my slumber, as the breaking up of our intercourse was the date of its commencement. To speak of myself, that most grateful of topics, is therefore out of the question ; as it would only be to expose the day dreams of this my lethargy to one whose active mind has no sympathy with listlessness and drowsiness, and this subject being excluded, where shall I find materials for this letter ?

I could detail to you the mineralogy of the Campsey hills, and tell you of the overlying formation of porphyry above the green stone, and of the nearly horizontal bed of lime-

stone on the green stone which supplies the greater part of
Stirling, Dumbarton, and Strathearn, and of a curious quarry
of stone which is carried far and near for building stoves and
setting grates, with an account of its singular virtue of
resisting heat; but well I know you are weary unto death
of such jargon. And I could relate to you one most sentimental incident that did befall me on that journey, whereby
hangs a tale which might furnish matter for a novel or even
a modern tragedy; but then I suspect you have already put
me down for an adventure hunter, which is too near a stage
to a story-teller to fall in with my fancy.

Now the truth is, to throw in a word of self-defence, if I
have a turn for the romantic, it is not for the vanity of being
the actor of a strange part, or the spouter of a strange tale,
in the various scenes of the great drama of this mortal state;
but rather to be a spectator of those who are so, more especially if they be unfortunate withal; and occasionally I confess to have the privilege of the ancient chorus, of moralising
a little, or rather not a little, upon the passing events; and
occasionally to reach an admonition or a consolation to the
suffering hero or heroine of the piece. But see, I am letting
you into some of the vagaries which came and went across
my fancy during the interval of apathy which has passed
away since I was separated from your conversation for which
I have not yet found a substitute.

And I could dwell upon the rich harvest of insight into
character, which I gathered from the debates of the General
Assembly; and of the lack of genius and honesty which
took from its value, and of the rankness and superfluity of
vulgarity and bad temper and party zeal, which were as the
thistles and ragworts and tares of the crop, but that I know
your mind is incurious of these things, engaged as it is with
much higher contemplations.

Of the men of Edinburgh and their employments I know

as little as of those of Canton in China ; save that Christieson rather inclines to fall in with Lord Lauderdale's views of the Bullion question, than the Committee's, and that he is as sure as ever that all men have mistaken the meaning of Aristotle—which, it seems, is wonderfully wrapped up in the power of the particle ἀν—and that Galloway is as ill-bred, and stares as full, and wears his hair hanging over the ample circumference of his globular skull, as usual ; like the thatch of those round rustic Chinese-roofed cottages which gentlemen sometimes plant at the outer gates of their grounds. As to Dickson, he plays quoits with Chartres, and at times with me, and has got his mouth always filled with wit at me for admiring those beautiful lines of Milton's Hymn on the Nativity :—

> It was no season then for her [nature]
> To wanton with the Sun, her lusty paramour.

I need not tell you where the wit lies ; and you know when he is primed anything will do for a match. He is just in the predicament of a spring-gun in a garden which has ropes in every direction—you cannot stir a foot, but twitch goes one of its ropes ; round it turns full-mouthed upon you, and, hit or miss, off it goes.

Weary not then, my dear Carlyle, of the country. I am here in the midst of the busy world, and its business only interrupts me and would vex me if I would let it. Fill up with the softness of rural beauty, and the sincerity of rural manners, and the contentment of rural life, those strong impressions of nature and of men which are already in your mind ; till the pictures become more mellow and joyous, and yield to yourself more delight in forming, and to others more pleasure in viewing them.

I would I were along with you to charm the melancholy of solitude, and in your company to carry my eye into those marks of beneficence and love which every part of nature exhibits, and win from the contemplation of them a portion of that beneficence ; so that the restless and evil passions of my heart might be charmed if not shamed into repose, and I might go forth again into the world of busy speech resolved to mar the enjoyment of no one, but in my little sphere to do all the good it would allow, to wish for a wider sphere, and to live in hope of that wider and better existence, which, when it is revealed, I pray that you and I and all we love and should love may be prepared for.

Don't be so tardy in writing to me as I have been in writing to you. Arrange the plan of a correspondence which may be useful to us both. You proposed it first, and now I reckon myself entitled to press it. Remember me kindly to your father and mother, and to Sandy and the rest.

Your faithful friend,

EDWARD IRVING.

CHAPTER VI.

A.D. 1819.   ÆT. 24.

IN November Carlyle was back at Edinburgh again, with his pupils and his law lectures, which he had not yet deserted, and still persuaded himself that he would persevere with. He did not find his friend; Irving had gone to Glasgow to be assistant to Dr. Chalmers; and the state of things which he found in the metropolis was not of a sort to improve his humour.

1819 (he says) was the year of the Radical rising in Glasgow, and the kind of (altogether imaginary) fight they attempted on Bonnymuir against the yeomanry—a time of great rages and absurd terrors and expectations; a very fierce Radical and anti-Radical time; Edinburgh endlessly agitated by it all round me, not to mention Glasgow in the distance; gentry people full of zeal and foolish terror and fury, and looking disgustingly busy and important. Courier hussars would come in from the Glasgow region, covered with mud, breathless, for headquarters, as you took your walk in Princes Street; and you would hear old powdered gentlemen in silver spectacles talking in low-toned but exultant voice about 'Cordon of troops, sir,' as you went along. The mass of the people, not the populace alone, had a quite different feeling, as if the danger was small or imaginary and their grievances dreadfully real, which was, with emphasis, my own poor private notion of it. One bleared Sunday morning I had gone out, perhaps seven to eight A.M., for my walk. At the riding-house in Nicolson Street was a kind of straggly group or small crowd, with red-coats interspersed. Coming up, I perceived it was the Lothian yeomanry (Mid or East I know not), just getting under way for Glasgow, to be part of 'the cordon.' I halted a moment, they took the road, very ill ranked, not numerous, or very dangerous-looking men of war ; but there rose from the little crowd, by way of farewell cheer to them, the strangest shout I have heard human throats utter ; not very loud, or loud even for the small numbers ; but it said, as plain as words, and with infinitely more emphasis of sincerity : ' May the devil go with *you*, ye peculiarly contemptible and dead to the distresses of your fellow-creatures.' Another morning, months after, spring and sun now come, and the 'cordon,' &c., all over, I met a gentleman, an advocate, slightly of my acquaintance, hurrying along, musket in hand, towards ' the Links,' there to be drilled as an item of the ' gentlemen volunteers ' now afoot. ' You should have the like of this,' said he, cheerily patting his musket. ' H'm yes ; but I haven't yet quite settled on which side ! ' which, probably, he hoped was quiz, though it really expressed my feeling. Irving, too, and all of us juniors, had the same feeling in different intensities, and spoken of only to one another : a sense that revolt against such a load of unvera-cities, impostures, and quietly inane formalities would one day become indispensable—sense which had a kind of rash, false, and quasi-insolent joy in it ; mutiny, revolt, being a light matter to the young.[1]

The law lectures went on, and Carlyle wrote to his mother about his progress with them. 'The law,' he said, 'I find to be a most complicated subject, yet I

[1] *Reminiscences,* vol. i. p. 152.

like it pretty well, and feel that I shall like it better as
I proceed. Its great charm in my eyes is that no mean
compliances are requisite for prospering in it.' To
Irving he had written a fuller, not yet completely full,
account of himself, complaining perhaps of his obstructions and difficulties. Irving's advice is not what
would have been given by a cautious attorney. He
admired his friend, and only wished his great capabilities to be known as soon as possible.

Edward Irving to Thomas Carlyle.

34, Kent Street, Glasgow: December 28, 1819.

Dear Carlyle,—I pray that you may prosper in your legal
studies, provided only you will give your mind to take in all
the elements which enter into the question of the obstacles.
But remember, it is not want of knowledge alone that im-
pedes, but want of instruments for making that knowledge
available. This you know better than I. Now my view of
the matter is that your knowledge, likely very soon to sur-
pass in extent and accuracy that of most of your compeers,
is to be made saleable, not by the usual way of adding friend
to friend, which neither you nor I are enough patient of, but
by a way of your own. Known you must be before you can
be employed. Known you will not be for a winning, attach-
ing, accommodating man, but for an original, commanding,
and rather self-willed man. Now establish this last character,
and you take a far higher grade than any other. How are
you to establish it ? Just by bringing yourself before the
public as you are. First find vent for your notions. Get
them tongue ; upon every subject get them tongue, not
upon law alone. You cannot at present get them either
utterance or audience by ordinary converse. Your utterance
is not the most favourable. It convinces, but does not per-

suade ; and it is only a very few (I can claim place for
myself) that it fascinates. Your audience is worse. They
are generally (I exclude myself) unphilosophical, unthinking
drivellers who lay in wait to catch you in your words, and
who give you little justice in the recital, because you give
their vanity or self-esteem little justice, or even mercy, in
the rencounter. Therefore, my dear friend, *some other way
is to be sought for*. Now pause, if you be not convinced of
this conclusion. If you be, we shall proceed. If you be not,
read again, and you will see it just, and as such admit it.
Now what way is to be sought for ? I know no other than
the press. You have not the pulpit as I have, and where
perhaps I have the advantage. You have not good and
influential society. I know nothing but the press for your
purpose. None are so good as these two, the ' Edinburgh
Review ' and ' Blackwood's Magazine.' Do not start away and
say, The one I am not fit for, the other I am not willing for.
Both pleas I refuse. The ' Edinburgh Review ' you are perfectly fit for ; not yet upon law, but upon any work of
mathematics, physics, general literature, history, and politics,
you are as ripe as the average of their writers. ' Blackwood's
Magazine' presents bad company, I confess ; but it also fur-
nishes a good field for fugitive writing, and good introduc-
tions to society on one side of the question. This last advice,
I confess, is against my conscience, and I am inclined to blot
it out ; for did I not rest satisfied that you were to use your
pen for your conscience I would never ask you to use it for
your living. Writers in the encyclopædias, except of leading
articles, do not get out from the crowd ; but writers in the
Review come out at once, and obtain the very opinion you
want, opinion among the intelligent and active men in every
rank, not among the sluggish *savants* alone.

It is easy for me to advise what many perhaps are as
ready to advise. But I know I have influence, and I am

willing to use it. Therefore, again let me entreat you to
begin a new year by an effort continuous, not for getting
knowledge, but for communicating it, that you may gain
money, and favour, and opinion. Do not disembark all your
capital of thought, and time, and exertion into this concern,
but disembark a portion equal to its urgency, and make the
experiment upon a proper scale. If it succeed, the spirit of
adventure will follow, and you will be ready to embark more ;
if it fail, no great venture was made ; no great venture is
lost : the time is not yet come. But you will have got a
more precise view by the failure of the obstacles to be sur-
mounted, and time and energy will give you what you
lacked. Therefore I advise you as a very sincere friend, that
forthwith you choose a topic, not that you are best informed
on, but that you are most likely to find admittance for, and
set apart some portion of each day or week to this object and
this alone, leaving the rest free for objects professional and
pleasant. This is nothing more than what I urged at our
last meeting, but I have nothing to write I reckon so important. Therefore do take it to thought. Depend upon
it, you will be delivered by such present adventure from
those harpies of your peace you are too much tormented
with. You will get a class with whom society will be as
pleasant as we have found it together, and you will open up
ultimate prospects which I trust no man shall be able to
close.

I think our town is safe for every leal-hearted man to
his Maker and to his fellow-men to traverse without fear of
scaith. Such traversing is the wine and milk of my present
existence. I do not warrant against a Radical rising, though
I think it vastly improbable. But continue these times a
year or two, and unless you unmake our present generation,
and unman them of human feeling and of Scottish intelligence, you will have commotion. It is impossible for them

to die of starvation, and they are making no provision to have them removed. And what on earth is for them ? God and my Saviour enable me to lift their hearts above a world that has deserted them, though they live in its plenty and labour in its toiling service, and fix them upon a world which, my dear Carlyle, I wish you and I had the inheritance in ; which we may have if we will. But I am not going to preach, else I would plunge into another subject which I rate above all subjects. Yet this should not be excluded from our communion either.

I am getting on quietly enough, and, if I be defended from the errors of my heart, may do pretty well. The Doctor (Chalmers) is full of acknowledgments, and I ought to be full—to a higher source.

Yours affectionately,
EDWARD IRVING.

Carlyle was less eager to give his thoughts 'tongue' than Irving supposed. He had not yet, as he expressed it, 'taken the Devil by the horns.' He did not mean to trouble the world with his doubts, and as yet he had not much else to trouble it with. But he was more and more restless. Reticence about his personal sufferings was at no time one of his virtues. Dyspepsia had him by the throat. Even the minor ailments to which our flesh is heir, and which most of us bear in silence, the eloquence of his imagination flung into forms like the temptations of a saint. His mother had early described him as 'gey ill to deal wi',' and while in great things he was the most considerate and generous of men, in trifles he was intolerably irritable. Dyspepsia accounts for most of it. He did not know what was the matter with him, and when

the fit was severe he drew pictures of his condition
which frightened everyone belonging to him. He
had sent his family in the middle of the winter
a report of himself which made them think that
he was seriously ill. His brother John, who had
now succeeded him as a teacher in Annan School, was
sent for in haste to Mainhill to a consultation, and
the result was a letter which shows the touching
affection with which the Carlyles clung to one
another.

John A. Carlyle to Thomas Carlyle.

Mainhill: February, 1820.

I have just arrived from Annan, and we are all so uneasy
on your account that at the request of my father in particular, and of all the rest, I am determined to write to call on
you for a speedy answer. Your father and mother, and all
of us, are extremely anxious that you should come home
directly if possible, if you think you can come without danger. And we trust that, notwithstanding the bitterness of
last summer, you will still find it emphatically a home. My
mother bids me call upon you to do so by every tie of affection, and by all that is sacred. She esteems seeing you
again and administering comfort to you as her highest feli-
city. Your father, also, is extremely anxious to see you
again at home. The room is much more comfortable than
it was last season. The roads are repaired, and all things
more convenient; and we all trust that you will yet recover,
after you shall have inhaled your native breezes and escaped
once more from the unwholesome city of Edinburgh, and its
selfish and unfeeling inhabitants. In the name of all, then,
I call upon you not to neglect or refuse our earnest wishes:
to come home and experience the comforts of parental and

brotherly affection, which, though rude and without polish,
is yet sincere and honest.

The father adds a postscript :—

My dear Tom,—I have been very uneasy about you ever
since we received your moving letter, and I thought to have
written to you myself this day and told you all my thoughts
about your health, which is the foundation and copestone of
all our earthly comfort. But, being particularly engaged
this day, I caused John to write. Come home as soon as
possible, and for ever oblige

Dear son, your loving father,
JAMES CARLYLE.

The fright had been unnecessary. Dyspepsia, while
it tortures body and mind, does little serious injury.
The attack had passed off. A letter from Carlyle
was already on the way, in which the illness was
scarcely noticed: it contained little but directions
for his brothers' studies, and an offer of ten pounds
out of his scantily filled purse to assist 'Sandy' on the
farm. With his family it was impossible for him to
talk freely, and through this gloomy time he had but
one friend, though this one was of priceless value. To
Irving he had written out his discontent. He was now
disgusted with law, and meant to abandon it. Irving,
pressed as he was with work, could always afford
Carlyle the best of his time and judgment.

Edward Irving to Thomas Carlyle.

Glasgow: March 14, 1820.

Since I received your last epistle, which reminded me of
some of those gloomy scenes of nature I have often had the

greatest pleasure in contemplating, I have been wrought almost to death, having had three sermons to write, and one of them a charity sermon ; but I shall make many sacrifices before I shall resign the entertainment and benefit I derive from our correspondence.

Your mind is of too penetrating a cast to rest satisfied with the frail disguise which the happiness of ordinary life has thrown on to hide its nakedness, and I do never augur that your nature is to be satisfied with its sympathies. Indeed, I am convinced that were you translated into the most elegant and informed circle of this city, you would find it please only by its novelty, and perhaps refresh by its variety ; but you would be constrained to seek the solid employment and the lasting gratification of your mind elsewhere. The truth is, life is a thing formed for the average of men, and it is only in those parts of our nature which are of average possession that it can gratify. The higher parts of our nature find their entertainment in sympathising with the highest efforts of our species, which are, and will continue, confined to the closet of the sage, and can never find their station in the drawing-rooms of the talking world. Indeed, I will go higher and say that the higher parts of our nature can never have their proper food till they turn to contemplate the excellencies of our Creator, and not only to contemplate but to imitate them. Therefore it is, my dear Carlyle, that I exhort you to call in the finer parts of your mind, and to try to present the society about you with those more ordinary displays which they can enjoy. The indifference with which they receive them,[1] and the ignorance with which they treat them, operate on the mind like gall and wormwood. I would entreat you to be comforted in the possession of your treasures, and to study more the times

---

[1] *I.e.*, the talk to which you usually treat your friends.

and persons to which you bring them forth. When I say your treasures, I mean not your information so much, which they will bear the display of for the reward and value of it, but of your feelings and affections, which, being of finer tone than theirs, and consequently seeking a keener expression, they are apt to mistake for a rebuke of their own lameness, or for intolerance of ordinary things, and too many of them, I fear, for asperity of mind.

There is just another panacea for your griefs (which are not imaginary, but for which I see a real ground in the too penetrating and, at times perhaps, too severe turn of your mind) ; but though I judge it better and more worthy than reserve, it is perhaps more difficult of practice. I mean the habit of using our superiority for the information and improvement of others. This I reckon both the most dignified and the most kindly course that one can take, founded upon the great principles of human improvement, mutual communication, and founded upon what I am wont, or at least would wish, to make my pattern, the example of the Saviour of men, who endured, in His errand of salvation, the contradiction of men. But I confess, on the other hand, one meets with so few that are apt disciples, or willing to allow superiority, that will be constantly fighting with you upon the threshold, that it is very heartless, and forces one to reserve. And besides, one is so apt to fancy a superiority where there is none, that it is likely to produce overmuch self-complacency. But I see I am beginning to prose, and therefore shall change the subject—with only one remark, that your tone of mind reminds me more than anything of my own when under the sense of great religious imperfection, and anxiously pursuing after higher Christian attainments.

I have read your letter again, and, at the risk of further prosing, I shall have another hit at its contents. You talk of renouncing the law, and you speak mysteriously of hope springing up from another quarter. I pray that it may soon be turned into enjoyment. But I would not have you renounce the law unless you coolly think that this new view contains those fields of happiness, from the want of which the prospect of law has become so dreary. Law has within it scope ample enough for any mind. The reformation which it needs, and which with so much humour and feeling you describe,[1] is the very evidence of what I say. Did Adam Smith find the commercial system less encumbered ? (I know he did not find it more) ; and see what order the mind of one man has made there. Such a reformation must be wrought in law, and the spirit of the age is manifestly bending that way. I know none who, from his capacity of remembering and digesting facts, and of arranging them into general results, is so well fitted as yourself. . . .

With regard to my own affairs, I am becoming too much of a man of business, and too little a man of contemplation. I meet with few minds to excite me, many to drain me off, and, by the habits of discharging and receiving nothing in return, I am run off to the very lees, as you may easily discern. I have a German master and a class in college. I have seen neither for a week ; such is the state of my engagements—engagements with I know not what ; with preaching in St. John's once a week a hasty production, and employing the rest of the week in visiting objects from which I can learn nothing, unless I were collecting for a new series of Tales of my Landlord, which should range among Radicals and smugglers.

Dr. Chalmers, though a most entire original by himself, is surrounded with a very prosaical sort of persons, who please me something by their zeal to carry into effect his

---

[1] Carlyle's letters to Irving are all unfortunately lost.

philosophical schemes, and vex me much by their idolatry of
him. My comforts are in hearing the distresses of the
people, and doing my mite to alleviate them. They are not
in the higher walks (I mean as to wealth) in which I am
permitted to move, nor yet in the greater publicity and
notoriety I enjoy. Every minister in Glasgow is an oracle
to a certain class of devotees. I would not give one day
in solitude or in meditation with a friend as I have enjoyed it often along the sands of Kirkcaldy for ages in this
way. . . .

Yours most truly,
EDWARD IRVING.

It does not appear what the 'other quarter' may
have been on which the prospect was brightening.
Carlyle was not more explicit to his mother, to whom
he wrote at this time a letter unusually gentle and
melancholy.

Thomas Carlyle to Mrs. Carlyle.

Edinburgh: March 29, 1820.

To you, my dear mother, I know that I can never be
sufficiently grateful, not only for the common kindness of a
mother, but for the unceasing watchfulness with which you
strove to instil virtuous principles into my young mind ; and
though we are separated at present, and may be still more
widely separated, I hope the lessons which you taught will
never be effaced from my memory. I cannot say how I have
fallen into this train of thought, but the days of childhood
arise with so many pleasing recollections, and shine so
brightly across the tempests and inquietudes of succeeding
times, that I felt unable to resist the impulse.

You already know that I am pretty well as to health, and

also that I design to visit you again before many weeks elapse. I cannot say that my prospects have got much brighter since I left you ; the aspect of the future is still as unsettled as it ever was ; but some degree of patience is behind, and hope, the charmer, that 'springs eternal in the human breast,' is yet here likewise. I am not of a humour to care very much for good or evil fortune, so far as concerns myself ; the thought that my somewhat uncertain condition gives you uneasiness chiefly grieves me. Yet I would not have you despair of your *ribe* of a boy. He *will* do something yet. He is a shy stingy soul, and very likely has a higher notion of his parts than others have. But, on the other hand, he is not incapable of diligence. He is harmless, and possesses the virtue of his country—thrift ; so that, after all, things will yet be right in the end. . . . . My love to all the little ones.

Your affectionate son,
T. CARLYLE.

The University term ends early in Scotland. The expenses of the six months which the students spend at college are paid for in many instances by the bodily labours of the other six. The end of April sees them all dispersed, the class rooms closed, the pupils no longer obtainable; and the law studies being finally abandoned, Carlyle had nothing more to do at Edinburgh, and migrated with the rest. He was going home; he offered himself for a visit to Irving at Glasgow on the way, and the proposal was warmly accepted. The Irving correspondence was not long continued; and I make the most of the letters of so remarkable a man which were written while he was still himself, before his intellect was clouded.

Edward Irving to Thomas Carlyle.

34 Kent Street, Glasgow: April 15, 1820.

My dear Carlyle,—Right happy shall I be to have your company and conversation for ever so short a time, and the longer the better; and if you could contrive to make your visit so that the beginning of the week should be the time of your departure, I could bear you company on your road a day's journey. I have just finished my sermon—Saturday at six o'clock—at which I have been sitting without interruption since ten; but I resolved that you should have my letter to-morrow, that nothing might prevent your promised visit, to which I hold you now altogether bound.

It is very dangerous to speak one's mind here about the state of the country. I reckon, however, the Radicals have in a manner expatriated themselves from the political co-operation of the better classes; and at the same time, I believe there was sympathy enough in the middle and well-informed people to have carried a melioration of our political evils, had they taken time and legal measures. I am very sorry for the poor; they are losing their religion, their domestic comfort, their pride of independence, their every-thing; and if timeous remedies come not soon, they will sink, I fear, into the degradation of the Irish peasantry; and if that class goes down, then along with it sinks the morality of every other class. We are at a complete stand here; a sort of military glow has taken all ranks. They can see the houses of the poor ransacked for arms without uttering the poor tribute of an interjection of grief on the fallen great-ness of those who brought in our Reformation and our civil liberty, and they will hardly suffer one sympathising word from anyone. Dr. Chalmers takes a safe course in all these difficulties. The truth is, he does not side with any party. He has a few political nostrums so peculiar that they serve to detach his ideal mind both from Whigs and Tories and Radicals—that Britain would have been as flourishing and full of capital though there had been round the island a brazen wall a thousand cubits high ; that the national debt does us neither good nor ill, amounting to nothing more or less than a mortgage upon property, &c. The Whigs dare not speak. The philanthropists are so much taken up each with his own locality as to take little charge of the general concern ; and so the Tories have room to rage and talk big about armaments and pikes and battles. They had London well fortified yesterday by the Radicals, and so forth.

Now it will be like the unimprisoning of a bird to come and let me have free talk. Not that I have anything to say in favour of Radicalism, for it is the very destitution of philosophy and religion and political economy ; but that we may lose ourselves so delightfully in reveries upon the emendation of the State, to which, in fact, you and I can bring as little help as we could have done against the late inundation of the Vallois.

I like the tone of your last letter ; for, remember, I read your very tones and gestures, at this distance of place, through your letter, though it be not the most diaphanous of bodies. I have no more fear of your final success than Noah had of the Deluge ceasing ; and though the first dove returned, as you say you are to return to your father's shelter, without even a leaf, yet the next time, believe me, you shall return with a leaf ; and yet another time, and you shall take a flight who knows where ? But of this and other things I delay further parley.

Yours affectionately,
EDWARD IRVING.

Carlyle went to Glasgow, spent several days there, and noted, according to his habit, the outward signs of men and things. He saw the Glasgow merchants in the Tontine, he observed them, fine, clean, opulent with their shining bald crowns and serene white heads, sauntering about or reading their newspapers. He criticised the dresses of the young ladies, for whom he had always an eye, remarking that with all their charms they had less taste in their adornments than were to be seen in Edinburgh drawing-rooms. He saw Chalmers too, and heard him preach. 'Never preacher went so into one's heart.' Some private talk, too, there was with Chalmers, 'the Doctor' explaining to him 'some new scheme for proving the truth of Christianity,' 'all written in us already *in sympathetic ink*; Bible awakens it, and you can read.'

But the chief interest in the Glasgow visit lies less in itself than in what followed it—a conversation between two young, then unknown men, strolling alone together over a Scotch moor, seemingly the most trifling of incidents, a mere feather floating before the wind, yet, like the feather, marking the direction of the invisible tendency of human thought. Carlyle was to walk home to Ecclefechan. Irving had agreed to accompany him fifteen miles of his road, and then leave him and return. They started early, and breakfasted on the way at the manse of a Mr. French. Carlyle himself tells the rest.[1]

Drumclog Moss is the next object that survives, and Irving and I sitting by ourselves under the silent bright skies among the 'peat hags' of Drumclog with a world all silent round us. These peat hags are still pictured in me;

---

[1] *Reminiscences*, vol. i. p. 177.

brown bog all pitted and broken into heathy remnants and
bare abrupt wide holes, four or six feet deep, mostly dry at
present ; a flat wilderness of broken bog, of quagmire not to
be trusted (probably wetter in old days then, and wet still at
rainy seasons). Clearly a good place for Cameronian preaching, and dangerously difficult for Claverse and horse soldiery
if ' the suffering remnant ' had a few old muskets among them !
Scott's novels had given the Claverse skirmish here, which
all Scotland knew of already, a double interest in those days.
I know not that we talked much of this ; but we did of many
things, perhaps more confidentially than ever before ; a col-
loquy the sum of which is still mournfully beautiful to me
though the details are gone. I remember us sitting on the
brow of a peat hag, the sun shining, our own voices the one
sound. Far, far away to the westward over our brown horizon,
towered up, white and visible at the many miles of distance,
a high irregular pyramid. ' Ailsa Craig ' we at once guessed,
and thought of the seas and oceans over yonder. But we did
not long dwell on that—we seem to have seen no human
creature, after French, to have had no bother and no need of
human assistance or society, not even of refection, French's
breakfast perfectly sufficing us. The talk had grown ever
friendlier, more interesting. At length the declining sun
said plainly, you must part. We sauntered slowly into the
Glasgow Muirkirk highway. Masons were building at a
wayside cottage near by, or were packing up on ceasing for
the day. We leant our backs to a dry stone fence, and
looking into the western radiance continued in talk yet a
while, loth both of us to go. It was just here as the sun was
sinking, Irving actually drew from me by degrees, in the
softest manner, the confession that I did not think as he of
the Christian religion, and that it was vain for me to expect
I ever could or should. This, if this was so, he had pre-
engaged to take well of me like an elder brother, if I

would be frank with him, and right loyally he did so, and to
the end of his life we needed no concealments on that head,
which was really a step gained.

The sun was about setting when we turned away each on
his own path. Irving would have a good space further to
go than I, perhaps fifteen or seventeen miles, and would not
be in Kent Street till towards midnight. But he feared no
amount of walking, enjoyed it rather, as did I in those young
years. I felt sad, but affectionate and good, in my clean,
utterly quiet little inn at Muirkirk, which and my feelings
in it I still well remember. An innocent little Glasgow
youth (young bagman on his first journey, I supposed) had
talked awhile with me in the otherwise solitary little sitting
room. At parting he shook hands, and with something of
sorrow in his tone said, ' Good night. I shall not see *you*
again.' I was off next morning by four o'clock.

CHAPTER VII.

A.D. 1820.   ÆT. 25.

NOTHING further has to be recorded of Carlyle's history for some months. He remained quietly through the spring and summer at Mainhill, occupied chiefly in reading. He was beginning his acquaintance with German literature, his friend Mr. Swan, of Kirkcaldy, who had correspondents at Hamburg, providing him with books. He was still writing small articles, too, for 'Brewster's Encyclopædia' unsatisfactory work, though better than none.

I was timorously aiming towards literature (he says, perhaps in consequence of Irving's urgency). I thought in audacious moments I might perhaps earn some trifle that way by honest labour, somehow to help my finance; but in that too I was painfully sceptical (talent and opportunity alike doubtful, alike incredible to me, poor downpressed soul), and in fact there came little enough of produce or finance to me from that source, and for the first years absolutely none, in spite of my diligent and desperate efforts, which are sad to me to think of even now. *Acti labores.* Yes, but of such a futile, dismal, lonely, dim, and chaotic kind, in a scene all ghastly chaos to me. Sad, dim, and ugly as the shore of Styx and Phlegethon, as a nightmare dream become real. No more of that; it did not conquer me, or quite kill me, thank God.[1]

[1] *Reminiscences,* vol i. p. 143.

August brought Irving to Annan for his summer holidays, which opened possibilities of companionship again. Mainhill was but seven miles off, and the friends met and wandered together in the Mount Annan woods, Irving steadily cheering Carlyle with confident promises of ultimate success. In September came an offer of a tutorship in a 'statesman's'[1] family, which Irving urged him to accept.

You live too much in an ideal world (Irving said), and you are likely to be punished for it by an unfitness for practical life. It is not your fault but the misfortune of your circumstances, as it has been in a less degree of my own. This situation will be more a remedy for that than if you were to go back to Edinburgh. . . . Try your hand with the respectable illiterate men of middle life, as I am doing at present, and perhaps in their honesty and hearty kindness you may be taught to forget, and perhaps to undervalue the splendours, and envies, and competitions of men of literature. I think you have within you the ability to rear the pillars of your own immortality, and, what is more, of your own happiness, from the basis of any level in life, and I would always have any man destined to influence the interests of men, to have read these interests as they are disclosed in the mass of men, and not in the few who are lifted upon the eminence of life, and when there too often forget the man to ape the ruler or the monarch. All that is valuable of the literary caste you have in their writings. Their conversations, I am told, are full of jealousy and reserve, or, perhaps to cover that reserve, of trifling.

Irving's judgment was perhaps at fault in this

[1] 'Statesman,' or small freeholder farming his own land, common still in Cumberland, then spread over the northern counties.

advice. Carlyle, proud, irritable and impatient as he was, could not have remained a week in such a household. His ambition (downtrodden as he might call himself) was greater than he knew. He may have felt like Halbert Glendinning when the hope was held out to him of becoming the Abbot's head keeper—'a body servant, and to a lazy priest!' At any rate the proposal came to nothing, and with the winter he was back once more at his lodgings in Edinburgh, determined to fight his way somehow, though in what direction he could not yet decide or see.

Thomas Carlyle to Alexander Carlyle.

Edinburgh: December 5, 1820.

I sit down with the greatest pleasure to answer your most acceptable letter. . . . The warm affection, the generous sympathy displayed in it go near the heart, and shed over me a meek and kindly dew of brotherly love more refreshing than any but a wandering forlorn mortal can well imagine. Some of your expressions affect me almost to weakness, I might say to pain, if I did not hope the course of events will change our feelings from anxiety to congratulation, from soothing adversity to adorning prosperity. I marked your disconsolate look. It has often since been painted in the mind's eye; but believe me, my boy, these days will pass over. We shall all get to rights in good time, and long after, cheer many a winter evening by recalling such pensive, but yet amiable and manly thoughts to our minds. And in the meanwhile let me utterly sweep away the vain fear of our forgetting one another. There is less danger of this than of anything. We Carlyles are a clannish people because we have all something original in our formation, and find

therefore less than common sympathy with others ; so that
we are constrained, as it were, to draw to one another, and
to seek that friendship in our own blood which we do not
find so readily elsewhere. Jack and I and you will respect
one another to the end of our lives, because I predict that
our conduct will be worthy of respect, and we will love one
another, because the feelings of our young days—feelings
impressed most deeply on the young heart—are all intertwined and united by the tenderest yet strongest ties of our
nature. But independently of this your fear is vain. Continue to cultivate your abilities, and to behave steadily and
quietly as you have done, and neither of the two literati[1] are
likely to find many persons more qualified to appreciate their
feelings than the farmer their brother. Greek words and
Latin are fine things, but they cannot hide the emptiness
and lowness of many who employ them.

Brewster has printed my article. He is a pushing man
and speaks encouragingly to me. Tait (the bookseller) is
loud in his kind anticipations of the grand things that are
in store for me. But in fact I do not lend much ear to
those gentlemen. I feel quite sick of this drivelling state of
painful idleness. I am going to be patient no longer, but
quitting study or leaving it in a secondary place I feel *determined*, as it were, to find something stationary, some local
habitation and some name for myself, ere it be long. I shall
turn and try all things, be diligent, be assiduous in season
and out of season to effect this prudent purpose ; and if
health stay with me I still trust I shall succeed. At worst
it is but narrowing my views to suit my means. I shall
enter the writing life, the mercantile, the lecturing, any life
in short but that of country schoolmaster ; and even that
sad refuge from the storms of fate rather than stand here in

---

[1] His brother John and himself.

frigid impotence, the powers of my mind all festering and
corroding each other in the miserable strife of inward will
against outward necessity.

I lay out my heart before you, my boy, because it is
solacing for me to do so ; but I would not have you think
me depressed. Bad health does indeed depress and under-
mine one more than all other calamities put together ; but
with care, which I have the best of all reasons for taking,
I know this will in time get out of danger. Steady then,
steady ! as the drill-sergeants say. Let us be steady unto
the end. In due time we shall reap if we faint not. Long
may you continue to cherish the manly feelings which you
express in conclusion. They lead to respectability at least
from the world, and, what is far better, to sunshine within
which nothing can destroy or eclipse.

In the same packet Carlyle encloses a letter to his
mother.

I know well and feel deeply that you entertain the most
solicitous anxiety about my temporal, and still more about
my eternal welfare ; as to the former of which, I have still
hopes that all your tenderness will yet be repaid ; and as to
the latter, though it becomes not the human worm to boast,
I would fain persuade you not to entertain so many doubts.
Your character and mine are far more similar than you
imagine ; and our opinions too, though clothed in different
garbs, are, I well know, still analogous at bottom. I respect
your religious sentiments and honour you for feeling them
more than if you were the highest woman in the world
without them. Be easy, I entreat you, on my account ; the
world will use me better than before ; and if it should not,
let us hope to meet in that upper country, when the vain
fever of life is gone by, in the country where all darkness

shall be light, and where the exercise of our affections will not be thwarted by the infirmities of human nature any more. Brewster will give me articles enough. Meanwhile my living here is not to cost me anything, at least for a season more or less. I have two hours of teaching, which both gives me a call to walk and brings in four guineas a month.

Again, a few weeks later :—

Thomas Carlyle to Mrs. Carlyle

January 30, 1821.

My employment, you are aware, is still very fluctuating and uncertain, but this I trust will improve. I am advancing, I think, though leisurely, and at last I feel no insuperable doubts (at least when healthy) of getting honest bread, which is all I want. For as to fame and all that, I see it already to be nothing better than a meteor, a will-o'-the-wisp which leads one on through quagmires and pitfalls to catch an object which, when we have caught it, turns out to be nothing. I am happy to think in the meantime that you do not feel uneasy about my future destiny. Providence, as you observe, will order it better or worse, and with His award, so nothing mean or wicked lie before me, I shall study to rest satisfied. . . .

It is a striking thing, and an alarming to those who are at ease in the world, to think how many living beings that had breath and hope within them when I left Ecclefechan are now numbered with the clods of the valley! Surely there is something obstinately stupid in the heart of man, or the flight of threescore years, and the poor joys or poorer cares of this our pilgrimage would never move as they do. Why do we fret and murmur, and toil, and consume ourselves for objects so transient and frail? Is it that the soul living here as in her prison-house strives after something boundless like herself, and finding it nowhere still renews the search ? Surely we are fearfully and wonderfully made. But I must not pursue these speculations, though they force themselves upon us sometimes even without our asking.

To his family Carlyle made the best of his situation ; and indeed, so far as outward circumstances were concerned, there was no special cause for anxiety. His farmhouse training had made him indifferent to luxuries, and he was earning as much money as he required. It was not here that the pinch lay ; it was in the still uncompleted 'temptations in the wilderness,' in the mental uncertainties which gave him neither peace or respite. He had no friend in Edinburgh with whom he could exchange thoughts, and no society to amuse or distract him. And those who knew his condition best, the faithful Irving especially, became seriously alarmed for him. So keenly Irving felt the danger, that in December he even invited Carlyle to give up Edinburgh and be his own guest for an indefinite time at Glasgow.

You make me too proud of myself (he wrote) when you connect me so much with your happiness. Would that I could contribute to it as I most fondly wish, and one of the richest and most powerful minds I know should not now be struggling with obscurity and a thousand obstacles. And yet if I had the power I do not see by what means I should cause it to be known ; your mind, unfortunately for its present peace, has taken in so wide a range of study as to be almost incapable of professional trammels ; and it has nourished so uncommon and so unyielding a character, as first unfits you for, and then disgusts you with, any accommodations which for so cultivated and so fertile a mind would easily procure favour and patronage. The race which you have run these last years pains me even to think upon it, and if it should be continued a little longer, I pray God to give you strength to endure it. . . . We calculate upon seeing you at Christmas, and till then you can think of what I now propose—that instead of wearying yourself with endless vexations which are more than you can bear, you will consent to spend not a few weeks, but a few months, here under my roof, where enjoying at least wholesome conversation and the sight of real friends, you may undertake some literary employment which may present you in a fairer aspect to the public than any you have hitherto taken before them. Now I know it is quite Scottish for you to refuse this upon the score of troubling me : but trouble to me it is none ; and if it were a thousand times more, would I not esteem it well bestowed upon you and most highly rewarded by your company and conversation ? I should esteem it an honour that your first sally in arms went forth from my habitation.

Well might Carlyle cherish Irving's memory. Never had he or any man a truer-hearted, more generous friend. The offer could not be accepted. Carlyle was determined before all things to earn his own bread, and he would not abandon his pupil work. Christmas he did spend at Glasgow, but he was soon back again. He was corresponding now with London booksellers, offering a complete translation of Schiller for one thing, to which the answer had been an abrupt No. Captain Basil Hall, on the other hand, having heard of Carlyle, tried to attach him to himself, as a sort of scientific companion on easy terms—Carlyle to do observations which Captain Hall was to send to the Admiralty as his own, and to have in return the advantage of philosophical society, &c., to which his answer had in like manner been negative. His letters show him still suffering from mental fever, though with glimpses of purer light.

Thomas Carlyle to John Carlyle.

Edinburgh : March 9, 1821.

It is a shame and misery to me at this age to be gliding about in strenuous idleness, with no hand in the game of life where I have yet so much to win, no outlet for the restless faculties which are thus up in mutiny and slaying one another for lack of fair enemies. I must do or die then, as the song goes. Edinburgh, with all its drawbacks, is the only scene for me. In the country I am like an alien, a stranger and pilgrim from a far-distant land. . . . I must endeavour most sternly, for this state of things cannot last, and if health do but revisit me as I know she will, it shall ere long give place to a better. If I grow seriously ill, indeed, it will be different ; but when once the weather is settled and dry, exercise and care will restore me completely. I am considerably clearer than I was, and I should have been still more so had not this afternoon been wet, and so prevented me from breathing the air of Arthur's Seat, a mountain close beside us, where the atmosphere is pure as a diamond, and the prospect grander than any you ever saw. The blue majestic everlasting ocean, with the Fife hills swelling gradually into the Grampians behind ; rough crags and rude precipices at our feet (where not a hillock rears its head unsung), with Edinburgh at their base clustering proudly over her rugged foundations, and covering with a vapoury mantle the jagged black venerable masses of stone-

7—2

work that stretch far and wide and show like a city of Fairyland. . . . I saw it all last evening when the sun was going down, and the moon's fine crescent, like a pretty silver creature as it is, was riding quietly above me. Such a sight does one good. But I am leading you astray after my fantasies when I should be inditing plain prose.

The gloomy period of Carlyle's life—a period on which he said that he ever looked back with a kind of horror—was drawing to its close, this letter among other symptoms showing that the natural strength of his intellect was asserting itself. Better prospects were opening; more regular literary employment; an offer, if he chose to accept it, from his friend Mr. Swan, of a tutorship at least more satisfactory than the Yorkshire one. His mother's affection was more precious to him, however simply expressed, than any other form of earthly consolation.

Mrs. Carlyle to Thomas Carlyle.

Mainhill: March 21, 1821.

Son Tom—I received your kind and pleasant letter. Nothing is more satisfying to me than to hear of your welfare. Keep up your heart, my brave boy. You ask kindly after my health. I complain as little as possible. When the day is cheerier, it has a great effect on me. But upon the whole I am as well as I can expect, thank God. I have sent a little butter and a few cakes with a box to bring home your clothes. Send them all home that I may wash and sort them once more. Oh, man, could I but write! I'll tell ye a' when we meet, but I must in the meantime content myself. Do send me a long letter; it revives me greatly : and tell me honestly if you read your chapter e'en and morn, lad.

You mind I hod if not your hand, I hod your foot of it. Tell me if there is anything you want in particular. I must run to pack the box, so I am

Your affectionate mother,

MARGARET CARLYLE.

Irving was still anxious. To him Carlyle laid himself bare in all his shifting moods, now complaining, now railing at himself for want of manliness. Irving soothed him as he could, always avoiding preachment.

I see (he wrote)[1] you have much to bear, and perhaps it may be a time before you clear yourself of that sickness of the heart which afflicts you; but strongly I feel assured it will not master you, that you will rise strongly above it and reach the place your genius destines you to. Most falsely do you judge yourself when you seek such degrading similitudes to represent what you call your 'whining.' And I pray you may not again talk of your distresses in so desperate, and to me disagreeable, manner. My dear Sir, is it to be doubted that you are suffering grievously the want of spiritual communion, the bread and water of the soul? and why, then, do you, as it were, mock at your calamity or treat it jestingly? I declare this is a sore offence. You altogether mistake at least *my* feeling if you think I feel anything but the kindest sympathy in your case, in which sympathy I am sure there is nothing degrading, either to you or to me. Else were I degraded every time I visit a sick bed in endeavouring to draw forth the case of a sufferer from his own lips that I may if possible administer some spiritual consolation. But oh! I would be angry, or rather I should have a shudder of unnatural feeling, if the sick man were to make

March 15, 1821.

a mockery to me of his case or to deride himself for making it known to any physician of body or mind. Excuse my freedom, Carlyle. I do this in justification of my own state of mind towards your distress. I feel for your condition as a brother would feel, and to see you silent about it were the greatest access of painful emotion which you could cause me. I hope soon to look back with you over this scene of trials as the soldier does over a hard campaign, or the restored captives do over their days of imprisonment.

Again, on the receipt of some better account of his friend's condition, Irving wrote on April 26 :—

I am beginning to see the dawn of that day when you shall be plucked by the literary world from my solitary, and therefore more clear, admiration ; and when from almost a monopoly I shall have nothing but a mere shred of your praise. They will unearth you, and for your sake I will rejoice, though for my own I may regret. But I shall always have the pleasant superiority that I was your friend and admirer, through good and through bad report, to continue, so I hope, unto the end. Yet our honest Demosthenes,[1] or shall I call him Chrysostom (Boanerges would fit him better), seems to have caught some glimpse of your inner man, though he had few opportunities ; for he never ceases to be inquiring after you. You will soon shift your quarters, though for the present I think your motto should be, ' Better a wee bush than na bield.' If you are going to revert to teaching again, which I heartily deprecate, I know nothing better than Swan's conception, although success in it depends mainly upon offset and address, and the studying of humours, which, though it be a good enough way of its kind, is not the way to which I think you should yet condescend.

[1] Dr. Chalmers.

Friends and family might console and advise, but
Carlyle himself could alone conquer the spiritual
maladies which were the real cause of his distraction.
In June of this year 1821 was transacted what in
'Sartor Resartus' he describes as his 'conversion,' or
'new birth,' when he 'authentically took the Devil by
the nose,' when he began to achieve the convictions,
positive and negative, by which the whole of his later
life was governed.

Nothing in 'Sartor Resartus' (he says) is fact ; symboli-
cal myth all, except that of the incident in the Rue St.
Thomas de l'Enfer, which occurred quite literally to myself
in Leith Walk, during three weeks of total sleeplessness, in
which almost my one solace was that of a daily bathe on the
sands between Leith and Portobello. Incident was as I went
down ; coming up I generally felt refreshed for the hour. I
remember it well, and could go straight to about the place.

As the incident is thus authenticated, I may borrow
the words in which it is described, opening, as it does,
a window into Carlyle's inmost heart.

Shut out from hope in a deeper sense than we yet dream
of (for as the professor wanders wearisomely through this
world, he has lost all tidings of another and a higher), full
of religion, or at least of religiosity, as our friend has since
exhibited himself, he hides not that in those days he was
totally irreligious. 'Doubt had darkened into unbelief,'
says he : 'shade after shade goes grimly over your soul, till
you have the fixed starless Tartarean black.' To such
readers as have reflected (what can be called reflecting) on
man's life, and happily discovered, in contradiction to much

profit and less philosophy, that soul is not synonymous with
stomach, who understand, therefore, in our friend's words,
'that for man's well-being faith is properly the one thing
needful, how with it martyrs, otherwise weak, can cheerfully
endure the shame and the cross, and without it worldlings
puke up their sick existence by suicide in the midst of
luxury;' to such it will be clear that for a pure moral nature
the loss of his religious belief was the loss of everything.
Unhappy young man! All wounds, the crush of long-con-
tinued destitution, the stab of false friendship and of false
love, all wounds in thy so genial heart, would have healed
again, had not its life-warmth been withdrawn. Well might
he exclaim in his wild way: 'Is there no God then? but, at
best, an absentee God sitting idle ever since the first Sabbath,
at the outside of his universe, and seeing it go? Has the
word "duty" no meaning? Is what we call Duty no divine
messenger and guide, but a false earthly fantasm, made up
of desire and fear, of emanations from the gallows and Dr.
Graham's celestial bed? Happiness of an approving conscience! Did not Paul of Tarsus, whom admiring men have
since named saint, feel that *he* was the chief of sinners; and
Nero of Rome, jocund in spirit, spend much of his time in
fiddling? Foolish wordmonger and motive grinder, who in
thy logic mill hast an earthly mechanism for the godlike
itself, and wouldst fain grind me out virtue from the husks
of pleasure. I tell thee Nay! To the unregenerate Prometheus Vinctus of a man, it is ever the bitterest aggrava-
tion of his wretchedness that he is conscious of virtue, that
he feels himself the victim not of suffering only, but of injustice. What then? Is the heroic inspiration we name
Virtue but some passion, some bubble of the blood bubbling
in the direction others profit by? I know not; only this I
know. If what thou namest Happiness is our true aim,
then are we all astray. With stupidity and sound digestion

man may front much. But what in these dull unimaginative days are the terrors of conscience to the diseases of the liver! Not on morality but on cookery let us build our stronghold. Then brandishing our frying-pan as censer, let us offer sweet incense to the Devil, and live at ease on the fat things *he* has provided for his elect!'

Thus has the bewildered wanderer to stand, as so many have done, shouting question after question into the Sibyl-cave of destiny, and receive no answer but an echo. . . . No pillar of cloud by day and no pillar of fire by night any longer guides the pilgrim. To such length has the spirit of inquiry carried him. 'But what boots it?' cries he; 'it is but the common lot in this era. Not having come to spiritual majority prior to the 'Siècle de Louis Quinze,' and not being born purely a loghead, thou hadst no other outlook. The whole world is like thee sold to unbelief. Their old temples of the godhead, which for long have not been rain-proof, crumble down; and men ask now, where is the god-head; our eyes never saw him.'

Pitiful enough were it for all these wild utterances to call our Diogenes wicked. Unprofitable servants as we all are, perhaps at no era of his life was he more decisively the servant of goodness, the servant of God, than even now when doubting God's existence. 'One circumstance I note,' says he; 'after all the nameless woe that Inquiry, which for me, what it is not always, was genuine love of truth, had wrought me, I nevertheless still loved Truth, and would bate no jot of my allegiance to her.' 'Truth!' I cried, 'though the heavens crush me for following her: no Falsehood! though a whole celestial Lubberland were the price of apostasy.' In conduct it was the same. Had a divine messenger from the clouds, or miraculous handwriting on the wall, convincingly proclaimed to me *This thou shalt do*, with what passionate readiness, as I often thought, would I have done it, had it been leaping into the infernal fire. Thus in spite of all motive grinders and mechanical profit and loss philosophies, with the sick ophthalmia and hallucination they had brought on, was the infinite nature of duty still dimly present to me : living without God in the world, of God's light I was not utterly bereft. If my as yet scaled eyes with their unspeakable longing could nowhere see Him, nevertheless in my heart he was present, and his Heaven-written law still stood legible and sacred there.'

Meanwhile, under all these tribulations and temporal and spiritual destitutions, what must the wanderer in his silent soul have endured !

The painfullest feeling (writes he), is that of your own feebleness ; even as the English Milton says, 'to be weak is the true misery.' And yet of your strength there is and can be no clear feeling, save by what you have prospered in, by what you have done. Between vague wavering capability and fixed indubitable performance, what a difference ! A certain inarticulate self-consciousness dwells dimly in us, which only our works can render articulate and decisively discernible. Our works are the mirror wherein the spirit first sees its natural lineaments. Hence, too, the folly of that impossible precept, *Know thyself*, till it be translated into this partially possible one, *Know what thou canst work at.*

But for me, so strangely unprosperous had I been, the net result of my workings amounted as yet simply to-- nothing. How, then, could I believe in my strength when there was as yet no mirror to see it in ? Ever did this agitating, yet, as I now preceive, quite frivolous question remain to me insoluble : Hast thou a certain faculty, a certain worth, such as even the most have not ; or art thou the completest dullard of these modern times ? Alas, the fearful unbelief is unbelief in yourself ; and how could I believe ?

Had not my first last faith in myself, when even to me the Heavens seemed laid open, and I dared to love, been all too cruelly belied? The speculative mystery of life grew ever more mysterious to me: neither in the practical mystery had I made the slightest progress, but been everywhere buffeted, foiled, and contemptuously cast out. A feeble unit in the middle of a threatening infinitude, I seemed to have nothing given me but eyes whereby to discern my own wretchedness. Invisible yet impenetrable walls, as of enchantment, divided me from all living. Now when I looked back it was a strange isolation I then lived in. The men and women round me, even speaking with me, were but figures; I had practically forgotten that they were alive, that they were not merely automatic. In the midst of their crowded streets and assemblages, I walked solitary, and (except as it was my own heart, not another's, that I kept devouring), savage also as the tiger in his jungle. Some comfort it would have been could I, like Faust, have fancied myself tempted and tormented of the devil; for a hell as I imagine, without life, though only diabolic life, were more frightful: but in our age of downpulling and disbelief, the very devil has been pulled down, you cannot so much as believe in a devil. To me the universe was all void of life, of purpose, of volition, even of hostility: it was one huge, dead, immeasurable steam-engine, rolling on in its dead indifference, to grind me limb from limb. Oh, the vast, gloomy, solitary Golgotha and mill of death! Why was the living banished thither companionless, conscious? Why, if there is no devil, nay, unless the devil is your god? . . . From suicide a certain aftershine (Nachschein) of Christianity withheld me, perhaps also a certain indolence of character; for was not that a remedy I had at any time within reach? Often, however, there was a question present to me: should someone now at the turning of that corner blow thee sud-

denly out of space into the other world or other no-world by
pistol-shot, how were it ? . . .

So had it lasted, as in bitter protracted death-agony
through long years. The heart within me, unvisited by any
heavenly dewdrop, was smouldering in sulphurous slow-
consuming fire. Almost since earliest memory I had shed
no tear ; or once only when I, murmuring half audibly,
recited Faust's death-song, that wild ' Selig der, den er im
Siegesglanze findet,' Happy, whom *he* finds in battle's splendour, and thought that of this last friend even I was not
forsaken, that destiny itself could not doom me not to die.
Having no hope, neither had I any definite fear, were it of man
or devil ; nay I often felt as if it might be solacing could
the arch-devil himself, though in Tartarean terrors, but rise
to me, that I might tell him a little of my mind. And yet,
strangely enough, I lived in a continual indefinite pining
fear ; tremulous, pusillanimous apprehension of I knew not
what. It seemed as if all things in the heavens above and
the earth beneath would hurt me ; as if the heavens and
the earth were but boundless jaws of a devouring monster,
wherein I palpitating waited to be devoured.

Full of such humour was I one sultry dogday after much
perambulation toiling along the dirty little Rue St. Thomas
de l'Enfer in a close atmosphere and over pavements hot as
Nebuchadnezzar's furnace ; whereby doubtless my spirits were
little cheered ; when all at once there rose a thought in me,
and I asked myself : ' What *art* thou afraid of ? wherefore,
like a coward, dost thou for ever pip and whimper, and go
cowering and trembling ? Despicable biped ! what is the sum
total of the worst that lies before thee ? Death ? Well, death ;
and say the pangs of Tophet too, and all that the devil and man
may, will, or can do against thee ! Hast thou not a heart ?
canst thou not suffer whatsoever it be ; and as a child of
freedom, though outcast, trample Tophet itself under thy feet,

while it consumes thee ? Let it come, then, and I will meet it and defy it.' And as I so thought, there rushed like a stream of fire over my whole soul, and I shook base fear away from me for ever. I was strong ; of unknown strength ; a spirit ; almost a god. Ever from that time, the temper of my misery was changed ; not fear or whining sorrow was it, but indignation and grim fire-eyed defiance.

Thus had the everlasting No ('das ewige Nein') pealed authoritatively through all the recesses of my being, of my ME ; and then it was that my whole ME stood up in native God-created majesty, and with emphasis recorded its protest. Such a protest, the most important transaction in my life, may that same indignation and defiance, in a psychological point of view, be fitly called. The everlasting No had said : Behold, thou art fatherless, outcast, and the universe is mine (the devil's) ; to which my whole ME now made answer : *I* am not thine but free, and for ever hate thee.

It is from this hour I incline to date my spiritual new birth ; perhaps I directly thereupon began to be a man.[1]

---

[1] *Sartor* p. 116, *et seq.*

CHAPTER VIII

CRAIGENPUTTOCK, craig, or whinstone hill of the put-tocks,[1] is a high moorland farm on the watershed between Dumfriesshire and Galloway, sixteen miles from the town of Dumfries. The manor house, solid and gaunt, and built to stand for centuries, lies on a slope protected by a plantation of pines, and surrounded by a few acres of reclaimed grass land—a green island in the midst of heathery hills, sheep-walks, and un-drained peat-bogs. A sterner spot is hardly to be found in Scotland. Here for many generations had resided a family of Welshes, holding the rank of small gentry. The eldest son bore always the same name—John Welsh had succeeded John Welsh as far back as tradition could record; the earliest John of whom authentic memory remained being the famous Welsh, the minister of Ayr, who married the daughter of John Knox. This lady it was who, when her husband was banished, and when she was told by King James that he might return to Scotland if he would acknowledge the authority of bishops, raised her apron and said, 'Please your Majesty I'd rather kep his head there.'

---

[1] Small hawks, so named still in Galloway, and once throughout England.

> Who finds the partridge in the puttock's nest,
> But may imagine how the bird was dead.'
>
> — *Shakespeare.*

The king asked her who she was. 'Knox and Welsh,' he exclaimed, when she told him her parentage, 'Knox and Welsh! The devil never made such a match as that.' 'It's right like, sir,' said she, 'for we never speered his advice.'

A family with such an ancestry naturally showed remarkable qualities. 'Several blackguards among them, but not one blockhead that I ever heard of,' was the account of her kinsfolk given to Jane Welsh [1] by her grandfather.

In the rebellion of 1745 the laird of Craigenputtock had been among the sympathisers, though he escaped committing himself. Some of his friends who had been more deeply implicated, had taken shelter with him when they were inquired for after Culloden. Informers betrayed their hiding-place, and a party of dragoons were sent up from Dumfries to arrest them. The alarm was given; before the dragoons arrived the objects of their pursuit were away across the hills in Galloway. 'Such and such men with you, aren't they?' said the officer to the laird, as he rode to the door. 'Truly they were three hours ago,' the laird answered; 'and they were rebels, say you? Fie, the villains! had I but known! But come, let us chase immediately. Once across the Orr yonder, and the swamps' (which looked green enough from the house), 'you will find firm road, and will soon catch the dogs.' Welsh mounted, and volunteered to guide; guided the dragoons into a spot where he and his pony, who knew the road, could pass, and the heavy dragoon horses sank

---

[1] Afterwards Mrs. Carlyle.

to their girths. Having provided them with work which would last till dark, he professed profound regrets, rode off, and left them.

The son of this laird died young, leaving a widow at Craigenputtock with a single child, another John, who was born in 1757. The mother, desiring to give the boy a better education than was to be had on the moors, sent him down to a tutor in Nithsdale. There he fell in love with a Miss Hunter, daughter of a neighbouring grazier, and married her, he being seventeen and the lady a year younger. They returned to the Craig together, and produced one after the other fourteen children. The large family brought expenses. The income was small. The laird drifted into difficulties, sold part of the Craigenputtock property, and being unable to make a living out of the rest, left it and took a farm by the riverside in Nith valley, above Dumfries. Here he was fairly successful, as indeed he deserved to be.

A valiant sensible man (says Carlyle), solidly devout, truth's own self in what he said and did; had dignity of manners too, in fact a really brave, sincere, and honourable soul; reverent of talent, honesty, and sound sense beyond all things; was silently respected and honestly esteemed in the district where he lived.

'Not however without a grin here and there,' for he had his peculiarities. He was a tall man himself; he had a fixed notion that size of body and size of mind went together, and he would never admit a new friend till he had measured him. This old John Welsh (or

Penfillan, as he was called from the name of his farm, did not die till 1823, outliving his distinguished son who was the father of Carlyle's wife.

This next John Welsh was the eldest of the fourteen. He was born at Craigenputtock in 1776, and spent his childish years there. Scotch boys learn early to take care of themselves. He was sent to Edinburgh University when a mere lad to study medicine. While attending the classes he drew attention to himself by his intelligence, and was taken as an apprentice by the then celebrated Dr. Benjamin Bell. Dr. Bell saw his extraordinary merit, and in 1796, when he was but twenty, recommended him for a commission as regimental surgeon to the Perthshire Fencibles. This post he held for two years, and afterwards, in 1798, he succeeded either by purchase or otherwise to the local practice of the town and neighbourhood of Haddington. His reputation rose rapidly, and along with it he made a rapid fortune. To help his brothers and sisters he purchased Craigenputtock from his father, without waiting till it came to him by inheritance. He paid off the encumbrances, and he intended eventually to retire thither when he should give up business.

In 1800 Dr. Welsh married, the wife whom he chose being a Welsh also, though of another family entirely unrelated to his own. She, too, if tradition might be trusted, came of famous blood. John Welsh was descended from Knox. Grace or Grizzie Welsh traced her pedigree through her mother, who was a Baillie, to Wallace. Her father was a well-to-do stock farmer, then living at Caplegill on Moffat Water. Walter Welsh (this was his name), when his daughter left him to go to Haddington, moved himself into Nithsdale, and took a farm then known as Templand, near **Penfillan**. Thus Jane Welsh's two grandfathers, old Walter and old John, Welshes both of them, though connected only through their children's marriage, became close neighbours and friends. Walter of Templand lived to a great age, and Carlyle after his marriage knew him well. He took to Carlyle, indeed, from the first, having but two faults to find with him, that he smoked tobacco, and would not drink whisky punch; not that old Walter drank to excess himself, or at all cared for drinking, but he thought that total abstinence in a young man was a sign of conceit or affectation.

He was a man (Carlyle writes)[1] of much singularity and intellect too, a microcosm of old Scottish life as it *had* been. Hot, impatient temper, breaking out into flashes of lightning if you touched him the wrong way; but they were flashes only, never bolts. Face uncommonly fine, serious yet laughing eyes as if inviting you in, bushy eyebrows picturesquely shaggy, abundant grey hair, beard imperfectly shaved, features massive yet soft, honesty, quick ingenuity, kindliness and frank manhood as the general expression, a most simple man of stunted utterance, burred with his rr's, had a chewing kind of way with his words which rapid or few were not extremely distinct till you attended a little, and then aided by the face they were distinct and memorable. Clever things Walter never said or attempted to say, nor wise things either in any shape beyond that of sincerely accepted commonplace; but he well knew when such were said by others, and had a bright dimpling chuckle—smudge of laughter the Scotch call it, one of the prettiest words and

[1] *Reminiscences,* vol. ii. (abridged).

ditto things, and on the whole hated no kind of talk but the unwise kind. He was serious, pensive, not mournful or sad in those old times. He had the prettiest laugh that I can remember, not the loudest. My own father's still rarer laugh was louder far, though not perhaps more complete. But his was all of artillery thunder—*feu de joie* from all guns as the main element ; while in Walter there was audible something as of infinite flutes and harps, as if the vanquished themselves were invited or compelled to partake of the triumph. 'Radiant ever young Apollo,' &c. &c. of Teufelsdröckh's laugh is a reminiscence of that. He had an immense fund of articulate gaiety in his composition, a truly fine sense of the ridiculous ; excellent sense in a man, especially if he never cultivate it or be conscious of it, as was Walter's case. It must have been from him that my Jane derived that beautiful light humour, never going into folly, yet full of tacit fires which spontaneously illuminated all her best hours. Thanks to Walter ! . . . she was like him in this respect. My father's laugh is mainly mine : a grimmer and inferior kind. Of my mother's beautifully sportive vein (which was a third kind, also hereditary I am told) I seem to have inherited less, though not nothing either, nay, perhaps at bottom not even less, had my life chanced to be easier and joyfuller. 'Sense of the ridiculous'—worth calling such—i.e. brotherly sympathy with the downward side, is very indispensable to a man. Hebrews have it not, hardly any Jew creature—not even a blackguard Heine to any real length ; hence various misqualities of theirs, perhaps most of their qualities too which have become historical. This is an old remark of mine, though not yet written anywhere.

The beautiful Miss Baillie, Walter's wife, who came of Wallace, died early. Their son, called also John (the many John Welshes may cause some confusion

in this biography unless the reader can remember the
distinctions), went into business at Liverpool, and was
prospering as a merchant there, when a partner who was
to have been his brother-in-law proved dishonest, ran
off with all the property that he could lay hands on,
and left John Welsh to bankruptcy and a debt of
12,000*l*. The creditors were lenient, knowing how the
catastrophe had been brought about. John Welsh
exerted himself, remade his fortune, and after eight
years invited them all to dinner, where each found
under his cover a cheque for the full amount of his
claim. He was still living at Liverpool long after Carlyle settled in London with his niece, and will be heard
of often in her correspondence.

His sister Grace, or Grizzie, was the wife of Dr.
Welsh at Haddington. In appearance she was like her
mother, tall, aquiline, and commanding.

She had a goodish, well-tending intellect (says Carlyle),
with something of real drollery in it, which her daughter
inherited. Your mother, my dear, I once said, has narrowly
missed being a woman of genius. But she was sensitive,
fanciful, capricious. Old Penfillan, who was on a visit at
Haddington once after his son's marriage, reported that he
had seen her one evening in fifteen different humours. She
was not easy to live with for one wiser than herself, though
very easy for one more foolish, especially if a touch of
hypocrisy and perfect admiration was superadded. The
married life at Haddington was loyal and happy, but because
the husband took the command and knew how to keep it;
he had much loved his wife, but none could less love what of
follies she had. She was unusually beautiful, but strangely
sad. Eyes bright as if with many tears behind them.

Dr. Welsh himself did not live to know Carlyle. He died in 1819, while still only forty-three, of a fever caught from a patient, three years before Carlyle's acquaintance with the family began. His daughter was so passionately attached to him, that she rarely mentioned his name even to her husband. From others, however, Carlyle gathered a general account of his character.

Dr. Welsh's success (he writes)[1] appears to have been swift and constant, till before long the whole sphere or section of life he was placed in had in all senses, pecuniary and other, become his own, and there remained nothing more to conquer in it: only very much to retain by the methods that had acquired it, and to be extremely thankful for as an allotment in this world: a truly superior man according to all the evidence I from all quarters have—a very valiant man Edward Irving once called him in my hearing. He was of noble and distinguished presence, tall, highly graceful, self-possessed, spontaneously dignified, so that people, if he entered a theatre or the like, asked Who is it? black hair, bright hazel eyes, bright, lively, steadily expressive features. His medical sagacity was reckoned at a higher and higher rate, medical and other honesty as well; for it was by no means as a wise physician only, but as an honourable, exact, and quietly-dignified man, punctual, faithful in all points, that he was esteemed over the county. It was three years after his death when I first came into the circle which had been his, and nowhere have I met with a posthumous reputation that seemed to be more unanimous or higher among all ranks of men. The brave man himself I never saw; but my poor Jeannie in her best moments

---

[1] *Reminiscences*, vol. ii. p. 114.

often said to me about this or that, 'Yes, he would have done it so!' 'Ah, he would have liked you!' as her highest praise. Punctuality, Irving described as a thing he much insisted on. Gravely inflexible wherever right was concerned, and very independent where mere rank attempted to avail upon him. One anecdote I always remember. Riding along one day on his multifarious business, he noticed a poor wounded partridge fluttering and struggling about, wing or leg, or both, broken by some sportsman's lead. He alighted in his haste, gathered up the poor partridge, looped it gently in his handkerchief, brought it home, and by careful splint and salve and other treatment had it soon on wing and sent it forth healed. This in so grave and practical a man had always in it a fine expressiveness to me.

Such was the genealogy of the young lady to whom Carlyle was now about to be introduced by Irving, and who was afterwards to be his wife. Tradition traced her lineage to Knox and Wallace. Authentic history connected her with parents and kindred of singular, original, and strikingly superior quality. Jane Baillie Welsh was an only child, and was born in 1801. In her earliest years she showed that she was a girl of no common quality. She had black hair, large black eyes shining with soft mockery, pale complexion, broad forehead, nose not regularly formed, but mocking also like the eyes, figure slight, airy, and perfectly graceful. She was called beautiful, and beautiful she was even to the end of her life, if a face be beautiful which to look at is to admire. But beauty was only the second thought which her appearance suggested; the first was intellectual vivacity. Precious as she was to parents who had

no other child, she was brought up with exceptional
care. Strict obedience in essentials was the rule of
the Haddington household. But the stories of her
young days show that there was no harsh interference
with her natural playfulness. Occasional visits were
allowed to Templand, to her grandfather Walter, who
was especially fond of her. In that house she was
called *Pen* (short for Penfillan) to distinguish her from
a second Jane Welsh of the other family. On one of
these occasions, when she was six years old, her
grandfather took her out for a ride on a quiet little
pony. When they had gone as far as was desirable,
Walter burring his rr's and intoning his vowels as
usual said, 'Now we will go back by so and so, to
vahery the shane.' 'Where did you ride to, Pen?'
the company asked at dinner. 'We rode to *so* and
then to *so*,' answered she punctually, 'and then from
so returned by *so* to *vahery the shane*,' at which, says
Carlyle, the old man burst into his cheeriest laugh at
the mimicry of tiny little Pen.

She was a collected little lady, with a fine readiness in difficulties. The Welshes were the leading
family at Haddington, and were prominent in the
social entertainments there. When she was about
the same age there was to be a children's ball at the
dancing-school.

Of this (Carlyle writes)[1] I often heard in the daintiest
style, how the evening was so great, all the higher public,
especially the maternal and paternal sections of it, there
to see their children dance : and Jeannie Welsh, then about

[1] *Reminiscences*, vol. ii. p. 99.

six, had been selected to perform some pas-seul, beautiful and difficult, the jewel of the evening, and was privately anxious in her little heart to do it well : how she was dressed to perfection with elegance, with simplicity, and at the due hour was carried over in a clothes-basket (streets being muddy and no carriage), and landed safe, pretty silks and pumps uninjured. Through the ball everything went well and smoothly, nothing to be noted till the pas-seul came. My little woman, with a look that I can still fancy, appeared upon the scene, stood waiting for the music. Music began, but, alas ! it was the wrong music. Impossible to dance that pas-seul to it. She shook her little head, looked or made some sign of distress ; music ceased, took counsel, scraped, began again : again wrong hopelessly ; the pas-seul flatly impossible. Beautiful little Jane alone against the world, forsaken by the music, but not by her presence of mind, plucked up her little skirt, flung it over her head, and, curtseying in that veiled manner, withdrew from the adventure, amidst general applause.

She learned rapidly the usual young lady's accomplishments—music, drawing, modern languages ; and she had an appetite for knowledge not easily to be satisfied. A girl's education was not enough. She demanded 'to learn Latin like a boy.' Her mother was against it. Her father, who thought well of her talents, inclined to let her have her way. The question was settled at last in a characteristic fashion by herself. She found some lad in Haddington who introduced her to the mysteries of nouns of the first declension. Having mastered her lesson, one night when she was thought to be in bed, she had hidden herself under the drawing-room table. When an opportunity offered, the small voice was heard from below the cover, '*Penna*, a pen; *pennæ*, of a pen,' &c. &c. She crept out amidst the general amusement, ran to her father, and said, 'I want to learn Latin; please let me be a boy.'

Haddington school was a furlong's distance from her father's house. Boys and girls were taught together there; and to this accordingly she was sent.

Thither daily at an early hour (records Carlyle again) might be seen my little Jeannie tripping nimbly and daintily along, satchel in hand, dressed by her mother, who had a great talent that way, in tasteful simplicity, neat bit of pelisse (light blue sometimes), fastened with black belt, dainty little cap, perhaps like beaverkin, with flap turned up, and I think once at least with modest little plume in it. Fill that figure with electric intellect, love, and generous vivacity of all kinds, where in nature will you find a prettier? At home was opulence without waste, elegance, good sense, silent, practical affection, and manly wisdom From threshold to roof tree no paltriness or unveracity admitted into it. I often told her how very beautiful her childhood was to me; so authentic looking withal in her charmingly naïve and humorous way of telling, and that she must have been the prettiest little Jenny Spinner [1] that was dancing on the summer rays in her time.

A fiery temper there was in her too. Boys and girls were kept for the most part in separate rooms at the school, but arithmetic and algebra, in which she was especially proficient, they learnt together,—or perhaps she in her zeal for knowledge was made an exception.

---

[1] Scotch name for a long-winged, long-legged, extremely bright and airy insect.—T. C.

The boys were generally devoted to her, but differences rose now and then. A lad one day was impertinent. She doubled her little fist, struck him on the nose, and made it bleed. Fighting in school was punished by flogging. The master came in at the instant, saw the marks of the fray and asked who was the delinquent. All were silent. No one would betray a girl. The master threatened to *tawse* the whole school, and being a man of his word would have done it, when the small Jeannie looked up and said, 'Please it was I.' The master tried to look grave, failed entirely, and burst out laughing. He told her she was 'a little deevil,' and had no business there, and bade her 'go her ways' to the girls' room.

Soon after this there was a change in the school management. Edward Irving, then fresh from college honours, came as master, and, along with the school, was trusted with the private education of Jane Welsh. Dr. Welsh had recognised his fine qualities, and took him into the intimacy of his household, where he was treated as an elder son. He watched over the little lady's studies, took her out with him on bright nights to show her the stars and teach her the movements of them. Irving was then a young man, and his pupil was a child. A few years were to make a difference. She worked with feverish eagerness, getting up at five in the morning and busy with her books at all hours. She was soon *dux* in mathematics. Her tutor introduced her to 'Virgil' and the effect of 'Virgil' and of her other Latin studies was 'to change her religion and make her into a sort of Pagan.' In one of her old note-books I find an allusion to this.

It is strictly true (she says), and it was not my religion alone that these studies influenced, but my whole being was imbued with them. Would I prevent myself from doing a selfish or cowardly thing, I didn't say to myself, ' You mustn't, or if you do you will go to hell hereafter ;' nor yet, ' If you do you will be whipt here ;' but I said to myself simply and grandly, ' A Roman would not have done it,' and that sufficed under ordinary temptations. Again, when I had done something heroic—when, for instance, I had caught a gander which hissed at me by the neck and flung him to the right about, it was not a good child that I thought myself, for whom the half-crown bestowed on me was fit reward—in my own mind I had deserved well of the Republic, and aspired to a ' civic crown.' But the classical world in which I lived and moved was best indicated in the tragedy of my doll. It had been intimated to me by one whose wishes were law, that a young lady in ' Virgil' should for consistency's sake drop her doll. So the doll being judged, must be made an end of ; and I, ' doing what I would with my own,' like the Duke of Newcastle, quickly decided how. She should end as Dido ended, that doll ! as the doll of a young lady in ' Virgil' should end ! With her dresses, which were many and sumptuous, her four-posted bed, a faggot or two of cedar allumettes, a few sticks of cinnamon, a few cloves and a—nutmeg ! I *non ignara futuri* constructed her funeral pyre—*sub auras*, of course ; and the new Dido, having placed herself in the bed, with help, spoke through my lips the last sad words of Dido the first, which I had then all by heart as pat as A B C, and have now forgotten all but two lines—

Vixi et quem dederat cursum fortuna peregi ;
Et nunc magna mei sub terras ibit imago.

And half a line more—

Sic, sic juvat ire sub umbras.

The doll having thus spoken, *pallida morte futurâ*, kindled the pile and stabbed herself with a penknife by way of Tyrian sword.   Then, however, in the moment of seeing my poor doll blaze up—for being stuffed with bran she took fire and was all over in no time—in that supreme moment my affection for her blazed up also, and I shrieked and would have saved her and could not, and went on shrieking till everybody within hearing flew to me, and bore me off in a plunge of tears—an epitome of most of one's 'heroic sacrifices' it strikes me, magnanimously resolved on, ostentatiously gone about, repented of at the last moment, and bewailed with an outcry.   Thus was my inner world at that period three-fourths old Roman and one-fourth old Fairy.

In the same notebook there is a long story of her first child love, told with the same grace, which need not be extracted here.   When she was fourteen she wrote a tragedy, rather inflated, but extraordinary for her age.   She never repeated the experiment, but for many years she continued to write poetry.   She had inherited from her mother the gift of verse-making. Mrs. Welsh's lyrics were soft, sweet, passionate, musical, and nothing besides.   Her daughter had less sweetness, but touched intellectual chords which her mother never reached.

The person 'whose wishes were law,' and whose suggestion occasioned the sacrifice of the doll, if it was not Irving, was probably her father.

Of him (says her friend Miss Jewsbury) she always

spoke with reverence. He was the only person who had any
real influence over her. However wilful she might be,
obedience to her parents unquestioning and absolute lay at
the foundation of her life. She used to say that this habit
was her salvation, and that she owed to it all that was of
value in her character. She always spoke of any praise her
father gave her as a precious possession. She loved him
passionately, and never spoke of him except to friends whom
she valued. It was the highest token of her regard when
she told anyone about her father.

She lost him, as has been said, at an age when she
most needed his guiding hand. Had Dr. Welsh lived,
her life would have been happier, whether more useful
it is unprofitable to conjecture. The patient from whom
he caught the fever which killed him was at some
distance from Haddington. She being then eighteen
had accompanied him in the carriage in this his last
drive, and it was for ever memorable to her. Carlyle
writes[1] :—

The usually tacit man, tacit especially about his bright
daughter's gifts and merits, took to talking with her that
day in a style quite new, told her she was a good girl,
capable of being useful and precious to him, and to the
circle she would live in ; that she must summon her utmost
judgment and seriousness to choose her path and be what he
expected of her ; that he did not think he had ever seen the
life-partner that would be worthy of her ; in short, that he
expected her to be wise as well as good-looking and good—
all this in a tone and manner which filled her poor little
heart with surprise and a kind of sacred joy coming from the
man she of all men revered. Often she told me about this,

[1] *Reminiscences*, vol. ii. p. 93.

for it was her last talk with him; on the morrow, perhaps that evening, certainly within a day or two, he caught from some poor old woman patient a typhus fever, which under injudicious treatment killed him in three or four days, and drowned the world for her in the very blackness of darkness. In effect it was her first sorrow, and her greatest of all. It broke her health permanently, and in a sense almost broke her heart. A father so loved and mourned I have never seen. To the end of her life, his title even to me was ' *He* ' and ' *Him.* ' Not above twice or thrice, quite in later years, did she ever mention, and then in what a sweet tone—my father.

Dr. Welsh's illness being of so deadly a kind, he gave orders that she should not be allowed to enter his room. Persons who were in the house at the time have said that Miss Welsh's agitation was convulsive in its violence. ' I will see him,' she cried. ' I will see my father.' She forced her way to his bedside. He sent her out, and she lay all night on the stairs outside the door, refusing to be moved. Dr. Welsh's end was hastened on, perhaps caused, by the unskilfulness of his brother, a medical man like himself, who bled him too profusely. The first letter of Jane Welsh which has been preserved, is one which she wrote a fortnight later to her Penfillan grandmother, her father's mother. She had spoken laughingly of her paganism; her nature at the bottom was of a seriousness too deep for words, and her real character only showed itself when she was passionately moved.

To Mrs. Welsh, Penfillan.

Haddington: October 5, 1819.

My dear Grandmother,—I cannot allow my uncle to return

to you without writing to assure you that the example
of resignation to the will of God which you have given has
not been totally lost upon us. It has been a great consolation to me under this dreadful trial to see my poor mother
support it so well. From the very delicate state of her
health for some time past, from the great fatigue she under-
went during my dear father's illness, and above all from the
acuteness of her feelings on the most ordinary occasions,
I had little reason to expect so much fortitude. I will ever
be grateful to her for the exertion which she has made (I am
convinced in a great measure on my account), and still more
grateful to Him who has enabled her to make them.

This has indeed been an unexpected and overwhelming
blow. My father's death was a calamity I almost never
thought of. If on any occasion the idea did present itself
to me, it was immediately repelled as being too dreadful to
be realised for many many years, and too painful to occupy
any present place in my thoughts. Until this misfortune
fell upon me I never knew what it was to be really unhappy.
The greatest error and misfortune of my life hitherto has been
not being sufficiently grateful for the happiness I enjoyed.

You, my dear grandmother, have had many trials ; but
if I mistake not, you will still remember the bitterness of
the *first* above all others ; you will still be able to recall the
feeling of disappointment and despair which you experienced
when calamity awoke you from your dream of security, and
dispelled the infatuation which led you to expect that you
alone were to be exempted from this world's misery. But
you are good, and I am judging of your feelings by my own ;
when young as I am perhaps you were not as I was, thoughtless and unprepared for the chastisement of the Divine
Power. The ways of the Almighty are mysterious ; but in
this instance, *though* He has left thousands in the world
whose existence is a burden to themselves and to those

around them, *though* He has cut off one who was the glory
of his family, a most useful member of society, one who was
respected and beloved by all who knew him, and *though* He
has afflicted those who we thought deserved to be happy, yet
His intention appears to me clear and intelligible.   Could
the annihilation of a thousand useless and contemptible
beings have sent such terror and submission to the hearts of
the survivors, as the sudden death of one whom their love
would, if possible, have gifted with immortality ?   Oh, no !
Hard it is, but we must acknowledge the wisdom of his
sentence, even while we are suffering under it—we must
kiss the rod even while we are writhing under the tortures
which it inflicts.

We shall be in Dumfriesshire in a month or three weeks.
My mother will answer your kind letter as soon as she feels
able for it.   With kind love to my grandfather and my
aunts, and with every wish for your health, and the restoration of your peace of mind,

I remain, my dear Grandmother,

Your very affectionate child,

JANE BAILLIE WELSH.

After her father's death, Miss Welsh continued with
her mother at Haddington.   With the exception of
some small annuity for his widow, Dr. Welsh had left
everything belonging to him to his daughter.   Craigenputtock became hers ; perhaps other money investments
became hers ; and though the property altogether was
not large according to modern estimates of such things,
it was sufficient as long as mother and child remained
together to enable them to live with comfort and even
elegance.   Miss Welsh was now an heiress.   Her wit
and beauty added to her distinctions, and she was

called the flower of Haddington. Her hand became an object of speculation. She had as many suitors as Penelope. They were eligible, many of them, in point of worldly station. Some afterwards distinguished themselves. She amused herself with them, but listened favourably to none, being protected perhaps by a secret attachment, which had grown up unconsciously between herself and her tutor. There were difficulties in the way which prevented them from acknowledging to one another, or even to themselves, the condition of their feelings. Edward Irving had been removed from Haddington to Kirkcaldy, where he had entered while Jane Welsh was still a child into a half-formed engagement with the daughter of the Kirkcaldy minister, Miss Isabella Martin. In England young people often fancy themselves in love. They exchange vows which as they grow older are repented of, and are broken without harm to either party. In Scotland, perhaps as a remains of the ecclesiastical precontract which had legal validity, these connections had a more binding character. They could be dissolved by mutual consent; but if the consent of both was wanting, there was a moral stain on the person escaping from the bond. Irving had long been conscious that he had been too hasty, and was longing for release. But there was no encouragement on the side of the Martins. Marriage was out of the question till he had made a position for himself, and he had allowed the matter to drift on, since immediate decision was unnecessary. Jane Welsh meanwhile had grown into a woman. Irving, who was a constant visitor at Haddington, discovered when he looked into

his heart that his real love was for his old pupil, and
the feeling on her part was—the word is her own—
'passionately' returned.   The mischief was done before
they became aware of their danger.   Irving's situation
being explained, Miss Welsh refused to listen to any
language but that of friendship from him until Miss
Martin had set him free.   Irving, too, was equally
high principled, and was resolved to keep his word.
But there was an unexpressed hope on both sides that
he would not be held to it, and on these dangerous
terms Irving continued to visit at Haddington, when he
could be spared from his duties.   Miss Welsh was
working eagerly at literature, with an ambition of
becoming an authoress, and winning name and fame.
Unable or too much occupied himself to be of use to
her, Irving thought of his friend Carlyle, who was
living in obscurity and poverty at Edinburgh, as a fit
person to assist and advise her.   The acquaintance, he
considered, would be mutually agreeable.   He obtained
leave from Mrs. Welsh to bring him over and introduce
him.   The introduction was effected a little before
Carlyle had 'taken the Devil by the nose,' as he
describes in 'Sartor Resartus;' and perhaps the first
visit to Haddington had contributed to bringing him off
victorious from that critical encounter.

In June, 1821 (says Carlyle, but it was rather in the last
week of May), Edward Irving, who was visiting and re-
cruiting about Edinburgh, on one of his occasional holiday
sallies from Glasgow, took me out to Haddington.   We
walked cheerily together, not always by the highway, but
meandering at our will pleasantly and multifariously talking, as

has been explained elsewhere,[1] and about sunset of that same day I first saw her who was to be so important to me thenceforth ; a red, dusky evening, the sky hanging huge and high, but dim as with dust or drought over Irving and me, as we walked home to our lodging at the George Inn.

The visit lasted three or four days, and included Gilbert Burns and other figures, besides the one fair figure most of all important to me. We were often in her mother's house ; sat talking with the two for hours almost every evening. The beautiful bright and earnest young lady was intent on literature as the highest aim in life, and felt imprisoned in the dull element which yielded her no commerce in that kind, and would not even yield her books to read. I obtained permission to send at least books from Edinburgh. Book parcels naturally included bits of writing to and from, and thus an acquaintance and correspondence was begun which had hardly any interruption, and no break at all while life lasted. She was often in Edinburgh on visit with her mother to 'Uncle Robert,' in Northumberland Street, to 'old Mrs. Bradfute, in George's Square,' and I had leave to call on these occasions, which I zealously enough, if not too zealously sometimes, in my awkward way took advantage of. I was not her declared lover, nor could she admit me as such in my waste and uncertain posture of affairs and prospects ; but we were becoming thoroughly acquainted with each other ; and her tacit, hidden, but to me visible friendship for me, was the happy island in my otherwise dreary, vacant, and forlorn existence in those years.

Eager as was the interest which Carlyle was taking in his new acquaintance, he did not allow it to affect the regulation of his life, or to drive him into the beaten

[1] *Reminiscences,* vol. i. p. 174.

roads of the established professions on which he could
arrive at fortune. His zeal for mathematics had
by this time cooled. He had travelled, as he said,
into more 'pregnant inquiries.' Inquiry had led to
doubt and doubt had enfeebled and dispirited him
till he had grappled with it and conquered it. Tradi-
tionary interpretations of things having finally broken
down with him, he was now searching for some
answer which he could believe to the great central
question, What this world is, and what is man's
business in it? Of classical literature he knew little,
and that little had not attracted him. He was not
living in ancient Greece or Rome, but in modern
Europe, modern Scotland, with the added experiences
and discoveries of eighteen centuries; and light, if
light there was, could be looked for only in the writers
of his own era. English literature was already widely
familiar to him. He had read every book in Irving's
library at Kirkcaldy, and his memory had the tenacity
of steel. He had studied Italian and Spanish. He
had worked at D'Alembert and Diderot, Rousseau and
Voltaire. Still unsatisfied, he had now fastened
himself upon German, and was devouring Schiller and
Goethe. Having abandoned the law, he was becoming
conscious that literature must be the profession of his
life. He did not suppose that he had any special gift
for it. He told me long after, when at the height of
his fame, that he had perhaps less capability for literature than for any other occupation. But he was
ambitious to use his time to honourable purpose.
He was impatient of the trodden ways which led only
to money or to worldly fame, and literature was the

single avenue which offered an opening into higher
regions. The fate of those who had gone before him
was not encouraging. 'The biographies of English
men of letters,' he says somewhere, 'are the wretchedest
chapters in our history, except the Newgate Calendar.'
Germany, however, and especially modern Germany,
could furnish brighter examples. Schiller first took
hold of him: pure, innocent, consistent, clear as the
sunlight, with a character in which calumny could
detect neither spot nor stain. The situation of Schiller
was not unlike his own. A youth of poverty, surrounded
by obstructions; long difficulty in finding a road on
which he could travel; bad health besides, and
despondent fits, with which Carlyle himself was but
too familiar. Yet with all this Schiller had conquered
adversity. He had raised himself to the second, if not
to the highest place, in the admiration of his countrymen; and there was not a single act in his whole
career which his biographer would regret to record.
Schiller had found his inherited beliefs break down
under him, and had been left floating in uncertainties.
But he had formed moral convictions of his own,
independent of creeds and churches, and had governed
his thought and conduct nobly by them. Nothing
that he did required forgiveness, or even apology. No
line ever fell from his pen which he could have wished
unwritten when life was closing round him. Schiller's
was thus an inspiriting figure to a young man tremu-
lously launching himself on the same waters. His
work was high and serene, clear and healthy to the last
fibre, noble thought and noble feeling rendered into
words with true artistic skill.

Nevertheless, the passionate questionings which were rising in Carlyle's mind could find no answer which would satisfy him in Schiller's prose or consolation in Schiller's lyrics. Schiller's nature was direct and simple rather than profound and many-sided. Kant had spoken the last word in philosophy to him. His emotions were generous, but seldom subtle or penetrating. He had never looked with a determined eye into the intellectual problems of humanity. He worked as an artist with composed vigour on subjects which suited his genius, and while his sentiments are lofty and his passion hearty and true, his speculative insight is limited. Thus Schiller is great, but not the greatest; and those who have gone to him for help in the enigmas social and spiritual which distract modern Europe, have found generally that they must look elsewhere. From Schiller Carlyle had turned to Goethe, and Goethe had opened a new world to him. Schiller believed in the principles for which Liberals had been fighting for three centuries. To him the enemy of human warfare was spiritual and political tyranny, and Don Carlos, William Tell, the revolt of the Netherlands, or the Thirty Years' War, were ready-made materials for his workshop. He was no vulgar politician. He soared far above the commonplaces of popular orators and controversialists. He was a poet, with a poet's sympathies. He could admire greatness of soul in a Duke of Friedland; he could feel for suffering if the sufferer was a Mary Stuart. But the broad articles of faith professed by the believers in liberal progress were Schiller's also, and he never doubted their efficacy for man's salvation. Goethe had no such beliefs

—no beliefs of any kind which could be reduced to
formulas. If he distrusted priests, he distrusted still
more the *Freiheit's Apostel* and the philosophic critics.
He had studied his age on all its sides. He had shared its
misgivings; he had suffered from its diseases; he had
measured its possibilities; he had severed himself from
all illusions; and held fast to nothing but what he
could definitely recognise as truth. In 'Werter,' in
'Faust,' in 'Prometheus,' Carlyle found that another
as well as he had experienced the same emotions with
which he was himself so familiar. In 'Wilhelm
Meister,' that menagerie of tame creatures, as Niebuhr
called it, he saw a picture of society, accurate precisely
because it was so tame, as it existed in middle-class
European communities; the ardent, well-disposed
youth launched into the middle of it, beginning his
apprenticeship in the false charms of the provincial
theatre, and led at last into a recognition of the divine
meaning of Christianity. Goethe had trod the thorny
path before Carlyle. He had not rushed into atheism.
He had not sunk into superstition. He remained true
to all that intellect could teach him, and after facing
all the spiritual dragons he seemed to have risen
victorious into an atmosphere of tranquil wisdom. On
finishing his first perusal of 'Meister,' and walking out
at midnight into the streets of Edinburgh to think
about it, Carlyle said to himself, 'with a very mixed
feeling in other respects, that here lay more insight
into the elements of human nature, and a more poeti-
cally perfect combining of them, than in all the other
fictitious literature of our generation.'

Having been charged by Irving with the direction of

Miss Welsh's studies, he at once introduced her to his German friends. Irving, of the nature of whose interest in her welfare Carlyle had no suspicion, was alarmed at what he had done. His own religious convictions were profound and sincere. He had occasioned unexpected mischief already with his 'Virgil.' He had laboured afterwards with all his energies to lead his pupil to think about Christianity as he thought himself, and when he heard of the books which she was set to read, he felt that he had been imprudent. Two months after the introduction at Haddington he wrote to Carlyle to confess his uneasiness.

Edward Irving to Thomas Carlyle.

July 24, 1821.

I did not follow your injunctions of transmitting to our fair acquaintance my German grammar and dictionary, her own being as much to the purpose. But I did not fail to instruct her to make all progress through the preliminaries to an easy perusal of the German poets. I am not competent to judge of their value towards the development of thought and character. You are—and therefore I should be silent. But if they should tend to cut our young friend off from any of the wholesome intercourse of those amongst whom she is cast without being able to raise her to a better, I should be very sorry, as it seems to me she is already unhinged from many of the enjoyments her condition might afford her. She contemplates the inferiority of others rather from the point of ridicule and contempt than from that of commiseration and relief; and by so doing she not only leaves objects in distress and loses the luxury of doing good, but she contracts in her own mind a degree of coldness and

bitterness which suits ill with my conception of female
character and a female's station in society. But I am speaking perhaps away from the truth. The books may not be
what they are reported of. At the same time I am daily
becoming more convinced that in all the literature of our
own which, it is said, holds of the German school, there is
something most poisonous to all that in this country has
been named virtue, and still more to the distinctions of conduct which religion makes. It seems to me there is a jumble
or confusion of former distinctions as if they were preparing
for some new ones. They have the language of the highest
purity, even of the most sacred religion, in communion with
the blackest crimes; and the presence of the former is
thought somehow or other to compensate for the latter.
There is an attempt, too, I think, at two standards of moral
judgment—one for the man of genius and literature, the
other for the vulgar. But I dare say these are rather the
extravagances of imitators than the errors of the masters.

Another letter is to the same purpose, while it
throws interesting light on Irving's opinion of Carlyle.

There is too much of that furniture about the elegant
drawing-room of Jane Welsh. I could like to see her surrounded with a more sober set of companions than Rousseau
(your friend), and Byron, and such like. They will never
make different characters than they were themselves, so
deeply are they the prototypes of their own conceptions of
character. And I don't think it will much mend the matter
when you get her introduced to Von Schiller and Von Goethe
and your other nobles of German literature. I fear Jane
has already dipped too deep into that spring already, so that
unless some more solid food be afforded I fear she will escape
altogether out of the region of my sympathies and the sym-

pathies of honest, home-bred men. In these feelings I know
you will join me ; and in giving to her character a useful
and elegant turn you will aid me as you have opportunity.

I have been analysing, as I could, the origin of my esteem
and affection for you. You are no more a general favourite
than I am, and in the strong points of character we are not
alike, nor yet alike in the turn of our general thoughts ; and
we are both too intrepid to seek in each other pity or consolation, and too independent to let anything sinister or selfish
enter into our attachments. How comes it to pass then,
that we have so much pleasant communion ? I'll tell you
one thing. High literature is exiled from my sphere, and
simple principle is very much exiled from yours. Thus we
feel a blank on both sides, which is supplied in some measure
when we meet. I'll tell you another thing. Severed from
the ordinary stays of men, influence, place, fortune, each in
his way has been obliged to hang his hopes upon something
higher ; and though we have not chosen the same thing, in
both cases it is pure and unearthly, and next to his own the
thing which the other admires most. I can easily see that
in the progress of our thoughts and characters there will be
ample room for toleration and charity, which will form the
touchstone of our esteem.

Irving identified 'principle' with belief in the
formulas of the Church, and therefore supposed Carlyle
to be without it. He considered his friend no doubt
to be playing with dangerous weapons, and likely to
injure others with them besides himself. But Carlyle's
principles when applied to the common duties of life
were as rigid as Irving's. He had been struck by his
new acquaintance at Haddington, but he was too wise
to indulge in dreams of a nearer relation—which their
respective positions seemed to put out of the ques-

tion—and he was too much in earnest to allow
himself to be disturbed in the course of life which
he had adopted, or forget the dearer friends at
Mainhill to whom he was so passionately attached.
He had remained this summer in Edinburgh longer
than usual, and he and Irving had meditated a small
walking tour together at the end of it. Irving, however, was unable to take a holiday. Carlyle went home
alone, walking as he always did, and sending his box
by the carrier. For him, as for so many of his student
countrymen, coaches were rarely tasted luxuries.
They tramped over moor and road with their bundles
on their shoulder, sleeping by the way at herdsmen's
cottages; and journeys which to the rich would be a
delightful adventure, were not less pleasing to the
sons of Scottish peasants because forced on them by
honest poverty. Mainhill had become again by this
time the happiest of shelters to him, and between his
family and himself the old clear affection and mutual
trust had completely re-established themselves. The
passing cloud had risen only out of affectionate
anxiety for his eternal well-being. Satisfied of the
essential piety of his nature, his mother had been
contented to believe that the differences between
herself and her son were differences of expression
merely, not of radical conviction. His father was
beginning to be proud of him, and was sensible enough
to leave him to his own guidance. Three quiet
months were spent with his brothers and sisters while
he was writing articles for Brewster's Encyclopædia.
In November he was in Edinburgh again with improving prospects.

Things look as if they would go smoothly with me this winter (he wrote on November 17 to his father). I saw Brewster the other day, who received me kindly, and spread out his bank draft for fifteen guineas like a man. He told me further that a translation was *for certain* to be set about, and that I as certainly should have the first offer of it. The work is a French one, Legendre's ' Elements of Geometry,' which Jack knows well and has in his possession. It is a thing I can work at, if the ' *gea of life* ' be in me at all, and for that cause alone I purpose to accept it. There is plenty of Encyclopædia work besides, and the worthy Review men seem to the full as desirous that I should write for them, as I am willing to write for anything in honour that will pay me well. That poor article which you saw [1] has done me some good I find already, and though I respect neither them nor their cause among the highest, I have thoughts of complying for a time. From the whole of this you will be happy to conclude that I am free of danger if I keep a sound body, which I shall surely do to a certain extent.

The first use which Carlyle made of his improved finance was to send his father a pair of spectacles, and his mother ' a little sovereign to keep the fiend out of her hussif.'

You will tell me I am poor (he said to her in a note which went with his present), and have so few myself of these coins ; but I am going to have plenty by and by ; and if I had but one I cannot see how I could purchase more enjoyment with it than if I shared it with you. Be not in want of anything, I entreat you, that I can possibly get for you.

---

[1] Perhaps one of the short biographies which Carlyle was writing for Brewster. He never republished these sketches, which are little more than exercises.

It would be hard indeed if in the autumn of a life—the spring and summer of which you have spent well in taking care of us—we should know what would add to your frugal enjoyments and not procure it. . . . [1] The stockings and other things you have sent me are of additional value in my eyes, as proofs of the unwearied care with which you continue to watch over me. I still hope to see the day when I may acknowledge all this more effectually. I think you wanted a bonnet when I was at home. Do not buy any till after the box returns.

His father and mother were not Carlyle's only thought. His brother John was working hard at school, hoping that means might offer to enable him to attend the medical classes at Edinburgh. Power rather than will was alone wanting for Carlyle to take the expense upon himself. He was watching for an opportunity, and meanwhile he encouraged John to persevere with all his energy.

Thomas Carlyle to John Carlyle.

Edinburgh : December 11, 1821.

I send many a thought southward to you ; often in the mind's eye you appear seated at your mahogany tippet with the various accoutrements of a solitary student, labouring in secret at the task which—fear it not, my boy—will yet be rewarded openly. Few such quiet things in nature have so much of the sublime in them as the spectacle of a poor but honourable-minded youth, with discouragement all around him, but never-dying hope within his heart ; forging, as it were, the armour with which he is destined to resist and

---

[1] This last paragraph is from another letter.

overcome the hydras of this world, and conquer for himself in due time a habitation among the sunny fields of life. Like every other virtue this effort may almost be called its own reward, even though success should never crown it. How poor, how beggar poor compared with this, is the vulgar rioting, punch-drinking, oyster-eating existence often led by your borough procurator or embryo provost. Truly, Jack, you have chosen the better part, and as your brother I rejoice to see you persevere in it. I perused with deep interest and pleasure your graphic account of the style in which our father received the spectacles. It is a cheap way of purchasing pleasure to make those that love us happy at so small an expense.

Your affectionate brother,

T. CARLYLE.

CHAPTER IX.

A.D. 1822.   ÆT. 27.

AN important change was now to take place in Carlyle's circumstances, which not only raised him above the need of writing articles for bread or hunting after pupils, but enabled him to give his brother the lift into the University in which he had so ardently desired to enter him. It came about in this way, through the instrumentality of his constant friend, Edward Irving. Irving's position at Glasgow, Carlyle says, was not an easy one. Theological Scotland was jealous of originality, and Irving was always inclined to take a road of his own. He said himself that 'from the Westland Whigs he had but toleration: when praised it was with reservation, often with cold and unprofitable admonition.' Even Chalmers sometimes, in retailing the general opinion of him, 'made him feel all black in his prospects.' He was growing dispirited about himself, when, just at that time, he received an invitation to go to London on experimental trial. The Caledonian Chapel in Hatton Garden was in need of a minister. 'Certain Glasgow people,' who thought more favourably of Chalmers's assistant than their neighbours thought, or than Chalmers himself, named him to the trustees, and Irving was sent for that his 'gifts' might be ascertained. The gifts proved to be what London wanted. He was

brilliantly successful. There was no jealousy of originality in Hatton Garden, but ardent welcome rather to a
man who had something new to say on so worn a
subject as the Christian religion.

I have preached (he reported to Carlyle after three weeks'
experience), but I shall not repeat the compliments which
burst upon me. It is so new a thing to me to be praised
in my preaching, I know not how to look. I have been
hailed with the warmest reception. They anticipate great
things. The Duke of York was present at a Charity sermon
Sunday week ; and much more which it is needless to repeat.
One thing would have made your heart feel. My audience
was almost entirely young Scotchmen. No fathers, no
mothers, no sisters ; seats full of youth—and how grave !
how attentive !

Not the Duke of York only, but great persons of all
kinds were brought to the Caledonian Chapel by the
report of a new man of genius who really believed in
Christianity. It happened that among the rest there
came Mrs. Strachey, wife of a distinguished East Indian
director, and her sister, Mrs. Charles Buller. Mr. Buller
was also a retired Anglo-Indian of eminence. Mrs.
Strachey was devout and evangelical, and had been led
to Hatton Garden by genuine interest; Mrs. Buller
had accompanied her in languid curiosity; she was
struck, like the rest of the world, by Irving's evident
ability, and she allowed herself to be afterwards introduced to him. She had three sons—one the Charles
Buller who won so brilliant a place for himself in Parliament, and died as he was beginning to show to what a
height he might have risen ; another, Arthur, the Sir

Arthur of coming years, an Indian judge; and a third,
Reginald, who became a clergyman. Charles was then
fifteen having just left Harrow, and was intended perhaps for Cambridge; Arthur was a year or two younger,
and Reginald was a child. The Bullers were uncertain
about the immediate education of the two elder boys.
Mrs. Buller consulted Irving, and Irving recommended
the University of Edinburgh, adding that he had a
friend of remarkable quality there who would prove an
excellent tutor for them. Mrs. Buller was prompt in
her decisions, if not always stable in adhering to them.
A negotiation was opened and was readily concluded.
Carlyle's consent having been obtained, he was instructed
to expect the arrival of his pupils as soon as arrangements could be made for their board. The family intended to follow, and reside themselves for a time in
Scotland. Those who remember Charles Buller will read
with revived interest Irving's first impressions of him.

Edward Irving to Thomas Carlyle.

London: January 4, 1822.
... My opinion is that in the mother you will meet
a most pleasant, elegant, and sensible woman. In the eldest
boy, whom I have conversed with, you will meet a rather
difficult subject: clever and acute, and not ill-informed for
his age; but his tastes are all given to Boxiana, Bond Street,
and pleasure, gathered out of the speculations and ambitions
of Harrow School. But while he argued for that style of
life against his mother and me, he displayed a soul far above
it, and sporting with it, and easily to be dislodged from it;
and he confessed, when his mother was gone, that he could
apply himself with great good will for several years to study,

and would delight to travel.   I told him and his mother that
I should like myself to be his tutor, and I spoke *bonâ fide*,
for nothing I perceive is wanting but a superior mind to give
him higher tastes and to breed admiration of excellence.
You could soon master him and easily direct him, though at
the outset it might be a trial of your patience.   But I think
you ought to submit to such a trial.   You would be no worse
by it.   You labour upon a good subject, for a most accomplished, quite a gallant and noble woman, and gracious
withal, and willing to recompense your labours.

The salary was to be 200*l.* a year.   The offer, so
desirable in many ways, came opportunely, and at
Mainhill was warmly welcomed.   The times were
hard; the farm was yielding short returns.   For once
it was Carlyle who was to raise the spirits of the
family.

Thomas Carlyle to James Carlyle.

Edinburgh : January 12, 1822.

. . . As to the times, it is an evil which must be
promptly and effectually met, and many will fail for want of
a remedy ; perhaps ninety-nine hundredths of the British
farmers before *you* need fear greatly.   And if the issue prove
unfortunate, what then ?   You can stand it better than
many—many whom it would leave without resources.   The
worst is over ; we are all past childhood, and with so many
brave sons to stand between you and danger, why should
you be afraid ?   For myself, the eldest and least profitable of
them, I do sometimes think that Fate is about to lift its heavy
hand off me, and that I shall yet have it in my power to be
useful to you all.   My health is considerably better than it
was last winter.   It will return completely, I trust, and my

hopes are infinitely more extensive and better founded than they were at that period. I have abundance of employment, and the expectation of more, and more lucrative in process of time. There is a place in particular about which Irving wrote to me the other day, that promises exceedingly well. It is a tutorship in a London family, who have two sons intended to reside with their parents in Edinburgh till their education is completed. The mother, Irving says, is an excellent person; the sons likely to be more troublesome; but the yearly salary is 200*l*., a round solid sum for which a man would submit to much. Accordingly I have engaged to attend the youths when they arrive, which they are to do shortly, in quality of 'teacher in the interim,' for three months, till their parents arrive, with the understanding that if I like them, and they me, I am to undertake the office permanently.

To his mother Carlyle wrote at the same date :—

The woman, Irving says, is a gallant, accomplished person, and will respect me well. He warned her that I had seen little of life, and was disposed to be rather high in the humour if not well used. The place, if I like it and be fit for it, will be advantageous for me in many aspects. I shall have time for study and convenience for it, and plenty of cash. At the same time, as it is uncertain, I do not make it my bower anchor by any means. If it go to nothing altogether I shall snap my finger and thumb in the face of all the Indian judges of the earth, and return to my poor desk and quill with as hard a heart as ever.

John Carlyle replies from Mainhill :—

We were all glad to hear from you. The 200*l*. figures largely in the eyes of our father, but not so largely and exclusively, perhaps, as you would be supposed to think, considering all the bearings of his character. He seems to entertain a very great deal more of respect towards you of late than he was wont to cherish when you were strolling about the moors. You can excuse him for doing so. He is one of the most wonderful persons in these parts, considering the manner in which he was brought up.

The young Bullers arrived at Edinburgh early in the spring. They lodged with a Dr. Fleming in George Square, Carlyle being in daily attendance.

From the first (he says), I found my Charles a most manageable, intelligent, cheery, and altogether welcome and agreeable phenomenon—quite a bit of sunshine in my dreary Edinburgh element. I was in waiting for his brother and him when they landed at Fleming's. We set instantly out on a walk round by the foot of Salisbury Crags, up from Holyrood by the Castle and Law Courts, home again to George Square; and really I recollect few more pleasant walks in my life—so all-intelligent, seizing everything you said to him with such a prompt recognition, so loyal hearted, chivalrous, guileless, so delighted evidently with me as I was with him. Arthur, two years younger, kept mainly silent, being slightly deaf too. But I could perceive that he also was a fine little fellow, honest, intelligent, and kind, and that apparently I had been much in luck in this didactic adventure, which proved abundantly the fact. The two youths took to me with unhesitating liking, and I to them, and we never had anything of quarrel, or even of weariness and dreariness between us—such teaching as I never had in any sphere before or since. Charles, by his qualities, his ingenuous curiosities, his brilliancy of faculty and character, was actually an entertainment to me rather than a labour.

If we walked together, which I remember sometimes happening, he was the best company which I could find in Edinburgh. I had entered him in Dunbar's third Greek class at College. In Greek and Latin, in the former in every respect, he was far my superior, and I had to prepare my lessons by way of keeping him to his work at Dunbar's. Keeping him to work was my one difficulty, if there was one, and my essential function. I tried to guide him into reading, into solid inquiry and reflection. He got some mathematics from me, and might have had more. He got, in brief, what expansion into wider fields of intellect and more manful modes of thinking and working my poor possibilities could yield him, and was always generously grateful to me afterwards. Friends of mine in a fine frank way, beyond what I could be thought to merit, he, Arthur, and all the family remained, till death parted us.[1]

Carlyle was now at ease in his circumstances. He could help his brother; he had no more money anxieties. He was living independently in his own rooms in Moray Street. His evenings were his own, and he had leisure to do what he pleased. Yet it was not his nature to be contented. He was full of thoughts which were struggling for expression, and he was beginning that process of ineffectual labour so familiar to every man who has risen to any height in literature, of trying to write something before he knew what the something was to be; of craving to give form to his ideas before those ideas had taken an organic shape. The result was necessarily failure, and along with it self-exasperation. He translated his Legendre

[1] *Reminiscences,* vol. i. p. 196.

easily enough, and made a successful book out of it;
but he was aspiring to the production of an original
work, and what it should be he could not decide. Now
it was an essay on Faust, now a history of the English
Commonwealth, now a novel to be written in concert
with Miss Welsh. An article on Faust was finished,
but it was crude and unsatisfactory. The other
schemes were commenced and thrown aside. The
workings of his mind appear in his letters to his
brother.

Thomas Carlyle to John Carlyle.

Edinburgh : March 15, 1822.

Your two letters came to hand about a fortnight ago.
I read them with the pleasure that all your letters give me.
They exhibit the same picture of young ardour, honest
affection and inflexible perseverance, in worthy though difficult pursuits, for which I have always loved you. The last
quality, perseverance, I particularly respect ; it is the very
hinge of all virtues. On looking over the world the cause
of nine parts in ten of the lamentable failures which occur
in men's undertakings, and darken and degrade so much of
their history, lies not in the want of talents or the will to
use them, but in the vacillating and desultory mode of
using them, in flying from object to object, in starting away
at each little disgust, and thus applying the force which
might conquer any one difficulty to a series of difficulties so
large that no human force can conquer them. The smallest
brook on earth by continuing to run has hollowed out for
itself a considerable valley to flow in. The wildest tempest
overturns a few cottages, uproots a few trees, and leaves
after a short space no mark behind it. Commend me,
therefore, to the Dutch virtue of perseverance. Without it

all the rest are little better than fairy gold, which glitters in
your purse, but when taken to market proves to be slate or
cinders.

This preaching, my beloved Jack, is directed against
myself, who have need of it—not against you, who have
none. 'Improve the passing hour, for it will never, never
return,' is a precept which you not only assent to but
practise. For myself study has in a measure ceased to be a
thing of which I am capable. At no period of my life did
I spend my time more unprofitably than at present. Sciences
and arts and book-learning no longer inspire me with any
suitable interest, and my ignorance, my indecision, my
weakness of all kinds, prevent me from fixing my heart on
any one object of my own inventing. Well did old Crispus
say, 'Truly that man lives and enjoys existence who is intent
on some undertaking and aims at the glory of some excellent
attainment.' It is in fact certain that I must write a *book*.
Would to Heaven that I had a subject which I could discuss,
and at the same time loved to discuss. I cannot say for
certain whether I have the smallest genius; but I know
I have unrest enough to serve a parish. Pity me, but
I hope I shall not always be so pitiful a thing. As for my
employment, it goes on pretty fairly. The Bullers are boys
of many good qualities and many faults. I am too little
beside them at present to grapple on fair terms with their
inattentions and frequent peccadillos. However, in the
main they are very superior boys, both in head and heart,
and I think the undertaking will succeed ultimately.

Again, a few days later, *à propos* of the translation
of Legendre :—

I am anxious to get all these mechanical things off my
hand, so that I may be able to embark fairly in some more

honourable enterprise. I have had a faint purpose for some weeks of writing some essay on the Genius and Character of Milton, if I could. It is not quite the subject I should like, but better than none, so that I am still thinking of it, and determined at least to read the works that relate to it. I am already through Clarendon's 'History of the Rebellion.' To-morrow I shall try to get hold of Ludlow's Memoirs, or some other of them. My condition is rather strange at present. I feel as if I were impelled to write; as if I had also very little power to do it; but at the same time as if I had altogether lost the faculty of exerting that power. It is these 'coorsed nervous disorders.' If I had but strong health! But what is the use of talking? If I had a super-eminent genius, the end would be still better attained, and the wish is perhaps just about as reasonable. Should I never be healthy again, it will not aid me to complain, to sit and whine, 'put finger in the eye and sob,' because my longings are not gratified. Better to do what I can while it is called to-day; and if the edifice I create be but a dog-hutch, it is more honourable to have built a dog-hutch than to have dreamed of building a palace. Therefore, Jack, I mean to try if I can bestir myself. Art is long and life is short; and of the three score and ten years allotted to the liver, how small a portion is spent in anything but vanity and vice, if not in wretchedness, and worse than unprofitable struggling with the adamantine laws of fate! I am wae when I think of all this, but it cannot be helped.

CHAPTER X.

A.D. 1822. ÆT. 27.

THE correspondence with Haddington meanwhile grew more intimate. The relations between tutor and pupil developed, or promised to develop, into literary partnership. Miss Welsh sent Carlyle her verses to examine and correct. Carlyle discussed his plans and views with her, and they proposed to write books in concert. But the friendship, at least on her part, was literary only. Carlyle, in one of his earliest letters to her, did indeed adopt something of the ordinary language of gallantry natural in a young man when addressing a beautiful young lady. But she gave him to understand immediately that such a tone was disagreeable to her, and that their intimacy could only continue on fraternal and sisterly terms. Carlyle obeyed without suspecting the reason. He had known that Irving was engaged to Miss Martin. It never occurred to him as possible that he could be thinking of anyone else, or anyone else of him.

As for Irving himself, the reception which he had met with in London was all that he could desire. A brilliant career appeared to be opening before him, and ardent and enthusiastic as he was, he had allowed his future in all points to be coloured by his wishes. There could be no doubt that the Hatton Garden committee would confirm his London appointment. He

would then be able to marry, and his fate would have
to be immediately decided.   He was to return to Scotland in the spring to be ordained—he was as yet only
in his noviciate; meanwhile he was in high spirits, and
his letters were of the rosiest colour.

Edward Irving to Thomas Carlyle.

February 19, 1822.

I have taken new wing by my visit to London.   I see my
way distinctly.   My intellect is putting forth new powers, at
least I fancy so; and if God endow me with His grace, I
foresee service to His Church.   My ambition—a sanctified
one, I trust—is taking another direction: no less than an
endeavour to bring the spirit and power of the ancient
eloquence into the pulpit, which appears to me the only
place in modern manners for its revival.   I would like to
hear your thoughts upon this subject, both as to the correctness of the idea and its proper execution.

It is for an audience chiefly I am so fond of London;
perhaps as much for a school to learn in by conversation and
observation, for which I think nature has fitted me more
than by books.   I have a wonderful aptitude to sympathise
with men.   Their manner of feeling, of thinking also, is
clear to me, and, even when false, is interesting from a desire
to set them right.   Jane Welsh accuses me of intolerance,
but I think she is wrong, although I think I have some little
skirmishes for approbation.   But this is not deep, and will
yield according as I receive the share which is my due.

And so will yours, my dear Carlyle; you have within you
powers of good the world is not alive to, and which shall yet
shine out to the confusion of many who discredit them.
Your natural power of devotion will yet have utterance;
and your deep-seated reverence of religion—the largest ex-

pansion and highest attainment of the soul, which makes your mother so superior to those around her—will yet make her son superior among the rich and literary men that are hereafter to company with him.

In March the trial period had ended. The trustees were satisfied; Irving was to be minister of the Hatton Garden chapel. He returned to Glasgow in March to prepare for his ordination. On April 29 he wrote to Carlyle again:—

It is now at length determined that I go to London. I have received the call, most respectably signed; and, what with subscriptions and the first of the seat-rents, the security of 500*l.* a year. I go to Annan this day three weeks, where I am to abide during the month of June and obtain ordination, then to London, without seeing Edinburgh; and yet I would like to see you could you come through at the time of the sacrament. Many things oppress my spirit at the present moment, nothing more than parting with these most worthy and kind-hearted people. Some other things also which I cannot render into language unto my own mind. There is an independence about my character, a want of resemblance especially with others of my profession, that will cause me to be apprehended ill of. I hope to come through honestly and creditably. God grant it!

I am not writing Irving's history, save so far as it intersects with that of Carlyle, and I must hasten to the catastrophe of their unconscious rivalry. The 'other things' which he could not render into language, the 'independence of character which might cause him to be apprehended ill of,' referred to his engagement, and to his intentions with respect to it.

Miss Martin had been true to him through many
years of tedious betrothal, and he was bound to her
by the strictest obligations of honour and conscience.
But it is only in novels that a hero can behave with
entire propriety.   Folded among Irving's letters to
Miss Welsh is a passionate sonnet addressed to her,
and on the other side of it (she had preserved his
verses and so much of the accompanying letter as
was written on the opposite page of the paper) a frag-
ment, written evidently at this period, in which he
told her that he was about to inform Miss Martin and
her father of the condition of his feelings.   It seems
that he did so, and that the answer was unfavourable
to his hopes.   The Martins stood by their contract,
as justice and Scotch custom entirely entitled them to
do.   Miss Welsh had refused to listen to his addresses
until he was free ; and Irving, though he confessed
afterwards (I use his own words) that the struggle
had almost ' made his faith and principles to totter,'
submitted to the inevitable.   He must have carried the
news to Haddington in person ; what had passed there
may be gathered from a letter which he wrote to her
from Carlyle's lodgings in Edinburgh, to which he had
gone after all.

Edward Irving to Miss Welsh.

My well-beloved Friend and Pupil,—When I think of
you my mind is overspread with the most affectionate and
tender regard, which I neither know to name nor to describe.
One thing I know, it would long ago have taken the form
of the most devoted attachment but for one intervening circumstance, and showed itself and pleaded itself before your

heart by a thousand actions from which I must now restrain
myself. Heaven grant me its grace to restrain myself ; and,
forgetting my own enjoyment, may I be enabled to combine
into your single self all that duty and plighted faith leave at
my disposal. When I am in your company my whole soul
would rush to serve you, and my tongue trembles to speak
my heart's fulness. But I am enabled to forbear, and have
to find other avenues than the natural ones for the overflowing of an affection which would hardly have been able to
confine itself within the avenues of nature if they had all
been opened. But I feel within me the power to prevail,
and at once to satisfy duty to another and affection to you.
I stand truly upon ground which seems to shake and give
way beneath me, but my help is in Heaven. Bear with thus
much, my early charge and my present friend, from one who
loves to help and defend you, who would rather die than
wrong you or see you wronged. Say that I shall speak no
more of the painful struggle that I am undergoing, and I
shall be silent. If you allow me to speak, then I shall reveal
to you the features of a virtuous contention, to be crowned, I
pray and trust, with a Christian triumph. It is very extraordinary that this weak nature of mine can bear two affections, both of so intense a kind, and yet I feel it can. It
shall feed the one with faith, and duty, and chaste affection ;
the other with paternal and friendly love, no less pure, no
less assiduous, no less constant—in return seeking nothing
but permission and indulgence.

I was little comforted by Rousseau's letters, though
holding out a most admirable moral ; but much comforted
and confirmed by the few words which your noble heart dictated the moment before I left you. Oh, persevere, my
admirable pupil, in the noble admirations you have taken up.
Let affectionateness and manly firmness be the qualities to
which you yield your love, and your life shall be honourable ;

advance your admiration somewhat higher, and it shall be
everlastingly happy. Oh, do not forbid me from rising in
my communications with one so capable of the loftiest conceptions. Forbid me not to draw you upwards to the love
and study of your Creator, which is the beginning of wisdom.
I have returned Rousseau. Count for ever, my dear Jane,
upon my last efforts to minister to your happiness, present
and everlasting,

From your faithful friend and servant,
EDWARD IRVING.

I should not unveil a story so sacred in itself, and
in which the public have no concern, merely to amuse
their curiosity; but Mrs. Carlyle's character was
profoundly affected by this early disappointment, and
cannot be understood without a knowledge of it.
Carlyle himself, though acquainted generally with
the circumstances, never realised completely the intensity of the feeling which had been crushed.
Irving's marriage was not to take place for a year,
and it was still possible that something might happen
in the interval. He went back to his place in London,
flung himself into religious excitement as grosser
natures go into drink, and took popularity by storm.
The fashionable world rushed after him. The streets
about Hatton Garden were blocked with carriages.
His chapel was like a theatre, to which the admission
was by tickets. Great statesmen went with the stream.
Brougham, Canning, Mackintosh bespoke their seats,
that they might hear the new actor on the theological stage. Irving concluded that he had a divine
mission to re-establish practical Christianity. He
felt himself honoured above all men, yet he bore

his honours humbly, and in his quiet intervals his thoughts still flowed towards Haddington. Miss Welsh's husband he could not be; but he could still be her guide, her spiritual father—some link might remain which would give him an excuse for writing to her. As long as he was actually unmarried there was still hope, but he tried to avoid hinting at so remote a possibility.

Edward Irving to Miss Welsh.

London : September 9, 1822

My dearest Friend,—I said in the last walk which we enjoyed together on a Sabbath evening—when by the solemn stillness of the scene, no less than the pathetic character of our discourse, my mind was in that solemn frame which is my delight—that in future I was to take upon me in my letters the subject of your moral and religious improvement, leaving to other correspondents matters of literature, taste, and entertainment. But I have not forgot that you discharged me from preaching to you in my letters, and I fear that what you humorously call preaching is the very thing which I shall have to do if I fulfil my resolution. Now I can chat, though somewhat awkwardly I confess ; and ten years agone I had a little humour, which has now nearly deceased from neglect. My mind was then light and airy, and loved to utter its conceptions, and to look at them and laugh at them when uttered. Then I could have written letters trippingly, and poured out whatever was uppermost in my mind ; but I can do that no longer. I am aiming from morning till night to be a serious and wise man, though God knows how little I succeed. The shortness of life is evermore in my eye, the wasting of it before my conscience ;

the responsibility of it overwhelms me, and the vanity of it
ashames me.   I cannot make a mock heroic of these things,
or laugh them away.   I was never so far lost to good sense
and good feeling as to try.   So they hang over me, and I
must either sink down into a melancholy forlorn creature,
weeping and sighing and talking over the difficulties of
living well, or I must rise up in the strength of Him who
made me, and endeavour to work my passage through the
best and surest way I can.   This last I have chosen, like the
wise men who have gone before me, and by God's help I
will fulfil it.

Now, my dear, dear friend, bear with me if I violate the
law of letter-writing you imposed on me by daring to be
serious, and to speak to you whom I love of those things and
that strain which most I love.   The fine promise of your
mind has been to me the theme of much conversation and of
far more delightful thought.   It is not a part of my character
to withhold my admiration from others, or even from those
I admire, and you yourself have often charged me with
exaggerating your gifts.   Your industry to get knowledge,
and to accomplish your mind with elegant learning, no one
can exaggerate.   Your enthusiasm towards the excellent and
rare specimens of human genius is beyond that of any other
I know ; and your desire to be distinguished by achievements of mind is equalled only by your contempt of all other
distinctions.   Now there is in these qualities of character
not only promise but assurance of the highest excellence, if
God give time for all to ripen, and you give ear to his
directions for bringing the human character to perfection.
Now it does give me great hope that God will yet be pleased
to open your mind to the highest of all knowledge, the knowledge of his Blessed Son, and give therewith the highest of
all delights, of being like his Son in character and in destiny,
when I see you not alienated from men of genius by their

being men of religion, but attracted to them I think rather
the more.

I could wish, indeed—and forgive me when I make free
to suggest it—that your mind were less anxious for the distinction of being enrolled amidst those whom this world
hath crowned with their admiration, than among those whom
God hath crowned with his approval. There are two things
to be kept in view in judging of the worth of men—first
what powers they had, and then what uses they turned them
to. You and I agree always when we meet with a person of
power, but you do not go so far as I in exacting from them
a good use of it. I do not wish it turned to arts of cruelty,
which satire and ridicule and scorn are. I can endure this
no more than I can endure the tyranny of a despot or the
wilfulness of a man of power. They prey upon the physical
rights and comforts of their underlings; the others prey
upon the feelings, by far the tenderer and nobler part. I
do not wish it turned to the aggrandisement and adulation
of its possessor; for he doth not possess it by virtue of himself, but by his Maker and his Preserver. Keep away these
two things, the cruel treatment of another, and the deifica-
tion of one's self, and I will not be offended with the exercise
of mental power; but to satisfy me I seek for much besides:
I must have it husbanded and not wasted in indolence, for
that is as bad almost as the indulgence of superiority. Then
I must have it turned to the discovery of truth, and to the
undeceiving of men, then to lead them into the way of their
well-being. Then finally, which should have been first, or
rather which should be the moving principle of the whole, to do
honour unto God who has made us masters of our powers.
Find people of this kind from the annals of the world;
admire them, love them, be like them, and God enrol you
among them. Oh, how few I find, my dear Jane, hardly
have I found a single one, who can stand the intoxication of

high talents, or resist presuming to lord it over others.
They cry out against kings for their arbitrary tempers.   I
think men of talents are more so.   Nothing can overcome it
but the power and wisdom of God, which is in the gospel of
his dear Son, your Saviour and mine, and the Saviour of all
who believe ; who though the brightness of his Father's
glory and the express image of his person, and speaking as
no man spoke, took upon Him the form of a servant, and
submitted to the death of the cross.   Therefore God highly
exalted Him, and hath given Him a name above every name.
So also will He exalt all others who like Him use those their
high gifts and appointments to the service of God and their
fellows.

Enough of this, for I have much more to speak of.   Of
my own condition I can speak with great satisfaction, in as
far as favour and friendship are concerned, and the outward
prosperity of my calling.   I have no evidence to judge by
farther than that my Chapel is filled, and that their patient
hearing of discourses, each an hour and a quarter long,
testifies they are not dissatisfied with the stuff they are
made of.   In another respect I have reason to be thankful
that God has revealed to me of late the largeness of my own
vanity and the worthlessness of my own services, which, if
He follows up with further light upon the best way for me
to act in future, and with strength to act as He teaches me,
then I have no doubt of a great increase both of happiness
and fruit.

I have made no acquaintance in London of any literary
eminence, but I shall, I doubt not, in good time.   I derive
little advantage from my acquaintances, my course is so
different from theirs.   The next moment I have unemployed
I devote to my friend Carlyle, to whom I have not yet found
time to write.   Oh that God would give rest to his mind,
and instruct him in his truth.   I meditate a work upon the

alienation of clever men from their Maker. But this shall not hinder me from taking up the life of St. Paul, which deserves certainly the highest strain of poetry, but I am utterly unable for such a task.

My love to your mother. Oh, how I would like to see you both, to live with you in the quietness and love which I have so often ——.[1] The next time I come to live with you I hope I shall be more worthy of your kindness, being more satisfied with myself, and standing firmer in the favour of my God, whom that my dear Jane may always set before her is the first and last prayer of her most true and faithful friend,

EDWARD IRVING.

This letter is one of Irving's best, simple, true, and from his heart, while it is kept firmly within the lines which he had prescribed for himself. Others were less collected, and perhaps less resigned. He would lie on his sofa in the December midnight, listening to the music of the streets, and then pour out his emotions to Mrs. Welsh, telling her how Haddington had been a haven of peace to him; how the happiest days of his life had been spent under her roof; how 'nowhere had thoughts of piety and virtue come to him so little sought as with her and his dear pupil.' Every day in his walk he passed a window where there was a portrait of Miss Kelly as Juliet. 'It had the cast of Miss Welsh's eye,' he said, 'in one of its most piercing moods which he could never stand to meet, the roundness of her forehead, and somewhat of the archness of her smile.' He was very miserable at times, but he

---

[1] Word omitted.

struggled with his weakness. His duty was plain and peremptory, and should be done, let the cost be what it might.

Though he seldom found time to write to Carlyle, he had not forgotten him. He was eager to see him in the position which of right belonged to him; especially to see him settled in London. 'Scotland breeds men,' he said, 'but England rears them.' He celebrated his friend's praises in London circles. He had spoken of him to Mr. Taylor, the proprietor of the 'London Magazine.' Carlyle had meditated a series of 'portraits of men of genius and character.' Taylor, on Irving's recommendation, undertook to publish these sketches in monthly numbers, paying Carlyle sixteen guineas a sheet. Carlyle closed with the proposal, and a 'Life of Schiller' was to be the first to appear. Irving's unwearied kindness unfortunately did not help him out of his own entanglements. The year passed, and then he married, and from that time the old, simple, unconscious Irving ceased to exist. His letters, once so genial and transparent, became verbose and stilted. Though 'faith and principle' escaped un-scathed, his intellect was shattered. He plunged deeper and deeper into the great ocean of unrealities. When his illusions failed him his health gave way, and after flaming for a few years as a world's wonder, he died, still young in age, worn out and broken-hearted. 'There would have been no tongues,' Mrs. Carlyle once said, 'had Irving married me.'

Carlyle, meanwhile, was working with his pupils, and so far as circumstances went, had nothing to complain of. The boys gave him little trouble. He was no longer obliged to write articles for Brewster to support himself. The Legendre was well done—so well that he was himself pleased with it.

I still remember (he says) a happy forenoon (Sunday, I fear) in which I did a Fifth book (or complete Doctrine of Proportion) for that work. Complete really and lucid, and yet one of the briefest ever known. It was begun and done that forenoon, and I have, except correcting the press next week, never seen it since; but still feel as if it was right enough and felicitous in its kind. I got only 50*l.* for my entire trouble in that Legendre, and had already ceased to be the least proud of mathematical prowess; but it was an honest job of work honestly done, though perhaps for bread-and-water wages, and that was such an improvement upon wages producing, in Jean Paul's phrase, 'only water without the bread.'

He ought to have been contented; but content was not in him. Small discomforts were exaggerated by his imagination till they actually became the monsters which his fancy represented. He was conscious of exceptional power of some kind, and was longing to make use of it, yet was unable as yet to find out what sort of power it was, or what to do with it.

If I fail (he wrote to Miss Welsh at the beginning of the Buller engagement) to effect anything in my day and generation, anything to justify Providence for having called me into His universe, the weakness of my ability, not of my will, shall be to blame. I have much to strive with, much to do. The few conceptions that actually exist within me are scattered in a thousand directions, distracted, dis-

membered, without form and void ; and I have yet gained
no right mastery of my pen, no right familiarity with the
public, to express them even if worth expressing. Nevertheless I must persevere. What motives have I not which
man can have ? The brightest hopes and the darkest fears.
On the one side obscurity and isolation, the want of all that
can render life endurable, and death, ' sad refuge from the
storms of fate,' without even an approving conscience to dis-
arm it of its sting. On the other is ———. I tell you, my
friend, to be in no pain for me. Either I shall escape from
this obscure sojourn, or persist as I ought in trying it. The
game is deep, but I must play it out. I can no other, so
away with fear.

Meanwhile I am not unhappy. It is true I have none to
love me *here*, none that I can love. But I have long been
studying the painful lesson to live alone, and the task is
easier than it was. I enjoy quiet and free air and returning
health. I have business in abundance for the present, and
the future lies before me vaguely, but with some glimpses
of a solemn beauty irradiating all its gloom. When I compare the aspect of the world to me now with what it was
twelve months ago, I am far from desponding or complaining.

If he could not express himself to his satisfaction
when trying to write for the public, he could describe
well enough anything which happened to him, when
telling it in a private letter. To his mother he was
the best of correspondents. Here is a little incident
characteristic both in manner and matter.

Thomas Carlyle to Mrs. Carlyle, Mainhill.

3 Moray Street, Edinburgh : June 2, 1822.
It will give you pleasure to know that I continue im-

proving in that most important of qualities, good health. The bathing does me great good, and you need be under no apprehension of my drowning. Unfortunately my mode of sleeping is too irregular to admit of my bathing constantly before breakfast. Small noises disturb me and keep me awake, though I always get to sleep at last, and happily such disturbances occur but rarely. Some two weeks ago I had a little adventure with an ugly *messin*, which a crazy half-pay captain had thought proper to chain in his garden, or, rather, grass-plot, about twenty yards from my window. The pug felt unhappy in its new situation, began repining very pitifully in its own way; at one time snarling, grinning, yelping, as if it cared not whether it were hanged then or to-morrow; at another, whining, howling, screaming, as if it meant to excite the compassion of the earth at large—this, at intervals, for the whole night. By five o'clock in the morning I would have given a guinea of gold for its hind legs firm in my right hand by the side of a stone wall.[1] Next day the crazy captain removed it, being threatened by the street at large with prosecution if he did not. But on the evening of the second day, being tired of keeping the cur in his kitchen, he again let it out, and just as I was falling asleep, about one o'clock, the same musical, 'most musical, most melancholy' serenade aroused me from my vague dreamings. I listened about half an hour, then rose indignantly, put on my clothes, went out, and charged the watchman to put an instant stop to the accursed thing. The watchman *could* not for the world interfere with a gentleman's rest at that hour, but next morning he would certainly, &c. &c. I asked to be shown the door, and pulling the crazy captain's bell about six times, his servant at length awoke, and inquired with a tremulous voice, *what was it?* I alluded

---

[1] Carlyle's mode of speech: he was exceptionally tender to animals.

to the dog and demanded the instant, the total, the everlasting removal of it, or to-morrow I would see whether
justice was in Edinburgh, or the shadow of British law in
force. 'Do you hear that?' said the Irish knight of the
rattle and lanthorn. She heard it and obeyed, and no
wretched *messin* has since disturbed my slumbers.

You ask about my home coming (he continues, the dog
being disposed of); but this must be a very uncertain story
for a while. I cannot count on any such thing till the
Buller people[1] are arrived, and in the event of my further
engaging with them, my period of absence must of course
be short. However, there is good and cheap conveyance to
Dumfries daily, and it shall go hard if I do not steal a week
or so to spend at home. It is the dearest blessing of my
life that I have you to write to and to care for me. . . .

June 29.—I am in very fair health considering everything:
about a hundred times as well as I was last year, and as
happy as you ever saw me. In fact I want nothing but
steady health of body (which I shall get in time) to be one
of the comfortablest persons of my acquaintance. I have
also books to write and things to say and do in this world
which few wot of. This has the air of vanity, but it is not
altogether so. I consider that my Almighty Author has given
me some glimmerings of superior understanding and mental
gifts; and I should reckon it the worst treason against Him
to neglect improving and using to the very utmost of my
power these his bountiful mercies. At some future day it
shall go hard but I will stand above these mean men whom
I have never yet stood *with*. But we need not prate of this.
I am very much satisfied with my teaching. In fact, it is a
pleasure rather than a task. The Bullers are quite another
sort of boys than I have been used to, and treat me in another

[1] Mr. and Mrs. C. Buller

sort of manner than tutors are used to. When I think of General Dixon's brats,[1] and how they used to vex me, I often wonder I had not broken their backs at once, and left them. This would not have done, to be sure ; but the temptation was considerable. The eldest Buller is one of the cleverest boys I have ever seen. He delights to inquire and argue and be demolished. He follows me almost nigh home every night. Very likely I may bargain finally with the people, but I have no certain intimation on the subject ; and, in fact, I do not care immensely whether or not. There is bread for the diligent to be gained in a thousand ways.

In July the London season ended, and the parent Bullers arrived in Edinburgh with their youngest boy. They took a large house and settled for the autumn and winter. They made acquaintance with Carlyle, and there was immediate and agreeable recognition of one another's qualities, both on his side and theirs. Mrs. Buller was clever and cultivated.[2] In her creed she was Manichæan. In her youth she had been a beauty, and was still handsome, and was in London

---

[1] Past pupils, of whom I find no other notice.

[2] Mrs. Buller had been celebrated at Calcutta. Among Carlyle's papers I find the following fine lines by John Leyden, which have never, I believe, before been printed :—

Verses to Mrs. Buller on seeing her in a Highland dress, by Doctor John Leyden.

(From a copy in Mrs. Buller's handwriting, January 1821.)

> That bonnet's pride, that tartan's flow,
>   My soul with wild emotion fills ;
> Methinks I see in Fancy's glow
>   A princess from the land of hills.

the centre of an admiring circle of intellectual politicians and unbelieving Radicals. She was first amused, then charmed and really interested in a person so distinctly original and remarkable as her son's tutor. Her husband, though of different quality, liked him equally well. Mr. Buller was practical and hard-headed; a Benthamite in theory, in theology negative and contemptuous. He had not much sympathy with literature, but he had a keen understanding; he could see faculty, and appreciate it whenever it was genuine, and he forgave Carlyle's imagination for the keenness of his sarcasms. Thus it was not only settled that he was to continue to be the tutor, but he was admitted into the family as a friend, and his presence was expected in the drawing-room in the evenings more often than he liked. The style of society was new to him, and he could not feel himself at ease. The habits of life were expensive, and the luxuries were not to his taste.

Tea (he wrote) I now consume with urns and china and splendid apparatus all around me, yet I often turn from these grandeurs to the little 'down the house' at Mainhill, where kind affection makes amends for all deficiencies. Often, often, my dear mother, in coming years, we shall yet

> Oh for a fairy's hand to trace
>   The rainbow tints that rise to view,
> That slender form of sweeter grace
>   Than e'er Malvina's poet drew!
>
> Her brilliant eye, her streaming hair,
>   Her skin's soft splendours do display;
> The finest pencil must despair
>   Till it can paint the solar ray.

Calcutta, 1811

drink tea there, enjoy our pipes and friendly chat together, and pity all the empty gorgeousness of the earth.

On the other hand, he found Mrs. Buller, naturally enough, 'one of the most fascinating, refined women he had ever seen.' The 'goodman' he did not take to quite so readily, but he thought him at least 'an honest, worthy, straightforward English gentleman.' His comfort was considered in every way. They would have liked to have him reside in their house, but he wished to keep his lodgings in Moray Street, and no difficulty was made. Even his humours, which were not always under restraint, were endured without resentment.

The people treat me (he wrote to his brother John in September) with a degree of respect which I do not deserve. They have submitted implicitly to all my ideas about a lodging place. They have delivered me, without even a hint on my part, from the drudgery of teaching their youngest boy,[1] and our arrangements for the other two have been formed with a view to my convenience as much as to that of any other. The boys, too, behave well ; and though I clearly perceive that the management of my duties will require the whole of my slender stock of prudence and discretion, yet this stock, I expect, will suffice to carry me through without discredit.

Again, a little later :—

I am well and comfortable as I could wish. Buller's house is becoming more and more a kind of home to me. The elders treat me almost like a son in many respects, the

---

[1] Reginald, then ten years old.

younger members almost like a brother. Our studies are
going on moderately well. There is nothing but good
agreement as yet, and I think the thing will do.

Not the least of the advantages of this tutorship was
the power which it gave Carlyle of being useful to his
family. John Carlyle came in the autumn to live with
him in Moray Street and attend the University lectures,
Carlyle taking upon himself the expenses. With himself, too, all was going well. He had paid a hasty visit
to Mainhill in October; where, perhaps, as was likely
enough, in some of their midnight smokes together, he
had revived the anxieties of his mother about his
spiritual state. His constant effort was to throw his
own thoughts into her language, and prevent her from
distressing herself about him.

Thomas Carlyle to Mrs. Carlyle, Mainhill.

Edinburgh: November 14, 1822.

You have not sent me a line since I went away. I am
not surprised at this, knowing how you are circumstanced,
but it keeps me very much in the dark with regard to your
situation. I can only hope you are in your usual state of
health and spirits, fighting as formerly against the incon-
veniences of your present life, and brightening all its dreariness by the hopes of a better. There is nothing else that
can keep the happiest of us in a state of peace, worth calling
by the name of peace; and 'with this anchor of the soul
both sure and steadfast' the unhappiest man alive is to be
envied. You think I am a very thoughtless character, careless of eternity, and taken up with the vain concerns of time
alone. Depend upon it, my dear mother, you misjudge me.
These thoughts are rooted in every reflecting mind, in mine

perhaps more deeply than in many that make more noise about them ; and of all the qualities that I love in you, there is none I so much love as that heroic feeling of devotion which elevates you so much above the meanness of ordinary persons in your situation, which gives to the humble circumstances of your lot a dignity unborrowed of earthly grandeur as well as far superior to the highest state of it ; and which ornaments a mind untrained in worldly education and accomplishments with sentiments after which mere literature and philosophy with all their pretensions would for ever strive in vain. The dress of our opinions, as I have often told you, may be different, because our modes of life have been different ; but fundamentally our sentiments are completely the same. We should tolerate each other, therefore, in this world, where all is weak and obscure, trusting meanwhile that we shall comprehend all things more perfectly in that clearer land where faith is changed into vision ; where the dim though fervent longings of our minds from this their dark prison-house are changed for a richness of actual grandeur, beyond what the most ardent imagination has ventured to conceive. Long may these hopes be yours, my dearest mother. Whoever entertains them is richer than kings.

The young Bullers are gone to college [1] a few days ago, and I do not go near them till two o'clock in the afternoon. By this means I not only secure a competent space of time for my own studies, but find also that my stomach troubles me a good deal less after breakfast than it used to do when I had a long hurried walk to take before it.

My duties are of an easy and brief sort. I dine at half-past three with a small and very civil youth, little Reginald, contracted into Reggy, and I have generally done with the

---

[1] The University term having begun.

whole against six. I find Jack immersed in study when I return. He cooks the tea for us, and we afterwards devote ourselves to business till between eleven and twelve. My brotherly love to all the younkers about home, to each by name. Why do they never write? Will you not write?

I am, ever affectionately your son—thy son!!

T. CARLYLE.

Once more before the year closed:—

To the Same.

December 4.

It is already past twelve o'clock, and I am tired and sleepy, but I cannot go to rest without answering the kind little note which you sent me, and acknowledging these new instances of your unwearied attention to my interests and comfort. I am almost vexed at these shirts and stockings. My dear mother, why will you expend on superfluities the pittance I intended for very different ends? I again assure you, and would swear it if needful, that you cannot get me such enjoyment with it in any way as by convincing me that it is adding to your own. Do not therefore frustrate my purposes. I send you a small screed of verses which I made some time ago. I fear you will not care a doit for them, though the subject is good—the deliverance of Switzerland from tyranny by the hardy mountaineers at the battle of Morgarten above five hundred years ago.

This is my birthday. I am now seven and twenty years of age. What an unprofitable lout I am! What have I done in this world to make good my place in it, or reward those that had the trouble of my upbringing? Great part of an ordinary lifetime is gone by, and here am I, poor trifler, still sojourning in Meshech, still dwelling among the tents of Kedar. May the great Father of all give me strength to do better in time remaining, to be of service in the good cause in my day and generation ; and, having finished the work which was given me to do, to lie down and sleep in peace and purity in the hope of a happy rising.

The 'screed of verses' was not thought worthy of a place among the few fragments of his poetry which Carlyle afterwards published, though they are as good as any of the rest. Long and patiently he had toiled at verse-making. Infinite loose sheets of paper remain covered with the memorials of his efforts. It was the received opinion that in verse alone fine emotion and spiritual thought could be clothed in adequate form. The poets, so far as Carlyle could see, had been the wisest men. Inspiration meant poetry, and poetry inspiration, and if he had any genius in him worth considering, he thought it his duty to master the mechanical difficulties of the art. He never entirely succeeded. Rhyme and metre were to Carlyle like Saul's armour to David, and the intended vase turned out usually no better than an earthen pitcher. The 'screed' is good as an echo of Campbell or Byron, or of both combined, but there is no trace in it of original native power.

Proud Hapsburgh came forth in the gloom of his wrath,
    With his banners of pomp and his Ritters in mail,
For the herdsmen of Uri have fronted his path,
    And the standard of freedom is raised in the vale.

All scornful advancing, he thought as he came
    How the peasants would shrink at the glance of his eye ;
How their heath-covered chalets in ruin must flame,
    And the hope of the nation must wither and die.

But marked he the moment when thundering and vast
   The voice of the Switzers in echoes arose,
When the rocks of the glen from the hill summits cast,
   Carried vengeance and death on the heads of their foes.

Now charge in your fury, ye sons of the Fell,
   Now plunge ye your blades in the hearts of his men ;
If ye conquer, all time of your glory shall tell,
   And conquered ye ne'er shall arouse ye again.

'Tis done, and the spoilers are crushed and o'erthrown,
   And terror has struck through the souls of the proud,
For the Despot of Austria stoops from his throne,
   And the war-cry of Uri is wrathful and loud.

In speed they came on, but still faster they go,
   While ruin and horrour around them are hurled,
And the field of Morgarten in splendour shall grow,
   Like Marathon's field, to the end of the world.

Once only Carlyle did better than this, when love
came to assist his inspiration. Miss Welsh's injunctions,
though they subdued the tone of his letters, could not
prevent a confidential intercourse with a young, fascinating woman from producing its natural effect. Perhaps, after Irving was lost to her, though she gave
Carlyle no encouragement, she was less peremptorily
cold. He on his part regarded her as the most perfect
of women, beyond his practical hopes, but not beyond
his adoration, and he indulged in the usual flights of
musical imagining :—

They chide thee, fair and fervid one,
　At Glory's goal for aiming,
Does not Jove's bird, its flight begun,
Soar up against the beaming sun,
　Undazed in splendour flaming.

Young brilliant creature, even so
　A lofty instinct draws thee,
Heaven's fires within thy bosom glow,
Could earth's vain fading vulgar show
　One hour's contentment cause thee?

The gay saloon 'twas thine to tread,
　Its stateliest scenes adorning,
Thine be, by nobler wishes led,
With bays to crown thy lofty head,
　All meaner homage scorning.

Bright maid, thy destiny as I view,
　Unuttered thoughts come o'er me ;
Enrolled among earth's chosen few,
Lovely as morning, pure as dew,
　Thy image stands before me.

Oh, that on Fame's far shining peak,
　With great and mighty numbered,
Unfading laurels I could seek ;
This longing spirit then might speak
　The thoughts within that slumbered.

Oh, in the battle's wildest swell,
　By hero's deeds to win thee,
To meet the charge, the stormy yell,
The artillery's flash, its thundering knell,
　And thine the light within me.

> What man in Fate's dark day of power,
>   While thoughts of thee upbore him,
> Would shrink at danger's blackest lour
> Or faint in Life's last ebbing hour,
>   If tears of thine fell o'er him ?

These lines are noteworthy for the emotion which they express, but not even they have the ring of genuine gold. The feeling did not seek the metre because it could not otherwise find fit expression. The metre was rather laboriously adapted to the feeling, because the metrical form was assumed to be the right and appropriate one. Had Carlyle struggled on upon the false track, he might have written good artificial verses, showing from time to time a mind impatient of its fetters, but he would scarcely have risen to true greatness. Happily he was himself under no illusions. His object was to write out the truth that was in him : he saw his mistake, and he left his ideas to take the shape that was most natural to him. Taylor's offer for the ' London Magazine ' came to the help of his resolution, and he began his Life of Schiller as the commencement of the intended series. Goethe was designed to follow. But the biography of Goethe was soon exchanged for a translation of ' Wilhelm Meister.'

Thus opened the year 1823. The Buller connection continued to be agreeable. John Carlyle's companionship relieved the loneliness of the Edinburgh lodgings, while spare moments were occupied with writing letters to Miss Welsh or correcting her exercises.

We lead a quiet life at present (he wrote to his brother

Alexander). No incident breaks the smooth current of our history. None meddles with us, we meddle with none. Jack is studying bones, and the like. I write nonsense all the morning, then go and teach from two till six, then come home and read till half-past eleven, and so the day is done. I am happy while I can keep myself busy, which, alas! is not by any means always. The other day I went with Murray to call upon Macculloch, the *Scotsman*. He was sitting like a great Polar bear, chewing, and vainly trying to digest, the doctrines of Adam Smith and Ricardo, which he means to vomit forth again next spring in the shape of lectures to 'the thinking public' of this city. He eyed me with suspicion and distrust; would not come forth into open parley at all. What ailed the great Macculloch I could not tell. Did he ever feel fear? or might I be come to spy out the nakedness of his land?—I would not give a rush to know.

Communications more interesting than political economy came in weekly by the carrier from Mainhill. His father wrote to him on the 1st of January.

James Carlyle to Thomas Carlyle.

Mainhill: Jan. 1, 1823.

I take the pen in hand once more to write to you, though you may look for nothing but a few ill-arranged thoughts. But however that may be, I can tell you that I am in as good health as any of my age can expect to enjoy. In spite of bad times we are fighting away, and by feeding cattle, selling our barley, and one thing and another, we think we can meet our landlord at Candlemas this year as formerly; and when we can do that, you know we may go on so long as we are in any measure of health. How long that may be we cannot say. He who knows all things only knows

12—2

what is before us ; but we may know, both by Scripture and
by our own observation, that before long we must leave the
place we now occupy for a place in eternity, and only one of
two places can we look for, as there is not a third ; and the
Apostle tells us that, as we spend our time here, so will our
eternal state be. May the Lord make us all wise to consider these things, and to think on our latter end.

I forgot the last time I wrote to tell you that I had got
the book of sermons safe which you sent me, and I like
them very well. When I was reading Balmer's sermon on
the Resurrection, it brought into my mind a sermon preached
by Mr. William Glen nearly on the same subject. He said
many things about the eternity of the body that would rise
at the day of judgment, and the subject was disputed about
by Robert Scott and George MacIvin. Robert Scott was for
the same body rising again. The arguments were talked
over one morning at the meeting house door. I was present, and was rather involved in the dispute. I observed
that I thought a stinking clogg of a body like Robert Scott
the weaver's would be very unfit to inhabit those places.

Your mother wishes you a happy new year, and she
wishes it may be the best you ever have seen, and the worst
you ever may see.

I am, dear Son,

Your loving father,

JAMES CARLYLE.

The family, young and old, often contributed their
scraps to the carrier's budget on these occasions. The
youngest child of all, Jane, called the Craw, or Crow,
from her black hair, and not yet able even to write,
was heard composing in bed in the morning, to be
enclosed in her father's letter, 'a scrap of doggerel from
his affectionate sister Jane Carlyle.'

Of Carlyle's brothers, Alexander had the most natural genius. Of his sisters, the eldest, Margaret, had a tenderness, grace, and dignity of character which, if health and circumstances had been more kind, would have made her into a distinguished woman. But Jane was peculiar and original. She, when the day's work was over, and the young men wandered out in the summer gloaming, would cling to 'Tom's' hand and trot at his side, catching the jewelled sentences which dropped from his lips. She now, when he was far away, sent, among the rest, her little thoughts to him, composing the 'meanest of the letter kind' instinctively in rhyme and metre; her sister Mary, who had better luck in having been at school, writing down the words for her.

'Surely a very singular little crow,' was Carlyle's observation on reading her characteristic lines. 'Meanest of the letter kind' became a family phrase, to be met with for many years when an indifferent composition seemed to require an apology. Carlyle, in return, thought always first of his mother. He must send her a present. She must tell him what she needed most. 'Dear bairn,' she might answer, 'I want for nothing.' But it was not allowed to serve. 'She must understand that she could not gratify him so much as by enabling him to promote her comfort.'

Life (he wrote to her) is still in prospect to Jack and me. We are not yet what we hope to be. Jack is going to become a large gawsie broad-faced practiser of physic, to ride his horse in time, to give aloes by the rule, to make money and be a large man; while I, in spite of all my

dyspepsias and nervousness and hypochondrias, am still bent
on being a very meritorious sort of character, rather noted
in the world of letters, if it so please Providence, and useful,
I hope, whithersoever I go, in the *good old cause*, for which I
beg you to believe that I cordially agree with you in feeling
my chief interest, however we may differ in our modes of
expressing it.

CHAPTER XI.

A.D. 1823. ÆT. 28.

THE BULLERS after a winter's experience grew tired of
Edinburgh, and in the spring of 1823 took Kinnaird
House, a large handsome residence in Perthshire.
Carlyle during the removal was allowed a holiday. He
had been complaining of his health again. He had been
working hard on Schiller, and was beginning his translation of 'Meister.' His brother had gone home when
the University session was over, and describes the
anxiety of the family with a degree of humour unusual
with him.

John Carlyle to Thomas Carlyle.

May 5, 1823.

I found all the Mainhill people well in body and mind,
all very cheerful, and all disposed to give me a hearty welcome and receive me in their 'choicest mood.'[1] They all
inquired after you. Question followed question anxiously.
'Thou'se a vast deal leaner, lad, sin' thou gaed away!' 'Is
Tom got better? Does he sleep well yet? It gaed to my
heart when he told me in the last letter that he couldna sleep
without his finger in his ear. Poor fellow, he has had a
terrible time o't. I see by thee thou'se no telling me the
worst'—before I could get a word said. She thanks you for

---

[1] A phrase of Edward Irving's.

the large quantity of tea you sent her. It was the best she had had for a long while. Our father is cheerful and vigorous, and in the very best health. He has got every ounce weight of his corn sown, his potatoes set and covered, and has wherewith to meet his landlord with an 'impudent face.' I gave him Paley's 'Horæ Paulinæ,' with which he was considerably pleased. He told me he had often heard of it, but never could get it. He read a little of it yesterday, and was much pleased. Jane's muse has not visited her frequently of late. The 'letter poetic' which she sent you was entirely her own production. She made it in her bed one night exactly in the form in which you got it.

Kinnaird House is a beautiful place in the midst of woods near Dunkeld on the Tay. Carlyle spent a week in Annandale, and rejoined the Bullers there at the end of May.

I spent a joyful week in Annandale (he reported to Miss Welsh) amidst scenes in themselves unattractive or repulsive, but hallowed in my thoughts by the rude but genuine worth and true affection of those who people them. I think I am going to be comfortable enough in my new quarters. The Bullers are good people ; and, what is better, the first hour when they treat me uncivilly shall likewise be the last. So we live together in that easy style of cheerful indifference which seems to be the fit relation between us. For the rest, I have balmy air to breathe, fine scenery to look at, and stillness deeper than I have ever before enjoyed. My apartments are in a house detached from the larger building, which, except at meals and times of business, I intend to frequent but seldom. My window opens into a smooth bowling green, surrounded with goodly trees, and the thrushes have been singing amongst them, though it has rained every moment since I came. Here I purpose to spend my leisure and to think sweetly of friends that are far away.

Of these friends, Miss Welsh was naturally the most frequently in his mind. Her relations with him were drifting gradually in the direction in which friendships between young men and young women usually do drift. She had no thought of marrying him, but she was flattered by his attachment. It amused her to see the most remarkable person that she had ever met with at her feet. His birth and position seemed to secure her against the possibility of any closer connection between them. Thus he had a trying time of it. In serious moments she would tell him that their meeting had made an epoch in her history, and had influenced her character and life. When the humour changed, she would ridicule his Annandale accent, turned his passionate expressions to scorn, and when she had toned him down again she would smile once more, and enchant him back into illusions. She played with him, frightened him away, drew him back, quarrelled with him, received him again into favour as the fancy took her, till the poor man said, 'My private idea is that you are a witch like Sapphira in the New Testament, concerning whom Dr. Nimmo once preached in my hearing, "It seems probable, my friends, that Ananias was tempted into this by some spirit more wicked than his wife."' At last, in the summer of 1823, just after he was settled at Kinnaird, she was staying in some house which she particularly disliked, and on this occasion, in a fit of impatience with her surroundings— for she dated a letter which she wrote to him thence,

very characteristically, as from 'Hell'—she expressed a
gratitude for Carlyle's affection for her, more warm than
she had ever expressed before. He believed her serious,
and supposed that she had promised to be his wife.
She hastened to tell him, as explicitly as she could,
that he had entirely mistaken her.

My friend (she said), I love you. I repeat it, though I
find the expression a rash one. All the best feelings of my
nature are concerned in loving you. But were you my
brother I should love you the same. No. Your friend I
will be, your truest, most devoted friend, while I breathe the
breath of life. But your wife, never. Never, not though
you were as rich as Crœsus, as honoured and renowned as
you yet shall be.

Carlyle took his rebuke manfully. 'My heart,' he
said, 'is too old by almost half a score of years, and is
made of sterner stuff than to break in junctures of this
kind. I have no idea of dying in the Arcadian shepherd's style for the disappointment of hopes which I
never seriously entertained, or had no right to entertain seriously.' Could they have left matters thus, it
had been better for both of them. Two diamonds do
not easily form cup and socket. But Irving was gone.
Miss Welsh was romantic; and to assist and further the
advance of a man of extraordinary genius, who was kept
back from rising by outward circumstances, was not
without attraction to her. Among her papers there is
a curious correspondence which passed about this time
between herself and the family solicitor. Her mother
had been left entirely dependent on her. Her marriage,

she said, was possible, though not probable ; and ' she did not choose that her husband, if he was ever to be so disposed, should have it in his power to lessen her mother's income.' She executed an instrument, therefore, by which she transferred the whole of her property to her mother during Mrs. Welsh's life. By another she left it to Carlyle after her own and her mother's death. It was a generous act, which showed how far she had seen into his character and the future which lay before him, if he could have leisure to do justice to his talents. But it would have been happier for her and for him if she could have seen a little further, and had persevered in her refusal to add her person to her fortune.

Men of genius are ' kittle folk,' as the Scotch say. Carlyle had a strange temper, and from a child was ' gey ill to deal wi'.' When dyspepsia was upon him he spared no one, least of all those who were nearest and dearest to him. Dearly as he loved his brother John, yet he had spoken to him while they were lodging together in language which he was ashamed to remember. 'Often in winter,' he acknowledged ruefully to the poor John, ' when Satanas in the shape of bile was heavy upon me, I have said cruel things to thee, and bitterly, though vainly, do I recollect them ; but at bottom I hope you never doubted that I loved you.' Penitence, however, sincere as it might be, was never followed by amendment, even to the very end of his life.

But enough will be heard hereafter on this sad subject. The life at Kinnaird went on smoothly. The translation of ' Meister' prospered. An Edinburgh publisher undertook to publish it and pay well for it. There is a letter from Carlyle to his mother, dated June 10 of this year. Half a page is cut off, and contained evidently a cheque for a small sum of money.

Thomas Carlyle to Mrs. Carlyle, Mainhill.

Kinnaird House : June 10, 1823.

This letter may operate as a spur on the diligence of my beloved and valuable correspondents at Mainhill. There is a small blank made in the sheet for a purpose which you will notice. I beg you to accept the little picture which fills it without any murmuring. It is a poor testimonial of the grateful love I should ever bear you. If I hope to get a moderate command of money in the course of my life's operations, I long for it chiefly that I may testify to those dear to me what affection I entertain for them. In the meantime we ought to be thankful that we have never known what it was to be in fear of want, but have always had wherewith to gratify one another by these little acts of kindness, which are worth more than millions unblest by a true feeling between the giver and receiver. You must buy yourself any little odd things you want, and think I enjoy it along with you, if it add to your comfort. I do indeed enjoy it with you. I should be a dog if I did not. I am grateful to you for kindness and true affection such as no other heart will ever feel for me. I am proud of my mother, though she is neither rich nor learned. If I ever forget to love and reverence her, I must cease to be a creature myself worth remembering. Often, my dear mother, in solitary pensive moments does it come across me like the cold shadow of death that we two must part in the course of time. I shudder at the thought, and find no refuge except in humbly trusting that the great God will surely appoint us a meeting in that far country to which we are tending. May He bless you for ever, my good mother, and keep up in your heart those sublime hopes which at present serve as a pillar of cloud by day and a pillar of fire by night to guide your footsteps through the wilderness of life. We are in his hands. He will not utterly forsake us. Let us trust in Him.

I have no news of myself to send you except what are good. The boys are going on very fairly with me. They are excellent creatures in the main. With the rest of the family I am on the best footing. We talk together cheerfully whenever we meet. They show themselves anxious to promote my comfort by every rational arrangement. When with them I forget that there is any difference in worldly rank. They have their wealth, and birth, and connections and accomplishments to brag of. I too have my little stock of vanities within myself. My health was scarcely so good as you saw it for some days after I arrived. The air is pure as may be, and I am quiet as when at home; but I did not sleep well for some nights, and began to fear that I was again going down hill. On considering what the matter might be, it struck me it was, perhaps, my dining so late, at five o'clock, and fasting so long before dinner. A new regulation took place instantly, and now except on Sabbath days, when from choice I eat with the family, my meals are served up in a very comfortable manner at the hours I myself selected. The boys and I are up at breakfast a little before nine. We begin work half an hour after it, continuing till one. Then I go out and walk, or smoke, or amuse myself till half-past two, when dinner is waiting for me in the parlour, after which teaching recommences till near five, and then I am free as air for the night. I go into my own room and do whatsoever seemeth me good. I go out of it and walk and sometimes ride, and Donovan, the smart, whisking,

and very trustworthy butler, has a dish of tea standing
ready for me at seven. By this means I have brought myself round again. I like the arrangement also because I
have more time to myself, and am less restricted in my
movements. I have begun translating the German work
which Jack knows of. I am busy, I shall be healthy, and in
the meantime I am as comfortable as I could hope to be.

To John Carlyle.

Kinnaird: June 24.

Tell our mother I have a fire every night, and that all
things I want are supplied to me abundantly. We have
no incidents in our menage. Buller fishes and rides, and
eschews heart(ache).[1]   The lady saunters about on the back
of a grey stalking pony, and fights against *ennui* as fiercely as
she can. Both are uniformly civil and even kind to me.
We have got two visitors from the south with us at present,
Anna Pole and Reginald Pole her brother ; but they produce
no change in our mode of life. The lady is fully arrived at
the years of discretion, at least if these are under thirty.
She is good-humoured, understands all cookery from the
mixture of water-gruel up to the composition of the choicest
curry. She has a cornelian necklace, and kind blue eyes,
and a bit *nimble-yarn* tongue. Reginald has been at
Oxford studying the nature of horses. Philosophy is all a
hum ; but the short back, and the shoulder, and the hands
of height, and the price, and the speed—these are the points
for a future parson of the English Church. My own boys in
general behave admirably well to me and not *very* ill to
themselves. . . . Under this fine climate and among these
beautiful scenes I am at no loss to pass my time with profit

· Paper torn.

to my body, if not my mind. I wander by the copses on the shores of the Tay, or stroll over these black, interminable solitary moors, and meditate on many foolish things.

Later in the season, when London began to empty itself, other guests appeared at Kinnaird. The first glimpse into the great world did not please Carlyle.

I see something of fashionable people here (he wrote to Miss Welsh), and truly to my plebeian conception there is not a more futile class of persons on the face of the earth. If I were doomed to exist as a man of fashion, I do honestly believe I should swallow ratsbane, or apply to hemp or steel before three months were over. From day to day and year to year the problem is, not how to use time, but how to waste it least painfully. They have their dinners and their routs. They move heaven and earth to get everything arranged and enacted properly ; and when the whole is done what is it ? Had the parties all wrapped themselves in warm blankets and kept their beds, much peace had been among several hundreds of his Majesty's subjects, and the same result, the uneasy destruction of half a dozen hours, had been quite as well attained. No wonder poor women take to opium and scandal. The wonder is rather that these queens of the land do not some morning, struck by the hopelessness of their condition, make a general finish by simultaneous consent, and exhibit to coroners and juries the spectacle of the whole world of *ton* suspended by their garters, and freed at last from *ennui* in the most cheap and complete of all possible modes. There is something in the life of a sturdy peasant toiling from sun to sun for a plump wife and six eating children ; but as for the Lady Jerseys and the Lord Petershams, peace be with them.

There was a glimpse, too, of modern sporting, which
was as little admirable as the fine ladies and gentlemen.

To John Carlyle.

Kinnaird : September 17.

I got your letter last Friday on returning from a roe
hunt, which we had all been assisting at in the wood on the
hill beside us. A sorrier piece of entertainment, I may
observe, is not to be met with in this kingdom. They went
hallooing and beating the bushes, and talking Gaelic, the
gun-men standing at certain determined points with their
pieces ready, and I driving on Mrs. Buller and a wretched
old clout of a white pony she was riding on, or doing my
best to keep her in talk while we sat for hours in open
places among the heath. In the course of the day they got
two fawns about as large as your long-eared warlock, in
value somewhere about sixpence a piece, and thought it
royal sport. Reginald de la Pole shot them both, and never
was victor at the Olympic games more charmed with his
laurels. Richard Buller,[1] the other Oxford scholar, declared
on the first occasion 'he would have given a sovereign for
that shot.' After the second he became chop-fallen, and spoke
little more for four and twenty hours. *Sic itur ad astra.*

Sporting was not the only amusement at Kinnaird.
There was literature also and literary discussion.
Irving's popularity had taken fire, as Carlyle called it,
and he had become the rage of fashionable London.
He had published an argument for judgment to come,
written in great excitement and under some imagined
quasi inspiration.

[1] Nephew of Mr Buller, on a visit at Kinnaird.

Irving's book (Carlyle wrote) is come three days ago. Mrs. Buller bought it. I fear it will hardly do. There is a fierce and very spiteful review of it and him in the last 'Blackwood.' There is strong talent in it, true eloquence and vigorous thought, but the foundation is rotten, and the building itself a kind of monster in architecture, beautiful in parts, vast in dimensions, but on the whole decidedly a monster. Buller has stuck in the middle of it, 'Can't fall in with your friend at all, Mr. C.' Mrs. Buller is very near sticking ; sometimes I burst right out laughing when reading it. At other times I admired it sincerely.

I am sorry (he wrote a little later to Miss Welsh) that Irving's preaching has taken such a turn ; he had been much better if, without the pleasure of being a newspaper lion and a season's wonder, he had gradually become what he must ultimately pass for—a preacher of first-rate abilities, of great eloquence, with a head fertile above all others in sense and nonsense, and a heart of the most honest and kindly sort. As it is, our friend incurs the risk of many vagaries and disasters, and at best the certainty of much disquietude. His path is steadfast and manly only when he has to encounter opposition and misfortune. When fed with flatteries and prosperity his progress soon changes into 'ground and lofty tumbling,' accompanied with all the hazards and confusion that usually attend this species of movement. With three newspapers to praise him and three to blame, with about six peers and six dozen right honourables introduced to him every Sunday, tickets issuing for his church as if it were a theatre, and all the devout old women in the capital treating him with comfits and adulation, I know that ere now he is striking the stars with his sublime head—well if he do not break his shins among the rough places of the ground. I wish we saw him safely down again, and walking as other men walk. . . , I have meant

to write to him very frequently for almost three months, but
I know not well how to effect it. He will be talking about
'the Lord,' and twenty other things which he himself only
wishes to believe, and which to one that knows and loves
him are truly painful to hear. . . . Happy Irving, after all,
that is fitted with a task which he loves and is equal to.
He entertains no doubt that he is battering to its base the
fortress of the Alien, and he lies down every night to dream
of planting the old true blue Presbyterian flag upon the
summit of the ruins.

'Happy Irving, that is fitted with a task that he
loves.' Without any tinge of envy Carlyle could not
but contrast his friend's lot with his own; and the
sense of this was perhaps the more painful, because his
friend was winning fame and name on a course which
he knew to be a wrong one. But a few years since they
were poor schoolmasters together at Kirkcaldy, and now
Irving was the theological lion of the age, the passing
wonder of lawyers, statesmen, and men of the world,
who, having set religion aside as no longer worthy of
serious consideration, were awakened by him to a
languid belief that there might be something in it
after all. Carlyle saw the hollowness of the success;
yet for all that his friend had been lifted into a blaze of
distinction, while he was still unnoticed, was still in his
own conscience undeserving of notice, and unable to
turn to account the talents which he knew that he
possessed. He would have been more than mortal if
he had not at times repined at the inequalities of Fate.
Poor Irving! Little Carlyle knew or could measure
his friend's real condition. So far from 'standing on

tiptoe on Fortune's wheel,' he was just then getting married, and trying to forget Haddington. Carlyle saw him on his wedding tour in the Highlands. He has given an account of their meeting in his 'Reminiscences' which need not be repeated here. It had been intended that Miss Welsh should pay Irving and his wife a visit in London as soon as they were settled. But Irving could not face the trial; he only hoped that a time might come when he might be able to face it.

My dear Isabella (he wrote to her) has succeeded in healing the wounds of my heart by her unexampled affection and tenderness; but am I hardly yet in a condition to expose them. My former calmness and piety are returning. I feel growing in grace and holiness; and before another year I shall be worthy in the eye of my own conscience to receive you into my house and under my care, which till then I should hardly be.

Carlyle's lot was happy compared to Irving's, and yet he was already quarrelling with it. The Bullers, as he admitted, were most kind and considerate; yet he must have tried their patience. He was uneasy, restless, with dyspepsia and intellectual fever. He laid the blame on his position, and was already meditating to throw up his engagement.

To John Carlyle.

September 2.

I sleep irregularly here, and feel a little, very little, more than my usual share of torture every day. What the cause is would puzzle me to explain within the limits I could here

assign it. I take exercise sufficient daily ; I attend with
vigorous minuteness to the quality of my food ; I take all
the precautions that I can, yet still the disease abates not.
I should be an unreasonable blockhead did I complain of the
conduct of Mr. and Mrs. Buller towards me. Any arrangement that I could suggest would, I have not a doubt, be
most cheerfully complied with. Much trouble they have
already had with me. But their good resolutions and enact-
ments require to be executed by a pack of lazy, careless, and
irregular waiting men and women, and often in this wasteful
transmission their good will comes my length almost void.
It is the hundred petty omissions and commissions of this
canaille, coupled with the small inquietudes and vexations,
small but often returning, of my official employments that
chiefly act against me, and render this Kinnaird a worse
place for me than Mainhill. Pity that it were so. I might
else be very happy. Here am I sitting in this far highland
glen, under a fair autumn night, with my clear fire of oak
sticks blazing near me, my books and my tackle all around
me, and no sound at all but now and then the twang of
honest James Gow's fiddle, who is solacing his labours by
this not usual gratification ; partly, I suppose, because he sees
the sky beautiful and mild and kind, and feels in spirits, he
knows not why. The boys and old people and all seem to
grow in their esteem for me. It is very hard. But what
avails its hardness or softness either ? Let us have done with
whining and consider what steps can be taken to remedy it.
Often and long have I meditated that point since I came
hither. I have cudgelled my brains till they are sore to seek
deliverance ; for, like Joseph of Austria, *par ma tête seule*
must I get help if I get help at all. This, then, Jack, I have
in view at present. The Bullers—I mean the old gentry,
with Miss Pole—are gone to Aberdeen to some Caledonian
hunt or other, and will not be back for ten days. At their

return, if I am not better than I have been lately, I shall say to them, ' My very noble and approved good masters, allow me to ask you what you purpose doing through the winter with your boys ? If to go to Edinburgh, can I be any way accommodated there, so that I shall have the entire command of my eating and drinking, sleeping, waking, and general regimen ? If so, then I shall be very glad to serve you. To stay here as you once proposed ? This plan I doubt not may be attended with a thousand benefits ; but for my poor share of it, I have distinctly ascertained that my *kerkage* cannot stand it without manifest and permanent injury, and therefore, with the most profound dorsoflexions, I beg to wish you all good morning as soon as may be.'

So here, you see, the matter rests. I care not the tossing of a halfpenny whether I go or stay. If I go, I have money enough to keep me for a year or two. I can obtain plenty of literary tasks, and get them done about five times as effectually as now. If I stay I shall gather a hundred or two additional pounds, and have the privilege of living for the winter in Edinburgh, where my engagements call me to be, at any rate. I shall leave it in spring with books and pens and fresh undertakings. We shall get some accommodation furbished up at Mainhill (the old peat-house or some hole), where, by the aid of Bardolph[1] and my faithful mother, I am nearly certain I can recover my health. I shall be very busy, and we can all live together as merry as maltmen ; so I cast my cap into the air in defiance of all things yet ; for the spirit that is in me is still unbroken as the spirit of that old lame duck you have at home, who trusts, though at present winged and mashed in both her limbs, that she shall yet by the blessing of Providence lay above five shillings worth of eggs, and be useful in her day and generation.

[1] A horse bought for Carlyle by his brother Alexander, and with him at Kinnaird.

In better moments Carlyle recognised that the mischief was in himself, and that the spot did not exist upon earth where so sensitive a skin would not be irritated. He wrote a fortnight after :—

I find the Bullers are determined to stay here with us all the winter. If I had any quiet place to retire to I believe I should be tempted to throw up my commission to-morrow, and set forth to try the voyage on another tack, as I must ere long do at any rate. But there is none. Mainhill must be full of bustle and confusion at this time,[1] unfit for purposes of literary labour. Of Edinburgh, of living in lodgings with Mantic[2] and stenches and horrors more than tongue can tell to drive me to despair, I cannot think without a cold shudder which scarcely the prospect of the gallows could bring over me. Many a man, I am sure, has been tried by fifteen of his peers, and fairly doomed and hanged, and quartered by the doctors, with less torment than I have suffered in that fatal city for no cause at all. What then shall I do ? In days when wrecked with want of sleep and all its infernal *et cæteras*, I am sometimes within an inch of writing to Buller to signify my resolution of departing ; but their kindness to me and the reflection of my inability to mend the matter certainly, and the risk I run of making it considerably worse, always shuts my mouth. Next day, perhaps, I shall sleep better and become as lively as a hawk, and think I might exist here long enough very comfortably. Thus I vary and vacillate. Most probably it will long be so. It seems likely I shall just *thring on* here till I get desperate, and then cut and run.

[1] Harvest.

[2] Mantic was the name of his least-loved landlady.

Meanwhile I make a point of going on with Goethe.[1] Ten pages I find more than I can almost ever execute, for it is very hard, and I scarcely get fairly into the spirit of it till I must leave off. Nevertheless, I *gar myself* (as our father would do) go on with this thing. I am now more than half through the first volume. It will all be ready long ere spring. You and I could do it in four weeks if we had quiet quarters, and the fiend would give me any respite. I am sometimes tempted to sally off and get it done and then have it printed in winter ; then take something different and better, down to Mainhill, to work and toil as if I were a brownie, not a man, till I have conquered all these mean impediments that hem in the free-born, heaven-tending soul. I say, Jack, thou and I must never falter. Work, my boy, work unweariedly. I swear that all the thousand miseries of this hard fight, and ill health, the most terrific of them all, shall never chain us down. By the river Styx it shall not. Two fellows from a nameless spot in Annandale shall yet show the world the pluck that is in Carlyles.

Mrs. Buller must have been a most forbearing and discerning woman. She must have suffered, like every-one who came in contact with Carlyle, from his strange humours, but she had mind enough to see what he was, and was willing to endure much to keep such a man at her sons' side.

---

[1] The translation of *Meister*.

IF Carlyle complained, his complaints were the impatience of a man who was working with all his might. If his dyspepsia did him no serious harm, it obstructed his efforts and made him miserable with pain. He had written the first part of Schiller, which was now coming out in the 'London Magazine.' He was translating 'Meister,' and his translation, though the production of a man who had taught himself with grammar and dictionary, and had never spoken a word of German, is yet one of the very best which has ever been made from one language into another. In everything which he undertook he never spared labour or slurred over a difficulty, but endeavoured with his whole strength to do his work faithfully. A journal which he kept intermittently at Kinnaird throws light into the inner regions of his mind, while it shows also how much he really suffered. Deeply as he admired his German friends, his stern Scotch Calvinism found much in them that offended him. Goethe and even Schiller appeared to think that the hope of improvement for mankind lay in culture rather than morality—in æsthetics, in arts, in poetry, in the drama, rather than in obedience to the old rugged rules of right and wrong; and this perplexed and displeased him.

Schiller (he writes) was a very worthy character, possessed

of great talents, and fortunate in always finding means to
employ them in the attainment of worthy ends. The
pursuit of the Beautiful, the representing it in suitable
forms, and the diffusion of the feelings arising from it,
operated as a kind of religion in his soul. He talks in some
of his essays about the æsthetic being a necessary means of
improvement among political societies. His efforts in this
cause accordingly not only satisfied the restless activity, the
desire of creating and working upon others which forms the
great want of an elevated mind, but yielded a sort of balsam
to his conscience. He viewed himself as an apostle of the
Sublime. Pity that he had no better way of satisfying it.
A playhouse shows but indifferently as an arena for the
moralist. It is even inferior to the synod of the theologian.
One is tired to death with his and Goethe's *palabra* about
the nature of the fine arts. Did Shakespeare know anything
of the æsthetic ? Did Homer ? Kant's philosophy has a
gigantic appearance at a distance, enveloped in clouds and
darkness, shadowed forth in types and symbols of unknown
and fantastic derivation. There is an apparatus, and a
flourishing of drums and trumpets, and a tumultuous *Markt-
schreyerei*, as if all the earth were going to renew its youth ;
and the *Esoterics* are equally allured by all this pomp and
circumstance, and repelled by the hollowness and airy
nothingness of the ware which is presented to them. Any of
the results which have been made intelligible to us turn out
to be—like Dryden in the ' Battle of the Books '—a helmet
of rusty iron large as a kitchen pot, and within it a head
little bigger than a nut. What is Schlegel's great solution
of the mystery of life ?—' the strife of necessity against the
will.' Nothing earthly but the old old story that all men
find it difficult to get on in the world, and that one never
can get all his humours out. They pretend that Nature
gives people true intimations of true beauty and just prin-

ciples in Art; but the *bildende Künstler* and the *richtende*
ought to investigate the true foundation of these obscure
intimations, and set them fast on the basis of reason. Stuff
and nonsense I fear it is. People made finer pieces of work-
manship when there was not a critic among them, just as
people did finer actions when there was no theory of the
moral sentiments among them. Nature is the sure guide in
all cases; and perhaps the only requisite is that we have
judgment enough to apply the sentiment implanted in us
without an effort to the more complex circumstances that
will meet us more frequently as we advance in culture
or move in a society more artificial. Poor silly sons of
Adam! you have been prating on these things for two or
three thousand years, and you have not advanced a hair's
breadth towards the conclusion. Poor fellows, and poorer
me, that take the trouble to repeat such insipidities and
truisms.

Here, on the same page, Carlyle sketched the emblem of the
wasting candle, with the motto
written on it, '*Terar dum prosim.*' 'May I be wasted, so that
I be of use.' He goes on:—

But what if I do not *prosum?* Why then *terar* still, so
I cannot help it. This is the end and beginning of all
philosophy, known even to Singleton the blacksmith; we
must just do the best we can. Oh, most lame and impotent
conclusion! I wish I fully understood the philosophy of
Kant. Is it a chapter in the history of human folly? or the
brightest in the history of human wisdom? or both mixed?
and in what degree?

This was written on May 23. The next entry begins :—

It is now November ; six weary months have passed away, another portion from my span of being ; and here am I, in a wet, dreary night at Kinnaird, with no re-collections or acquisitions to fill up that span with ; but the recollection of agonised days and nights, and the ac-quisition of a state of health worse than ever it was. My time ! my time ! my peace and activity ! where are they ? I could read the curse of Ernulphus, or something twenty times as fierce, upon myself and all things earthly. What will become of me ? Happiness ! Tophet must be happier than this ; or they——but, *basta !* it is no use talking. Let me get on with Schiller, then with Goethe. 'They that meaned at a gowden gown gat aye the sleeve.' I shall not get even the listing. Schiller is in the wrong vein—laborious, partly affected, meagre, bombastic. Too often it strives by lofty words to hide littleness of thought. Would I were done with it ! Oh, Carlyle ! if thou ever become happy, think on these days of pain and darkness, and thou wilt join trembling with thy mirth.

———

There is something in reading a weak or dull book very nauseous to me. Reading is a weariness of the flesh. After reading and studying about two scores of good books there is no new thing whatever to be met with in the generality of libraries ; repetitions a thousand times repeated of the same general idea. Feelings, opinions, and events, all is what we might anticipate. No man without Themistocles' gift of forgetting can possibly spend his days in reading. Generally about the age of five and twenty he should begin to put the little knowledge he has acquired (it can be but little) from books to some practical use. If I could *write*, that were my practical use. But, alas! alas! Oh Schiller! what secret hadst thou for creating such things as Max and Thekla when thy body was wasting with disease? I am well nigh *done*, I think. To die is hard enough at this age. To die by inches is very hard. But I *will* not. Though all things human and divine are against me, I will not.

December 14.—Schiller, part ii. is off to London three weeks ago. It was very bad. Part iii. I am swithering to begin; would it were finished!

I spent ten days wretchedly in Edinburgh and Haddington. I was consulting doctors, who made me give up my dear nicotium and take to mercury. I am to write letters, and then begin Schiller. May God bless all my friends! my poor mother at the head of them. It sometimes comes on me like the shadow of death that we *are* all parting from one another—each moving his several, his inevitable way; fate driving us on—inexorable, dread, relentless fate. No deliverance! (*Mit dem Fusse stampfend.*) No help? Alas, poor sons of Adam!

December 31.—The year is closing. This time eight and twenty years I was a child of three weeks old, sleeping in my mother's bosom.

> Oh! little did my mither think
> That day she cradled me,
> The lands that I should travel in,
> The death I was to dee.

Another hour and 1823 is with the years beyond the flood. What have I done to mark the course of it? Suffered the pangs of Tophet almost daily; grown sicker and sicker; alienated by my misery certain of my friends, and worn out from my own mind a few remaining capabilities of enjoyment; reduced my world a *little* nearer the condition of a

bare, rugged desert, where peace and rest for me is none.
Hopeful youth, Mr. C. ! Another year or two and it will do.
Another year or two and thou wilt wholly *be*—this *caput
mortuum* of thy former self ; a creature ignorant, stupid,
peevish, disappointed, broken-hearted, the veriest wretch
upon the surface of the globe. My curse seems deeper and
blacker than that of any man : to be immured in a rotten
carcase, every avenue of which is changed into an inlet of
pain, till my intellect is obscured and weakened, and my
head and heart are alike desolate and dark. How have I
deserved this ? Or is it mere fate that orders these things,
caring no jot for merit or demerit, crushing our poor mortal
interests among its ponderous machinery, and grinding us
and them to dust relentlessly ? I know not. Shall I ever
know ? Then why don't you kill yourself, sir ? Is there
not arsenic ? is there not ratsbane of various kinds ? and
hemp ? and steel ? Most true, Sathanas, all these things
are ; but it will be time enough to use them when I have
lost the game which I am as yet but *losing.* You observe,
sir, I have still a glimmering of hope ; and while my friends,
my mother, father, brothers, sisters live, the duty of not
breaking their hearts would still remain to be performed
when hope had utterly fled. For which reason—even if
there were no others, which, however, I believe there are—
the benevolent Sathanas will excuse me. I do not design to
be a suicide. God in heaven forbid ! That way I was never
tempted. But where is the use of going on with this ? I
am not writing like a reasonable man. If I am miserable
the more reason there is to gather my faculties together, and
see what can be done to help myself. I want health,
health, health ! On this subject I am becoming quite
furious ; my torments are greater than I am able to bear.
If I do not soon recover, I am miserable for ever and ever.
They talk of the benefit of ill health in a moral point of

view. I declare solemnly, without exaggeration, that I impute nine-tenths of my present wretchedness, and rather more than nine-tenths of all my faults, to this infernal disorder in the stomach.

But if it were once away, I think I could snap my fingers in the face of all the world. The only good of it is the friends it tries for us and endears to us. Oh, there is a charm in true affection that suffering cannot weary, that abides by us in the day of fretfulness and dark calamity, a charm which almost makes amends for misery. Love to friends—alas! I may almost say relatives—is now almost the sole religion of my mind.

I have hopes of 'Meister,' though they are still very faint. Schiller, part iii. I began just three nights ago. I absolutely could not sooner. These drugs leave me scarcely the consciousness of existence. I am scribbling, not writing, Schiller. My mind will not catch hold of it. I skim it, do it as I will, and I am as anxious as possible to get it off my hands. It will not do for publishing separately. It is not in my natural vein. I wrote a very little of it to-night, and then went and talked ineptitudes at the house. Alas! there is mercurial powder in me, and a gnawing pain over all the organs of digestion, especially in the pit and left side of the stomach. Let this excuse the wild absurdity above.

Half-past eleven.—The silly Donovan is coming down (at least so I interpreted his threat) with punch or 'wishes,' which curtails the few reflections that mercury might still leave it in my power to make. To make none at all will perhaps be as well. It exhibits not an interesting, but a true picture of my present mood—stupid, unhappy, by fits wretched, but also dull—dull and very weak.

> Now fare thee well, old twenty-three,
>   No powers, no arts can thee retain;
> Eternity will roll away,
>   And thou wilt never come again.

And welcome thou, young twenty-four,
  Thou bringest to men of joy and grief ;
Whatever thou bringest in sufferings sour,
  The heart in faith will hope relief.

Here thou art, by Jove. Donny is not come. Good-night—
to whom ?

January 7.—Last Sunday came the ' Times ' newspaper
with the commencement of Schiller, part ii. extracted. So
Walter thought it on this side zero. I believe this is about
the first compliment (most slender as it is) that ever was paid
me by a person who could have no interest in hoodwinking
me. I am very weak. It kept me cheerful for an hour.
Even yet I sometimes feel it. Certainly no one ever wrote
with such tremendous difficulty as I do. Shall I ever learn
to write with ease ?

There can be no doubt that Carlyle suffered and perhaps suffered excessively. It is equally certain that
his sufferings were immensely aggravated by the treatment to which he was submitted. ' A long hairy-eared
jackass,' as he called some eminent Edinburgh physician,
had ordered him to give up tobacco, but he had ordered
him to take mercury, as well ; and he told me that
along with the mercury he must have swallowed whole
hogsheads of castor oil. Much of his pain would be so
accounted for ; but of all the men whom I have ever
seen, Carlyle was the least patient of the common woes
of humanity. Nature had, in fact, given him a constitution of unusual strength. He saw his ailments
through the lens of his imagination, so magnified by
the metaphors in which he described them as to seem
to him to be something supernatural ; and if he was a

torment to himself, he distracted every one with whom he came in contact. He had been to Edinburgh about the printing of ' Meister,' and had slept in the lodgings which he had longed for at Kinnaird. 'There was one of those public guardians there,'[1] he says in a letter, ' whose throat I could have cut that night; his voice was loud, hideous, and ear and soul piercing, resembling the voices of ten thousand gib cats all molten into one terrific peal.' He had been given rooms in a separate house at Kinnaird for the sake of quiet. This did not content him either. When the winter came he complained of the cold.

My bower (he said) is the most polite of bowers, refusing admittance to no wind that blows from any quarter of the shipmate's card. It is scarcely larger than your room at Mainhill; yet has three windows, and of course, a door, all shrunk and crazy. The walls, too, are pierced with many crevices, for the mansion has been built by Highland masons, apparently in a remote century. I put on my gray duffle sitting jupe. I bullyrag the sluttish harlots of the place, and cause them to make fires that would melt a stithy. . . .

Poor Mrs. Buller's household management pleased him as little.

This blessed stomach I have lost all patience with (he wrote to his brother Alexander). The want of health threatens to be the downdraught of all my lofty schemes. My heart is burnt with fury and indignation when I think of being cramped and shackled and tormented as never man till me was. 'There is too much fire in my belly,' as Ram Dass said, to permit my dwindling into a paltry valetu-

---

[1] A watchman.

dimarian. I must and will be free of these despicable fetters, whatever may betide. . . . I could almost set my house in order, and go and hang myself like Judas. If I take any of their swine-meat porridge, I sleep ; but a double portion of stupidity overwhelms me, and I awake very early in the morning with the sweet consciousness that another day of my precious, precious time is gone irrevocably, that I have been very miserable yesterday, and shall be very miserable to-day. It is clear to me that I can never recover or retain my health under the economy of Mrs. Buller. Nothing, therefore, remains for me but to leave it. This kind of life is next to absolute starvation, only slower in its agony. And if I had my health even moderately restored, I could earn as much by my own exertions.

So it would be one day. The next, the pain would be gone, the sun would be shining again, and nothing would remain but a twinge of remorse for the anxiety which his clamours might have caused. He apologised in a letter to his father with characteristic coolness.

I often grieve for the uneasiness my complaining costs you and my dear mother, who is of feebler texture in that re- spect than you. But by this time she must be beginning to understand me ; to know that when I shout ' murder,' I am not always being killed. The truth is, complaint is the natural resource of uneasiness, and I have none that I care to complain to, but you. After all, however, I am not so miserable as you would think. My health is better than it was last year, but I have lost all patience with it ; and when ever any retrograde movement comes in view, I get quite desperate in the matter ; being determined that I must get well—cost what it will. On days when moderately well, I feel as happy as others ; happier perhaps, for sweet is pleasure after pain.

I have dwelt more fully on these aspects of Carlyle's character than in themselves they deserve, because the irritability which he could not or would not try to control followed him through the greater part of his life. It was no light matter to take charge of such a person, as Miss Welsh was beginning to contemplate the possibility of doing. Nor can we blame the anxiety with which her mother was now regarding the closeness of the correspondence between Carlyle and her daughter. Extreme as was the undesirableness of such a marriage in a worldly point of view, it is to Mrs. Welsh's credit that inequality of social position was not the cause of her alarm, so much as the violence of temper which Carlyle could not restrain even before her. The fault, however, was of the surface merely, and Miss Welsh was not the only person who could see the essential quality of the nature which lay below. Mrs. Buller had suffered from Carlyle's humours as keenly as anyone, except, perhaps, her poor ' sluttish harlots ; ' yet she was most anxious that he should remain with the family and have the exclusive training of her sons. They had been long enough at Kinnaird ; their future plans were unsettled. They thought of a house in Cornwall, of a house in London, of travelling abroad, in all of which arrangements they desired to include Carlyle. At length it was settled—so far as Mrs. Buller could settle anything—that they were to stay where they were till the end of January, and then go for the season to London. Carlyle was to remain behind in Scotland till he had carried ' Meister ' through the press. Irving had invited him to be his guest at any time in the spring which might suit him, and further plans could then be arranged. For the moment his mind was taken off from his own sorrows by the need of helping his brothers. His brother Alick was starting in business as a farmer. Carlyle found him in money, and refused to be thanked for it. ' What any brethren of our father's house possess,' he said, ' I look on as common stock, from which all are entitled to draw whenever their convenience requires it. Feelings far nobler than pride are my guides in such matters.'

He was already supporting John Carlyle at college, and not supporting only, but directing and advising. His counsels were always wise. As a son and brother his conduct in all essentials was faultlessly admirable. Here is a letter on the value of a profession. John, it seems, was shrinking from drudgery, and inclining to follow the siren of literature.

Thomas Carlyle to John Carlyle.

Kinnaird: Jan. 1, 1824.

I am glad to learn that your repugnance to medicine is gradually wearing away. Persist honestly in the study, and you will like it more and more. Like all practical sciences, medicine is begirt with a tangled border of minute, technical, uninteresting, or, it may be, disgusting details, the whole of which must be mastered before you penetrate into the philosophy of the business, and get the better powers of your understanding at all fastened on the subject. You are now, I suppose, getting across these brambly thickets into the green fields of the science. Go on and prosper, my dear

14—2

Jack ! Let not the difficulties repulse you, nor the little contentions of natural taste abate your ardour. To conquer our inclinations of whatever sort is a lesson which all men have to learn, and the man who learns it soonest will learn it easiest. This medicine your judgment says is to be useful to you. Do you assail it and get the better of it, in spite of all other considerations. It is a noble thing to have a profession by the end : it makes a man independent of all mortals. He is richer than a lord, for no *external* change can destroy the possession which he has acquired for himself. Nor is there any weight in the fears you labour under about failing in more interesting acquisitions by your diligence in following after this. It appears to me that a man who is not born to some independency, if he means to devote himself to literature properly so called, even ought to study some profession which as a first preliminary will enable him to live. It is galling and heartburning to live on the precarious windfalls of literature ; and the idea that one has not time for practising an honest calling is stark delusion. I could have studied three professions in the time I have been forced, for want of one, to spend in strenuous idleness. I could practise the most laborious doctor's occupation at this moment in less time than I am constrained to devote to toiling in that which cannot permanently profit, and serves only to make a scanty provision for the day that is passing over me : but I will preach no more, for you are a reasonable youth, Jack, and are already bent on persevering.

The life at Kinnaird was running out. The last roes were shot on the mountains, and the last visitors were drifting away. Carlyle too was longing to be gone, but the move was continually postponed.

He wad need to have a lang ladle that sups with the

Deil (he said), and he wad need to have a long head that predicts the movements of aught depending on Mrs. Buller. . . . This accursed Schiller is not finished yet. Patience, patience ; or, rather, fortitude and action, for patience will not do. . . . It is impossible for anything to be more stagnant and monotonous than our life here is. We are all very agreeable together, but there is no new topic among us ; and now, grouse shooting having failed, the good people are weary of their abode here. Two or three squires of the neighbourhood have looked in upon us of late, but their minds are what Pump Sandy calls a ' vaacuum.' *Nailer and airt working together* have rendered them dull. We had the other night a Sir John something—I forget what— perhaps Ogilvie,—' one of the numerous baronets of the age,' as Arthur Buller described him. Thurtell being hanged last week, we grew duller than ever, till yesterday Mrs. Buller turned off all the servants except two at one swoop. This keeps up our hearts for the time. On the whole, however, I have been happier than I usually was throughout the summer and autumn. My health, I think, is little worse or better than it was ; but I have the prospect of speedy deliverance, and my mind has been full, disagreeably so often, of this miserable Schiller.

He was looking forward to London, though far from sharing the enthusiastic expectations which Irving had formed for him. Irving, it seems, had imagined that his friend had but to present himself before the great world to carry it by storm as he had himself done, and when they met in the autumn had told him so. Carlyle was under no such illusion.

We spoke about this project of his and my share in it (he wrote), but could come to no conclusion. He figured

out purposes of unspeakable profit to me. He seemed to
think that, if set down in London streets, some strange
development of genius would take place in me; that by conversing with Coleridge and the Opium-eater I should find
out new channels of speculation and soon learn to speak with
tongues. There is but a very small degree of truth in all
this. Of genius (bless the mark!) I never imagined in the
most lofty humour that I possessed beyond the smallest
possible fraction; and this fraction, be it little or less, can
only be turned to account by rigid and stern perseverance
through long years of labour, in London as any other spot in
the universe. Unrelenting perseverance, stubborn effort, is
the remedy. Help cometh not from the hills or valleys.
My own poor arm, weak and shackled as it is, must work out
my deliverance, or I am for ever captive and in bonds.
Irving said I had none to love or reverence in Scotland.
Kind, simple Irving. I did not tell him of the hearts in
Scotland I will love till my own has ceased to feel, whose
warm, pure and generous affection I would not exchange for
the maudlin sympathy of all the peers and peeresses and
prim saints and hypochondriacal old women of either sex in
the creation. I told him that love concentered on a few
objects, or a single one, was like a river flowing within its
appointed banks, calm, clear, rejoicing in its course. Diffused
over many, it was like that river spread abroad upon a
province, stagnant, shallow, cold and profitless. He puckered
up his face into various furrowy peaks at this remark, and
talked about the Devil and universal benevolence, reproving
me withal because I ventured to laugh at the pretensions of
the Devil.

The Bullers went at last. Carlyle returned to his
lodgings at Edinburgh, finished his Schiller, and was
busy translating the last chapters of 'Meister' while

the first were being printed. Miss Welsh came into
the city to stay with a friend. They met and
quarrelled. She tormented her lover till he flung out
of the room, banging the door behind him. A note of
penitence followed. 'I declare,' she said, 'I am very
much of Mr. Kemp's way of thinking, that certain
persons are possessed of devils at the present time.
Nothing short of a devil could have tempted me to
torment you and myself as I did on that unblessed day.'
There was no engagement between them, and under
existing circumstances there was to be none; but she
shared Irving's conviction that Carlyle had but to be
known to spring to fame and fortune; and his fortune,
as soon as it was made, she was willing to promise to
share with him. Strict secrecy was of course desired.
Her mother and his mother were alone admitted to the
great mystery; but the 'sorrows of Teufelsdröckh,'
bodily and mental, were forgotten for at least three
months.

To James Carlyle, Mainhill.

3 Moray Street: April 2, 1824.

My dear Father,—I feel thankful to learn that you are still
in moderate health, having little to complain of except the
weariness of increasing years, and being supported under the
feeling of this by such comforts as it has been your care in
life to lay up. To all men journeying through the wilderness
of the world religion is an inexhaustible spring of nourishment
and consolation; the thorns and flinty places of our path become soft when we view them as leading to an everlasting
city, where sorrow and sin shall be alike excluded. To a
religious man, and to a mere worldling, the frailties of age

speak in very different tones : to the last they are the judgment voice that warns him to an awful reckoning, a dark and dreary change ; to the first they are kind assurances of a father, that a place of rest is made ready where the weary shall find refreshment after all their toils.

Judging from your years and past and present health, I expect that we shall yet be all spared together for a long, long season, shall live and see good here below.   But it gives me real pleasure to know that you have such approved resources against the worst that can befall.   I often think of death, as all reasonable creatures must ;   but with such prospects there is little in it to be feared.   I have many a time felt that without the expectation of it life would be in its brightest station a burden too heavy to be borne.   But these are topics too serious for this light handling.   We are in the hands of an All-merciful Father.   Let us live with hope in Him, and try to fill rightly the parts he has assigned us.   Here is an anchor of the soul both sure and steadfast. By this let us abide, and vex ourselves with no needless fear.

Jack, poor Jack ! I feel convinced is going to make a figure yet ; he inherits a good head and an honest heart from his parents, and no bad habit of any kind has perverted these invaluable gifts.   His only faults at present are his in-experience and the very excess of his good qualities.   Our only subject of disagreement is the relative importance of worldly comforts and mental wealth.   Jack decides, as a worthy fellow of twenty always will decide, that mere external rank and convenience are nothing ; the dignity of the mind is all in all.   I argue as every reasonable man of *twenty-eight*, that this is poetry in part, which a few years will mix pretty largely with prose.   And there we differ and chop logic, an art for which Jack has been famous from his very cradle.   Sometimes I make free to settle him with your finisher, 'Thou natural thou !'   But on the whole he is getting more rational. His jolly presence has been of no small benefit to myself on many sad occasions. I have often absolutely wondered at the patience with which he has borne my black humours, when bad health and disturbance vexed me too much. He is certainly a prime honest 'Lord Moon,'[1] with all his faults.

Carlyle did not stay long in Edinburgh. He remained only till he had settled his business arrangements with Boyd, his publisher, and then went home to Mainhill to finish his translation of 'Meister' there. He was to receive 180*l*. on publication for the first edition. If a second edition was called for, Boyd was to pay him 250*l*. for a thousand copies, and after that the book was to be Carlyle's own. 'Any way, I am paid sufficiently for my labours,' he said. 'Am I a genius? I was intended for a horsedealer, rather.' The sheets of 'Meister' were sent to Haddington as they were printed. Miss Welsh refused to be interested in it, and thought more of the money which Carlyle was making than of the great Goethe and his novel. Carlyle admitted that she had much to say for her opinion.

There is not (he said), properly speaking, the smallest particle of historical interest in it except what is connected with Mignon, and her you cannot see fully till near the very end. Meister himself is perhaps one of the greatest *ganaches* that ever was created by quill and ink. I am going to write a fierce preface disclaiming all concern with the literary or the moral merit of the work, grounding my claims to recompense

---

[1] Name by which John Carlyle went in the family from the breadth of his face.

or toleration on the fact that I have accurately copied a striking portrait of Goethe's mind—the strangest, and in many points the greatest, now extant. What a work! Bushels of dust and straws and feathers, with here and there a diamond of the purest water.

Carlyle was very happy at this time at Mainhill. He had found work that he could do, and had opened, as it seemed, successfully his literary career. The lady whom he had so long worshipped had given him hopes that his devotion might be rewarded. She had declined to find much beauty even in Mignon; but she might say what she pleased now without disturbing him.

To Miss Welsh.

Mainhill: April 15.

So you laugh at my venerated Goethe and my *Herzen's Kind* poor little Mignon. Oh, the hardness of man's, and still more of woman's heart! If you were not lost to all true feeling your eyes would be a fountain of tears in the perusing of 'Meister.' Have you really no pity for the hero, or the Count, or the Frau Melina, or Philina, or the Manager? Well, it cannot be helped. I must not quarrel with you. Do what you like. Seriously, you are right about the book. It is worth next to nothing as a novel. Except Mignon, who will touch you yet perhaps, there is no person in it one has any care about. But for its wisdom, its eloquence, its wit, and even for its folly and its dullness, it interests me much, far more the second time of reading than it did the first. I have not got as many ideas from any book for six years. You will like Goethe better ten years hence than you do at present. It is pity the man were not known among us. The English have begun to speak about him of late years, but no light has yet been thrown upon him ; 'no light but only darkness visible.' The syllables Goethe excite an idea as vague and monstrous as the words Gorgon or Chimera.

It would do you good to see with what regularity I progress in translating. Clockwork is scarcely steadier. Nothing do I allow to interfere with me. My movements might be almost calculated like the moon's. It is not unpleasant work, nor is it pleasant. Original composition is ten times as laborious. It is an agitating, fiery, consuming business, when your heart is in it. I can easily conceive a man writing the soul out of him—writing till it evaporate like the snuff of a farthing candle when the matter interests him properly. I always recoil from again engaging with it. But this present business is cool and quiet. One feels over it as a shoemaker does when he sees the leather gathering into a shoe—as any mortal does when he sees the activity of his mind expressing itself in some external material shape. You are facetious about my mine of gold. It has often struck me as the most accursed item in men's lot that they had to toil for filthy lucre ; but I am not sure now that it is not the *ill-best* way it could have been arranged. Me it would make happy at least for half a year, if I saw the certain prospect before me of making 500*l.* per annum. A pampered Lord— *e.g.* Byron—would turn with loathing from a pyramid of ingots. I *may* be blessed in this way : he never. Let us be content.

It would edify you much to see my way of life here—how I write and ride and delve in the garth and muse on things new and old. On the whole I am moderately happy. There is rough substantial plenty here. For me there is heartfelt kindness in the breast of every living thing, from the cur that vaults like a kangaroo whenever he perceives me, and

the pony that prances when he gets me on his back, up to
the sovereign heads of the establishment. Better is a
dinner of herbs with peace, than a stalled ox with contention.
Better is affection in the smoke of a turf cottage than indifference amidst the tapestries of palaces.

I am often very calm and quiet. I delight to see these
old mountains lying in the clear sleep of twilight, stirless as
death, pure as disembodied spirits, or floating like cærulean
islands, while the white vapours of the morning have hidden
all the lower earth.

They are my own mountains. Skiddaw and Helvellyn,
with their snowy cowls among their thousand azure brethren,
are more to me than St. Gothard and Mont Blanc. Hartfell
and Whitecomb raise their bald and everlasting heads into
my native sky, and far beyond them, as I often picture, are
Jane and her mother, sometimes thinking of me, cheering
this dull earth for me with a distant spot of life and kindliness. . . . But, bless me ! the sweet youth is growing quite
poetical. *C'est assez.*

In this mood Carlyle heard of the end of Lord Byron.
He had spoken slightingly of Byron in his last letter ;
he often spoke in the same tone in his own later years ;
but he allowed no one else to take the same liberties.
Perhaps in his heart he felt at fourscore much what he
wrote when the news came from Missolonghi. Both he
and Miss Welsh were equally affected. She wrote 'I
was told it all alone in a room full of people. If they
had said the sun or the moon was gone out of the
heavens, it could not have struck me with the idea of
a more awful and dreary blank in the creation than the
words, " Byron is dead." '

Carlyle answered—

Poor Byron! alas, poor Byron! the news of his death came upon my heart like a mass of lead ; and yet, the thought of it sends a painful twinge through all my being, as if I had lost a brother. Oh God ! that so many souls of mud and clay should fill up their base existence to its utmost bound ; and this the noblest spirit in Europe should sink before half his course was run. Late so full of fire and generous passion and proud purposes ; and now for ever dumb and cold. Poor Byron ! and but a young man, still struggling amidst the perplexities and sorrows and aberrations of a mind not arrived at maturity, or settled in its proper place in life. Had he been spared to the age of threescore and ten, what might he not have done ! what might he not have been ! But we shall hear his voice no more. I dreamed of seeing him and knowing him ; but the curtain of everlasting night has hid him from our eyes. We shall go to him ; he shall not return to us. Adieu. There is a blank in your heart and a blank in mine since this man passed away.

CHAPTER XIII.

THE time for Carlyle's departure for London had now arrived. A letter came from Mrs. Buller begging his immediate presence. 'Meister' was finished and paid for. A presentation copy was secured for Mainhill, and there was no more reason for delay. The expedition was an epoch in Carlyle's life. There was, perhaps, no one of his age in Scotland or England who knew so much and had seen so little. He had read enormously —history, poetry, philosophy; the whole range of modern literature—French, German, and English—was more familiar to him, perhaps, than to any man living of his own age; while the digestive power by which all this spiritual food had been assimilated and converted into intellectual tissue was equally astonishing. And yet all this time he had never seen any town larger than Glasgow, or any cultivated society beyond what he had fallen in with at occasional dinners with Brewster, or with the Bullers at Kinnaird. London had hovered before him rather as a place of doubtful possibilities than of definite hope. The sanguine Irving would have persuaded him that it would open its arms to a new man of genius. Carlyle knew better. He had measured his own capabilities. He was painfully aware that they were not of the sort which would win

easy recognition, and that if he made his way at all it
would be slowly, and after desperate and prolonged
exertion. He would never go to bed unknown and
wake to find himself famous. His own disposition was
rather towards some quiet place in Scotland, where with
fresh air and plain food he could possess his soul in
peace and work undisturbed and unconfused. Still
London was to be seen and measured. He was to go
by sea from Leith, and for the first week or two after
his arrival he was to be Irving's guest at Pentonville.
A few happy days were spent at Haddington, and on
Sunday morning, June 6, he sailed—sailed literally.
Steamers had begun to run, but were not yet popular;
and the old yacht, safe if tedious, was still the usual
mode of transit for ordinary travellers. His fellow-
passengers were—a Sir David Innes, a Captain Smith
from Linlithgow; a M. Dubois, land-steward to Lord
Bute; and two ladies who never left their cabins.
This is Carlyle's account of his voyage.

To Miss Welsh.

I had the most melancholy sail to London. Cross winds,
storms, and, what was ten times worse, dead calms, and the
stupidest society in nature. Sir David Innes, if, indeed, he be
a knight of flesh and blood, and not a mere shadowy personifi-
cation of dullness, snored assiduously beside me all night, and
talked the most polite ineptitudes all day. He had a large
long head like a sepulchral urn. His face, pock-pitted, hirsute
and bristly, was at once vast and hatchet-shaped. He stood
for many hours together with his left hand laid upon the
boat on the middle of the deck, and the thumb of his right
hand stuck firmly with its point on the hip joint; his large

blue and rheumy eyes gazing on vacancy, the very image of thicklipped misery. Captain Smith was of quite an opposite species, brisk, lean, whisking, smart of speech, and quick in bowing ; but if possible still more inane than Dullness . . . . These two, Dullness and Inanity, contrived to tell me in the course of the voyage nearly all the truisms which natural and moral science have yet enriched the world withal. They demonstrated to me that sea-sickness was painful, that sea-captains ought to be expert, that London was a great city, that the Turks eat opium, that the Irish were discontented, that brandy would intoxicate. Oh, I thought I should have given up the ghost ! M. Dubois, a Strasburger, Lord Bute's factotum, with his flageolet, his 'Vaillant Troubadour,' and his 'Es hatt' ein Bauer ein schönes Weib,' alone con-tributed to save me. I laughed at him every day about an hour. On Sunday do you suppose I was very gay ? The Bass was standing in sight all day, and I recollected where the Sunday before I had been sitting beside you in peace and quietness at home ! But time and hours wear out the roughest day. Next Friday at noon we were winding slowly through the forest of masts in the Thames up to our station at Tower Wharf. The giant bustle, the coalheavers, the bargemen, the black buildings, the ten thousand times ten thousand sounds and movements of that monstrous harbour formed the grandest object I had ever witnessed. One man seems a drop in the ocean : you feel annihilated in the immensity of that heart of all the earth.

Carlyle has described in his 'Reminiscences' his arrival in London, his reception in Irving's house, and his various adventures during his English visit. When written evidence rises before us of what we said and did in early life, we find generally that memory has played false to us, and has so shaped and altered past scenes that our actions have become legendary even to ourselves. Goethe called his autobiography ' Wahrheit und Dichtung,' being aware that facts stand in our recollection as trees, houses, mountains, rivers stand in the landscape; that lights and shadows change their places between sunrise and sunset, and that the objects are grouped into new combinations as the point of vision alters. But none of these involuntary freaks of memory can be traced in Carlyle's ' Reminiscences.' After two and forty years the scenes and persons which he describes remain as if photographed precisely as they are to be found in his contemporary letters. Nothing is changed. The images stand as they were first printed, the judgments are unmodified, and are often repeated in the same words. His matured and epitomised narrative may thus be trusted as an entirely authentic record of the scenes which are recorded at fuller length in the accounts which he sent at the time to his family and friends. With Irving he was better pleased than he expected. Uneasiness Carlyle had felt about him—never, indeed, that the simplicity and truth of Irving's disposition could be impaired or tarnished, but that he might be misled and confused by the surroundings in which he was to find him. 'The orator,' he wrote, ' is mended since I saw him at Dunkeld. He begins to see that his honours are not supernatural, and his honest, practical warmth of heart is again becoming the leading feature of his character.' He was thrown at once into Irving's circle, and made acquaintance with various persons whom he had previously heard celebrated. Mrs. Strachey, Mrs.

Buller's sister, he admired the most. Her husband, too, he met and liked, and her niece, Miss Kirkpatrick. To Miss Welsh he wrote a few days after his arrival :—

I have seen some notable characters. Mrs. Montagu[1] (do not tremble) is a stately matron, with a quick intellect and a taste for exciting sentiments, which two qualities, by dint of much management in a longish life, she has elaborated into the materials of a showy, tasteful, clearsighted, rigid, and I fancy, cold manner of existence, intended rather for itself and being looked at than for being used to any useful purpose in the service of others. She loves and admires the Orator beyond all others : me she seems to like better than I like her. I have also seen and scraped acquaintance with Procter—Barry Cornwall. He is a slender, rough-faced, palish, gentle, languid-looking man, of three or four and thirty. There is a dreamy mildness in his eye ; he is kind and good in his manners, and I understand in his conduct. He is a poet by the ear and the fancy, but his heart and intellect are not strong. He is a small poet. I am also a nascent friend of Allan Cunningham's—my most dear, modest, kind, good-humoured Allan. He has his Annandale accent as faithfully as if he had never crossed the border. He seems not to know that he is anything beyond a reading mason. Yet I will send you his books and tell you of him, and you will find him a genuis of no common make. I have also seen Thomas Campbell. Him I like worst of all. He is heartless as a little Edinburgh advocate. There is a smirk on his face which would befit a shopman or an auctioneer. His very eye has the cold vivacity of a conceited worldling,

---

[1] Mrs. Basil Montagu, of whom there is a full account in the *Reminiscences*, called by Irving ' the noble lady,' and already known through Irving's letters to Miss Welsh.

His talk is small, contemptuous, and shallow. The blue frock and trousers, the eye-glass, the wig, the very fashion of his bow, proclaim the literary dandy. His wife has black eyes, a fair skin, a symmetrical but vulgar face ; and she speaks with that accursed Celtic accent—a twang which I never yet heard associated with any manly or profitable thought or sentiment, which to me is but the symbol of Highland vanity and filth and famine. 'Good heavens !' cried I, on coming out, 'does literature lead to this ? Shall I, too, by my utmost efforts realise nothing but a stupid Gaelic wife, with the pitiful gift of making verses, and affections cold as those of a tinker's cuddie, with nothing to love but my own paltry self and what belongs to it ? My proudest feelings rivalled, sur-passed by Lord Petersham and the whole population of Bond Street ? God forbid ! Let me be poor and wretched if it must be so, but never, never let the holy feeling of affection leave me. Break my heart a hundred times, but never let it be its own grave !' The aspect of that man jarred the music of my mind for a whole day. He promised to invite me to his first 'literary *déjeuner.*' Curiosity attracts, disgust repels. I know not which will be stronger when the day arrives. Perhaps I am hasty about Campbell. Perhaps I am too severe. He was my earliest favourite. I hoped to have found him different. Of Coleridge and all the other originals I will not say a word at present. You are sated and more.

Coleridge naturally was an object of more than curiosity. He was then at the height of his fame— poet, metaphysician, theologian, accomplished, or sup-posed to be accomplished, in the arts in which Carlyle was most anxious to excel. Carlyle himself had formed a high if not the highest opinion of the merits of

Coleridge, who was now sitting up at Highgate receiving the homage of the intellectual world, and pouring out floods of eloquence on all who came to worship in a befitting state of mind. The befitting state was not universal even in those who sincerely loved the great man. Leigh Hunt and Lamb had sate one night in the Highgate drawing-room for long hours listening to the oracle discoursing upon the Logos. Hunt, as they stood leaning over a stile in the moonlight, on their way home, said, 'How strange that a man of such indisputable genius should talk such nonsense!' 'Why, you see,' said Lamb, stammering, 'C-c-coleridge has so much f-f-fun in him.' The finished portrait of Coleridge is found in Carlyle's 'Life of Sterling.' The original sketch is a letter of the 24th of June to his brother John.

I have seen many curiosities; not the least of them I reckon Coleridge, the Kantian metaphysician and quondam Lake poet. I will tell you all about our interview when we meet. Figure a fat, flabby, incurvated personage, at once short, rotund, and relaxed, with a watery mouth, a snuffy nose, a pair of strange brown, timid, yet earnest-looking eyes, a high tapering brow, and a great bush of grey hair; and you have some faint idea of Coleridge. He is a kind good soul, full of religion and affection and poetry and animal magnetism. His cardinal sin is that he wants *will*. He has no resolution. He shrinks from pain or labour in any of its shapes. His very attitude bespeaks this. He never straightens his knee-joints. He stoops with his fat, ill-shapen shoulders, and in walking he does not tread, but shovel and slide. My father would call it 'skluiffing.' He is also always busied to keep, by strong and frequent inhalations, the water of his mouth from overflowing, and his eyes have a look of anxious impotence. He *would* do with all his heart, but he knows he dares not. The conversation of the man is much as I anticipated—a forest of thoughts, some true, many false, more part dubious, all of them ingenious in some degree, often in a high degree. But there is no method in his talk : he wanders like a man sailing among many currents, whithersoever his lazy mind directs him ; and, what is more unpleasant, he preaches, or rather soliloquises. He cannot speak, he can only *tal-k* (so he names it). Hence I found him unprofitable, even tedious ; but we parted very good friends, I promising to go back and see him some evening—a promise which I fully intend to keep. I sent him a copy of 'Meister,' about which we had some friendly talk. I reckon him a man of great and useless genius : a strange, not at all a great man.

While Carlyle was studying the leaders of literature in London with such indifferent satisfaction, the family at Mainhill were busy over his own first book. Never had Goethe's novel found its way into a stranger circle than this rugged, unlettered Calvinist household. But they had all strong natural understandings. Young and old alike read it, and in their way appreciated it, the mother most of all.

John Carlyle to Thomas Carlyle.

Mainhill : June 24.

You did well to send our father the neckerchief and tobacco with the spluichan, for he was highly pleased at the sight of them. The shawl, our mother says, suits very well, though she has no particular need of one at present. She bids me tell you she can never repay you for the kind-

ness you have all along shown her, and then she has advices
about religion to give you, the best of gifts in her estimation
that she has to offer. She is sitting here as if under some
charm, reading 'Meister,' and has nearly got through the
second volume. Though we are often repeating honest Hall
Foster's denouncement against readers of 'novels,' she still
continues to persevere. She does not relish the character of
the women, and especially of Philina : ' They are so wanton.'
She cannot well tell what it is that interests her. I defer
till the next time I write to give a full account of the
impression it has made upon us all, for we have not got it
fairly studied yet. We are unanimous in thinking it should
succeed.

The Bullers were still uncertain about their future
movements. One day they were to take a house at
Boulogne, the next to settle in Cornwall, the next to
remain in London, and send Carlyle with the boys into
the country. As a temporary measure, ten days after
his arrival he and Charles found themselves located in
lodgings at Kew Green, which Carlyle soon grew
weary of and Charles Buller hated ; while Carlyle,
though he appreciated, and at times even admired,
Mrs. Buller's fine qualities, was not of a temper to
submit to a woman's caprices.

To John Carlyle.

Kew Green : June 24, 1824.

The Bullers are essentially a cold race of people. They
live in the midst of fashion and external show. They love no
living creature. Our connection, therefore, has to sit a little
loosely. I attach no portion of my hopes or thoughts of affec-

tion towards them : they none to me. Nevertheless, I have
engaged to go with them whithersoever they list for the next
three months. After that, with regard to the France project,
I shall pause before deciding. Indeed, so fitful and weather-
cock-like in their proceedings are they, that it is very
possible the whole scheme of Boulogne-sur-Mer may be
abandoned long before the time for trying it comes round.
Meanwhile, Mrs. B. has settled us here *for a fortnight only*
in lodgings, and we have begun our studies. It is a pleasant
village. We are within a bowshot of a Royal Palace, close
by the south bank of the Thames, about six miles to the
westward of London. A village here is not what it is with
you. Here it is a quantity of houses scattered over a whole
parish, each cluster connected with the rest by lanes of trees,
with meadows and beautiful greens interspersed, sometimes
ponds and lakes and hedges of roses, and commons with
sheep and cuddies grazing on them. Many of the houses
belong to rich people, and the whole has a very smart and
pleasing air. Such is the village of Kew, especially the
Green, the part of it which lies on the south side of the
river, connected by the bridge with Kew proper. We form
part of the periphery of an irregular square, measuring, perhaps, two furlongs in diagonal, intersected with one large
and many foot roads, and into portions by thick, low, painted
wooden paling, with breaks in it to admit the freest ingress
and egress. The parish church, with its cluster of grave-
stones, stands a little to the right of our windows. Beyond
it the north-west corner of the square is occupied by the
Palace and the barracks of soldiers. This, with the many
barges and lighters of the river, and the shady woods and
green places all around, makes the place very pretty. What
is better, our lodging seems to be very respectable. I have
a good, clean, quiet bed, and the landlady, Mrs. Page, and
her pretty granddaughter (sweet Anne Page), almost become

as dead women every time we speak to them, so reverential are they and so prompt to help.

Mrs. Page was unlike the dames who had driven Carlyle so distracted in Edinburgh, and the contrast between the respectful manners of English people and the hard familiarity of his countrywomen struck him agreeably. Time and progress have done their work whether for good or evil, and it would at present be difficult to find reverential landladies either at Kew Green or anywhere in the British dominions; Kew Green has become vulgarised, and the grace has gone from it; the main points of the locality can be recognised from Carlyle's picture, but cockneys and cockney taste are now in possession. The suburban sojourn came to an early end, and with it Carlyle's relations with Mr. Buller and his family. He describes the close of the connection in words which did not express his deliberate feeling. He knew that he owed much to Mrs. Buller's kindness; and her own and Mr. Buller's regard for him survived in the form of strong friendship to the end of their lives. But he was irritated at the abruptness with which he conceived that he had been treated. He was proud and thin-skinned. His next letter is dated from Irving's house at Pentonville, which was again immediately opened to him, and contains the history of the Buller break up, and of a new acquaintance which was about to take him to Birmingham.

4 Myddelton Terrace, Pentonville : July 6, 1824.

My dear Mother,—I suppose you are not expecting to

hear from me so soon again, and still less to hear the news I
have got to tell you. The last letter was dated from Kew'
Green ; there will be no more of mine dated thence. Last
time I was complaining of the irresolute and foolish fluctua-
tions of the Bullers : I shall never more have reason to complain of them and their proceedings. I am now free of them
for ever and a day. I mentioned the correspondence which
had taken place between ' the fair Titania ' (as the Calcutta
newspapers called her) and myself on the subject of her
hopeful son, and how it was arranged that we should live
together till October, and then *see* about proceeding to
Boulogne, in France, or else abandoning our present engagement altogether. The shifting and trotting about which
she managed with so total a disregard to my feelings, joined
to the cold and selfish style of the lady's general proceedings,
had a good deal disaffected me ; and when, in addition to all
this, I reflected that nothing permanent could result from
my engagement with them, and considered the horrid weariness of being in seclusion from all sense and seriousness, in
the midst of sickness on my own part, mingled with frivolous
and heartless dissipation on theirs, I had well nigh silently
determined *not* to go to Boulogne, or even to stay with the
people though they remained in England. My determination was called for sooner than I had anticipated. After a
week spent at Kew in the most entire tedium, by which my
health had begun to deteriorate rapidly, but which I determined to undergo without repining till October, Mrs. Buller
writes me a letter signifying that they must know directly
whether I would go with them to France or not ; that if I
could not, the boy might be sent to prepare for Cambridge ;
and that if I could, we must instantly decamp for Royston,
a place in Hertfordshire about fifty miles off. I replied that
the expected time for deciding was not yet arrived, but that
if they required an immediate decision, of course there

was nothing for it but to count on my declining the offer. Next day we met in town by appointment; there seemed to be the best understanding in the world betwixt us; it was agreed that I should quit them—an arrangement not a little grievous to old Buller and his son, but no wise grievous to his wife, one of whose whims was Cambridge University, in which whim, so long as she persists, she will be ready to stake her whole soul on the fulfilment of it. Buller offered me twenty pounds for my trouble. With an excess of generosity which I am not quite reconciled to since I thought of it maturely, I pronounced it to be too much, and accepted of *ten*. The old gentleman and I shook hands with dry eyes. Mrs. Buller gave me one of those 'Good mornings' with which fashionable people think it right to part with friends and foes alike. Charlie was in a passion of sadness and anger, to be forgotten utterly in three hours, and I went my way and they saw me no more. Such is my conclusion with the Bullers. I feel glad that I have done with them; their family was ruining my mind and body. I was selling the very quintessence of my spirit for 200*l*. a year. Twelve months spent at Boulogne in the midst of drivelling and discomfort would have added little to my stock of cash, and fearfully diminished my remnant of spirits, health, and affection. The world must be fronted some time, soon as good as *syne!* Adieu, therefore, to ancient dames of quality, that flaunting, painting, patching, nervous, vapourish, jigging, skimming, scolding race of mortals.[1] Their clothes are silk, their manners courtly, their hearts are *kipper*. I have left the Bullers twelve months sooner than they would have parted with me had I liked. I am glad that we have parted in friendship; very glad that we are parted at

[1] Poor Mrs. Buller! a year back 'one of the most fascinating women he had ever met.' She was about forty, and probably had never flaunted, painted, or patched in her life.

all. She invited me to a rout (a grand, fashionable affair) next night. I did not go a foot length. I want to have no further trade with her or hers at least except in the way of cold civility; for as to what affection means I do not believe there is one of them that even guesses what it means. Her sister, indeed (Mrs. Strachey),[1] likes me; but she is as opposite as day from night.

Thus you see, my dear mother, I am as it were once more upon the waters. I got my trunks hither last night, after having kept them just one week at Kew, and paid fourteen shillings for the trip to and fro. So much for having a spirited commander like Titania. I am settled with Irving, who presses me to stay with him all winter. That I certainly will not do, though I honour the kindness that prompts even an *invitation* of this sort. Irving and I are grown very intimate again, and have had great talking matches about many things. He speaks in glorious language of the wonderful things I am to accomplish here, but my own views are much more moderate.

Meanwhile let me assure you that I have not been so happy for a long while. I am at no loss for plans of proceeding, nor is the future overcast before me with any heavy clouds that I should feel or fear. I am once more free; and I must be a weak genius indeed if I cannot find an honest living in the exercise of my faculties, independently of favour from anyone. My movements for a while must be rather desultory. My first is to be northward. Among the worthy persons whom I have met with here is a Mr. Badams, a friend of Irving's, a graduate in medicine, though his business is in chemical manufactures in Birmingham, where

---

[1] Of this lady he says in another letter: 'My chief favourite is Mrs. Strachey, a sister of Mrs. Buller; but she is serious and earnest and religious and affectionate, while the other is light, giddy, vain and heartless. She and I will be sworn friends by and by.'

I understand he is rapidly realising a fortune. This man, one of the most sensible, clear-headed persons I have ever met with, seems also one of the kindest. After going about for a day or two talking about pictures and stomach disorders, in the cure of which he is famous, and from which he once suffered four years of torment in person, what does the man do but propose that I should go up to Birmingham and live for a month with him, that he might find out the make of me and prescribe for my unfortunate inner man. I have consented to go with him. I understand he keeps horses, &c., and is really the frank hospitable fellow he seems. Of his skill in medicine I augur favourably from his general talent, and from the utter contempt in which he holds all sorts of drugs as applied to persons in my situation. Regimen and exercise are his specifics, assisted by as little gentlest medicine as possible ; on the whole I think I never had such a chance for the recovery of health. I intend to set off in about a week. There is a fine coach that starts from our very door, and carries one up between seven in the morning and seven at night for one guinea. I am going to take books and read and ride and stroll about Birmingham, and employ or amuse myself as seemeth best. Sometimes I think of beginning another translation, sometimes of setting about some original work. 'Meister,' I understand, is doing very well. Jack tells me you are reading 'Meister.' This surprises me. If I did not recollect your love for me, I should not be able to account for it.

CHAPTER XIV.

A.D. 1824.   ÆT. 29.

CARLYLE was now once more his own master, adrift
from all engagements which made his time the property
of others, and without means or prospect of support
save what his pen could earn for him. Miss Welsh had
expected with too sanguine ignorance that when his
first writings had introduced him to the world, the
world would rush forward to his assistance; that he
would be seized upon for some public employment, or
at worst would be encouraged by a sinecure. The
world is in no such haste to recognise a man of original
genius. Unless he runs with the stream, or with some
one of the popular currents, every man's hand is at
first against him. Rivals challenge his pretensions;
his talents are denied; his aims are ridiculed; he is
tried in the furnace of criticism, and it is well that it
should be so. A man does not know himself what is in
him till he has been tested; far less can others know;
and the metal which glitters most on the outside most
often turns out to be but pinchbeck. A longer and
more bitter apprenticeship lay before Carlyle than even
he, little sanguine as he was, might at this time have
anticipated. His papers on Schiller had been well
received and were to be collected into a volume; a
contemptuous review of 'Meister' by De Quincey

appeared in the 'London Magazine,' but the early sale
was rapid. He had been well paid for the first specimens of jewels which he had brought out of the
German mines. An endless vein remained unwrought,
and the field was for the present his own. Thus he
went down to Birmingham to his friend with a light
heart, anxious chiefly about his health, and convinced
that if he could mend his digestion, all else would be
easy for him. Birmingham with its fiery furnaces and
fiery politics was a new scene to him, and was like the
opening of a fresh volume of human life. He has
given so full a history of his experiences when he was
Mr. Badams' guest that there is no occasion to dwell
upon it. The visit lasted two months instead of one.
His first impression of the place, as he described it in
a letter to his brother, is worth preserving as a speci-
men of his powers of minute word-painting, and as a
description of what Birmingham was sixty years ago.

To John Carlyle.

Birmingham : August 10, 1824.

Birmingham I have now tried for a reasonable time, and
I cannot complain of being tired of it. As a town it is pitiful enough—a mean congeries of bricks, including scarcely
one or two large capitalists, some hundreds of minor ones,
and, perhaps, a hundred and twenty thousand sooty artisans
in metals and chemical produce. The streets are ill-built,
ill-paved, always flimsy in their aspect—often poor, sometimes miserable. Not above one or two of them are paved
with flagstones at the sides ; and to walk upon the little egg-
shaped, slippery flints that supply their places is something
like a penance. Yet withal it is interesting from some of

the commons or lanes that spot or intersect the green, woody, undulating environs to view this city of Tubal Cain. Torrents of thick smoke, with ever and anon a burst of dingy flame, are issuing from a thousand funnels. 'A thousand hammers fall by turns on the red son of the furnace.' You hear the clank of innumerable steam-engines, the rumbling of cars and vans, and the hum of men interrupted by the sharper rattle of some canal-boat loading or disloading ; or, perhaps, some fierce explosion when the cannon founders are proving their new-made ware. I have seen their rolling-mills, their polishing of teapots, and buttons, and gun-barrels, and fire-shovels, and swords, and all manner of toys and tackle. I have looked into their iron works where 150,000 men are smelting the metal in a district a few miles to the north ; their coal-mines, fit image of Avernus ; their tubs and vats, as large as country churches, full of copperas and aqua fortis and oil of vitriol ; and the whole is not without its attractions, as well as repulsions, of which, when we meet, I will preach to you at large.

But all the while Carlyle's heart was in Scotland, at Haddington—and less at Haddington than at Mainhill. The strongest personal passion which he experienced through all his life was his affection for his mother. She was proud and wilful, as he. He had sent her, or offered her, more presents, and she had been angry with him. She had not been well, and she was impatient of doctors' regulations.

To Mrs. Carlyle, Mainhill.

Birmingham : August 29, 1824.
I must suggest some improvements in your diet and mode of life which might be of service to *you*, who I know too

well have much to suffer on your own part, though your affection renders you so exclusively anxious about me. You will say you cannot be *fashed*. Oh, my dear mother, if you did but think of what value your health and comfort are to us all, you would never talk so. Are we not all bound to you, by sacred and indissoluble ties? Am I not so bound more than any other? Who was it that nursed me and watched me in frowardness and sickness from the earliest dawn of my existence to this hour?—My mother. Who is it that has struggled for me in pain and sorrow with undespairing diligence, that has for me been up early and down late, caring for me, labouring for me, unweariedly assisting me? —My mother. Who is the *one* that never shrunk from me in my desolation, that never tired of my despondencies, or shut up by a look or tone of impatience the expression of my real or imaginary griefs? Who is it that loves me and will love me for ever with an affection which no chance, no misery, no crime of mine can do away?—It is you, my mother. As the greatest favour that I can beg of you, let me, now that I have in some degree the power, be of some assistance in promoting your comfort. It were one of the achievements which I could look back upon with most satisfaction from all the stages of my earthly pilgrimage, if I could make you happier. Are we not all of us animated by a similar love to you? Why then will you spare any trouble, any cost, in what is valuable beyond aught earthly to every one of us?

Eight weeks were passed with Badams, without, however, the advantage to Carlyle's health which he had looked for. There had been daily rides into the country, visits to all manner of interesting places— Hadley, Warwick, and Kenilworth. The society had

been interesting, and Badams himself all that was kind
and considerate. But the contempt of 'drugs' which
he had professed in London had been rather theoretic
than practical; and the doses which had been adminis-
tered perhaps of themselves accounted for the failure of
other remedies. At the beginning of September an
invitation came to Carlyle to join the Stracheys at
Dover. The Irvings were to be of the party. Irving
needed rest from his preaching. Mrs. Irving had been
confined and had been recommended sea air for herself
and her baby. The Stracheys and Miss Kirkpatrick
had taken a house at Dover; the Irvings had lodgings
of their own, but were to live with their friends, and
Carlyle was to be included in the party. Mrs. Strachey
was a very interesting person to him, still beautiful,
younger than Mrs. Buller, and a remarkable contrast to
her. Mrs. Buller was a sort of heathen; Mrs. Strachey
was earnestly religious. 'She is as unlike Mrs. Buller,'
Carlyle told his mother, 'as pure gold is to gilt copper;
she is an earnest, determined, warm-hearted, religious
matron, while the other is but a fluttering patroness of
routs and operas.' An invitation to stay with her had
many attractions for him. He wished to go, but was
undecided. The last letter from Birmingham was on
September 18.

To John Carlyle.

Badams and I go on very lovingly together. He calls
me 'philosopher' by way of eminence; and I discuss and
overhaul, and dissect all manners of subjects with him. A
closer acquaintance diminishes the sublimity, but scarcely

the pleasing quality of his character. A certain tendency to paint *en beau*, a sort of gasconading turn in describing his own achievements and purposes, is all the fault I can discover in him ; his kindheartedness, his constant activity, and good humour are more and more apparent. In spite of all his *long-bow* propensities (his running away with the harrows, as our father would call it) he is a man of no ordinary powers, nor has he any particle of dishonesty in his nature, however he may talk. In fact, if I admire the man less than I once expected, I like him more. Strange that so many men should say *the thing that is not* without perceptible temptation ! Hundreds do it out of momentary vanity—Frank Dickson and many others. It is the poorest of all possible resources in this world of makeshifts ; thou and I will never try it.

With regard to health, it often seems to me that I am better than I have been for several years, though scarcely a week passes without a relapse for a while into directly the opposite opinion. The truth is, it stands thus : I have been bephysicked and bedrugged. I have swallowed, say about two stoupfuls of castor oil since I came hither : unless I dose myself with that oil of sorrow every fourth day, I cannot get along at all. . . . My resources are more numerous than they have been, and I am free to use them. Am I a man and can do nothing to ameliorate my destiny ? Hang it, I will set up house in the country and take to gardening and translating, before I let it beat me. In general I am not unhappy—of late I have begun to grudge being so long idle. 'Schiller' is almost at a stand. I have been thinking of it and preparing improvements, but the Taylor creature is slow as a snail. . . . I wrote to Irving stating in distant terms a proposal to board with him through winter. He has not answered me, but I expect daily that he will. If he consent, I shall go with him and Mrs. Strachey to Dover.

If not, I think hardly. My better plan will be to go to London and take lodgings till this pitiful book is off my hands, then return to the north or stay in London as I reckon best.

The journey back on the coach through the midland counties, which in late September are usually so beautiful, was spoilt by bad weather. On his way, however, Carlyle saw Stratford, and was long enough in the town to form a clear picture of it. His letters are the journal of his experiences.

To John Carlyle.

London: September 27, 1824.

Taking leave of Badams, who strictly charged me to come back for another month till he had completed his doctorial and castor oil system with me, I left the city of Tubal Cain on Thursday morning. My passage was of a mixed character. Some of Badams' drugs had not prospered with me, and I fell below par in point of health. The morning also was damp and the day proved rainy. To complete the matter it cleared up just when I had shifted my place to the interior of the vehicle, and exchanged the sight of High Wycombe and the lawns of Buckinghamshire for the inane prattle of a little black-eyed pretty blue-stocking Genevese, my sole travelling companion ; so that when they set me down in Oxford Street, falsely said by the rascal guard to be the nearest point to Pentonville, from which it was three miles distant—Lad Lane being only one—I fell somewhat out of humour, a dissonance of spirit which increased to loud jarring as I followed my stout and fleet porter, who strode lustily along under cloud of night, through labyrinthine streets and alleys, with my portmanteau dan-

16—2

gling at his back, and a travelling bag to balance it in front. Stamp, stamp, amidst the rattling of wains and coaches, and the unearthly cries of fruiterers and oystermen and piemen and all the mighty din of London, till I verily thought he would never reach a point of the city which my eyes had seen before.

Nevertheless, I had not been without my enjoyments on the road. I had got another glance of the heart of 'merry England,' with its waving knolls and green woody fields and snug hamlets and antique boroughs and jolly ale-drinking, beef-eating people. . . . It was not without some pleasurable imaginations that I saw Stratford-upon-Avon, the very hills and woods which the boy Shakespeare had looked upon, the very church where his dust reposes, nay, the very house where he was born ; the threshold over which his staggering footsteps carried him in infancy ; the very stones where the urchin played marbles and flogged tops. . . . It is a small grim-looking house of bricks, bound, as was of old the fashion, with beams of oak intersecting the bricks which are built into it and fill up its interstices as the glass does in a window. The old tile roof is cast by age, and twisted into all varieties of curvature. Half the house has been modernised and made a butcher's shop. The street where it stands is a simple-looking, short, everyday village street, with houses mostly new, and consisting, like the Shakespeare house, of two low stories, or rather a story and a half. Stratford itself is a humble, pleasant-looking place, the residence as formerly of woolcombers and other quiet artisans, except where they have brought an ugly black canal into it, and polluted this classical borough by the presence of lighters or trackboats with famished horses, sooty drivers, and heaps of coke and coal. It seems considerably larger and less showy than Annan. Shakespeare, Breakspeare, and for aught I know sundry other spears, are still common names in Warwickshire,

I was struck on my arrival at Birmingham by a sign not far from Badams', indicating the abode of William Shakespeare, boot and shoe maker, which boots and shoes the modern Shakespeare also professed his ability to mend 'cheap and neatly.' Homer, I afterwards discovered, had settled in Birmingham as a button maker.

But I must not wander thus, or I shall never have done. Of Oxford, with its domes and spires and minarets, its rows of shady trees, and still monastic edifices in their antique richness and intricate seclusion, I shall say nothing till I see you. I must rather hasten to observe that I found the orator at Pentonville sitting sparrowlike, companionless, in— not on—the housetop alone. His wife had left him, and had taken all the crockery and bedding and other household gear along with her. He extended to me the right hand of fellowship notwithstanding, and even succeeded in procuring me some genial tea with an egg, only half rotten, which, for a London egg, is saying much. By-and-by, one Hamilton, a worthy and accomplished merchant from Sanquhar, came in and took me with him to his lodgings and treated me comfortably ; and there in a splendid bed, I contrived, in spite of agitation from within, and noise and bugs from without, to get six hours of deep slumber. Next morning I was fitter to do business.

On leaving Birmingham I had felt uncertain whether I should go to Dover with the Orator or not ; and I had partly determined to be regulated in my yea and no by his acceptance or rejection of my proposal to board with him while in London. On coming to discuss the subject orally I soon discovered that his reverence was embarrassed by a conflicting proposal (to board at a very high rate some medical youth from Glasgow) which was not yet decided on, and was consequently in the way of any definite arrangement with me. The good priest—for with all his vanities and affectations he is really a good man, an excellent man, as men go—puckered up his face and eyebrows in much distress, and was just commencing with various articulate and inarticulate preparations, when I, discovering rapidly how the matter stood, begged him to consider my proposal unmade, and never to say, or even think, one other word upon the subject. The puckers disappeared at this announcement, but were succeeded by a continuous cloud of gloom and regret as he set about advising me to go with him to Dover, and to put off the consideration of lodging and all such matters till my return. After much canvassing I assented, upon the proviso of my being allowed to bear my own share of the expense, and to be his fellow-lodger and not his guest. With this salvo to my pride, which I already almost begin to despise as a piece of cold selfishness, we struck the bargain that he should set out on Monday, and I should follow whenever my business was concluded.

The ' business ' I could have in London may well surprise you ; it was (alas ! it is) the most pitiful that ever man had : nothing but the collecting of a few books for the completing of my poor ' Schiller.' You cannot think what trotting to and fro I have had to get a book or two of the most simple character. Messrs. Taylor and Henry pay me somewhere on the verge of 90*l.* down upon the nail for this book, the day when it is published. In about ten weeks from this date I expect to be free of London, to have ascertained how it will suit me, what hopes, what advantages it offers, and to decide for continuance or departure as shall seem to me best. If my health improve I shall be for remaining, especially if I can fasten upon any profitable employment ; if not, scarcely. About the ultimatum I am by no means low-spirited, not often even dumpish. I feel pretty confident that I *can* recover my health in some considerable degree, perhaps wholly. If not here—*elsewhere.* While this is in progress I can at the worst translate for the London or Edinburgh market ; and if I were well, I feel that some considerable desire to write might rise within me. I might like Archy Halliday, 'fin' a kind of inclination to bark, and certainly there is no want of game. A miserable scrub of an author, sharking and writing 'articles' about town like Hazlitt, De Quincey, and that class of living creatures, is a thing which, as our mother says, 'I canna be.' Nor shall I need it. I have fifty better schemes.

As to not boarding with Irving, I hardly regret it now that it is past. His house would scarcely have been a favourable place for studying any science but the state of religion in general, and that of the Caledonian chapel in particular, as managed by various elders, delegates, and other nondescript personages. A very affected and not beautiful sister of ——'s is also to stay with them through the winter. Her I might have found it a task to love. 'Pray, Mr. Carlyle,' said she, in a mincing, namby-pamby tone, the night she arrived, when I was sitting with my powers of patience screwed to the sticking place, being in truth very miserable and very much indisposed to make complaints ; 'Pray, Mr. Carlyle, are you *really* sick now, or is it only fanciful ?' 'Fancy, ma'am, fancy, nothing more,' said I, half-turning round and immediately proceeding with some other topic, addressed to some other member of the company. Besides, Irving has a squeaking brat of a son, 'who indeed brings us many blessings,' but rather interrupts our rest at night. Bad luck to his blessings compared with natural rest ! In short, I shall be more completely master in my own lodgings.

Carlyle himself was not an inmate whom any mistress not directly connected with him would readily welcome into her household ; so it was well perhaps for all parties that the proposed arrangement was abandoned. The Dover visit, however, was accomplished, and the unexpected trip to Paris which grew out of it. For this, too, the reader is mainly referred to the ' Reminiscences,' which need no correction from contemporary letters ; and to which those letters, though written when the scenes were fresh, can still add little, save a further evidence of the extreme accuracy of his memory. But there is a humorous description of the gigantic Irving and his new-born baby, a pleasant sketch of others of the party, and an interesting account of the state of English farming and the English labourer, as Carlyle saw both before the days of economic progress. These, and some vivid pictures of the drive through France, justify a few extracts.

To James Carlyle, Mainhill.

Dover : October 4.

My dear Father,—I arrived in this corner of the seagirt land in the dusk of a bright and sharp autumnal day. There has been no fixed arrangement in our plans as yet. Mrs. Irving with her infant had come hither with a Miss Kirkpatrick, a cousin of Mrs. Strachey, in whose hired house we are all living till the rest arrive, when the Irvings and I shall evacuate the place and seek lodgings of our own. I expect to be very snug and comfortable while here. The sea-bathing seems to agree with me as well as ever, and the people are all anxious to treat me as a kind of established invalid, whose concerns are to be attended to as a prime object.

The young Miss Kirkpatrick, with whom I was already acquainted, is a very pleasant and meritorious person—one of the kindest and most modest I have ever seen. Though handsome and young and sole mistress of 50,000*l.*, she is meek and unassuming as a little child. She laughs in secret at the awkward extravagances of the Orator; yet she loves him as a good man, and busies herself with nothing so much as discharging the duties of hospitality to us all. . . . Of Irving, I have much kindness towards me to record. I like the man, as I did of old, without respecting him much less or more. He has a considerable turn for displays, which in reality are sheer vanity, though he sincerely thinks them the perfection of Christian elevation. But in these things he indulges very sparingly before me, and any little glimpses of them that do occur I find it easy without the slightest ill-nature arising between us to repress. We talk of religion and literature and men and things, and stroll about and smoke cigars, a choice stock of which he has been presented with by some friend. I reckon him much improved since winter. The fashionable people have totally left him, yielding like feathers and flying chaff to some new 'centre of attraction.' The newspapers also are silent, and he begins to see that there was really nothing supernatural in the former hurly-burly, but that he must content himself with patient well-doing, and liberal, though not immoderate, success; not taking the world by one fierce onslaught, but by patient and continual sapping and mining, as others do.

I for one am sincerely glad that matters have taken this change. I consider him a man of splendid gifts and good intentions, and likely in his present manner of proceeding to be of much benefit to the people among whom he labours. His Isabella also is a good, honest-hearted person and an excellent wife. She is very kind to me, and though without any notable gifts of mind or manners or appearance, contrives to be in general extremely agreeable. Irving and she are sometimes ridiculous enough at present in the matter of their son, a quiet *wersh gorb* of a thing, as all children of six weeks are, but looked upon by them as if it were a cherub from on high. The concerns of ' him ' (as they emphatically call it) occupy a large share of public attention. Kitty Kirkpatrick smiles covertly, and I laugh aloud at the earnest devotedness of the good Orator to this weighty affair. ' Isabella,' said he the other night, ' I would wash him, I think, with *warm* water to-night,' a counsel received with approving assent by the mother, but somewhat objected to by others. I declared the washing and dressing of *him* to be the wife's concern alone ; and that, were I in her place, I would wash him with oil of vitriol if I pleased, and take no one's counsel in it.

When Mrs. Strachey comes I expect some accession of enjoyment. She has taken a great liking to me, and is any way a singularly worthy woman. I had a very kind note from her this day.

Kent is a delightful region, fertile and well cultivated, watered with clear streams, sufficiently and not excessively besprinkled with trees, and beautifully broken with inequalities of surface. The whole country rests on chalk. They burn this mineral in kilns and use it as lime. In its native state it lies in immense masses, divided into strata or courses by lumps of flint distributed in parallel seams. The husbandry in Kent is beyond that in many counties in England, but a Scottish farmer would smile at many parts of it. They plough with five horses and two men (one ca-ing), and the plough has wheels. Many a time have I thought of Alick with his Lothian tackle and two horses setting these inefficient loiterers to the right about. Yet here they are much better than in Warwickshire, where farming may be said to be an unknown art, where the fields are sometimes of half an acre, and of all possible shapes but square, and a threshing mill is a thing nearly unheard of. Here a fifth part of the surface is not covered with gigantic and ill-kept fences ; but they grow their wheat and their beans and their hops on more rational principles. In all cases, however, the people seem to realise a goodly share of solid comfort. The English hind has his pork (often raw) or his beef, with ale and wheaten bread three times a day, and wears a ruddy and substantial look, see him where you will. I have looked into the clean, brick-built, tile-flagged little cottages, and seen the people dining, with their jug of ale, their bacon, and other ware, and a huge loaf, like a stithy clog, towering over it all. It is pleasant to see everyone so well provided for. There is nothing like the appearance of want to be met with anywhere.

To Miss Welsh, little dreaming of the relations between herself and Irving, Carlyle was still more dramatic in his sketches of the Orator. Miss Welsh, as she told him afterwards, had purposely misled him on the subject.

October 5.—The Orator is busy writing and bathing, persuading himself that he is scaling the very pinnacles of Christian sentiment, which in truth, with him, are little more than the very pinnacles of human vanity rising through an atmosphere of great native warmth and generosity. I find him much as he was before, and I suppose always will be, overspread with secret affectations, secret to himself, but kind and friendly and speculative and discursive as ever. It would do your heart good to look at him in the character of dry nurse to his first-born, Edward. Oh that you saw the Giant with his broad-brimmed hat, his sallow visage, and his sable, matted fleece of hair, carrying the little pepper-box of a creature folded in his monstrous palms along the beach, tick

ticking to it, and dandling it, and every time it stirs an eyelid
grinning horribly a ghastly smile, heedless of the crowds of
petrified spectators that turn round in long trains, gazing
in silent terror at the fatherly leviathan; you would laugh for
twelve months after, every time you thought of it. And yet
it is very wrong to laugh if one could help it. Nature is very
lovely: pity she should ever be absurd. On the whole I am
pleased with Irving, and hope to love him and admire him
and laugh at him as long as I live. There is a fund of
sincerity in his life and character which in these heartless,
aimless days is doubly precious. The cant of religion, conscious or unconscious, is a pitiable thing, but not the most
pitiable. It often rests upon a groundwork of genuine,
earnest feeling, and is, I think, in all except its very worst
phases, preferable to that poor and arid spirit of contemptuous *persiflage* which forms the staple of fashionable accom-
plishment so far as I can discern it, and spreads like a narcotic
drench over all the better faculties of the soul.

Mrs. Strachey came down after a few days. The
little party was always together—walking on the beach
or reading Fletcher's 'Purple Island.' Mrs. Strachey
herself was in full sympathy with Irving, if no one
else was. Then her husband came, who was especially wanting in sympathy. The difference of sentiment became perceptible. The French coast lay in-
vitingly opposite. The weather was beautiful. A trip
to Paris was proposed and instantly decided on. Mr.
Strachey, Miss Kirkpatrick, and Carlyle were to go.
Mrs. Strachey and the Irvings were to stay behind.
A travelling carriage was sent across the Channel, post-
horses were always ready on the Paris road, and
Carlyle, who had but left Scotland for the first time

four months before, and had been launched an entire
novice into the world, was now to be among the
scenes so long familiar to him as names. They went
by Montreuil, Abbeville, Nampont, with Sterne's
'Sentimental Journey' as a guide book, when Murray
was unknown. They saw the Cathedral at Beauvais,
for which Carlyle did not care at all; they saw French
soldiers, for which he cared a great deal. He himself
could speak a little French; Strachey, like most
Englishmen, almost none. Montmorency reminded
him of Rousseau. From Montmartre they looked
down on Paris : 'not a breath of smoke or dimness
anywhere, every roof and dome and spire and chimney-
top clearly visible, and the skylights sparkling like
diamonds.' 'I have never,' he says, 'since or before,
seen so fine a view of a town.' Carlyle, who could see
and remember so much of Stratford, where he stayed
only while the coach changed horses, coming on Paris
fresh, with a mind like wax to receive impressions, yet
tenacious as steel in preserving them, carried off
recollections from his twelve days' sojourn in the
French capital which never left him, and served him
well in after years when he came to write about the
Revolution. He saw the places of which he had read.
He saw Louis Dix-huit lying in state, Charles Dix,
Legendre (whose Geometry he had translated for
Brewster), the great Laplace, M. de Chezy the Persian
professor. He heard Cuvier lecture. He went to the
Théâtre Français, and saw and heard Talma in 'Œdipe.'
He listened to a sermon at Ste. Geneviève. A more
impressive sermon was a stern old grey-haired corpse
which he saw lying in the Morgue. He saw the French

people, and the ways and works of them, which interested him most of all. These images, with glimpses of English travellers, were all crowded into the few brief days of their stay; the richest in new ideas, new emotions, new pictures of human life, which Carlyle had yet experienced.

From the many letters which he wrote about it, I select one to his brother John.

To John Carlyle.

Dover: November 7.

My expedition to Paris was nearly as unexpected to myself as the news of it will be to you. Strachey, a little bustling, logic-chopping, good-hearted, frank fellow, came down to Dover three weeks ago, and finding himself, I suppose, rather dull in the region of the Cinque Ports, and tempted moreover, by the persuasions of his cousin Kitty, as well as by the daily sight of the French coast, he determined at last on a journey thither, and after infinite pleadings and solicitations I was prevailed upon to be of the party. They were to travel in their own carriage, Kitty and her maid inside, Strachey on the coach-box to see the country. The additional expense for me would be nothing; it would be *so* pleasant, and would do me *so* much good. In fine, after a world of perplexities and miscalculations and misadventures, I having first half consented, then wholly refused, then again consented, we at length all assembled by different routes on the sands of Boulogne in the afternoon of Thursday gone a fortnight, and set off with the utmost speed of three lean horses of the poste royale for Paris. After adventures and mistakes which will keep us laughing many a winter night when thou and I meet, we reached the capital on Saturday about four o'clock, and forthwith established ourselves in the

Hôtel de Wagram, and proceeded to the great purpose of our journey—the seeing of the many sights with which the metropolis of France abounds beyond any other spot on the surface of the earth. By degrees we got into proper train, and everything went on wonderfully well. Strachey and I went out singly or in company to purvey for dinners and breakfasts in the cafés and *restaurateur* establishments, &c.

Sated at length with wonders, we left Paris last Wednesday, and after a not unprosperous journey arrived here yesterday afternoon. Irving with his household had left Dover a few hours before.[1] On the whole I cannot say I regret this jaunt. I have seen many strange things which may people my imagination with interesting forms, and, perhaps, yield some materials for reflection and improvement. France, as it presented itself to me on a most cursory survey, seemed a place rather to be looked at than tarried in. Oh that I had space to paint to you the strange pilgarlic figures that I saw breakfasting over a few expiring embers on roasted apples, ploughing with three ponies, with ploughs like peat barrows, or folded together in long trough-shaped wicker carts, wearing night caps, and dresses of blue calico, with a black stump of a pipe stuck between their jaws, and a drop hanging at their long thin noses, and faces puckered together into the most *weepy mouse* aspect ; or the women riding on cuddies with wooden saddles ; or the postilions with their leather shovel hats and their boots like moderate churns ; often blind of an eye or broken-legged, and always the coolest liars in existence. But better than all was our own mode of treating them ; and Strachey's French when he scolded the waiters and hosts of the inns. ‘C'est bien imposante’ (said he at Beauvais), ‘c'est une—une—rascalité, vous dis-je ; vous avez chargé deux fois trop ; vous êtes,’ &c.

[1] In the *Reminiscences* he says that he found Irving still at Dover. This is the single error of fact which I have detected.

To all which they answered with the gravity of judges passing the sentence of death : ' Monsieur, c'est impossible ; on ne vous surfait nullement ; on ne,' &c. ' Où est les chevaux,' shrieked he at the end of every post. ' Vont venir, monsieur,' said they. Kitty and I were like to split with laughing. At length Strachey himself gave up the cause entirely and took to speaking French English without disguise. When a man asked him for 'quelque chose à boire ; je vous ai conduit très-bien,' Strachey answered, without looking at him, ' Nong ! vous avez drivé devilish slow,' which suited just as well.

Of Paris I shall say nothing till we meet. It is the Vanity Fair of the Universe, and cannot be described in many letters. With few exceptions the streets are narrow and crowded and unclean, the kennel in the middle, and a lamp hanging over it here and there on a rope from side to side. There are no footpaths, but an everlasting press of carriages and carts and dirty people hastening to and fro among them, amidst a thousand *gare-gares* and *sacrés* and other oaths and admonitions ; while by the side are men roasting chestnuts in their booths, fruitshops, wineshops, barbers ; silk merchants selling *à prix juste* (without cheating), *restaurateurs, cafés, traiteurs, magasins de bonbons,* billiard-tables, *estaminets* (gin-shops), *débits de tabac* (where you buy a cigar for a halfpenny and go out smoking it), and every species of *dépôt* and *entrepôt* and *magasin* for the comfort and refreshment of the physical part of the natural man, plying its vocation in the midst of noise and stink, both of which it augments by its produce and by its efforts to dispose of it. The Palais Royal is a spot unrivalled in the world, the chosen abode of vanity and vice, the true palace of the *tigre-singes* (tiger-apes), as Voltaire called his countrymen, a place which I rejoice to think is separated from me by the girdle of the ocean, and never likely to be copied in the British Isles. I dined in it often, and bought four little bone *étuis* (needle-cases) at a franc each for our four sisters at Mainhill. It is a sort of emblem of the French character, the perfection of the physical and fantastical part of our nature, with an absence of all that is solid and substantial in the moral, and often in the intellectual part of it. Looking-glasses and trinkets and fricassees and gaming tables seem to be the life of a Frenchman ; his home is a place where he sleeps and dresses ; he lives in the *salon du restaurateur* on the *boulevards*, or the garden of the Palais Royal. Every room you enter, destitute of carpet or fire, is expanded into boundlessness by mirrors ; and I should think about fifty thousand diceboxes are set a rattling every night, especially on Sundays, within the walls of Paris. There the people sit and chatter and fiddle away existence as if it were a raree show, careless how it go on so they have excitement, *des sensations agréables*. Their palaces and picture-galleries and triumphal arches are the wonder of the earth, but the stink of their streets is considerable, and you cannot walk on them without risking the fracture of your legs or neck.

But peace be to the French ! for here I have no room to express even my ideas about them, far less to do them any justice. Suffice it to observe that I contrived to see nearly all that could be seen within twelve days, and to carry off as much enjoyment as it was possible for sights to afford me at the expense of about five pounds sterling. I saw the Louvre gallery of pictures, the Tuileries palace, the Jardin des Plantes, the churches and cemeteries, and all that *could* be seen. I saw Talma the actor, and almost touched His Most Christian Majesty Charles X. What was most interesting, I heard Baron Cuvier deliver his introductory lecture on comparative anatomy. Cuvier himself pleased me much ; he seems about fifty, with a fair head of hair growing grey, a large broad, not very high head, a nose irregularly aquiline, receding mouth, peaked chin, blue eyes, which he casts upwards, puckering the eyebrows with a look of great sweetness and wisdom ; altogether the appearance of an accomplished, kind, and gentlemanly person. His lecture lasted an hour and a half. I made out nine-tenths of it, and thought it very good and wonderfully fluent and correct for an extempore one. Nay, what do you think ? I made bold to introduce myself to Legendre, and was by him taken to a sitting of the Institute, and presented to Dupin, the celebrated traveller in England. Here also I saw Laplace and Lacroix, and Poisson the mathematicians, and Vauquelin and Chaptal and Thénard the chemists, and heard Majendie read a paper. Dupin would have introduced me to Laplace and others, an honour which I declined, desiring only to impress myself with a picture of their several appearances.

Such was Carlyle's sudden visit to Paris—an incident of more importance to him than he knew at the moment. He complained before and he complained after of the hardness of fortune to him ; but fortune in the shape of friends was throwing in his way what very few young men better connected in life have the happiness of so early falling in with. The expedition created no small excitement at Mainhill. The old people had grown up under the traditions of the war. For a son of theirs to go abroad at all was almost miraculous. When they heard that he was gone to Paris, 'all the stoutness of their hearts' was required to bear it.

It matters little to the sufferers (wrote his brother Alexander) whether their evils are real or imaginary. Our anxiety was groundless, but this did little help till your letter to Jack arrived. We had inquired at the post-office every day for more than a fortnight before it came, and every new disappointment was, especially to our anxious mother, reason sufficient for darkening still deeper the catalogue of her fears about your welfare. I really believe that two or three days more of silence would have driven her distracted well nigh. She had laid aside singing for more than a fortnight; and even the rest of the women, if they attempted to sing or indulge in laughing, were reproached with unbecoming lightness of heart. But, thanks to heaven, we are all of us to rights again; and you have crossed and re-crossed the blue ocean—yea, visited the once-powerful kingdom of the great Napoleon, at whose frown Europe crouched in terror.

THE holiday was over. Carlyle returned to London with the Stracheys, and settled himself in lodgings in Southampton Street, near Irving. Here at any rate he intended to stay till Schiller was off his hands complete in the form of the book. That accomplished, the problem of his future life remained to be encountered. What was he to do? He was adrift, with no settled occupation. To what should he turn his hand? Where should he resolve to live? He had now seen London. He had seen Birmingham with its busy industries. He had seen Paris. He had been brought into contact with English intellectual life. He had conversed and measured strength with some of the leading men of letters of the day. He knew that he had talents which entitled him to a place among the best of them. But he was sick in body, and mentally he was a strange combination of pride and self-depreciation. He was free as air, but free only, as it seemed to him, because of his insignicance,—because no one wanted his help. Most of us find our course determined by circumstances. We are saved by necessity from the infirmity of our own wills. No necessity interfered with Carlyle. He had the world before him with no limitations but his poverty, and he was entirely at sea. So far only he was

determined, that he would never sell his soul to the
Devil, never speak what he did not wholly believe,
never do what in his inmost heart he did not feel to
be right, and that he would keep his independence,
come what might.

As old Quixote said (he wrote at this time), and as I have
often said after him, if it were but a crust of bread and a
cup of water that Heaven has given thee, rejoice that thou
hast none but Heaven to thank for it. A man that is not
standing on his own feet in regard to economical affairs soon
ceases to be a man at all. Poor Coleridge is like the hulk
of a huge ship—his masts and sails and rudder have rotted
quite away.

Literature lay open. Nothing could hinder a man
there save the unwillingness of publishers to take his
wares; but of this there seemed to be no danger.
'Meister' was approaching to a second edition; the
'Schiller,' such parts of it as had yet appeared, had
been favourably noticed; and Schiller's own example
was specially encouraging. Schiller, like himself,
had been intended for the ministry, had recoiled from
it, had drifted, as he had done, into the initial stages
of law, but had been unable to move in professional
harness. Schiller, like himself again, had been
afflicted with painful chronic disease, and, though
it killed him early, his spirit had triumphed over his
body. At the age at which Carlyle had now arrived,
Schiller's name was known in every reading household in Germany, and his early plays had been translated into half the languages in Europe. Schiller,

however, more fortunate than he, possessed the rare and glorious gift of poetry. Carlyle had tried poetry and had consciously failed. He had intellect enough. He had imagination—no lack of that, and the keenest and widest sensibilities; yet with a true instinct he had discovered that the special faculty which distinguishes the poet from other men, nature had not bestowed upon him. He had no correct metrical ear; the defect can be traced in the very best of his attempts, whether at translation or at original composition. He could shape his materials into verse, but without spontaneity, and instead of gaining beauty they lost their force and clearness. His prose at this time was, on the other hand, supremely excellent, little as he knew it. The sentences in his letters are perfectly shaped, and are pregnant with meaning. The more impassioned passages flow in rhythmical cadence like the sweetest tones of an organ. The style of the 'Life of Schiller' is the style of his letters. He was not satisfied with it; he thought it 'wretched,' 'bombastic,' 'not in the right vein.' It was in fact simple. Few literary biographies in the English language equal it for grace, for brevity, for clearness of portraiture, and artist-like neglect of the unessentials. Goethe so clearly recognised its merits, that in a year or two it was to be translated under his direction into German, and edited with a preface by himself. While England and Scotland were giving Carlyle at best a few patronising nods, soon to change to anger and contempt, Goethe saw in this young unknown Scotchman the characteristics of a true man of genius, and spoke of him 'as a new moral force, the extent and effects of which it was impossible to predict.'

The rewriting and arranging of the 'Life of Schiller' was more tedious than Carlyle expected. It was done at last, however, published and paid for. A copy was sent to Mainhill, with a letter to his mother.

I have at last finished that miserable book, on account of which I have been scolding printers and running to and fro like an evil spirit for the last three weeks. The 'Life of Schiller' is now fairly off my hands. I have not put my name to it, not feeling anxious to have the syllables of my poor name pass through the mouths of cockneys on so slender an occasion, though, if anyone lay it to my charge, I shall see no reason to blush for the hand I had in it. Sometimes of late I have bethought me of some of your old maxims about pride and vanity. I do see this same vanity to be the root of half the evil men are subject to in life. Examples of it stare me in the face every day.

The pitiful passion under any of the thousand forms which it assumes never fails to wither out the good and worthy parts of a man's character, and leave him poor and spiteful, an enemy to his own peace and that of all about him. There never was a wiser doctrine than that of Christian humility, considered as a corrective for the coarse unruly selfishness of man's nature. I know you will read the 'Schiller' with attention and pleasure. It contains nothing that I know of but truth of fact and sentiment, and I have always found that the honest truth of one mind had a certain attraction in it for every other mind that loved truth honestly. Various quacks, for instance, have exclaimed against the immorality of 'Meister;' and the person whom it delighted above all others of my acquaintance was Mrs.

Strachey, exactly the most religious, pure, and true-minded person among the whole number. A still more convincing proof of my doctrine was the satisfaction you took in it.

The 'Schiller' was as welcome at Mainhill as 'Meister' had been, but I have anticipated the completion of it. It was not finished till the middle of the winter, all which time Carlyle was alone in his London lodgings. His personal history from the time of his return from Dover is told in his letters.

To Mrs. Carlyle, Mainhill.

23 Southampton Street, Pentonville :
November 12, 1824.

The Stracheys took me with them in their carriage to Shooter's Hill, and I made my way to the hospitable mansion of the Orator at Pentonville by various coaches as I best could. Next morning no entreaties for delay could detain me. I set out in quest of lodgings, determined to take no rest till I had found some place which I could call my own, where I might at last collect my scattered thoughts and see what yet remained to me to be accomplished or avoided. I found the task of taking lodgings less abominable than I used to reckon it in Edinburgh. Irving and his wife went with me to one or two till I got into the way, after which I dismissed them, and proceeded on the search myself. Ere long I landed in Southampton Street, a fine, clean, quiet spot, and found a landlady and a couple of rooms almost exactly such as I was wanting.

Here I have fixed my abode for a space, and design to set seriously about remodelling my affairs. On the whole I am happy that I have got into a house of my own where I am lord and master, and can manage as I like without giving

an account to anyone. Irving could not take me to board
in his house, having engaged to admit one Parker from
Glasgow (at a *very* high rate), who is coming here to study
law. Indeed, after inspecting the state of his internal
economy, I more than ceased to desire it. He himself is of
rough and ready habits, and his wife is not by any means
the pink of housekeepers. For one like me their house and
table would have suited but indifferently in point of health,
and their visitors and other interruptions would have sadly
interfered with my standing business. Irving's kind and
interesting conversation was the only thing that tempted me,
and even this for the present could not have been got. The
Orator's whole heart and soul seem for a while to have been
set on two solitary objects—the Caledonian Chapel and the
squealing brat of a child which his dear Isabella brought
him three months ago. This smallest and *wershest* of his
Majesty's subjects the worthy preacher dandles and fondles
and dry-nurses and talks about in a way that is piteous to
behold. He speculates on the progressive development of
his senses, on the state of *his* bowels, on *his* hours of rest,
his pap-spoons and his hippings. He asks you twenty times a
day (me he dares not ask any longer) if *he* is not a pretty
boy. He even at times attempts a hideous chaunt to the
creature by way of lullaby. Unhappy *gorb!* I have wished
it farther than I need repeat at present. Its mewing used
to awaken me at night. Its history keeps me silent by day.
Now that I am gone from its sphere I can wish it well as
the offspring of my friend, whom after all I do not like much
the worse that he is over-fond and foolish as a father. In my
present state, too, I can enjoy all that is enjoyable in his
company and friendship. This house is within three minutes'
walk of his, where I design to be a frequent visitor. They
have been kind friends to me. I were a worthless creature
to forget them.

I expect to pass my time neither unpleasantly nor unprofitably in this city. I have people enough here whom I wish to see and may see. Some of them are attractive by their talent and knowledge, several by their kindness. The Stracheys I have found to be friendly in a high degree. Mrs. Montagu (Irving's 'noble lady,' whom I do not like as well as Mrs. S.), had a note lying for me in Dover inviting me in very warm and high-flown terms to come and live with them. The Bullers are here at present; they sent inviting me by Arthur their son to come and dine with them to-day. I would not *dine* with the King. But I engaged to go and take tea. Badams predicts that I will come back to him; but this I do not expect.

London pleased Carlyle less as he knew it better.

To John Carlyle.

23 Southampton Street : November 30, 1824.

Allis of York is here at present, setting up a sort of 'Asylum.' He wishes me to go out and live with him at his house in Epping Forest. He will board me and a horse for 40*l.* a year! That scheme will not answer. There is folly enough within my reach already without going to seek it among the professedly insane. Perhaps I may go and stay with him a week or so when I have finished the writing of this book. I have yet made but little progress in my survey of London. The weather has been very unpropitious, and I have had many things to do. I have several persons (Mrs. Montagu, Mrs. Strachey, Procter, &c.) whom I call on now and then, and might far oftener if I found it useful. They are kind persons, particularly the first two; but for rational employment of my mind in their company there is but very little. People of elevated minds and clear judgment seem to be as rare here as in the north. Anything approaching to a *great character* is a treasure I have yet to meet with. Yet such is life. The little that is good in it we ought to welcome, and forget how much better it might have been when we think how much worse it generally is. These two women and their families treat me as if I were a near relation, not a wandering stranger. I feel their kindness, and hope yet to profit more by it. Basil Montagu, the husband, was described to me as a philosopher. I find him to be an honest-hearted —— goose. Happy Irving, who sees in all his friends the pink of human excellence ; and when he has found the nakedness of the land, can turn him round and seek a fresh supply. He is still fighting away as valiantly as ever—nursing and preaching. His popularity is growing steadier, and I think will ultimately settle into something comfortable and accordant with the nature of things.

The fashionable people have long ago forgot that he exists ; and our worthy preacher has discovered, fortunately not too late, that many things since the Reformation have been more surprising than to grow a London lion for the space of three little months. I am glad with all my heart that this insane work is over. Irving is becoming known to men at large *as he is*. The sceptical and literary people find that he is *not* a quack ; and they honour him, or at least let him live at peace. There are many persons of warm hearts and half-cultivated heads who love him and admire him, and I think will stand by him firmly. All that have ever known him in private must and do like him. Delivered from the gross incense of preaching popularity, Irving will cultivate his mind in peace ; and may ray out a profitable mixture of light and darkness upon a much wider public than he has yet addressed by writing. After all he is a brave fellow— among the best, if not the very best, whom I have met in life. Success to him ! for though I laugh at him, I were a

dog if I did not love him. Speak not of his popularity.
Your words will be interpreted to mean, not that it is growing
rational, but that it is over. At present I reckon the appearance of it better than it has ever been.

The correspondence with Miss Welsh had continued
regularly since Carlyle left Scotland. Letters written
under such circumstances are in their nature private,
and so must for the most part remain. Miss Welsh, however, was necessarily a principal element in any scheme
which Carlyle might form for his future life, and to her
his views were exposed without the smallest reserve.
The pensions or sinecures of which her too sanguine
expectation had dreamt, he had known from the first
to be illusions. He must live, if he lived at all by his
own hand. He had begun to think that both for body
and mind London was not the place for him. He had
saved between two and three hundred pounds, beyond
what he had spent upon his brothers. His tastes were
of the simplest. The plainest house, the plainest food, the
plainest dress was all that he wanted. The literary men
whom he had met with in the metropolis did not please
him. Some, like Hazlitt, were selling their souls to
the periodical press. Even in Campbell and Coleridge
the finer powers were dormant or paralysed, under the
spell it seemed of London and its influences. Southey
and Wordsworth, who could give a better account of
their abilities, had turned their backs upon the world
with its vain distinctions and noisy flatteries, and were
living far away among the lakes and mountains.
Carlyle was considering that he, too, would be better in
Annandale. He would take a farm and stock it. His

brother Alexander would manage it for him, while he could study and write. From these two sources, means sufficient could easily be provided for a simple and honourable existence. Before taking any decided step, however, it was necessary to consult the person who had promised to be his wife when he should find himself in a condition to maintain her in tolerable comfort. It is possible—though speculations of an interested kind influenced Carlyle as little as they ever influenced any man—that among their resources he had calculated her fortune would pass for something. There had been no occasion for her to tell him precisely the disposition which she had made of it. He had written to her effusively, and she had laughed at him. She had been afterwards slightly unwell, and had expressed penitence for her levity.

To Miss Welsh.

23 Southampton Street, Pentonville: December —.

Your sickness I have striven to make light of. I will not let myself believe that it is more than temporary; and the serious mood you partly owe to it is that in which to me you are far most interesting.

Do not mock and laugh, however gracefully, when you can help it. For your own sake I had almost rather see you sad. It is the earnest, affectionate, warm-hearted, enthusiastic Jane that I love. The acute, sarcastic, clear-sighted, derisive Jane I can at best but admire. Is it not a pity that you had such a turn that way? 'Pity rather that the follies of the world, and yours among the number, Mr. Quack, should so often call for castigation.' Well, well! Be it so, then.

A wilful man, and still more a wilful woman, will have their way . . . . Now let us turn over a new leaf—a new leaf in the paper, and still more in the subject. I am meditating with as rigid an intensity as ever on the great focus of all purposes at present—the arranging of my future life. Here is no light business, and no want of eagerness in me to see it done. As yet I have made no way, or very little ; but already I am far happier than I was, from the mere consideration that my destiny, with all its manifold entanglements, perplexing and tormenting as they are, is now submitted to my own management. Of my projects I can give no description. They fluctuate from day to day, and many of them are not of a kind to be explained in writing. One item lies at the bottom of almost any scheme I form. It is determination to have some household of my own ; some abode which I may be lord of, though it were no better than the Cynic's tub ; some abiding home which I may keep myself in peace by the hope of improving—not of changing for another. I have lived too long in tents a wandering Bedouin, the fruit of my toils wasted or spent in the day that witnessed them. I am sick and must recover ; and if so, sickness itself provides the helps for getting out of it. Till then my mind lies spell-bound, the best of my talents (bless the mark) shut up even from my own view, and the thought of writing anything beyond mere drudgery is vain. I see all this, but I also see the plan of conquering it if it can be conquered. I must settle myself down within reach of Edinburgh or London. I must divide my time between mental and bodily exercises. If the latter could be turned to profit, could be regularly fixed and ordered by necessity of any kind, I should regard the point as gained. Had I land of my own, I should instantly be tempted to become a—farmer ! Laugh outright ! But it is very true. I think how I should mount a horseback in the grey of the morning and go forth like a destroying

angel among my lazy hinds,[1] quickening every sluggish hand,
cultivating and clearing, tilling and planting, till the place
became a very garden round me.   In the intermediate hours
I could work at literature ; thus compelled to live according
to the wants of nature, in one twelvemonth I should be the
healthiest man in three parishes, and then, if I said and did
nothing notable, it were my own blame or nature's only.

This you say is Utopian dreaming, not the sober scheme of
a man in his senses.   I am sorry for it—sorry that nothing
half so likely to save me comes within the circuit of my
capabilities.   A sinecure !   God bless thee, my darling !   I
could not touch a sinecure though twenty of my friends
should volunteer to offer it. *Keineswegs*. It is no part of my
plan to eat the bread of idleness so long as I have the force of
a sparrow left in me to procure the honest bread of industry.
Irving, too ! good Irving ! His thoughts are friendly, but he
expresses them like a goose. 'Help me to the uttermost' ?
If he can help himself to get along the path through life, it
is all that I shall ask of him.   If his own shins are safe at
the journey's end (a point on which there are many doubts),
let him hang a votive tablet up and go to bed in peace.   I
shall manage mine.   There is no use in 'helps.' The grown-
up man that cannot be his own help ought to solicit his discharge from the Church militant, and turn him to some
middle region by the earliest conveyance.   For affection, or
the faintest imitation of it, a man should feel obliged to his
very dog.   But for the gross assistances of patronage or
purse, let him pause before accepting them from anyone.
Let him utterly refuse them except from beings that are
enshrined in his heart of hearts, and from whom no chance

---

[1] This is like his 'sluttish harlots' at Kinnaird.   How did he
know that his hinds would be lazy ? But vehement language, which
implied nothing but the impatience and irritability of his own mind, was
as characteristic of Carlyle as it was of Johnson.

can divide him. It is the law in Yarmouth that every herring hang by its own head. Except in cases singularly wretched or singularly happy, that judicious principle I think should also govern life.

A few days later he writes again :—

Irving advises me to stay in London ; partly with a friendly feeling, partly with a half-selfish one, for he would fain keep me near him. Among all his followers there is none whose intercourse can satisfy him. Any other than him it would go far to disgust. Great part of them are blockheads, a few are fools. There is no rightly intellectual man among them. He speculates and speculates, and would rather have one contradict him rationally, than gape at him with the vacant stare of children viewing the Grand Turk's palace with his guards—all alive ! He advises me, not knowing what he says. He himself has the nerves of a buffalo, and forgets that I have not. His philosophy with me is like a gill of ditch-water thrown into the crater of Mount Ætna. A million gallons of it would avail me nothing.

On the whole, however, he is among the best fellows in London, by far the best that I have met with. Thomas Campbell has a far clearer judgment, infinitely more taste and refinement, but there is no living well of thought or feeling in him. His head is a shop, not a manufactory ; and for his heart, it is as dry as a Greenock kipper. I saw him for the second time the other night. I viewed him more clearly and in a kindlier light, but scarcely altered my opinion of him. He is not so much a man as the editor of a magazine. His life is that of an exotic. He exists in London, as most Scotchmen do, like a shrub disrooted and stuck into a bottle of water. Poor Campbell ! There were good things in him too, but fate has pressed too heavy on him, or he has resisted it too weakly. His poetic vein is failing, or has run out. He has a Glasgow wife, and their only son is in a state of idiotcy. I sympathised with him, I could have loved him, but he has forgot the way to love. Procter here has set up house on the strength of his writing faculties, with his wife, a daughter of the Noble Lady. He is a good-natured man, lively and ingenious, but essentially a small. Coleridge is sunk inextricably in the depths of putrescent indolence. Southey and Wordsworth have retired far from the din of this monstrous city; so has Thomas Moore. Whom have we left? The dwarf Opium-eater, my critic in the 'London Magazine,' lives here in lodgings, with a wife and children living, or starving, on the scanty produce of his scribble far off in Westmoreland. He carries a laudanum bottle in his pocket, and the venom of a wasp in his heart. A rascal (——), who writes much of the black-guardism in 'Blackwood,' has been frying him to cinders on the gridiron of 'John Bull.' Poor De Quincey! He had twenty thousand pounds, and a liberal share of gifts from nature. Vanity and opium have brought him to the state of 'dog distract or monkey sick.' If I could find him, it would give me pleasure to procure him one substantial beefsteak before he dies. Hazlitt is writing his way through France and Italy. The ginshops and pawnbrokers bewail his absence. Leigh Hunt writes 'wishing caps' for the 'Examiner,' and lives on the lightest of diets at Pisa. But what shall I say of you, ye ——, and ——, and ——, and all the spotted fry that 'report' and 'get up' for the 'public press,' that earn money by writing calumnies, and spend it in punch and other viler objects of debauchery? Filthiest and basest of the children of men! My soul come not into your secrets; mine honour be not united unto you! 'Good heavens!' I often inwardly exclaim, 'and is this the literary world?' This rascal rout, this dirty rabble, destitute not only of high feeling and knowledge or intellect, but even of common honesty! The very best of them are ill-natured weaklings. They are not red-blooded men at all. They are only things for writing articles. But I have done with them for once. In railing at them let me not forget that if they are bad and worthless, I, as yet, am nothing; and that he who putteth on his harness should not boast himself as he who putteth it off. Unhappy souls! perhaps they are more to be pitied than blamed. I do not hate them. I would only that stone walls and iron bars were constantly between us.

Such is the literary world of London; indisputably the poorest part of its population at present.

While in this humour with English men of letters, Carlyle was surprised and cheered by a letter from one of the same calling in another country, the man whom above all others he most honoured and admired, Goethe himself. He had sent a copy of his translation of 'Meister' to Weimar, but no notice had been taken of it, and he had ceased to expect any. 'It was like a message from fairyland,' he said. He could at first scarcely believe 'that this was the real hand and signature of that mysterious personage whose name had floated through his fancy like a sort of spell since his boyhood, whose thoughts had come to him in maturer years almost with the impressiveness of revelations.' An account of this angel visitation, with a copy of the letter itself, was forwarded to Mainhill.

To John Carlyle.

Southampton Street : December 18.

The other afternoon, as I was lying dozing in a brown study after dinner, a lord's lackey knocked at the door and presented me with a little blue parcel, requiring for it a note of delivery. I opened it, and found two pretty stitched little books, and a letter from Goethe! I copy it and send it for your edification. The patriarchal style of it pleases me much :—[1]

'My dearest Sir,—If I did not acknowledge on the spot the arrival of your welcome present, it was because I was unwilling to send you an empty acknowledgment merely, but I purposed to add some careful remarks on a work so honourable to me.

'My advanced years, however, burdened as they are with many indispensable duties, have prevented me from comparing your translation at my leisure with the original text— a more difficult undertaking, perhaps, for me than for some third person thoroughly familiar with German and English literature. Since, however, I have at the present moment an opportunity, through the Lords Bentinck, of forwarding this note safely to London, and at the same time of bringing about an acquaintance between yourself and the Lords B. which may be agreeable to both of you, I delay no longer to thank you for the interest which you have taken in my literary works as well as in the incidents of my life, and to entreat you earnestly to continue the same interest for the future also. It may be that I shall yet hear much of you. I send herewith a set of poems which you will scarcely have seen, but with which I venture to hope that you will feel a certain sympathy.

'With the most sincere good wishes,
'Your most obedient,
'J. W. GOETHE.'[2]

---

[1] The translation is mine: Carlyle copied the letter as it was written.

[2] In Goethe's German :—

'Wenn ich, mein werthester Herr, die glückliche Ankunft Ihrer willkommenen Sendung nicht ungesäumt anzeigte, so war die Ursache

This is the first of several letters which Carlyle received from Goethe; the earliest token of the attention which he had commanded from the leader of modern literature, an attention which deepened into regard and admiration when the 'Life of Schiller' reached Goethe's hands. The acquaintance which was to prove mutually interesting came of course to nothing. Carlyle heard no more of the 'Lords Bentinck.' The momentary consequence which attached to him as the correspondent of the poet-minister of the Duke of Weimar disappeared in England, where he seemed no more than an insignificant struggling individual, below the notice of the privileged circles.

dass ich nicht einen leeren Empfangschein ausstellen, sondern über Ihre mir so ehrenvolle Arbeit auch irgend ein geprüftes Wort beyzufügen die Absicht hatte.

' Meine hohen Jahre jedoch mit so vielen unabwendbaren Obliegenheiten immerfort beladen, hinderten mich an einer ruhigen Vergleichung Ihrer Bearbeitung mit dem Originaltext, welches vielleicht für mich eine schwerere Aufgabe seyn möchte, als für irgend einen dritten der deutschen und englischen Literatur gründlich Befreundeten. Gegenwärtig aber, da ich eine Gelegenheit sehe durch die Herren Grafen Bentinck gegenwärtiges Schreiben sicher nach London zu bringen, und zugleich beiden Theilen eine angenehme Bekanntschaft zu verschaffen, so versäume nicht meinen Dank für Ihre so innige Theilnahme an meinen literarischen Arbeiten, sowohl als an den Schicksalen meines Lebens, hierdurch treulich auszusprechen; und Sie um Fortsetzung derselben auch für die Zukunft angelegentlich zu ersuchen. Vielleicht erfahre ich in der Folge noch manches von Ihnen, und übersende zugleich mit diesem eine Reihe von Gedichten welche schwerlich zu Ihnen gekommen sind, von denen ich aber hoffen darf, dass sie Ihnen einiges Interesse abgewinnen werden.

' Mit den aufrichtigsten Wünschen,

' Ergebenst,

' J. W. GOETHE.

The annals of this year, so eventful in Carlyle's history, may close with a letter to him from the poor farm-house in Annandale.

To Thomas Carlyle.

Dear Son,—I take this opportunity to thank you for your unvarying kindness, though I fear it will hardly read. But never mind; I know to whom I am writing. It is a long time since we had a sight of each other; nevertheless I am often with you in thought, and I hope we shall meet at a throne of grace where there is free access to all who come in faith. Tell me if thou readest a chapter often. If not, begin; oh, do begin! How do you spend the Sabbath in that tumultuous city? Oh! remember to keep it holy; this you will never repent. I think you will be saying, 'Hold, mother!' but time is short and uncertain. Now, Tom, the best of boys thou art to me! Do not think I am melancholy, though I so speak. Be not uneasy on my account. I have great reason to be thankful. I am quite well, and happy too when I hear from London and Edinburgh. And pray do not let me want food: as your father says, I look as if I would eat your letters. Write everything and soon—I look for one every fortnight till we meet. I grudge taking up the sheet, so I bid thee good-night, and remain

Your affectionate mother,
MARGARET CARLYLE.

P.S. by Alexander Carlyle:—

You are very wise, we seriously think, in determining to live in the country, but how or where I do not pretend to say; perhaps in some cottage with a grass park or cow attached to it for the nonce, and our mother or Mag for housekeeper. Or what say you of farming (marrying, I dare not speak to you about at all) ? There are plenty of farms to let on all sides of the country. But tell me : are the warm hearts of Mainhill changed ? or are they less anxious to please ? I guess not. Yet after all, I do often think that you would be as comfortable here as anywhere.

CHAPTER XVI

GOETHE'S letter was more than a compliment.   Goethe, who did not throw away his words in unmeaning politenesses, had noticed Carlyle ; and notice was more welcome from such a source than if it had come from ministers or kings.   The master had spoken approvingly.   The disciple was encouraged and invigorated. He had received an assurance that his intellectual career would not be a wholly unfruitful one.   Pleasant as it was, however, it did not help the solution of the pressing problem, what was he immediately to do? The prospect of a farm in Scotland became more attractive the more he thought of it.   Freedom, fresh air, plain food, and the society of healthy, pious people, unspoilt by the world and its contagion—with these life might be worth having and might be turned to noble uses.   He had reflected much on his engagement with Miss Welsh.   He had felt that perhaps he had done wrong in allowing her to entangle herself with a person whose future was so uncertain, and whose present schemes, even if realised successfully, would throw her, if she married him, into a situation so unlike what she had anticipated, so unlike the surroundings to which she had been accustomed.   In his vehement way he had offered to release her if she wished it ; and she had unhesitatingly refused. As little, however, was her ambition gratified with the prospect of being mistress of a Scotch farm. She had mocked at his proposal. She had pointed out with serious truth his own utter unfitness for a farmer's occupation. She had jestingly told him that she had land of her own at Craigenputtock. The tenant was leaving. If he was bent on trying, let him try Craigenputtock. He took her jest in earnest. Why should he not farm Craigenputtock? Why should not she, as she was still willing to be his life companion, live with him there? Her father had been born in the old manor-house, and had intended to end his days there. To himself the moorland life would be only a continuance of the same happy mode of existence which he had known at Main-hill. In such a household, and in the discharge of the commonest duties, he had seen his mother become a very paragon of women. He did not understand, or he did not wish to understand, that a position which may be admirably suited to a person who has known no other, might be ill-adapted to one who had been bred in luxury and had never known a want uncared for. The longer he reflected on it, the more desirable the plan of taking Craigenputtock appeared to him to be.

To Miss Welsh.

Pentonville: Jan. 9, 1825.

I trust that the same cheerful spirit of affection which breathes in every line of your last charming letter still animates you, and disposes you kindly towards me. I have somewhat to propose to you which it may require all your love of me to make you look upon with favour. If you are not the best woman in the world, it may prove a sorry business for both of us.

You bid me tell you how I have decided—what I mean to do. It is you that must decide. I will endeavour to explain to you what I wish; it must rest with you to say whether it can ever be attained. You tell me you have land which needs improvement. Why not work on that? in one word, then, will you go with me? Will you be my own for ever? Say yes, and I embrace the project with my whole heart. I send my brother Alick over to rent that Nithsdale farm for me without delay; I proceed to it the moment I am freed from my engagements here; I labour in arranging it, and fitting everything for your reception; and the instant it is ready I take you home to my hearth, never more to part from me, whatever fate betide us.

I fear you think this scheme a baseless vision; and yet it is the sober best among the many I have meditated—the best for me, and I think also, so far as I can judge of it, for yourself. If it take effect and be well conducted, I look upon the recovery of my health and equanimity, and with these, of regular profitable and natural habits of activity, as things which are no longer doubtful. I have lost them by departing from nature; I must find them by returning to her. A stern experience has taught me this, and I am a fool if I do not profit by the lesson. Depend upon it, Jane, this literature which both of us are so bent on pursuing will not constitute the sole nourishment of any true human spirit. No truth has been forced upon me, after more resistance, or with more invincible impressiveness than this. I feel it in myself. I see it daily in others. Literature is the *wine* of life. It will not, cannot, be its food. What is it that makes blue-stockings of women, magazine hacks of men? They neglect household and social duties. They have no

household and social enjoyments. Life is no longer with
them a verdant field, but a *hortus siccus*. They exist pent
up in noisome streets, amid feverish excitements. They
despise or overlook the common blessedness which Providence
has laid out for *all* his creatures, and try to substitute for it
a distilled quintessence prepared in the alembic of painters
and rhymers and sweet singers. What is the result? This
ardent spirit parches up their nature. They become discontented and despicable, or wretched and dangerous.
Byron and all strong souls go the latter way. Campbell and
all the weak souls the former. ' Hinaus !' as the Devil says
to Faust. ' Hinaus ins freie Feld !' There is no soul in
these vapid ' articles ' of yours. Away ! be men before
attempting to be writers.

You, too, are unhappy, and I see the reason. You have
a deep, earnest, and vehement spirit, and no earnest task has
ever been assigned it. You despise and ridicule the meanness
of the things about you. To the things you honour you can
only pay a fervent adoration which issues in no practical
effect. Oh that I saw you the mistress of a house diffusing
over human souls that loved you those clear faculties of
order, judgment, elegance, which you are now reduced to
spend on pictures and portfolios ; blessing living hearts with
that enthusiastic love which you must now direct to the
distant and dimly seen. All this is in you. You have a
heart and an intellect and a resolute decision which might
make you the model of wives, however widely your thoughts
and your experience have hitherto wandered from that
highest distinction of even the noblest woman. I too have
wandered wide and far. Let us return ; let us return
together. Let us learn through one another what it is to
live. Let us set our minds and habitudes in order, and
grow under the peaceful sunshine of nature, that whatever
fruit or flowers have been implanted in our spirits may ripen

wholesomely and be distributed in due season. What is genius but the last perfection of true manhood? the pure reflection of a spirit in union with itself, discharging all common duties with more than common excellence; extracting from the many-coloured scenes of life in which it mingles the beautifying principle which more or less pervades them all? The rose in its full-blown fragrance is the glory of the fields; but there must be a soil and stem and leaves, or there will be no rose. Your mind and my own have in them many capabilities; but the first of all their duties is to provide for their own regulation and contentment. If there be an overplus to consecrate to higher ends it will not fail to show itself. If there be none, it were better it should never attempt to show itself.

But I must leave these generalities and avoid romance, for it is an earnest practical affair we are engaged in, and requires sense and regulation, not poetics and enthusiasm. 'Where then,' you ask me, 'are the means of realising these results, of mastering the difficulties and deficiencies that beset us both?' This too I have considered; the black catalogue of impediments have passed again and again in review before me, but on the whole I do not think them insurmountable. If you will undertake to be my faithful helper, as I will all my life be yours, I fear not to engage with them.

The first, the lowest, but a most essential point, is that of funds. On this matter I have still little to tell you that you do not know. I feel in general that I have ordinary faculties in me, and an ordinary degree of diligence in using them, and that thousands manage life in comfort with even slenderer resources. In my present state my income, though small, might to reasonable wishes be sufficient; were my health and faculties restored, it *might* become abundant. Shall I confess to you this is a difficulty which we are apt to overrate. The essentials of even elegant comfort are not difficult to procure. It is only vanity that is insatiable in consuming. To my taste cleanliness and order are far beyond gilding and grandeur, which without them are an abomination ; and for displays, for festivals, and parties I believe you are as indisposed as myself. What is the use of this same vanity ? Where is the good of being its slaves ? If thou and I love one another, if we discharge our duties faithfully and steadfastly, one labouring with honest, manful zeal to provide, the other with noble wife-like prudence in dispensing, have we not done all we can ? Are we not acquitted at the bar of our own conscience ? And what is it to us whether this or that Squire or Bailie be richer or poorer than we ?

Two laws I have laid down to myself—that I must and will recover health, without which to think or even to live is burdensome or unprofitable ; and that I will *not* degenerate into the wretched thing which calls itself an author in our capitals, and scribbles for the sake of lucre in the periodicals of the day. Thank Heaven, there are other means of living. If there were not, I for one should beg to be excused. . . . On the whole I begin to entertain a certain degree of contempt for the destiny which has so long persecuted me. I will be a man in spite of it. Yet it lies with you whether I shall be a *right* man, or only a hard and bitter Stoic. What say you ? Decide for yourself and me. Consent if you dare trust me, and let us live and die together. Yet fear not to deny me if your judgment so determine. It will be a sharp pang that tears away from me for ever the hope which now for years has been the solace of my existence ; but better to endure it and all its consequences than to witness and to cause the forfeit of your happiness. At times, I confess, when I hear you speak of your gay cousins, and contrast with their brilliant equipments my own simple exterior and scanty prospects, and humble, but to me most dear and honourable-minded kinsmen, whom I were the veriest dog if I ceased to love and venerate and cherish for their true affection and the rugged sterling worth of their character— when I think of all this I could almost counsel you to cast me utterly away, and to connect yourself with one whose friends and station are more analogous to your own. But anon in some moment of self-love, I say proudly there is a spirit in *me* which is worthy of this maiden, which shall be worthy of her. I will teach her, I will guide her, I will make her happy. Together we will share the joys and sorrows of existence.

Speak, then. . . . Think well of me, of yourself, of our circumstances, and determine—Dare you trust me, dare you trust your fate with me, as I trust mine with you? Judge if I wait your answer with impatience. I know you will not keep me waiting. Of course it will be necessary to explain all things to your mother, and take her serious advice respecting them. For your other friends, it is not worth while consulting one of them. I know not that there is one among them that would give you as disinterested advice as even I, judging in my own cause. May God bless you and direct you. Decide as you will.

Miss Welsh, after having lost Irving, had consented to be Carlyle's wife as soon as he was in a fair position to marry, in the conviction that she was connecting herself with a man who was destined to become brilliantly distinguished, whom she honoured for his character and admired for his gifts, in whose society and in whose triumphs she would find a compensation for the disappointment of her earlier hopes. She was asked in this letter to be the mistress of a moorland

farming establishment. Had she felt towards Carlyle
as she had felt towards his friend, she would perhaps
have encountered cheerfully any lot which was to be
shared with the object of a passionate affection. But
the indispensable feeling was absent. She was invited
to relinquish her station in society, and resign comforts
which habit had made necessary to her, and she was
apparently to sacrifice at the same time the very
expectations which had brought her to regard a
marriage with Carlyle as a possibility. She knew
better than he what was really implied in the situation
which he offered her. She knew that if farming on a
Scotch moor was to be a successful enterprise, it would
not be by morning rides, metaphorical vituperation of
'lazy hinds,' and forenoons and evenings given up to
poetry and philosophy. Both he and she would have
to work with all their might, and with their own hands,
with all their time and all their energy, to the extinc-
tion of every higher ambition. Carlyle himself also
she knew to be entirely unfit for any such occupation.
The privations of it might be nothing to him, for he
was used to them at home, but he would have to cease
to be himself before he could submit patiently to a life
of mechanical drudgery. She told him the truth with
the merciless precision which on certain occasions distinguished her.

To Thomas Carlyle.

Haddington : January 13, 1825.

I little thought that my joke about your farming Craigenputtock was to be made the basis of such a serious and

extraordinary project. If you had seen the state of per-
plexity which your letter has thrown me into, you would
have practised any self-denial rather than have written it.
But there is no use in talking of what is done. *Cosa fatta
ha capo.* The thing to be considered now is what to do.

You have sometimes asked me did I ever think? For
once in my life at least I have thought myself into a vertigo,
and without coming to any positive conclusion. However,
my mind, such as it is, on the matter you have thus precipitately forced on my consideration I will explain to you
frankly and explicitly, as the happiness of us both requires.
I love you, and I should be the most ungrateful and injudicious of mortals if I did not. But I am not *in love* with you;
that is to say, my love for you is not a passion which over-
clouds my judgment and absorbs all my regards for myself
and others. It is a simple, honest, serene affection, made
up of admiration and sympathy, and better perhaps to found
domestic enjoyment on than any other. In short, it is a love
which *influences*, does not *make*, the destiny of a life.

Such temperate sentiments lend no false colouring, no
' rosy light' to your project. I see it such as it is, with all
the arguments for and against it. I see that my consent
under existing circumstances would indeed secure to *me* the
only fellowship and support I have found in the world, and
perhaps, too, shed some sunshine of joy on your existence,
which has hitherto been sullen and cheerless; but, on the
other hand, that it would involve you and myself in number-
less cares and difficulties, and expose me to petty tribulations which I want fortitude to despise, and which, not
despised, would embitter the peace of us both. I do not
wish for fortune more than is sufficient for my wants—my
natural wants, and the artificial ones which habit has rendered nearly as importunate as the others. But I will not
marry to live on less; because in that case, every inconve

nience I was subjected to would remind me of what I had
quitted, and the idea of a sacrifice should have no place in a
voluntary union. Neither have I any wish for grandeur ;
the glittering baits of titles and honours are only for children
and fools.   But I conceive it a duty which everyone owes to
society, not to throw up that station in it which Providence
has assigned him, and, having this conviction, I could not
marry into a station inferior to my own with the approval of
my judgment, *which* alone could enable me to brave the
censures of my acquaintance.

And now let me ask you, have you any *certain* livelihood
to maintain me in the manner I have been used to live in ?
any *fixed* place in the rank of society I have been born
and bred in ?   No.   You have projects for attaining both,
capabilities for attaining both, and much more.   But as yet
you have not attained them.   Use the noble gifts which God
has given you.   You have prudence—though, by the way,
this last proceeding is no great proof of it.   Devise then how
you may gain yourself a moderate but *settled* income.   Think
of some more promising plan than farming the most barren
spot in the county of Dumfriesshire.   What a thing that would
be to be sure !   You and I keeping house at Craigenputtock !
I would as soon think of building myself a nest on the Bass
rock.   Nothing but your ignorance of the spot saves you
from the imputation of insanity for admitting such a thought.
Depend upon it you could not exist there a twelvemonth.
For my part I could not spend a month at it with an angel.
Think of something else then.   Apply your industry to carry
it into effect ; your talents, to gild over the inequality of our
births—and then we will talk of marrying.   If all this were
realised, I *think* I should have good sense enough to abate
something of my romantic ideal, and to content myself with
stopping short on this side idolatry.   At all events I will
marry no one else.   This is all the promise I can or will

make. A positive engagement to marry a certain person at a certain time, at all haps and hazards, I have always considered the most ridiculous thing on earth. It is either altogether useless or altogether miserable. If the parties continue faithfully attached to each other, it is a mere ceremony. If otherwise, it becomes a fetter, rivetting them to wretchedness, and only to be broken with disgrace.

Such is the result of my deliberations on this very serious subject. You may approve of it or not, but you cannot either persuade me or convince me out of it. My decisions, when I do decide, are unalterable as the laws of the Medes and Persians. Write instantly, and tell me that you are content to leave the event to time and destiny, and in the meanwhile to continue my friend and guardian, which you have so long faithfully been, and *nothing more*.

It would be more agreeable to etiquette, and perhaps also to prudence, that I should adopt no middle course in an affair such as this; that I should not for another instant encourage an affection which I may never reward, and a hope I may never fulfil, but cast your heart away from me at once, since I cannot embrace the resolution which would give me a right to it for ever. This I would assuredly do if you were like the generality of lovers, or if it were still in my power to be happy independent of your affection. But, as it is, neither etiquette nor prudence can obtain this of me. If there is any change to be made in the terms on which we have so long lived with one another, it must be made by you, not by me.

An ordinary person who had ventured to make such a proposal as Miss Welsh had declined, would have been supremely foolish if he had supposed that it could be acceded to; or supremely selfish if he had possessed

sufficient influence with the lady whom he was addressing to induce her to listen to it. But Carlyle was
in every way peculiar. Selfish he was, if it be selfishness to be ready to sacrifice every person dependent on
him, as completely as he sacrificed himself, to the aims
to which he had resolved to devote his life and talents.
But these objects were of so rare a nature, that the
person capable of pursuing and attaining them must
be judged by a standard of his own. His rejoinder to
this letter throws a light into the inmost constitution
of his character. He thanked Miss Welsh for her
candour; he was not offended at her resoluteness; but
also, he said, he must himself be resolute. She showed
that she did not understand him. He was simply conscious that he possessed powers for the use of which he
was responsible, and he could not afford to allow those
powers to run to waste any longer.

To Miss Welsh.

Pentonville: Jan. 20, 1825.

It were easy for me to plant myself upon the pinnacle of
my own poor selfishness, and utter a number of things proceeding from a very vulgar sort of pride. It were easy also
to pour out over the affair a copious effusion of sentimental
cant. But to express in simplicity the convictions of a man
wishing at least with his whole heart to act as becomes him,
is not easy. Grant me a patient hearing, for I have things
to say that require earnest consideration from us both.

In the first place, however, I must thank you heartily for
your candour. Your letter bears undoubted evidence within
itself of being a faithful copy of your feelings at the moment
it was written; and this to me is an essential point. Your

resoluteness does not offend me ; on the contrary I applaud it. Woe to us both if we cannot be resolute. The miserable man is he who halts between two opinions, who would and would not ; who longs for the merchandise and will not part with the price. He who has dared to look his destiny, however frightful, stedfastly in the face, to measure his strength with its difficulties, and once for all to give up what he cannot reach, has already ceased to be miserable.

Your letter is dictated by good sense and sincerity ; but it shows me that you have only an imperfect view of my present purposes and situation ; there are several mistakes in it, expressed or implied. It is a mistake to suppose that want of self-denial had any material share in causing this proposal. I hope that I should at all times rather suffer pain myself than transfer it to you ; but here was a very different case. For these many months the voice of every persuasion in my conscience has been thundering to me as with the Trump of the Archangel : Man ! thou art going to destruction. Thy nights and days are spent in torment ; thy heart is wasting into entire bitterness. Thou art making less of life than the dog that sleeps upon thy hearth. Up, hapless mortal ! Up and re-build thy destiny if thou canst ! Up in the name of God, that God who sent thee hither for other purposes than to wander to and fro, bearing the fire of hell in an unguilty bosom, to suffer in vain silence, and to die without ever having lived ! Now, in exploring the chaotic structure of my fortunes, I find my affection for you intertwined with every part of it ; connected with whatever is holiest in my feelings or most imperative in my duties. It is necessary for me to understand completely how this matter stands ; to investigate my own wishes and powers in regard to it ; to know of you both what you will do and what you will not do. These things once clearly settled, our line of conduct will be clear also. It was in such a spirit that I

19—2

made this proposal ; not, as you suppose, grounded on a
casual jest of yours, or taken up in a moment of insane
selfishness ; but deliberated with such knowledge as I had
of it for months, and calmly decided on, as with all its
strangeness absolutely the best for both of us. There was
nothing in it of the love and cottage theory, which none but
very young novel writers now employ their thoughts about.
Had you accepted it, I should not by any means have thought
the battle won.   I should have hailed your assent, and the
disposition of mind it bespoke, with a deep but serious joy ;
with a solemn hope as indicating the distinct possibility that
two true hearts might be united and made happy through
each other ; might by their joint unwearied efforts be trans-
planted from the barren wilderness, where both seemed out
of place, into scenes of pure and wholesome activity, such as
nature fitted both of them to enjoy and adorn.   You have
rejected it, I think wisely ; with your actual purposes and
views we should both have been doubly wretched had you
acted otherwise.   Your love of me is completely under the
control of judgment and subordinated to other principles of
duty or expediency.   Your happiness is not by any means
irretrievably connected with mine.   Believe me, I am not
hurt or angry.   I merely wished to know.   It was only in
brief moments of enthusiasm that I ever looked for a different
result.   My plan was no wise one if it did not include the
chance of your denial as well as that of your assent.

    The maxims you proceed by are those of common and
acknowledged prudence ; and I do not say that it is not wise
in you to walk exclusively by them.   But for me, my case is
peculiar ; and unless I adopt other than common maxims, I
look upon my ruin as already sure.   In fact I cannot but
perceive that the stations from which we have looked at life,
and formed our schemes of it, are in your case and mine
essentially different.   You have a right to anticipate excite-

ment and enjoyment. The highest blessing I anticipate is peace. You are bound to pay deference to the criticisms of others, and expect their approbation ; I, to pay comparatively little deference to their criticisms, and to overlook their contempt. This is not strange ; but it accounts for the wide discrepancy in our principles and intentions and demands the serious study of us both.

In your opinion about sacrifices, *felt to be such*, I entirely agree ; but at the same time need I remind your warm and generous heart that the love which will not make sacrifices to its object is no proper love ? Grounded in admiration and the feeling of enjoyment, it is a fit love for a picture or a statue or a poem ; but for a living soul it is not fit. Alas ! without deep sacrifices on both sides, the possibility of our union is an empty dream. It remains for us both to determine what extent of sacrifices it is worth. To me, I confess the union with such a spirit as yours might be, is worth all price but the sacrifice of those very principles which would enable me to deserve and enjoy it.

Then why not make an effort, attain rank and wealth, and confidently ask what is or might be so precious to me ? Now, my best friend, are you sure that you have ever formed to yourself a true picture of me and my circumstances ; of a man who has spent seven long years in *incessant* torture, till his heart and head are alike darkened and blasted, and who sees no outlet from this state but in a total alteration of the purposes and exertions which brought it on. I must not and cannot continue this sort of life ; my patience with it is utterly gone. It were better for me on the soberest calculation to be dead than to continue it much longer. Even of my existing capabilities I can make no regular or proper use till it is altered. These capabilities, I have long seen with regret, are painted in your kind fancy under far too favourable colours. I am not without a certain consciousness of the gifts that are in me ; but I should mistake their nature *widely,* if I calculated they would ever guide me to wealth and preferment or even certainly to literary fame. As yet the best of them is very immature ; and even if they should come forth in full strength, it must be to other and higher ends that they are directed. How then ? Would I invite a generous spirit out of affluence and respectability to share with me obscurity and poverty ? Not so. In a few months I might be realising from literature and other kindred exertions the means of keeping *poverty* at a safe distance. The elements of real comfort, which in your vocabulary and mine, I think, has much the same meaning, might be at my disposal ; and farther than this I should think it injudicious to expect that external circumstances could materially assist me in the conduct of life. The rest must depend upon myself and the regulation of my own affections and habits.

Now this is what I would do were it in my power. I would ask a generous spirit, one whose happiness depended on seeing me happy, and whose temper and purposes were of kindred to my own—I would ask such a noble being to let us unite our resources—not her wealth and rank merely, for these were a small and unessential fraction of the prayer, but her judgment, her patience, prudence, her true affection, to mine ; and let us try if by neglecting what was not important, and striving with faithful and inseparable hearts after what was, we could not rise above the miserable obstructions that beset us both into regions of serene dignity, living as became us in the sight of God, and all reasonable men, happier than millions of our brethren, and each acknowledging with fervent gratitude that to the other he and she owed all. You are such a generous spirit. But your purposes and feelings are not such. Perhaps it is happier for you that they are not.

This, then, is an outline intended to be true of my unhappy fortunes and strange principles of action. Both, I fear, are equally repulsive to you, yet the former was meant for a faithful picture of what destiny has done to me, and the latter are positively the best arms which my resources offer me to war with her. I have thought of these things till my brain was like to crack. I do not pretend that my conclusions are indubitable, I am still open to better light. But this at present is the best I have. Do you also think of all this ? not in any spirit of anger, but in the spirit of love and noblemindedness which you have always shown me. If we must part, let us part in tenderness and go forth upon our several paths lost to the future, but in possession of the past.

T. CARLYLE.

The functions of a biographer are, like the functions of a Greek chorus, occasionally at the important moments to throw in some moral remarks which seem to fit the situation. The chorus after such a letter would remark, perhaps, on the subtle forms of self-deception to which the human heart is liable, on the momentous nature of marriage, and how men and women plunge heedlessly into the net, thinking only of the satisfaction of their own immediate wishes. . . . Self-sacrifice it might say was a noble thing. But a sacrifice which one person might properly make, the other might have no reasonable right to ask or to allow. It would conclude, however, that the issues of human acts are in the hands of the gods, and would hope for the best in fear and trembling. Carlyle spoke of self-denial. The self-denial which he was prepared to make was the devotion of his whole life to the pursuit and setting forth of spiritual truth ; throwing aside every meaner ambition. But apostles in St. Paul's opinion were better unwedded. The cause to which they give themselves leaves them little leisure to care for the things of their wives. To his mother Carlyle was so loving,

> That he might not beteem the winds of heaven
> Visit her face too roughly.

This was love indeed—love that is lost in its object, and thinks first and only how to guard and foster it. His wife he would expect to rise to his own level of disinterested self-surrender, and be content and happy in assisting him in the development of his own destiny. And this was selfishness—selfishness of a rare and elevated kind, but selfishness still; and it followed him throughout his married life. He awoke only to the consciousness of what he had been, when the knowledge could bring no more than unavailing remorse. He admired Miss Welsh; he loved her in a certain sense; but, like her, he was not *in love*. In a note-book written long after I find the following curious entry in her hand.

What the greatest philosopher of our day execrates loudest in Thackeray's new novel—finds indeed 'altogether false and damnable in it'—is that love is represented as spreading itself over our whole existence, and constituting the one grand interest of it; whereas love—*the thing people call love*—is confined to a very few years of man's life; to, in fact, a quite insignificant fraction of it, and even then is but one thing to be attended to among many infinitely more important things. Indeed, so far as he (Mr. C.) has seen into it, the whole concern of love is such a beggarly futility, that in an heroic age of the world nobody would be at the pains of think of it, much less to open his mouth upon it.

A person who had known by experience *the thing called love*, would scarcely have addressed such a vehemently unfavourable opinion of its nature to the woman who had been the object of his affection. He admired Miss Welsh. Her mind and temper suited him. He had allowed her image to intertwine itself with all his thoughts and emotions; but with love his feeling for her had nothing in common but the name. There is not a hint anywhere that he had contemplated as a remote possibility the usual consequence of a marriage— a family of children. He thought of a wife as a companion to himself who would make life easier and brighter to him. But this was all, and the images in which he dressed out the workings of his mind served only to hide their real character from himself.

Miss Welsh's explanation of the limits of her regard had made so little impression that she found it necessary to be still more candid.

You assure me (she replied in answer to this long letter) that you are not hurt or angry. Does this imply that there is some room for your being hurt or angry—that I have done or said what might have angered another less generous than you? I think so. Now room for disappointment there *may* be, but surely there is none for mortification or offence. I have refused my immediate assent to your wishes because our mutual happiness seemed to require that I should refuse it. But for the rest I have not slighted your wishes; on the contrary, I have expressed my willingness to fulfil them at the expense of everything but what I deem essential to our happiness; and, so far from undervaluing you, I have shown you, in declaring that I would marry no one else, not only that I esteem you above all the men I have ever seen, but

also that I am persuaded I should esteem you above all the
men I may ever see. What, then, have you to be hurt or
angry at ?

The maxims I proceed by (you tell me) are those of
common and acknowledged prudence ; and you *do not say* it
is unwise in me to walk by them exclusively. The maxims
I proceed by are the convictions of my own judgment ; and
being so it would be unwise in me not to proceed by them
whether they are right or wrong. Yet I am prudent, I fear,
only because I am not strongly tempted to be otherwise.
My heart is capable (I feel it is) of a love to which *no*
deprivation would be a sacrifice—a love which would over-
leap that reverence for opinion with which education and
weakness have begirt my sex, would bear down all the
restraints which *duty* and *expediency* might throw in the way,
and carry every thought of my being impetuously along with
it. But the all-perfect mortal who could inspire me with a
love so extravagant is nowhere to be found ; exists nowhere
but in the romance of my own imagination. Perhaps it is
better for me as it is. A passion like the torrent in the
violence of its course might perhaps too, like the torrent,
leave ruin and desolation behind. In the meantime I should
be mad to act as if from the influence of such a passion while
my affections are in a state of perfect tranquillity. I have
already explained to you the nature of my love for *you* ; that
it is deep and calm, more like the quiet river which refreshes
and beautifies where it flows, than the torrent which bears
down and destroys : yet it is materially different from what
one feels for a statue or a picture.

' Then why not attain wealth and rank ? ' you say ; and it
is you who have said it, not I. Wealth and rank, to be sure,
have different meanings, according to the views of different
people ; and what is bare sufficiency and respectability in the
vocabulary of a young lady may be called wealth and rank in

that of a philosopher. But it certainly was not wealth or rank according to *my* views which I required you to attain. I merely wish to see you earning a certain livelihood, and exercising the profession of a gentleman. For the rest, it is a matter of great indifference to me whether you have hundreds or thousands a year; whether you are a 'Mr.' or a 'Duke.' To me it seems that my wishes in this respect are far from unreasonable, even when your peculiar maxims and situation are taken into account.

Nor was it wholly with a view to improvement in your external circumstances that I have made their fulfilment a condition to our union, but also with a view to some improvement in my sentiments towards you which might be brought about in the meantime. In withholding this matter in my former letter I was guilty of a false and ill-timed reserve. My tenderness for your feelings betrayed me into an insincerity which is not natural to me. I thought that the most decided objection to your circumstances would pain you less than the least objection to yourself. While, in truth, it is in some measure grounded on *both*. I must be sincere, I find: at whatever cost.

As I have said, then, in requiring you to better your fortune, I had some view to an improvement in my sentiments. I am not sure that they are proper sentiments for a husband. They are proper for a brother, a father, a guardian spirit; but a husband, it seems to me, should be dearer still. At the same time, from the change which my sentiments towards you have already undergone during the period of our acquaintance, I have little doubt but that in time I shall be perfectly satisfied with them. One loves you, as Madame de Staël said, in proportion to the ideas and sentiments which are in oneself. According as my mind enlarges, and my heart improves, I become capable of comprehending the goodness and greatness which are in you, and my affection for you increases. Not many months ago I would have said it was *impossible* that I should ever be your wife. At present I consider this the most probable destiny for me, and in a year or two perhaps I shall consider it the only one. *Die Zeit ist noch nicht da!*

From what I have said it is plain (to me at least) what ought to be the line of our future conduct. Do *you* what you can to better your external circumstances ; always, however, subordinately to your own principles, which I do not ask you to give up ; which I should despise you for giving up whether I approved them or no—while I, on the other hand, do what I can, subordinately to nothing, to better *myself ;* which I am persuaded is the surest way of bringing my wishes to accord with yours ; and let us leave the rest to fate.

Miss Welsh had been perfectly open ; and had she ended there, Carlyle—if persons in such situations were ever as wise as they ought to be—would have seen from this frank expression of her feelings that a marriage with himself was not likely to be a happy one for her. He had already dimly perceived that the essential condition was absent. She did not love him as she felt that she could love. As little, however, could she make up her mind to give him up or consent that, as he had said, 'they should go forth their several ways.' She refused to believe that he could mean it. 'How could I,' she said, 'part from the only living soul that understands me ? I would marry you to-morrow rather ; our parting would need to be brought about by death or some dispensation of Providence. Were you to will it, to part would no longer be bitter. The bitterness would be in thinking you unworthy.'

The serious tone changed; the mockery at the Craigenputtock farm project came back, with the strong sense playing merrily beneath it.

Will you be done with this wild scheme of yours? I tell you it will not answer, and you must play Cincinnatus somewhere else. With all your tolerance of places you would not find at Craigenputtock the requisites you require. The light of heaven to be sure is not denied it; but for green grass! Beside a few cattle fields there is nothing except a waste prospect of heather and black peat moss. Prune and delve will you? In the first place there is nothing to prune : and for delving, I set too high a value on your life to let you engage in so perilous an enterprise. Were you to attempt such a thing there are twenty chances to one that you would be swallowed up in the moss, spade and all. In short, I presume, whatever may be your *farming* talents, you are not an accomplished cattle-drover, and nobody but a person of this sort could make the rent of the place out of it. Were *you* to engage in the concern, we should all be ruined together.

Part with Carlyle, however, she would not, unless he himself wished it.

I know not (she says in a following letter) how your spirit has gained such a mastery over mine, in spite of my pride and stubbornness. But so it is. Though self-willed as a mule with others, I am tractable and submissive towards you. I hearken to your voice as to the dictates of a second conscience hardly less awful to me than that which nature has implanted in my breast. How comes it then that you have this power over me ? for it is not the effect of your genius

and virtue merely.   Sometimes in my serious moods I believe
it is a charm with which my good angel has fortified my
heart against evil.

Thus matters drifted on to their consummation.
The stern and powerful sense of duty in these two
remarkable persons held them true through a long and
trying life together to the course of elevated action
which they had both set before themselves.   He never
swerved from the high aims to which he had resolved
to devote himself.   She, by never failing toil and
watchfulness, alone made it possible for him to accomplish the work which he achieved.   But we reap as
we have sown.   Those who seek for something more
than happiness in this world must not complain if
happiness is not their portion.   She had the companionship of an extraordinary man.   Her character was
braced by the contact with him, and through the
incessant self-denial which the determination that he
should do his very best inevitably exacted of her.   But
she was not happy.   Long years after, in the late
evening of her laborious life, she said, 'I married for
ambition.   Carlyle has exceeded all that my wildest
hopes ever imagined of him—and I am miserable.'

CHAPTER XVII.

A.D. 1825. ÆT. 29.

By the beginning of January the 'Life of Schiller' was finished. Carlyle lingered in London for a few weeks longer. The London publishers had their eye on him, and made him various offers for fresh translations from the German; for a life of Voltaire; for other literary biographies. For each or all of these they were ready to give him, as they said, fair terms. He postponed his decision till these terms could be agreed on. Meanwhile he was as usual moody and discontented; in a hurry to be gone from London, and its 'men of letters,' whom he liked less and less.

To John Carlyle.

London: January 22, 1825.

With regard to my own movements after the conclusion of this most small of literary labours, there is yet nothing fixed determinately. That I shall return to Scotland pretty soon is, I think, the only point entirely decided. Here is nothing adequate to induce my continuance. The people are stupid and noisy, and I live at the easy rate of five and forty shillings per week! I say the people are stupid not altogether unadvisedly. In point either of intellectual and moral culture they are some degrees below even the inhabitants of the 'modern Athens.' I have met no man of true head and heart among them. Coleridge is a mass of richest spices putrefied into a dunghill. I never hear him *tawlk* without feeling ready to worship him, and toss him in a blanket. Thomas Campbell is an Edinburgh '*small*,' made still smaller by growth in a foreign soil. Irving is enveloped with delusions and difficulties, wending somewhat down hill, to what depths I know not ; and scarcely ever to be seen without a host of the most stolid of all his Majesty's Christian people sitting round him. I wonder often that he does not buy himself a tar-barrel, and fairly light it under the Hatton Garden pulpit, and thus once for all *ex fumo* giving *lucem*, bid adieu to the gross train-oil concern altogether. The poor little ———. I often feel that were I as one of these people, sitting in a whole body by the cheek of my own wife, my feet upon my own hearth, I should feel distressed at seeing myself so *very* poor in spirit. Literary men ! The Devil in his own good time take all such literary men. One sterling fellow like Schiller, or even old Johnson, would take half a dozen such creatures by the nape of the neck, between his finger and thumb, and carry them forth to the nearest common sink. Save Allan Cunningham, an honest Nithsdale peasant, there is not one *man* among them. In short, it does not seem worth while to spend five and forty shillings weekly for the privilege of being near such pen-men.

To live in London and become enrolled in the un-illustrious fellowship, Carlyle felt to be once for all impossible. But what was to be the alternative? Miss Welsh had condemned the farming project; but the opinion at Mainhill was not so unfavourable. If a good farm could be found, his brother Alexander was ready to undertake to set it going. His mother or a sister would manage the house and dairy. To his father, who was experienced in such matters, that Tom should take to

them as he had done appeared neither wild nor un-
feasible. He might, indeed, go back to Edinburgh and
take pupils again. Mr. Buller was prepared to send
his son Arthur to him, and go on with the 200*l.* a-year.
One of the Stracheys might come, and there were hopes
of others; but Carlyle hated the drudgery of teaching,
and was longing for fresh air and freedom.

He had sent 'Schiller' to his mother.

The point next to be considered (he wrote to her) is what
shall be done with the author of this mighty work? He is
a deserving youth, with a clear conscience, but a bad bad
stomach. What shall be done with him? After much consideration, I had resolved in the first instance to *come home.*
Irving wants a week of talk with me before I go. By the
time that is done I shall have settled my affairs here, taken
leave of the good people, and be about ready to take flight.
I am not coming by sea, so take no thought of it. My last
voyage satisfied me with sailing; with regard to my sub-
sequent proceedings there must be some consideration, but
not an hour of loitering. I have set out before my mind
distinctly what I *want*: and this, as Goethe says, is half the
game. I *will recover my health*, though all the books in the
universe should go to smoke in the process. I will be a
whole man; no longer a piping, pining wretch, though I
should knap stones by the wayside for a living. I had some
thoughts of setting up house at Edinburgh, and taking two
or three pupils whose education I might superintend at
college. But I already perceive this project will not suit my
chief purpose; I recur to the old plan of farming and living
in the country. This I really think might be made to do.
What might hinder Alick and me to take a farm and move
to it with you and some other of the younkers, furnishing up

an apartment in the house for my writing operations, and going on in our several vocations with all imaginable energy ? You must take counsel with the whole senate on this matter. I *must* have a house of my own (a bit haddin o' my ain ——), where I can enjoy quiet and free air, and have liberty to do as I list ; and I see no scheme so likely in the actual state of matters as this.   Tell Alick to look about him on all sides for such a thing ; a farm with a comfortable house to live in, and at a rent which we can front.   I shall have 200*l.* in my pocket when I return, notwithstanding the horrible expensiveness of this place ; and that, with what we have already, ought to put us on some sort of footing.   Were we once begun I could write at a moderate rate without injuring myself, and make a handsome enough thing of it within the year.   And for my health, with riding, gardening, and so forth, it would to a certainty improve.   Could I live without taking drugs for three months, I should even now be perfectly well.   But drenching oneself with castor oil and other abominations, how can one be otherwise than weak and feckless ?   I must and will come out of this despicable state ; nor on the whole have I any great doubts about succeeding. Often of late I have even begun to look upon my long dismal seven years of pain as a sort of blessing in disguise.   It has kept me clear of many temptations to degrade myself ; and really when I look back on my former state of mind, I scarcely see how, except by sickness or some most grinding calamity, I could have been delivered out of it into the state proper for a man in this world.   Truly, as you say, the ways of that Being who guides our destiny are wonderful, and past finding out.   Let us trust that for all of us this will prove the best.

The start of Schiller in the trade was less favourable than had been looked for and the offers from the booksellers for future work, when they came to be specified, were not satisfactory. Carlyle in consequence formed an ill opinion of these poor gentlemen.

The booksellers of the universe (he said) are bipeds of an erect form and speak articulately ; therefore they deserve the name of men, and from me at least shall always get it. But for the rest, their thoughts are redolent of 'solid pudding.' They are as the pack-horses of literature ; which the author should direct with a halter and a goad, and remunerate with clover and split beans. Woe to him if the process is reversed ; if he, with a noose about his neck, is tied to their unsightly tail, and made to plash and sprawl along with them through every *stank* to which their love of provant leads them. Better it were to be a downright hairy cuddy, and crop thistles and gorse on any of the commons of this isle.

He was more successful in making an arrangement with the publishers of 'Wilhelm Meister' for further translations. It was arranged that he should furnish them with selections from Goethe, Tieck, Hoffmann, Jean Paul, and several others, enough to form the considerable book, which appeared in the following year, as specimens of German romance. With this work definitely in prospect, which he felt that he could execute with ease as a mechanical task, Carlyle left London at the beginning of March, and left it with dry eyes. He regretted nothing in it but Irving ; and Irving having taken now to interpretation of prophecy, and falling daily into yet wilder speculations, was almost lost to him. Their roads had long been divergent—Irving straying into the land of dreams, Carlyle into the hard region of unattractive truth, which as yet presented itself to him in its sternest form. The distance was becoming too wide for intimacy, although their affection for each other, fed on recollections of what had been, never failed either of them. Carlyle went down to Scotland, staying a day or two at Birmingham, and another at Manchester to see an old schoolfellow. When the coach brought him to Ecclefechan he found waiting for him his little sister Jane, the poetess, who had been daily watching for his arrival. 'Her bonny little blush,' he wrote long after, 'and radiancy of look when I let down the window and suddenly disclosed myself, are still present to me.'

His relation with his family was always beautiful. They had been busy for him in his absence, and had already secured what he was longing after. Two miles from Mainhill, on the brow of a hill, on the right as you look towards the Solway, stands an old ruined building with uncertain traditions attached to it, called the Tower of Repentance. Some singular story lies hidden in the name, but authentic record there is none. The Tower only remains visible far away from the high slopes which rise above Ecclefechan. Below the Tower is the farm-house of Hoddam Hill, with a few acres of tolerable land attached to it. The proprietor, General Sharpe, was the landlord of whom the Carlyles held Mainhill. It had been occupied by General Sharpe's factor; but the factor wishing to leave, they had taken it at the moderate rent of 100*l.* a year for 'Tom,' and Alick was already busy putting in the crops, and the mother and sisters preparing the house to receive him. They would have made a home

for him among themselves, and all from eldest to
youngest would have done everything that affection
could prompt to make him happy. But the narrow
space, the early hours, the noises inseparable from the
active work of a busy household, above all, the necessity of accommodating himself to the habits of a large
family, were among the evils which he reckoned that
he must avoid. He required a home of his own where
he could be master of everything about him, and sit or
move, sleep or rise, eat or fast, as he pleased, with no
established order of things to interfere with him.
Thus Hoddam Hill was taken for him, and there he
prepared to settle himself.

This morning (he wrote to Miss Welsh from Mainhill on
March 23) they woke me with a tumult of loading carts
with apparatus for Hoddam, a farm of which I, or brother
Alick for me, am actually tenant. Think of this and reverence my *savoir faire*. I have been to see the place, and I
like it well so far as I am interested in it. There is a good
house where I may establish myself in comfortable quarters.
The views from it are superb. There are hard smooth roads
to gallop on towards any point of the compass, and ample
space to dig and prune under the pure canopy of a wholesome
sky. The ancient Tower of Repentance stands on a corner
of the farm, a fit memorial for reflecting sinners. My mother
and two little sisters go with us at Whitsunday—we expect
them to manage well. Here, then, will I establish my home
till I have conquered the fiend that harasses me, and afterwards my place of retreat till some more suitable one shall
come within my reach.

Miss Welsh had promised that as soon as he was

settled she would pay him and his mother a visit at Hoddam, that she might become acquainted with her future relations, and see with her eyes the kind of home which he was inviting her to share with him. His own imagination had made it into fairyland.

I will show you (he wrote) Kirkconnell churchyard and Fair Helen's grave. I will take you to the top of Burnswark and wander with you up and down the woods and lanes and moors. Earth, sea, and air are open to us here as well as anywhere. The water of Milk [1] was flowing through its simple valley as early as the brook Siloa, and poor Repentance Hill is as old as Caucasus itself. There is a majesty and mystery in nature, take her as you will. The essence of all poetry comes breathing to a mind that feels from every province of her empire. Is she not immovable, eternal and immense in Annandale as she is in Chamouni ? The chambers of the East are opened in every land, and the sun comes forth to sow the earth with orient pearl. Night, the ancient mother, follows him with her diadem of stars ; and Arcturus and Orion call *me* into the Infinitudes of space as they called the Druid priest or the shepherd of Chaldea. Bright creatures ! how they gleam like spirits through the shadows of innumerable ages from their thrones in the boundless depths of heaven.

> Who ever gazed upon them shining,
> And turned to earth without repining,
> Nor wished for wings to fly away
> To mix with their ethereal ray.

The calm grace and even loveliness of this passage goes further than all his arguments to justify Carlyle's

[1] One of the small tributaries of the Annan.

longing for a country home among his own people. It was already telling on the inmost fibres of his nature, and soothing into sleep the unquiet spirits that tormented him.

I avoid as far as possible quoting passages from the 'Reminiscences,' preferring the contemporary record of his letters which were written at the time ; and because what is already there related does not need repeating. But in this year, when he was living among his own people, the letters are wanting, and one brief extract summing up the effects and experiences of the life at Hoddam may here be permitted.

Hoddam Hill was a neat compact little farm, rent 100*l*., which my father had leased for me, on which was a prettyish little cottage for dwelling house ; and from the window such a view (fifty miles in radius from beyond Tyndale to beyond St. Bees, Solway Firth and all the fells to Ingleborough inclusive) as Britain or the world could hardly have matched. Here the ploughing, &c., was already in progress which I often rode across to see. Here I established myself,[1] set up my books and bits of implements, and took to doing German romance as my daily work—ten pages daily my stint, which I faithfully accomplish, barring some rare accidents. Brother Alick was my practical farmer ; my ever kind and beloved mother with one of the little girls was generally there. Brother John too, oftenest, who had just taken his degree— these with a little man and ditto maid were our establishment. . . . This year has a rustic dignity and beauty to me, and lies now like a not ignoble russet-coated idyll in my memory ; one of the quietest on the whole, and, perhaps,

[1] May 26, 1825.

the most triumphantly important of my life. I lived very silent, diligent, had long solitary rides on my wild Irish horse Larry, good for the dietetic part. My meditatings, musings, and reflections were continual ; my thoughts went wandering or travelling through eternity, through time and space so far as poor I had scanned or known, and were now to my infinite solacement coming back with tidings to me. This year I found that I had conquered all my scepticisms, agonising doubtings, fearful wrestlings with the foul, vile and soul-murdering mud-gods of my epoch ; had escaped as from a worse than Tartarus, with all its Phlegethons and Stygian quagmires, and was emerging free in spirit into the eternal blue of ether, where, blessed be Heaven, I have, for the spiritual part, ever since lived, looking down upon the welterings of my poor fellow creatures in such multitudes and millions still stuck in that fatal element, and have had no concern whatever in their Puseyisms, ritualisms, metaphysical controversies and cobwebberies, and no feeling of my own except honest silent pity for the serious or religious part of them, and occasional indignation for the poor world's sake at the frivolous, secular, and impious part with their universal suffrages, their nigger emancipations, sluggard and scoundrel protection societies, and unexampled prosperities for the time being. What my pious joy and gratitude then was, let the pious soul figure. In a fine and veritable sense, I, poor, obscure, without outlook, almost without worldly hope had become independent of the world. What was death itself from the world to what I come through ? I understood well what the old Christian people meant by conversion —by God's infinite mercy to them. I had in effect gained an immense victory, and for a number of years, in spite of nerves and chagrins, had a constant inward happiness that was quite royal and supreme, in which all temporal evil was transient and insignificant, and which essentially remains with me still, though far oftener eclipsed, and lying deeper down than then. Once more, thank Heaven for its highest gift. I then felt, and still feel, endlessly indebted to Goethe in the business. He in his fashion, I perceived, had travelled the steep rocky road before me—the first of the moderns. Bodily health itself seemed improving. Bodily health was all I had really lost in the grand spiritual battle now gained; and that too I may have hoped would gradually return altogether—which it never did, and was far enough from doing. Meanwhile my thoughts were very peaceable, full of pity and humanity as they had never been before. Nowhere can I recollect of myself such pious musings, communings silent and spontaneous with fact and nature, as in those poor Annandale localities. The sound of the kirk-bell once or twice on Sunday mornings (from Hoddam kirk, about a mile on the plains below me) was strangely touching, like the departing voice of eighteen hundred years.[1]

The industry which Carlyle describes did not show itself immediately on his settlement at Hoddam. The excitement of the winter months had left him exhausted; and for the first few weeks at least he was recovering himself in an idleness which showed itself in the improvement of his humour. In *June* he wrote to Miss Welsh:—

I am gradually and steadily gathering health, and for my occupations they amount to zero. It is many a weary year since I have been so idle or so happy. I read Richter and Jacobi; I ride and hoe cabbages, and, like Basil Montagu, am 'a lover of all quiet things.' Sometimes something in the shape of conscience says to me, 'You will please to

---

[1] *Reminiscences*, vol. i. p. 286 *et seq.*

observe, Mr. Tummas, that time is flying fast away, and you
are poor and ignorant and unknown, and verging towards
nine and twenty.[1]   What is to become of you in the long
run, Mr. Tummas?   Are you not partly of opinion that
you are an ass?   The world is running past you.   You are
out of the battle altogether, my pretty sir : no promotion,
knowledge, money, glory !'   To which I answer, 'And what
the devil is the matter?   What have knowledge, money,
glory, done for me hitherto?   Time, you say, is flying.   Let
it fly ; twice as fast if it likes.'   I hope this humour will not
be my final one.   It is rather a holy time—a *pax Dei*, which
exhausted nature has conquered for herself from all the fiends
that assaulted and beset her.   As strength returns, the
battle will again commence ; yet never I trust with such
fateful eagerness as of old.   I see the arena of my life lying
round me desolate and quiet as the ashes of Mount Ætna.
Flowers and verdure will again spring over its surface.   But
I know that fire is still beneath it, and that it, or I, have no
foundation or endurance.   Oh human life !   Oh soul of
man !   But my paper is concluded.

Carlyle could not long be idle.   The weariness
passed off.   He took up his translating work, and went
on with it as he has related.   An accident meanwhile
precipitated the relations between himself and Miss
Welsh, which had seemed likely to be long protracted,
and, after threatening to separate them for ever, threw
them more completely one upon the other.

When Irving first settled in London he had opened
the secrets of his heart to a certain lady with whom he
was very intimately acquainted.   He had told her of

---

[1] Thirty—he was born December 4, 1795.

his love for his old pupil, and she had drawn from him that the love had been returned. She had seen Irving sacrifice himself to duty, and she had heard that his resolution had been sustained by the person to whom the surrender of their mutual hopes had been as bitter as to himself. The lady was romantic, and had become profoundly interested. Flowing over with sympathy, she had herself commenced a correspondence with Haddington. To Carlyle she wrote occasionally, because she really admired him. To Miss Welsh she introduced herself as one who was eager for her confidence, who was prepared to love her for the many excellences which she knew her to possess, and to administer balm to the wounds of her heart.

Miss Welsh did not respond very cordially to this effusive invitation. It was not her habit to seek for sympathy from strangers; but she replied in a letter which her new friend found extremely beautiful, and which stirred her interest still deeper. The lady imagined that her young correspondent was still pining in secret for her lost lover, and she was tempted to approach closer to the subject which had aroused her sympathies. She thought it would be well slightly to disparage Irving. She painted him as a person whose inconstancy did not deserve a prolonged and hopeless affection. She too had sought to find in him the dearest of friends; but he had other interests and other ambitions, and any woman who concentrated her heart upon him would be disappointed in the return which she might meet with.

The lady's motive was admirable. She thought that she could assist in reconciling Miss Welsh to her dis-

appointment. In perfect innocence she wrote confidentially to Carlyle on the same subject. She
regarded him simply as the intimate friend both of
Miss Welsh and Irving. She assumed that he was
acquainted with their secret history. She spoke of the
affection which had existed between them as still
unextinguished on either side. For the sake of both
of them she wished that something might be done to
put an end to idle regrets and vain imaginings.
Nothing she thought could contribute more to dis-
enchant Miss Welsh than a visit to herself in London,
where she could see Irving as he was in his present
surroundings.[1]

Miss Welsh had for two years never mentioned
Irving to Carlyle except bitterly and contemptuously;
so bitterly indeed that he had often been obliged to
remonstrate. Had he been less singleminded, a tone
so marked and acid might have roused his suspicions.
But that Irving and she had been more than friends,
if he had ever heard a hint of it, had passed out of
his mind. Even the lady's letter failed to startle him.
He mentioned merely, when he next wrote to her, that
the writer laboured under some strange delusion about
her secret history, and had told him in a letter full of
eloquence that her heart was with Irving in London.

Miss Welsh felt that she must at least satisfy her
ecstatic acquaintance that she was not pining for

---

[1] No part of this language is the lady's own. The substance of her
letters was repeated in the correspondence which followed between
Carlyle and Miss Welsh. I have alluded to the subject only because
Mrs. Carlyle said afterwards that but for the unconscious action of a
comparative stranger her engagement with Carlyle would probably
never have been carried out.

another woman's husband. She was even more explicit.
She had made up her mind to marry Carlyle. She told
her intrusive correspondent so in plain words, desiring
her only to keep her secret. The lady was thunder-
struck. In ordinary life she was high-flown, and by
those who did not know her might have been thought
affected and unreal; but on occasions really serious she
could feel and write like a wise woman. She knew
that Miss Welsh could not love Carlyle. The motive
could only be a generous hope of making life dearer,
and want of health more endurable, to an honest and
excellent man, while she might be seeking blindly to
fill a void which was aching in her own heart. She
required Miss Welsh, she most solemnly adjured her,
to examine herself, and not allow one who had known
much disappointment and many sorrows to discover by
a comparison of his own feelings with hers that she had
come to him with half a heart, and had mistaken
compassion and the self-satisfaction of a generous act
for a sentiment which could alone sustain her in a
struggle through life. Supposing accident should set
Irving free, supposing his love to have been indestructible and to have been surrendered only in
obedience to duty, and supposing him, not knowing of
this new engagement, to come back and claim the
heart from which an adverse fate had separated him,
what in such a case would her feeling be? If she
could honestly say that she would still prefer Carlyle,
then let her marry him, and the sooner the better. If,
on the other hand, she was obliged to confess to herself
that she could still find happiness where she had hoped
to find it, Irving might still be lost to her: but in such

a condition of mind she had no right to marry anyone else.

With characteristic integrity Miss Welsh, on receiving this letter, instantly enclosed it to Carlyle. She had been under no obligation, at least until their marriage had been definitively determined on, to inform him of the extent of her attachment to Irving. But sincere as she was to a fault in the ordinary occasions of life, she had in this matter not only kept back the truth, but had purposely misled Carlyle as to the nature of her feelings. She felt that she must make a full confession. She had deceived him—wilfully deceived him. She had even told him that she had never cared for Irving. 'It was false,' she said. She had loved him—once passionately loved him. For this she might be forgiven. 'If she had shown weakness in loving a man whom she knew to be engaged to another, she had made amends in persuading him to marry the other, and save his honour from reproach.' But she had disguised her real feelings, and for this she had no excuse. She who had felt herself Carlyle's superior in their late controversy, and had been able to rebuke him for selfishness, felt herself degraded and humbled in his eyes. If he chose to cast her off, she said that she could not say he was unjust; but her pride was broken; and very naturally, very touchingly, she added that he had never been so dear to her as at that moment when she was in danger of losing his affection and, what was still more precious to her, his respect.

If Carlyle had been made of common stuff, so unexpected a revelation might have tried his vanity. The actual effect was to awaken in him a sense of his own unworthiness. He perceived that Miss Welsh was probably accepting him only out of the motives which her London correspondent suggested. His infirmities, mental and bodily, might make him an unfit companion for her or indeed for any woman. It would be better for her once for all to give him up. He knew, he said, that he could never make her happy. They might suffer at parting, but they would have obeyed their reason, and time would deaden the pain. No affection was unalterable or eternal. Men themselves, with all their passions, sank to dust and were consumed. He must imitate her sincerity. He said (and he spoke with perfect truth) that there was a strange dark humour in him over which he had no control. If she thought they were 'blue devils, weak querulous wailings of a mind distempered,' she would only show that she did not understand him. In a country town she had seen nothing of life, and had grasped at the shadows that passed by her. First, the rude, smoky fire of Edward Irving seemed to her a star from heaven; next, the quivering *ignis fatuus* of the soul that dwelt in himself. The world had a thousand noble hearts that she did not dream of. What was he, and what was his father's house, that she should sacrifice herself for him?

It was not in nature—it was not at least in Miss Welsh's nature—that at such a time and under such circumstances she should reconsider her resolution. She was staying with her grandfather at Templand when these letters were interchanged. She determined to use the opportunity to pay the Carlyles her promised visit, see him in his own home and his own circle, and there face to face explain all the past and form some scheme for the immediate future.   Like the lady in London, she felt that if the marriage was to be, or rather since the marriage was to be, the sooner it was over now the better for everyone.   Carlyle was to have met her on the road, and was waiting with horses; but there had been a mistake.   She was dropped by the coach the next morning at Kelhead Kilns, from which she sent him a little characteristic note.

To Thomas Carlyle.

Kelhead Kilns : Friday, September 3, 1825.

Good morning, Sir.   I am not at all to blame for your disappointment last night.   The fault was partly your own, and still more the landlady's of the Commercial Inn, as I shall presently demonstrate to you *virâ voce.*   In the meantime I have billeted myself in a snug little house by the wayside, where I purpose remaining with all imaginable patience till you can make it convenient to come and fetch me, being afraid to proceed directly to Hoddam Hill in case so sudden an apparition should throw the whole family into hysterics.   If the pony has any prior engagement, never mind.   I can make a shift to walk two miles in pleasant company.   Any way, pray make all possible despatch, in case the owner of these premises should think I intend to make a regular settlement in them.

Yours,

JANE.

The great secret, which had been known from the first to Mrs. Carlyle and suspected by the rest, was now the open property of the family; and all, old and young, with mixed feelings of delight and anxiety, were looking forward to the appearance of the lady who was soon to belong to them.

She stayed with us above a week (Carlyle writes), happy, as was very evident, and making happy. Her demeanour among us I could define as unsurpassable, spontaneously perfect. From the first moment all embarrassment, even my mother's, as tremulous and anxious as she naturally was, fled away without return. Everybody felt the all-pervading simple grace, the perfect truth and perfect trustfulness of that beautiful, cheerful, intelligent, and sprightly creature, and everybody was put at his ease. The questionable visit was a clear success. She and I went riding about, the weather dry and grey, nothing ever going wrong with us ; my guidance taken as beyond criticism ; she ready for any pace, rapid or slow, melodious talk never wanting. Of course she went to Mainhill, and made complete acquaintance with my father (whom she much esteemed and even admired, now and henceforth—a *reciprocal* feeling, strange enough), and with my two elder sisters, Margaret and Mary, who now officially kept house with my father there. On the whole, she came to know us all, saw face to face us and the rugged peasant element and way of life we had ; and was *not* afraid of it, but recognised, like her noble self, what of intrinsic worth it might have, what of real human dignity. She charmed all hearts, and was herself visibly glad and happy, right loath to end these halcyon days, eight or perhaps nine the utmost appointed sum of them.

Two little anecdotes she used to tell of this visit, showing that under peasants' dresses there was in the Carlyles the essential sense of delicate high breeding.

She was to use the girls' room at Mainhill while there; and it was rude enough in its equipments as they lived in it. Margaret Carlyle, doing her little best, had spread on the deal table for a cover a precious new shawl which some friend had given her. More remarkable was her reception by the father. When she appeared he was in his rough dress, called in from his farm work on the occasion. The rest of the family kissed her. The old man to her surprise drew back, and soon left the room. In a few minutes he came back again, fresh shaved and washed, and in his Sunday clothes. Now, he said, if Miss Welsh allows it, I am in a condition to kiss her too. When she left Hoddam, Carlyle attended her back to Dumfries.

As I rode with her (he says) she did not attempt to conceal her sorrow, and indeed our prospect ahead was cloudy enough. I could only say 'Espérons, espérons.' To her the Haddington element had grown dreary and unfruitful; no geniality of life possible there, and I doubt not many paltry frets and contradictions. We left our horses at the Commercial Inn; I walked with her, not in gay mood either, to her grandmother's threshold, and there had to say farewell. In my whole life I can recollect no week so like a sabbath as that had been to me—clear, peaceful, mournfully beautiful, and as if sacred.

A few days after she was gone Carlyle wrote the following entry in his most intermittent journal:—

Hoddam Hill, September 21, 1825.—A *hiatus valde deflendus.* Since the last line was written, what a wandering to and fro! how many sad vicissitudes of despicable

suffering and inaction have I undergone! This little book
and the desk that carries it have passed a summer and
winter in London since I last opened it ; and I, their foolish
owner, have roamed about the brick-built Babylon, the sooty
Brummagem, and Paris, the Vanity Vair of our modern
world. My mood of mind is changed. Is it improved?
Weiss nicht. This stagnation is not peace ; or is it the
peace of Galgacus's Romans : 'Ubi solitudinem faciunt,
pacem appellant.' How difficult it is to free one's mind
from cant ! How very seldom are the principles we act on
clear to our own reason ! Of the great nostrums, 'forgetfulness of self' and 'humbling of vanity,' it were better
therefore to say nothing. In my speech concerning them I
overcharge the impression they have made on me, for my
conscience, like my sense of pain and pleasure, has grown
dull, and *I secretly desire to compensate for laxity of feeling by intenseness of describing.* How much of these great
nostrums is the product of necessity ? Am I like a sorry
hack, content to feed on heather while rich clover seems to
lie around it at a little distance, because in struggling to
break the tether it has almost hanged itself ? Oh that I
could go out of the body to philosophise ! that I could ever
feel as of old the glory and magnificence of things, till my
own little *Me* (*mein kleines Ich*) was swallowed up and lost
in them. (Partly cant !) But I cannot, I cannot. Shall I
ever more ? *Gott weiss.* At present I am but an *abgerissenes
Glied*, a limb torn off from the family of man, excluded from
acting, with pain for my companion, and hope, that comes to
all, rarely visiting me, and, what is stranger, rarely desired
with vehemence. Unhappy man, in whom the body has
gained the mastery over the soul ! Inverse sensualist, not
drawn into the rank of beasts by pleasure, but driven into it
by pain ! Hush ! hush ! Perhaps this *is* the truce which
weary nature has conquered for herself to re-collect her scat-

tered strength. Perhaps, like an eagle (or a goose) she will 'renew her mighty youth' and fly against the sun; or at least fish haddocks with equanimity, like other birds of similar feather, and no more lie among the pots, winged, maimed, and plucked, doing nothing but chirp like a chicken in the croup for the livelong day. 'Jook and let the jaw gae by,' my pretty sir. When this solitude becomes intolerable to you it will be time enough to quit it for the dreary blank which society and the bitterest activity have hitherto afforded you. You deserve considerable pity, Mr. C., and likewise considerable contempt. Heaven be your comforter, my worthy sir! You are in a promising condition at this present: sinking to the bottom, yet laid down to sleep; destruction brandishing his sword above you, and you quietly desiring him to take your life but spare your rest. *Gott hilf Ihnen!* Now for Tieck and his Runenberg. But first one whiff of generous narcotic. 'How gladly we love to wander on the plain with the summit in our eye!' *Ach Du meine Einzige die Du mich liebst und Dich an mich anschmiegst, warum bin ich Dir wie ein gebrochenes Rohr! Sollst Du niemals glücklich werden? Wo bist Du heute Nacht? Mögen Friede und Liebe und Hoffnung deine Gefährten seyn! Leb' wohl.*

MISS WELSH had now seen with her own eyes the
realities of life in a small Scotch farm, and was no
longer afraid of it. She doubtless distrusted as much
as ever Carlyle's fitness in his own person for agricul-
tural enterprises. But if his brother would take the
work off his hands he could himself follow his own more
proper occupations. She had recognised the sterling
worth of his peasant family, and for her own part she
was willing to share their method of existence, sharply
contrasted as it was with the elegance and relative
luxury of her home at Haddington. It was far otherwise with her mother. Mrs. Welsh's romantic days
were not over. They were never over to the end of her
life; but she had no romance about Carlyle. She knew
better than her daughter how great the sacrifice would
be, and the experience of fifty years had taught her
that resolutions adopted in enthusiasm are often repented of when excitement has been succeeded by the
wearing duties of hard every-day routine. She was a
cultivated, proud, beautiful woman, who had ruled as
queen in the society of a Scotch provincial town. Many
suitors had presented themselves for her daughter's
hand, unexceptionable in person, in fortune, in social

standing. Miss Welsh's personal attractions, her talents,
the fair if moderate fortune which, though for the present
she had surrendered it, must be eventually her own,
would have entitled her to choose among the most
eligible matches in East Lothian. It was natural, it
was inevitable, independent of selfish considerations,
that a mother could not look without a shudder on this
purposed marriage with the son of a poor Dumfriesshire
farmer, who had no visible prospects and no profession,
and whose abilities, however great they might be,
seemed only to unfit him for any usual or profitable
pursuit. Added to this, Carlyle himself had not attracted
her. She was accustomed to rule, and Carlyle would
not be ruled. She had obstinate humours, and Carlyle,
who never checked his own irritabilities, was impatient
and sarcastic when others ventured to be unreasonable.
She had observed and justly dreaded the violence of his
temper, which when he was provoked or thwarted would
boil like a geyser. He might repent afterwards of these
ebullitions; he usually did repent. But repentance
could not take away the sting of the passionate expressions, which fastened in the memory by the metaphors with which they were barbed, especially as there
was no amendment, and the offence was repeated on
the next temptation. It will easily be conceived,
therefore, that the meeting between mother and
daughter after the Hoddam visit, and Miss Welsh's announcement of her final resolution, was extremely
painful. Miss Welsh wrote to Carlyle an account of
what had passed. His letter in reply bears the same
emblem of the burning candle, with the motto, '*Terar
dum prosim*,' which he had before sketched in his

journal. He was fond of a design which represented human life to him under its sternest aspect.[1]

To Miss Welsh.

Holdam Hill: November 4, 1825.

. . . Let us be patient and resolute, and trust in ourselves and each other. I maintain that the weal of every human being, not perhaps his enjoyment or his suffering, but his true and highest welfare, lies within himself. Oh that we had wisdom to put this weighty truth in practice : to know our duty—for a duty every living creature has—and to do it with our whole heart and our whole soul. This is the everlasting rock of man's security against which no tempest or flood shall prevail. 'Sufficiently provided for within,' the outward gifts or amercements of fortune are but the soft or the hard materials out of which he is to build his fairest work of art, a life worthy of himself and the vocation wherewith he is called. But I am verging towards cant, so I shall hasten to the right about.

Your mother is not wise or just in spoiling the stinted enjoyments of your present way of life by the reflections and remonstrances with which she pursues you. Her views of me and my connection with you I cannot justly blame : they coincide too nearly with my own. But what, one might ask her, does she mean you to *do?* Anything ? If so, it were better that she simply proposed it, and backed it out by all attainable reasons in simplicity and quiet, that if just and fit you might go through with it at all haps and hazards instantly and completely. If, nothing, then silence is the least that can be asked of her. Speech that leads not to action, still more that hinders it, is a nuisance on the earth. Let *us* remember this, as well as call on others to remember it. But,

[1] See p. 202.

after all, where is the mighty grief ? *Is* it ruin for you to think of giving yourself to me, here as I am, in the naked undissembled meanness of my actual state ? Consider this with a cold clear eye, not in the purple light of love, but in the sharp chill light of prudence. If your mind still have any wavering, follow the truth fearlessly, not heeding me, for I am ready with alacrity to forward your anticipated happiness in any way. Or was this your love of me no girlish whim, but the calm, deliberate, self-offering of a woman to the man whom her reason and her heart had made choice of ? Then is it a crime in you to love me, whose you are in the sight of God and man ?

The story of my temper is not worth much. I actually do not think myself an ill-natured man, nor even, all things considered, very ill-tempered ! Really it is wearisome to think of these things. What counsel to give you I know not. Submission has its limits. When not based on conviction it degenerates into hypocrisy, and encourages demands which perhaps ought to be resisted. But in asserting your rights be meek and reasonable. What is this caprice and sullenness in your mother but unhappiness in herself—an effort to increase her own scanty stock of satisfaction at your expense ; or rather to shift a portion of her own suffering upon you ? She *cannot* cease to love you, and this is saying much. For me I beg you to take no thought. Her anger at me, her aversion to me, shall never be remembered against her. She thinks of me in the main, to the full as highly as she ought ; and these gusts of unreasonable caprice should be met by increased equability, and steady forgiving self-possession, as angry gusts of wind are rendered harmless not by other conflicting gusts, but by a solid wall of stone and mortar.

While on the Haddington side the contemplated

alliance was so distasteful, two letters from Miss Welsh, one to Carlyle's mother, the other to his little sister Jane, show how playfully and prettily she had thrown herself into the ways of the Mainhill household, and adopted their expressions. With Jane she had assumed the privilege of an elder sister, and charged herself with the direction of her education. Carlyle has written a short preface to each.

To Mrs. Carlyle, Hoddam Hill.

[There are snatches of *coterie* speech in this letter, two quite of new date, brought from Hoddam Hill, which I must explain.

'Broad Atlantic of his countenance' was a phrase I had noticed in some stupidly adoring 'Life of Fox,' and been in use to apply to my brother John, whose face also was broad enough (and full of honesty and good humour, poor fellow!). From him also comes the other phrase, 'mixture of good and evil.' He was wont in his babbly way, while at breakfast with mother and me, to remark when the least thing was complained of or went wrong, 'Nothing but evil in the world, mother!' till one day mother took him sharply up on theological grounds. Ever onward from which he used to make it 'Nothing but a mixture of good and evil.' He had many mock utterances of this kind. 'Comes all to the same ultimately,' 'What d'ye think of life this morning?' &c., over which we had our laughing and counter-laughing, borne with perfect gravity always, and perfect patience, but producing no abatement of the practice. One morning, however, he did get a retort, which rather stuck to him. Addressing his mother with 'What d'ye think of life, mother?' 'What does t'ou (thou) think o' death tho'?'

answered she with a veritably serious and crypto-contemptu-
ous tone, which was not forgotten again.

'Christian *comfoart*' comes from a certain Mrs. Carruthers
of Haregills, a cousin of my mother; Bell by maiden name,
solid, rather stupid, farmer's wife by station. Meeting once
with Frank Dickson (a speculative Tartar he, unluckily for
her), she had been heard to wind up some lofty lilt with,
'Sir, it is the great *soorce* of Christian *comfoart*,' accent on
the last syllable and sound *oa*, Annandale only.—T.C.]

George Square, Edinburgh: November 14.

My dear Mrs. Carlyle,—In the busy idleness of my
present situation I have little leisure to write or to do any
rational thing; but it is best I should fulfil my promise to
you *now* rather than wait for a more quiet season, that you
may know that even the turmoil of a great city cannot seduce
me into forgetfulness of the Hill. Indeed, the more I am in
the way of what is commonly called pleasure, the more I
think of the calm days which I spent under your roof. I
have never been so happy since; though I have been at
several fine entertainments, where much thought and pains
and money were expended to assemble the ingredients of
enjoyment; and this is no wise strange, since affection is the
native element of my soul, and *that* I found in your cottage
warm and pure, while in more splendid habitations it is
chilled with vanity, affectation, and selfishness. For 'there
is nothing but a mixture of good and evil in the world,
mother;' and thus some have 'the dinner of herbs where love
is,' others 'the stalled ox and hatred therewith.'

I left Templand on Thursday last after many delays, but
in no such downcast mood as at my departure from the Hill.
Indeed, I was never in my life more pleased to turn my face
homewards, where, if I have not suitable society any more than
in Nithsdale, I can at least enjoy what is next best, solitude.

But all my impatience to see Haddington failed to make the journey hither agreeable, which was as devoid of 'Christian comfoart' as anything you can suppose. Never was poor damsel reduced to such 'extremities of fate.' I was sick, woefully sick, and notwithstanding that I had on four petticoats, benumbed with cold. To make my wretchedness as complete as possible, we did not reach Edinburgh till many hours after dark. Sixteen miles more, and my wanderings for this season are at an end. Would that my trials were ended also! But no! Tell Mr. Carlyle my handsome cousin is coming to Haddington with his sister Phoebe, and his valet Henley, and his great dog Toby, over and above Dash, Craigen, Fanny, and Frisk. My heart misgives me at the prospect of this inundation of company, for their ways are not my ways, and what is amusement to them is death to me. But I must just be patient as usual. Verily I should need to be Job, instead of Jane Welsh, to bear these everlasting annoyances with any degree of composure.

Mr. Carlyle must write next week without fail to Haddington, lest in vexation of spirit I curse God and die. Moreover, he must positively part with Larry, and get a horse of less *genius* in his stead, if he would not have me live in continual terror of his life.[1] If the fates are kind, and the good doctor[2] a man of his word, he will be in this city to-morrow, so that I have some hope to feast my eyes on 'the broad

---

[1] Larry had run away with Carlyle, thrown him, and dragged him some yards along the road. He rode up to a late period in his life; but he always had a loose seat, and his mind was busy with anything but attending to his horse. Fritz, his last, a present from Lady Ashburton, carried him safely for many years through the London streets, to the astonishment of most of his friends. I asked him once how he had escaped misadventure. 'It was Fritz,' he said. 'He was a very sensible fellow. I suppose he had not been brought up to think that the first duty of a horse was to say something witty.'

[2] John Carlyle.

Atlantic of his countenance,' and hear all about my dear friends at the Hill before I go. How does Jane's Latin prosper? Tell her to write a postscript in her brother's next letter. You must excuse this hurried epistle. I am writing under many eyes and in the noise of many tongues. God bless you.

I am always affectionately yours,

JANE B. WELSH.

The next letter is to Jean Carlyle, which is prefaced by Carlyle thus.

This Jean Carlyle is my second youngest sister, then a little child of twelve. The youngest sister, youngest of us all, was Jenny (Janet), now Mrs. Robert Hanning, in Hamilton, Canada West. These little beings in their bits of grey speckled (black and white) straw bonnets, I recollect as a pair of neat brisk items, tripping about among us that summer at the Hill, especially Jean (only by euphemism Jane), the bigger of the two, who was a constant quantity there. The small Jenny (I think in some pet) had unexpectedly flung herself off and preferred native independence at Mainhill. Jean, from her black eyes and hair, had got the name of ' Craw Jean ' among us, or often of ' Craw ' simply. That was my mother's complexion too ; but the other seven of us, like our father, were all of common blond. Jean was an uncommonly open-minded, gifted, ingenuous, and ingenious little thing, *true* as steel (never told a fib from her birth upwards), had, once or so, shown suddenly a *will* like steel too (when indisputably in the right, as I have heard her mother own to me), otherwise a most loving, cheerful, amenable creature, hungering and thirsting for all kinds of knowledge ; had a lively sense of the ridiculous withal, and already something of what you might call 'humour.' She was by this time in visible favour with me, which doubtless she valued sufficiently. One of the first things I had noted of her was five or six years ago in one of my rustications at Mainhill, when in the summer evenings brothers Alick and John and I used to go out wandering extensively and talking ditto till gloaming settled into dark, always I observed little Craw turned up, either at our starting or somewhere afterwards, trotting at my side, head hardly higher than my knee, but eagerly thrown back and listening with zeal and joy : no kind of ' sport ' equal to this, for her, pursuit of knowledge under difficulties. Poor little Craw !

My darling took warmly to her for my sake and the child's own. This was the first time they had met. ' Such a child ought to be educated,' said she, with generous emphasis, and felt steadily, and, indeed, took herself, for some years onwards, a great deal of trouble and practical pains about it, as this letter may still indicate. Little Jean was had to Comely Bank,[1] for a good few months, got her lessons, &c., attended us to Craigenputtock, hoping to try farther there too ; but in the chaos of *incipience* there (a rather dark and even dismal chaos, had not *my* Jane been a daughter of the Sun) this was found impracticable ; and Scotsbrig, father's place,[2] coveting and almost grudging the little Jean's bits of labour within doors and without, she had to give the project up and return to her own way of life, which she loyally did ; grew up a peasant girl, got no further special education, though she has since given herself consciously and otherwise not a little, both of the practical and speculative sort ; and is at this day to be named fairly a superior woman, superior in extent of reading, culture, &c., and still better in veracity of character, sound discernment, and

[1] Where Carlyle first lived, as will be seen, after his marriage.
[2] To which old Mr. Carlyle removed from Mainhill in the year following.

practical wisdom ; wife for above thirty-five years now [1] of
James Aitken, a prosperous, altogether honest, valiant, intelligent and substantial man, house-painter in Dumfries by
trade ; parents they, too, of my bright little niece, Mary C.
Aitken, who copies for me, and helps me all she can in this
my final operation in the world.

To Miss Jean Carlyle, Hoddam Hill.

Haddington : November, 1825.

My affectionate Child,—It grieved me to learn from your
good little postscript,[2] that the poor Latin was already come
to a stand ; for I would fain see the talents with which
nature has entrusted you not buried in ignorance, but made
the most of.　Nevertheless, I do not *blame* you, because you
have despaired of accomplishing an impossibility ; for it *is*
impossible for you, sure enough, to make any great attainment
of scholarship in the circumstances in which you are already
placed.　You must on no account, however, abandon the
idea of becoming a scholar, for good, because it is beyond
your ability to carry it into effect just as soon as you wish ;
for your circumstances, by the blessing of Heaven, may be in
process of time rendered more towardly ; but should the
noble desire of knowledge die away within you, you would
indeed cruelly disappoint my hopes.　Moreover, though the
acquirement of a foreign language has proved too difficult a
matter for you in the time being, I see nothing that there is
to hinder you from reading many instructive books in your
own.　For your mother cannot be so hard a task-mistress,
that she would refuse you two hours or so in the day to yourself, provided she saw that they were turned to a profitable

[1] Written in 1868.
[2] ‘ Doubtless of some letter to me.—T. C.’

account. Here is a copy of Cowper's Poems for you, with which I expect you will presently commence a regular course of reading. Your brother is able, and I am sure will be most willing, to direct you in the choice of books ; and on this account you ought to be exceedingly thankful, as many for want of such direction have to seek knowledge by a weary circuit.

Had Providence been less kind to you in the relation you hold in life, you should get many an epistle from me full of the best advices I have to give ; for I love you, my good little girl, from the bottom of my heart, and desire earnestly that it should be well with you in this world as well as in the world to come. But when I consider the piety and goodness of the mother who has you in her bosom, and that he whose wisdom I bow myself before is your brother, I feel it idle and presumptuous in me to offer you any counsel, when in the precepts and example of those about you, you have already such a light to your path. Do but continue, my dear Jean, a dutiful daughter and a loving sister, and you are sure to grow up an estimable woman. If we can make you also an accomplished woman, so much the better.

One thing more when I am about it. Look sharp that you fulfil the written promise which you gave me at parting ; for know that I am not disposed to remit you the smallest tittle of it. And now God bless and keep you.

I am always your attached friend,
JANE BAILLIE WELSH.

After the bright interlude of Miss Welsh's visit to Hoddam, life soon became as industrious as Carlyle has described. The mornings were spent in work over the German Tales, the afternoons in rides, Larry remaining still in favour notwithstanding his misdemeanours. In the evenings he and his mother perhaps smoked their

pipes together, as they used to do at Mainhill, she in
admiring anxiety labouring to rescue his soul from the
temptations of the intellect ; he satisfying her, for she
was too willing to be satisfied, that they meant the
same thing, though they expressed it in different
languages.   He was meditating a book, a real book of
his own, not a translation, though he was still unable
to fasten upon a subject ; while the sense that he was
in his own house, lord of it, and lord of himself, and
able if he pleased to shut his door against all comers,
was delightful to him.

It is inexpressible (he wrote) what an increase of happiness and of consciousness, wholesome consciousness of
inward dignity, I have gained since I came within the walls
of this poor cottage—my own four walls—for in this state
the primeval law of nature acts on me with double and
triple force ; and how cheaply it is purchased, and how
smoothly managed. They simply admit that I am *Herr im
Hause*, and act on this conviction.   There is no grumbling
about my habitudes and whims.   If I choose to dine on fire
and brimstone they will cook it for me to their best skill,
thinking only that I am an unintelligible mortal, perhaps
in their secret souls a kind of humourist, *facheux* to deal
with, but no bad soul after all, and *not* to be dealt with in
any other way. My own four walls !

This expression, repeated twice, suggests the possible
date of a poem—the only poem, perhaps, that Carlyle
ever wrote which is really characteristic of him. It was
written either at Hoddam or at Craigenputtock. In
some respects—in the mention of a wife, especially—
it suits Craigenputtock best. But perhaps his imagination was looking forward.

MY OWN FOUR WALLS.

The storm and night are on the waste,
    Wild through the wind the herdsman calls,
As fast on willing nag I haste
    Home to my own four walls.

Black tossing clouds with scarce a glimmer
    Envelope earth like sevenfold palls ;
But wifekin watches, coffee-pot doth simmer,
    Home in my own four walls.

A home and wife I too have got,
    A hearth to blaze whate'er befals ;
What wanteth a man that I have not
    Within my own four walls ?

King George has palaces of pride,
    And armed grooms must ward those halls ;
With one stout bolt I safe abide
    Within my own four walls.

Not all his men may sever this,
    It yields to friends', not monarchs', calls ;
My whinstone house my castle is—
    I have my own four walls.

When fools or knaves do make a rout
    With gigmen, dinners, balls, cabals,
I turn my back and shut them out :
    These are my own four walls.

The moorland house, though rude it be,
    May stand the brunt when prouder falls ;
'Twill screen my wife, my books, and me,
    All in my own four walls.

In the autumn of this year Carlyle had a glimpse of Irving at Annan.

I had next to no correspondence with Irving (he says); a little note or so on business, nothing more. Nor was Mrs. Montagu much more instructive on that head, who wrote me high-sounding amiable things which I could not but respond to more or less, though dimly aware of their quality. Nor did the sincere and ardent Mrs. Strachey, who wrote seldomer, almost ever touch upon Irving. But by some occasional unmelodious clang in all the newspapers (twice over I think in this year) we could sufficiently and with little satisfaction construe his way of life. Twice over he had leapt the barriers and given rise to criticisms of the customary idle sort, loudish universally and nowhere accurately just. Case first was of preaching to the London Missionary Society (Missionary I will call it, though it might be 'Bible,' or another). On their grand anniversary these people had assigned him the honour of addressing them, and were numerously assembled, expecting some flourishes of eloquence and flatteries to their illustrious, divinely blessed society, ingeniously done and especially with fit brevity; dinner itself waiting, I suppose, close in the rear. Irving emerged into his speaking place at the due moment; but instead of treating men and office-bearers to a short, comfortable dose of honey and butter, opened into strict, sharp inquiries, rhadamanthine expositions of duty and ideal, issuing, perhaps, in actual criticism and admonition; gall and vinegar instead of honey; at any rate, keeping the poor people locked up there 'for above two hours,' instead of an hour or less, with dinners hot at the end of it. This was much criticised: 'Plainly wrong, and produced by love of singularity and too much pride in oneself,' voted everybody. For, in fact, a man suddenly holding up the naked inexorable ideal in the face of the clothed (and in England generally plump, comfortable, and pot-bellied) reality is doing an unexpected and questionable thing.

The next escapade was still worse. At some public meeting, probably of the same 'Missionary Society,' Irving again held up his Ideal, I think not without murmurs from former sufferers by it, and ended by solemnly putting down, not his name to the subscription list, but an actual gold watch, which he said had just arrived to him from his beloved brother lately dead in India.[1] That of the gold watch tabled had in reality a touch of rash ostentation, and was bitterly crowed over by all the able editors for a time. On the whole one could gather too clearly that Irving's course was beset with pitfalls, barking dogs, and dangers and difficulties unwarned of ; and that for one who took so little counsel with prudence, he perhaps carried his head too high. I had a certain harsh kind of sorrow about poor Irving, and my loss of him (and his loss of me on such poor terms as these seemed to me), but I carelessly trusted in his strength against whatever mistakes and impediments, and felt that for the present it was better to be absolved from corresponding with him.

That same year, late in autumn, he was at Annan only for a night and a day, returning from some farther journey, perhaps to Glasgow or Edinburgh, and had to go on again for London next day. I rode down from Hoddam Hill before nightfall, found him sitting in the snug little parlour beside his father and mother, beautifully domestic. I think it was

---

[1] This brother was John, the eldest of the three, an Indian army surgeon, whom I remember once meeting on a common stair in Edinburgh, on return, I suppose, from a call on some comrade higher up : a taller man than even Edward, and with a blooming, placid, not very intelligent face. —T. C.

the last time I ever saw those good old people. We sat only a few minutes, my thoughts sadly contrasting the beautiful affectionate safety here and the wild tempestuous hostilities and perils yonder. He left his blessing to each by name in a low soft voice. There was something almost tragical to me as he turned round, hitting his hat on the little door lintel, and next moment was on the dark street followed only by me. His plan of journey was to catch the Glasgow London mail at Gretna, and to walk thither, the night being dry. We stept over to Robert Dickson's, his brother-in-law's, and sate there still talking for perhaps an hour. He looked sad and serious, not in the least downhearted; told us, probably in answer to some question of mine, that the projected London University seemed to be progressing towards fulfilment, and how, at some meeting, Poet Campbell, arguing loudly for a purely *secular* system, had on sight of Irving entering at once stopped short, and in the politest manner he could, sat down without another word on the subject. 'It will be *unreligious*, secretly *anti*-religious all the same,' said Irving to us.

When the time had come for setting out, and we were all on foot, he called for his three little nieces, having their mother by him, made them each successively stand on a chair, laid his hand on the head first of one, with a 'Mary Dickson, the Lord bless you,' then of the next by name, and of the next; 'the Lord bless you,' in a sad, solemn tone, with something of elaborate noticeable in it too; which was painful and dreary to me; a dreary visit altogether, though an unabatedly affectionate on both sides—in what a contrast, thought I, to the old sunshiny visits when Glasgow was head-quarters, and everybody was obscure, frank to his feelings, and safe. Mrs. Dickson, I think, had tears in her eyes. Her too he doubtless blessed, but without hand on head. Dickson and the rest of us escorted him a little way.

We parted in the howling of the north wind, and I turned back across the moors to Hoddam Hill to meditate in silence on the chances and changes of this strange whirlpool of a world.[1]

---

[1] The last paragraph is taken from a contemporary description of the scene. The rest, as most complete, is from the *Reminiscences*, vol. i. p. 290, and is a curious illustration of the minute exactness of Carlyle's memory.

THE life at Hoddam Hill, singularly happy while it lasted, and promising to last, was not after all of long continuance. Differences with the landlord, General Sharpe, rose to a quarrel, in which old Mr. Carlyle took his son's part. Hoddam Hill was given up; the lease of Mainhill, expiring at the same time, was not renewed, and the whole family, Carlyle himself with the rest, removed to Scotsbrig, a substantial farm in the neighbourhood of Ecclefechan, where the elder Carlyles remained to the end of their lives, and where their youngest son succeeded them.

The break-up at Hoddam precipitated the conclusion of Carlyle's protracted relations with Miss Welsh. He sums up briefly his recollections of the story of this year, which was in every way so momentous to him.

My translation (German Romance) went steadily on, the pleasantest labour I ever had; could be done by task in whatever humour or condition one was in, and was day by day (ten pages a day, I think) punctually and comfortably so performed. Internally, too, there were far higher things going on; a grand and ever joyful victory getting itself achieved at last! The final chaining down, trampling home 'for good,' home into their caves for ever of all my spiritual

SCOTSBRIG.

dragons, which had wrought me such woe, and for a decade past had made my life black and bitter.[1] This year 1826 saw the end of all that, with such a feeling on my part as may be fancied. I found it to be essentially what Methodist people call their 'conversion,' the deliverance of their souls from the Devil and the pit! precisely enough *that*, in new form. And there burnt accordingly a sacred flame of joy in me, silent in my inmost being, as of one henceforth superior to fate, able to look down on its stupid injuries, with contempt, pardon, and almost with a kind of thanks and pity. This 'holy joy,' of which I kept silence, lasted sensibly in me for several years in blessed counterpoise to sufferings and discouragements enough ; nor has it proved what I can call fallacious at any time since. My 'spiritual dragons,' thank heaven, do still remain strictly in their caves, forgotten and dead, which is indeed a conquest, and the beginning of conquests. I rode about a great deal in all kinds of weather that winter and summer, generally quite alone, and did not want for meditations, no longer of defiantly hopeless or quite impious nature.

Meanwhile, if on the spiritual side all went well, one poor item on the temporal side went ill : a paltry but essential item—our lease arrangements of Hoddam Hill. The lease had been hurriedly settled, on word of mouth merely, by my father, who stood well with his landlord otherwise, and had perfect trust in him. But when it came to practical settlement, to 'demands of outgoing tenant,' who was completely right as against his landlord, and completely wrong as against us, there arose difficulties which, the farther they were gone into, spread the wider. Arbitration was tried ; much was tried ; nothing would do. Arbitrators,

---

[1] First battle won in the Rue de l'Enfer—Leith Walk—four years before. Campaign not ended till now.

little farmers on the neighbouring estates, would not give a verdict, but only talk, talk. Honourable landlord owes outgoing tenant (his and his father's old factor) say 150*l.*, and other just decision there was none. Factor was foolish, superannuated, impoverished, pressingly in want of his money. Landlord was not wise or liberal. Arbitrary and imperious he tried to be ; wrote letters, &c., but got stiff answers ; over the belly of justice would not be permitted to ride. The end was, after much babbling, in which I meddled little, and only from the background,[1] complete break ensued ; Hoddam Hill to be given up, laid at his honour's feet May 26, 1826 ; ditto Mainhill when the lease also expired there. My father got, on another estate near by, the farm of Scotsbrig, a far better farm (where our people still are), farm well capable both of his stock and ours, with roomy house, &c., where, if anywhere in the country, I, from and after May 1826, must make up my mind to live. To stay there till German Romance was done—clear as to that—went accordingly, and after a week of joinering resumed my stint of ten daily pages, steady as the town clock, no interruption dreaded or occurring. Had a pleasant, diligent, and interesting summer ; all my loved kindred about me for the last time ; hottest and droughtiest summer I have ever seen, drier even than the last (of 1868), though seldom quite so intolerably hot. No rain from the end of March till the middle of August. Delightful morning rides (in the first months) are

---

[1] Not altogether. In a letter from Hoddam Hill Carlyle says : 'My kindred can now regard the ill-nature of our rural Ali Pacha with a degree of equanimity much easier to attain than formerly. Ali—I mean his honour General Sharpe—and I had such a *sclane* the other day at this door. I made Graham of Burnswark laugh at it yesterday all the way from Annan to Hoddam Bridge. In short, Ali sank, in the space of little more than a minute, from 212° of Fahrenheit's thermometer to 32°, and retired even below the freezing-point.'

still present to me, ditto breakfasts in the kitchen, an antique baronial one, roomy, airy, curious to me. Cookery, company, and the cow with her produce always friendly to me. Nothing to complain of but want of the old silence ; noise and bustle of business now round me, and like to increase, not diminish ; and this thought always too, here cannot be thy continuing city ! and then withal, my darling in noble silence getting so weary of dull Haddington. In brief, after much survey and consideration of the real interests and real feelings of both parties, I proposed, and it was gently acceded to, that German Romance once done (end of September or so) we should wed, settle at Edinburgh in some small suburban house (details and preparations there all left to her kind mother and her), and thenceforth front our chances in the world, not as two lots, but as one, for better for worse, till death us part !

In August Haddington became aware of what was toward, a great enough event there, the loss of its loved and admired 'Jeannie Welsh, the Flower o' Haddington' (as poor old Lizzie Baldy, a notable veteran sewing woman, humble heroine, then sadly said), 'gaun to be here na mair !' In Annandale, such my entire seclusion, nothing was yet heard of it for a couple of months. House in Comely Bank [1] suitable as possible had been chosen ; was being furnished from Haddington, beautifully, perfectly, and even richly, by Mrs. Welsh's great skill in such matters, aided by her daughter's, which was also great, and by the frank *wordless* generosity of both, which surely was very great ! Mrs. Welsh had decided to give up house, quit Haddington, and privately even never see it more ; to live at Templand thenceforth with her father and sister (Aunt Grizzie), where it was well

---

[1] A row of houses to the north of Edinburgh, then among open fields between the city and the sea.

judged her help might be useful. My brave little woman
had by deed of law two years before settled her little estate
(Craigenputtock) upon her mother for life, being clearly
indispensable *there*. Fee simple of the place she had at the
same time by will bequeathed to me if I survived her.

So Carlyle, at a distance of forty-two years, describes
the prelude to his marriage—accurately so far as substance went, and with a frank acknowledgment of Mrs.
Welsh's liberality, as the impression was left upon his
memory.   But exactly and circumstantially as he
remembered things which had struck and interested
him, his memory was less tenacious of some particulars
which he passed over at the time with less attention
than perhaps they deserved, and thus allowed to drop
out of his recollection.   Details have to be told which
will show him *not* on the most considerate side.   They
require to be mentioned for the distinct light which
they throw on aspects of his character which affected
materially his wife's happiness.   There were some
things which Carlyle was *constitutionally* incapable of
apprehending, while again there were others which he
apprehended perhaps with essential correctness, but on
which men in general do not think as he thought.   A
man born to great place and great visible responsibili-
ties in the world is allowed to consider first his position
and his duties, and to regard other claims upon him as
subordinate to these.   A man born with extraordinary
talents, which he has resolved to use for some great and
generous purpose, may expect and demand the same
privileges, but they are not so easily accorded to him.
In the one instance it is assumed as a matter of course

that secondary interests must be set aside ; even in marriage the heir of a large estate consults the advantage
of his family; and his wife's pleasure, even his wife's
comforts, must be postponed to the supposed demands of
her husband's situation. The claims of a man of genius
are less tolerantly dealt with ; partly perhaps because it
is held an impertinence in any man to pretend to genius
till he has given proof of possessing it ; partly because,
if extraordinary gifts are rare, the power of appreciating
them is equally rare, and a fixed purpose to make a
noble use of them is rarer still. Men of literary faculty,
it is idly supposed, can do their work anywhere in any
circumstances; if the work is left undone the world
does not know what it has lost ; and thus, partly by
their own fault, and partly by the world's mode of
dealing with them, the biographies of men of letters
are, as Carlyle says, for the most part the saddest
chapter in the history of the human race except the
Newgate Calendar.

Carlyle, restless and feverish, was convinced that no
real work could be got out of him till he was again in
a home of his own, and till his affairs were settled on
some permanent footing. His engagement, while it
remained uncompleted, kept him anxious and irritated.
Therefore he conceived that he must find some cottage
suited to his circumstances, and that Miss Welsh ought
to become immediately the mistress of it. He had
money enough to begin housekeeping ; he saw his way,
he thought, to earning money enough to continue it
on the scale on which he had himself been bred up—
but it was on condition that the wife that he took to
himself should do the work of a domestic servant as

his own mother and sisters did; and he was never able to understand that a lady differently educated might herself, or her friends for her, find a difficulty in accepting such a situation. He was in love, so far as he understood what love meant. Like Hamlet he would have challenged Miss Welsh's other lovers 'to weep, to fight, to fast, to tear themselves, to drink up Esil, eat a crocodile,' or ' be buried with her quick in the earth;' but when it came to the question how he was himself to do the work which he intended to do, he chose to go his own way, and expected others to accommodate themselves to it.

Plans had been suggested and efforts made to secure some permanent situation for him. A newspaper had been projected in Edinburgh, which Lockhart and Brewster were to have conducted with Carlyle under them. This would have been something; but Lockhart became editor of the ' Quarterly Review,' and the project dropped. A Bavarian Minister had applied to Professor Leslie for some one who could teach English literature and science at Munich. Leslie offered this to Carlyle, but he declined it. He had set his mind upon a cottage outside Edinburgh, with a garden and high walls about it to shut out noise. This was all which he himself wanted. He did not care how poor it was so it was *his own*, entirely his own, safe from intruding fools.

Here he thought that he and his wife might set themselves up together and wish for nothing more. It did, indeed, at moments occur to him that, although he could be happy and rich in the midst of poverty, ' for a woman to descend from superfluity to live in poverty with a sick, ill-natured man, and not be wretched, would be a miracle.' But though the thought came more than once, it would not abide. The miracle would perhaps be wrought; or indeed without a miracle his mother and sisters were happy, and why should anyone wish for more luxuries than they had?

Mrs. Welsh being left a widow, and with no other child, the pain of separation from her daughter was unusually great. Notwithstanding a certain number of caprices, there was a genuine and even passionate attachment between mother and daughter. It might have seemed that a separation was unnecessary, and that if Mrs. Welsh could endure to have Carlyle under her own roof, no difficulty on his side ought to have arisen. Mrs. Welsh indeed, romantically generous, desired to restore the property, and to go back and live with her father at Templand; but her daughter decided peremptorily that she would live with Carlyle in poverty all the days of her life sooner than encroach in the smallest degree on her mother's independence. She could expect no happiness, she said, if she failed in the first duty of her life. Her mother should keep the fortune, or else Miss Welsh refused to leave her.

All difficulties might be got over, the entire economic problem might be solved, if the family could be kept together. As soon as the marriage was known to be in contemplation this arrangement occurred to everyone who was interested in the Welshes' welfare as the most obviously desirable. Mrs. Welsh was as unhappy as ever at an alliance which she regarded as not imprudent only, but in the highest degree objectionable. Carlyle had neither family nor fortune nor prospect of preferment. He had no religion that she could comprehend, and she had seen him violent and unreasonable. He was the very last companion that she would have selected for herself. Yet for her daughter's sake she was willing to make an effort to like him, and, since the marriage was to be, either to live with him or to accept him as her son-in-law in her own house and in her own circle.

Her consent to take Carlyle into her family removed Miss Welsh's remaining scruples, and made her perfectly happy. It never occurred to her that Carlyle himself would refuse, and the reasons which he alleged might have made a less resolute woman pause before she committed herself further. It would never answer, he said; 'two households could not live as if they were one, and he would never have any right enjoyment of his wife's company till she was all his own.' Mrs. Welsh had a large acquaintance. He liked none of them, and 'her visitors would neither be diminished in numbers nor bettered in quality.' No! he must have the small house in Edinburgh; and 'the moment he was master of a house, the first use he would turn it to would be to slam the door against nauseous intrusions.' It never occurred to him, as proved too fatally to be the case, that he would care little for 'the right companionship' when he had got it; that he would be absorbed in his work; that, after all, his wife would see but little of him, and that little too often under trying conditions of temper; that her mother's companionship, and the 'intrusion' of her mother's old friends, might add more to her comfort than it could possibly detract from his own.

However deeply she honoured her chosen husband, she could not hide from herself that he was selfish—extremely selfish. He had changed his mind indeed about the Edinburgh house almost as soon as he had made it up—he was only determined that he would not live with Mrs. Welsh.

Surely (Miss Welsh wrote) you are the most tantalising man in the world, and I the most tractable woman. This time twelvemonth nothing would content you but to live in the country, and though a country life never before attracted my desires, it nevertheless became my choice the instant it seemed to be yours. In truth I discovered a hundred beauties and properties in it which had hitherto escaped my notice; and it came at last to this, that every imagination of the thoughts of my heart was love in a cottage continually. *Eh bien!* and what then? A change comes over the spirit of your dream. While the birds are yet humming, the roses blooming, the small birds rejoicing, and everything is in summer glory about our ideal cottage, I am called away to live *in prospectu* in the smoke and bustle and icy coldness of Edinburgh. Now this I call a trial of patience and obedience—and say, could I have complied more readily though I had been your wedded wife ten times over? Without a moment's hesitation, without once looking behind, without even bidding adieu to my flowers, I took my way with you out of our Paradise, to raise another in the howling wilderness. A very miracle of love! Oh mind of man! And this too must pass away. Houses and walled gardens pass away like the baseless fabric of a vision; and lo! we are once more a solitary pair, 'the world all before us where to choose our place of rest.' Be Providence our guide. Suppose we take different roads and try how that answers. There is ——, with 50,000*l.* and a princely lineage, and 'never was out of humour in her life'—with such a 'singularly pleasing creature' you could hardly fail to find yourself admirably well off—while I, on the other hand, might better my fortune in many quarters. A certain handsome stammering Englishman I know of would give his ears to carry me away south with him. My second cousin, too, the doctor at Leeds, has set up a fine establishment, and writes to me that 'I am the very first of my sex.' Or, nearer home, I have an interesting young widower in view, who has no scruple in making me mother to his three small children, blue stocking though I be. But what am I talking about? as if we were not already married, married past redemption. God knows in that case what is to become of us. At times I am so disheartened that I sit down and weep.

Carlyle could just perceive that he had not been gracious, that Mrs. Welsh's offer had deserved 'more serious consideration,' and at least a more courteous refusal. He could recognise also, proud as he was, that he had little to offer in his companionship which would be a compensation for the trials which it might bring with it. He again offered to set the lady free.

To Miss Welsh.

Oh Jane, Jane, your half-jesting enumeration of your wooers does anything but make me laugh. A thousand and a thousand times I have thought the same thing in deepest earnest. That you have the power of making many good matches is no secret to me; nay, it would be a piece of news for me to learn that I am not the very worst you ever thought of. And you add, with the same tearful smile, 'Alas! we

are married already.' Let me cut off the interjection, and
say simply what is true, that we are not married already ;
and do you hereby receive further my distinct and deliberate
declaration that it depends on yourself, and shall always
depend on yourself, whether ever we be married or not.
God knows I do not say this in a vulgar spirit of defiance,
which in our present relation were coarse and cruel ; but
I say it in the spirit of disinterested affection for you, and of
fear from the reproaches of my own conscience, should your
fair destiny be marred by me, and you wounded in the house
of your friend. Can you believe it with the good nature
which I declare it deserves ? It would absolutely give me
satisfaction to know that you thought yourself entirely free
of all ties to me but those, such as they might be, of your
own still renewed election. It is reasonable and right that
you should be concerned for your future establishment.
Look round with calm eyes on the persons you mention, or
may hereafter so mention, and if there is any one among
them whose wife you had rather be—I do not mean whom
you love better than me, but whose wife, all things considered,
you had rather be than mine—then I call upon you, I, your
brother and friend through every fortune, to accept that man
and leave me to my destiny. But if, on the contrary, my
heart and my hand, with the barren and perplexed destiny
which promises to attend them, shall after all appear the
best that this poor world can offer you, then take me and be
content with me, and do not vex yourself with struggling
to alter what is unalterable—to make a man who is poor and
sick suddenly become rich and healthy. You tell me you
often weep when you think what is to become of us. It is
unwise in you to weep. If you are reconciled to be *my* wife
(not the wife of an ideal *me*, but the simple actual prosaic
me), there is nothing frightful in the future. *I* look into it
with more and more confidence and composure. Alas ! Jane,

you do not know me.   It is not the poor unknown rejected Thomas Carlyle that you know, but the prospective rich, known, and admired.   I am reconciled to my fate as it stands, or promises to stand ere long.   I have pronounced the word *unpraised* in all its cases and numbers, and find nothing terrific in it, even when it means unmoneyed, and even by the mass of his Majesty's subjects neglected or even partially contemned.   I thank Heaven I have other objects in my eye than either their pudding or their breath.   This comes of the circumstance that my apprenticeship is ending, and yours still going on.   Oh Jane, I could weep too, for I love you in my deepest heart.

These are hard sayings, my beloved child, but I cannot spare them, and I hope, though bitter at first, they may not remain without wholesome influence.   Do not get angry with me.   Do not.   I swear I deserve it not.   Consider this as a true glimpse into my heart which it is good that you contemplate with the gentleness and tolerance you have often shown me.   If you judge it fit, I will take you to my heart as my wedded wife this very week.   If you judge it fit, I will this very week forswear you for ever.   More I cannot do; but all this, when I compare myself with you, it is my duty to do.   Adieu.   God bless you and have you in his keeping !

I am at your own disposal for ever and ever,

T. CARLYLE.

That Carlyle could contemplate with equanimity being unpraised, unmoneyed, and neglected all his life, that he required neither the world's pudding nor its breath, and could be happy without them, was pardonable and perhaps commendable.   That he should expect another person to share this unmoneyed, pudding-less, and rather forlorn condition, was scarcely consistent with such lofty principles. Men may sacrifice themselves, if they please, to imagined high duties and ambitions, but they have no right to marry wives and sacrifice them. Nor were these 'hard sayings which could not be spared' exactly to the point, when he had been roughly and discourteously rejecting proposals which would have made his *unmoneyed* situation of less importance.

He had said that Miss Welsh did not know him, which was probably true; but it is likely also that he did not know himself. She answered this last letter of his with telling him that she had chosen him for her husband, and should not alter her mind. Since this was so he immediately said 'she had better wed her wild man of the woods at once, and come and live with him in his cavern in the hope of better days.' The cavern was Scotsbrig. When it had been proposed that he should live with Mrs. Welsh at Haddington, he would by consenting have spared the separation of a mother from an only child, and would not perhaps have hurt his own intellect by an effort of self-denial. It appeared impossible to him, when Mrs. Welsh was in question, that two households could go on together. He was positive that he must be master in his own house, free from noise and interruption, and have fire and brimstone cooked for him if he pleased to order it. But the two households were not, it seemed, incompatible when one of them was his own family. If Miss Welsh would come to him at Scotsbrig, 'he would be a new man;' 'the bitterness of life would pass away like a forgotten tempest,' and he and she 'would walk in bright weather thenceforward' to the end of their

existence. This, too, was a mere delusion. The cause
of his unrest was in himself; he would carry with him
wherever he might go or be, the wild passionate spirit,
fevered with burning thoughts, which would make
peace impossible, and cloud the fairest weather with
intermittent tempests. Scotsbrig would not have
frightened Miss Welsh. She must have perceived his
inconsistency, though she did not allude to it. But if
Carlyle had himself and his work to consider, she had
her mother. Her answer was very beautiful.

To Thomas Carlyle.

Were happiness the thing chiefly to be cared for in this
world, I would put my hand in yours now, as you say, and
so cut the knot of our destiny. But oh ! have you not told
me a thousand times, and my conscience tells me also, that
happiness is a secondary consideration ? It must not, must
not, be sought out of the path of duty. Should I do well to
go into Paradise myself, and leave the mother who bore me
to break her heart ? She is looking forward to my marriage
with a more tranquil mind in the hope that our separation is
to be but nominal—that, by living where my husband lives,
she may at least have every moment of my society which he
can spare. And how would it be possible not to disappoint
her of this hope if I went to reside with your people in
Annandale ? Her presence there would be a perpetual
cloud. For the sake of all concerned, it would be necessary
to keep her quite apart from us, yet so near.[1] She would be
the most wretched of mothers, the most desolate woman in

---

[1] Templand, where Mrs. Welsh was to live if she returned to her
father, was about fifteen miles from Ecclefechan.

the world. Oh ! is it for me to make her so ? me who am so unspeakably dear to her in spite of all her caprice, who am her only, only child, and she a widow ? I love you, Mr. Carlyle, tenderly, devotedly. But I may not put my mother away from me, even for your sake. I cannot do it. I have lain awake whole nights trying to reconcile this act with my conscience. But my conscience will have nothing to say to it—rejects it with indignation.

What is to be done, then ? Indeed, I see only one way to escape out of all these perplexities. Be patient with me while I tell you what it is. My mother, like myself, has ceased to feel any contentment in this hateful Haddington, and is bent on disposing of our house here as soon as may be, and hiring one elsewhere. Why should it not be the vicinity of Edinburgh after all ? and why should not you live with your wife in your mother's house ? Because, you say, my mother would never have the grace to like you, or let you live with her in peace ; because you could never have any right enjoyment of my society, so long as you had me not all to yourself ; and finally because you must and will ' have a door of your own to slam in the face of all nauseous intrusions.' These are objections which sound fatal to my scheme ; but I am greatly mistaken if they are not more sound than substance. My mother would like you, assuredly she would, if you came to live with her as her son. Her terror is lest, through your means, she should be made childless, and a weak imagination that you regard her with disrespect—both which rocks of offence would be removed by this one concession. Besides, as my wedded husband, you would appear to her in a new light. Her maternal affection, of which there is abundance at the bottom of her heart, would of necessity extend itself to him with whom I was become inseparably connected ; and mere common sense would prescribe a kind motherly behaviour as

the only expedient to make the best of what could no longer
be helped.

The arrangement was at least as reasonable as that
which he had himself proposed, and Carlyle, who was
so passionately attached to his own mother, might have
been expected to esteem and sympathise with Miss
Welsh's affection for hers. At Scotsbrig he would have
had no door of his own 'to slam against nauseous intrusions;' his father, as long as he lived, would be
master in his own house; while the self-control which
would have been required of him, had he resided with
Mrs. Welsh as a son-in-law, would have been a discipline
which his own character especially needed. But he
knew he was 'gey ill to deal wi'.' His own family were
used to him, and he in turn respected them, and could,
within limits, conform to their ways. From others he
would submit to no interference. He knew that he
would not, and that it would be useless for him to try.
He felt that he had not considered Mrs. Welsh as he
ought to have done ; but his consideration, even after
he had recognised his fault, remained a most restricted
quantity.

To Miss Welsh.

April 2, 1826.

As we think mostly of our own wants and wishes alone
in this royal project, I had taken no distinct account of
your mother. I merely remembered the text of Scripture,
'Thou shalt leave thy father and mother and cleave unto
thy husband, and thy desire shall be towards him all the
days of thy life.' I imagined perhaps she might go to

Dumfriesshire and gratify her heart by increasing the accommodations of her father, which she would then have ample means to do; perhaps that she might even——[1] in short, that she might arrange her destiny in many ways in which my presence must be a hindrance rather than a furtherance. Here I was selfish and thoughtless. I might have known that the love of a mother to her only child is indestructible and irreplaceable; that forcibly to cut asunder such was cruel and unjust.

Perhaps, as I have told you, I may not yet have got to the bottom of this new plan so completely as I wished; but there is one thing that strikes me more and more the longer I think of it—this, the grand objection of all objections, the head and front of offence, the soul of all my counterpleading—an objection which is too likely to overset the whole project. It may be stated in a word : '*The man should bear rule in the house, and not the woman.*' This is an eternal axiom, the law of nature, which no mortal departs from unpunished. I have meditated on this many years, and every day it grows plainer to me. I must not, and I cannot, live in a house of which I am not head. I should be miserable myself, and make all about me miserable. Think not this comes of an imperious temper, that I shall be a harsh and tyrannical husband to thee. God forbid ! But it is the nature of a man, if he is controlled by anything but his own reason, that he feels himself degraded and incited, be it justly or not, to rebellion and discord. It is the nature of a woman again (for she is entirely passive, not active) to cling to the man for support and direction, to comply with his humours and feel pleasure in doing so, simply because they are his, to reverence while she loves him, to conquer him not by her force, but by her weakness, and perhaps, the cunning

---

[1] He probably was going to say 'marry again.' but checked himself.

gipsy, to command him by obeying him. . . . Your mother is of all women the best calculated for being a *wife*, and the worst for being a *husband*. I know her, perhaps better than she thinks ; and it is not without affection and sincere esteem that I have seen the fundamental structure of her character, and the many light capricious half graces, half follies, that sport on the surface of it. I could even fancy that she might love me also and feel happy beside me, if her own true and kindly character were to come into fair and free communion with mine, which she might then find was neither false nor cruel any more than her own. But this could only be (I will speak it out at once and boldly, for it is the quiet and kind conviction of my judgment, not the conceited and selfish conviction of my vanity)—this could only be in a situation where she looked up to me, not I to her.

Now think, Liebchen, whether your mother will consent to forget her own riches and my poverty, and uncertain, more probably my scanty, income, and consent, in the spirit of Christian meekness, to make *me* her guardian and director, and be a second wife to her daughter's husband. If she can, then I say she is a noble woman, and in the name of truth and affection *let* us all live together and be one household and one heart, till death or her own choice part us. If she cannot, which will do anything but surprise me, then also the other thing cannot be, must not be ; and for her sake no less than for yours and mine we must think of something else.

The Greek chorus would have shaken its head ominously, and uttered its musical cautions, over the temper displayed in this letter. Yet it is perfectly true that Carlyle would have been an unbearable inmate of any house, except his father's, where his will was not absolute. 'Gey ill to deal wi',' as his mother said. The condition which he made was perhaps not so much as communicated to Mrs. Welsh, for whom it would have furnished another text for a warning sermon. The 'judicious desperation' which Carlyle recommended to her daughter brought her to submit to going to live at Scotsbrig. Under the circumstances Mrs. Welsh, in desperation too, decided that the marriage should be celebrated immediately and an end made. She comforted herself with the thought that being at Templand with her father, she would at least be within reach, and could visit Scotsbrig as often as she pleased. Here, however, new difficulties arose. Carlyle, it seems, had made the proposition without so much as consulting his father and mother. They at least, if not he, were sensible, when they heard of it, of the unfitness of their household to receive a lady brought up as Miss Welsh had been. 'Even in summer,' they said, 'it would be difficult for her to live at Scotsbrig, and in winter impossible;' while the notion that Mrs. Welsh should ever be a visitor there seemed as impossible to Carlyle himself. He had deliberately intended to bring his wife into a circle where the suggestion of her mother's appearance was too extravagant to be entertained.

You have misconceived (he said) the condition of Scotsbrig and our only possible means of existence there. You talk of your mother visiting us. By day and night it would astonish her to see this household. Oh, no. Your mother must not visit mine. What good were it? By an utmost exertion on the part of both they might learn, perhaps, to tolerate each other, more probably to pity and partially dislike each other. Better than mutual tolerance I could anticipate nothing from them. The mere idea of such a visit argued too plainly that you *knew nothing* of the family circle in which, for my sake, you were ready to take a place.

It is sad to read such words. Carlyle pretended that he knew Mrs. Welsh. Human creatures are not all equally unreasonable; and he knew as little of her as he said that her daughter knew of Scotsbrig. The two mothers, when the family connection brought them together, respected each other, could meet without difficulty, and part with a mutual regard which increased with acquaintance. Had the incompatibility been as real as he supposed, Carlyle's strange oblivion both of his intended wife's and his wife's mother's natural feelings would still be without excuse.

His mind was fixed, as men's minds are apt to be in such circumstances. He chose to have his own way, and since it was impossible for Miss Welsh to live at Scotsbrig, and as he had on his side determined that he would not live with Mrs. Welsh, some alternative had to be looked for. Once more he had an opportunity of showing his defective perception of common things. Mrs. Welsh had resolved to leave Haddington and to give up her house there immediately. The associations of the place after her daughter was gone would necessarily be most painful. All her friends, the social circle of which she had been the centre, regarded the marriage with Carlyle as an extraordinary *mésalliance*. To them he was known only as an eccentric farmer's son without profession or prospects, and their pity or their sym-

pathy would be alike distressing. She had herself
found him moody, violent, and imperious, and she at
least could only regard his conduct as utterly selfish.
Men in the situation of lovers often are selfish. It is
only in novels that they are heroic or even considerate.
It occurred to Carlyle that since Mrs. Welsh was going
away the house at Haddington would do well for himself. There it stood, ready provided with all that was
necessary. He recollected that Edinburgh was noisy
and disagreeable, Haddington quiet, and connected with
his own most pleasant recollections. It might have
occurred to him that under such altered circumstances,
where she would be surrounded by a number of acquaintances, to every one of whom her choice appeared
like madness, Miss Welsh might object to living there
as much as her mother. She made her objections as
delicately as she could; but he pushed them aside as if
they were mere disordered fancies; and the fear of
'nauseous intrusions,' which had before appeared so
dreadful to him, he disposed of with the most sum-
mary serenity. 'To me,' he calmly wrote, 'among the
weightier evils and blessings of existence, the evil of
impertinent visitors, and so forth, seems but a small
drop of the bucket, and an exceedingly little thing. I
have nerve in me to despatch that sort of deer for ever
by dozens in the day.'

'That sort of deer' were the companions who had
grown up beside Miss Welsh for twenty years. She
was obliged to tell him peremptorily that she would
not hear of this plan. It would have been happier and
perhaps better both for her and for him had she taken
warning from the unconscious exhibition which he had

made of his inner nature. After forty years of life with
him—forty years of splendid labour, in which his
essential conduct had been pure as snow, and unblemished by a serious fault, when she saw him at
length rewarded by the honour and admiration of
Europe and America—she had to preach nevertheless
to her younger friends as the sad lesson of her own experience, 'My dear, whatever you do, never marry a
man of genius.' The mountain-peaks of intellect are
no homes for quiet people. Those who are cursed or
blessed with lofty gifts and lofty purposes may be gods
in their glory and their greatness, but are rarely tolerable as human companions. Carlyle consented to drop
the Haddington proposal, not, however, without showing
that he thought Miss Welsh less wise than he had
hoped.

The vacant house at Haddington (he said) occurred to
my recollection like a sort of godsend expressly suited to
our purpose. It seemed so easy, and on other accounts so
indispensable, to let it stand undisposed of for another year,
that I doubted not a moment but the whole matter was
arranged. If it turned out, which I reckoned to be impossible if you were not distracted in mind, that you really
liked better to front the plashes and puddles and the thousand inclemencies of Scotsbrig through winter than live
another six months in the house where you had lived all
your days, it was the simplest process imaginable to stay
where we were. The loss was but of a few months' rent for
your mother's house, and the certainty it gave us made its
great gain. Even yet I cannot, with the whole force of my
vast intellect, understand how my project has failed. I wish
not to undervalue your objections to the place, or your

opinion on any subject whatever, but I confess my inability with my present knowledge to reconcile this very peremptory distaste with your usual good sense.

Again the plans were all astray. An Annandale cottage was once more thought of, and once more, again, the difference in point of view became prominent.

I should have 200*l.* to begin with (Carlyle said), and many an honest couple has begun with less. I know that wives are supported, some in peace and dignity, others in contention and disgrace, according to their wisdom or their folly, on all incomes from 14*l.* a year to 200,000*l.*, and I trusted in Jane Welsh, and still trust in her, for good sense enough to accommodate her wants to the means of the man she has chosen before all others, and to live with him contented on whatever it should please Providence to allot him, keeping within their revenue, not struggling to get without it, and therefore *rich*, by whatever arithmetical symbol, whether tens, hundreds, or thousands, by which that same revenue might be expressed. This is not impossible, or even very difficult, provided the will be truly there. Say what we like, it is in general our stupidity that makes us straitened or contemptible. The sum of money is a very secondary matter. One of the happiest, most praiseworthy, and really most enviable families on the earth at present lives within two bowshots of me—that of Wightman, the hedger—on the produce of fifteenpence per diem, which the man earns peacefully with his mattock and bill, not counting himself any philosopher for so doing. Their cottage on our hill is as tidy as a cabinet. They have a black-eyed boy whom few squires can parallel. Their *girnel* is always full of meal. The man is a true, honest, most wisely-conditioned man, an elder of the congregation, and meekly but firmly persuaded that he shall go to heaven when his hedging here below is done. What want these knaves that a king should have ?

If Carlyle had looked into the economics of the Wightman household, he would have seen that the wife made her own and her husband's and the child's clothes, that she cooked the meals, swept and cleaned the house that was 'tidy as a cabinet,' washed the flannels and the linen, and weeded the garden when she required fresh air—that she worked in fact at severe bodily labour from sunrise to sunset. Had he inquired into this, it is possible (though it would have depended on his mood) that he might have asked himself whether Miss Welsh, setting aside her education and habits, was physically capable of these exertions, and whether he had a right to expect her to undertake them. Happily neither she nor her mother had completely parted with their senses. They settled the matter at last in their own fashion. The Haddington establishment was broken up. They moved to Edinburgh, and took the house in Comely Bank which Carlyle mentioned. Mrs. Welsh undertook to pay the rent, and the Haddington furniture was carried thither. She proposed to remain there with her daughter till October, and was then to remove finally to her father's house at Templand, where the ceremony was to come off. Carlyle when once married and settled in Edinburgh would be in the way of any employment which might offer for him. At Comely Bank, at any rate, Mrs. Welsh could be received occasionally as a visitor. For immediate expenses of living there was Carlyle's 200*l.*, and such additions to it as he could earn. Miss Welsh recovered hope and spirit, and wrote in June from the new home, describing it and its position.

It is by no means everything one might wish (she said); but it is by much the most suitable that could be got, particularly in situation, being within a few minutes' walk of the town, and at the same time well out of its smoke and bustle. Indeed it would be quite country-looking, only that it is one of a range; for there is a real flower garden in front, overshadowed by a fair spreading tree, while the windows look out on the greenest fields with never a street to be seen. As for interior accommodation, there are a dining room and a drawing room, three sleeping rooms, a kitchen, and more closets than I can see the least occasion for unless you design to be another Blue Beard. So you see we shall have apartments enough, on a small scale indeed, almost laughably small; but if this is no objection in your eyes, neither is it any in mine.

Carlyle was supremely satisfied. The knotty problem which had seemed so hopeless was now perfectly solved.

To Miss Welsh.

Scotsbrig: July 19, 1826.

It is thus the mind of man can learn to command the most complex destiny, and like an experienced steersman (to speak in a most original figure) to steer its barque through all imaginable currents, undercurrents, quicksands, reefs, and stormy weather. Here are two swallows in the corner of my window that have taken a house (not at Comely Bank) this summer; and in spite of drought and bad crops, are bringing up a family together with the highest contentment and unity of soul. Surely, surely, Jane Welsh and Thomas Carlyle here as they stand have in them conjunctly the wisdom of many swallows. Let them exercise it then, in God's name, and live happy as these birds of passage are doing. It is not nature that made men unhappy, but their own despicable perversities. The Deuce is in the people ! Have they not food and raiment fit for all the wants of the body ; and wives, and children, and brothers, and parents, and holiest duties for the wants of the soul ? What ails them then, the ninnies ? Their vanity, their despicable, very despicable *self-conceit*, conjoined with, or rather grounded on, their lowness of mind. They want to be happy, and by happiness they mean *pleasure*, a series of *passive* enjoyments. If they had a quarter of an eye they would see that there not only was not, but could not be such a thing in God's creation. I often seriously thank this otherwise very infernal distemper for having helped to teach me these things. They are not to be learned without sore affliction. Happy he to whom even affliction will teach them ! And here ends my present lecture.

The great business having been once arranged, the rest of the summer flew swiftly by. ' German Romance ' was finished, and paid for the marriage expenses. The world was taken into confidence by a formal announcement of what was impending : Miss Welsh, writing for the first time to her relations, sent a description of her intended husband to the wife of her youngest uncle, Mrs. George Welsh. She was not blinded by affection—no one ever less so in her circum-stances. I have not kept back what I believe to have been faults in Carlyle, and the lady to whom he was to be married knew what they were better than anyone else can know ; yet here was her deliberate opinion of him.—He stood there such as he had made himself : a peasant's son who had run about barefoot in Ecclefechan street, with no outward advantages, worn with many troubles bodily and mental. His life had been pure and without spot. He was an admirable son, a faithful and affectionate brother, in all private relations blamelessly innocent. He had splendid talents, which he rather felt than understood ; only he was determined, in the same high spirit and duty which had governed his personal conduct, to use them well, whatever they might be, as a trust committed to him, and never, never to sell his soul by travelling the primrose path to wealth and distinction. If honour came to him, honour was to come unsought. I feel as if in dwelling on his wilfulness

> I did him wrong, being so majestical,
> To offer him the show of violence.

But I learnt my duty from himself : to paint him as he was, to keep back nothing and extenuate nothing. I never knew a man whose reputation, take him for all in all, would emerge less scathed from so hard a scrutiny.

Miss Welsh's letter was sent to Carlyle after her death in 1866. It came to him, as he said, 'as a flash of radiance from above.' One or two slight notes which he attached are marked with his initials, T. C.

To Mrs. George Welsh, Boreland, Dumfries.

Templand : September, 1826.
My dear Mrs. Welsh,—You must think me just about

the most faithless character in the nation ; but I know, myself, that I am far from being so bad as I seem. The truth is, the many strange things I have had to do and think of in late months left me no leisure of mind for writing mere complimentary letters ; but still you, as well as others of my friends, have not been remembered by me with the less kindness that you have seen no expression of my remembrance on paper. So pray do not go to entertain any hard thoughts of me, my good little aunt, seeing that at bottom I deserve nothing but loving-kindness at your hands. Better add a spice of long-suffering to your loving-kindness, which will make us the very best friends in the world.

It were no news to you what a momentous matter I have been busied with. 'Not to know that would argue yourself unknown.' For a marriage is a topic suited to the capacities of all living ; and in this, as in every other known instance, has been made the most of. But, forasmuch as much breath has been wasted on 'my situation,' I have my own doubts whether they have given you any right idea of it. They would tell you, I should suppose, first and foremost, that my intended is *poor* (for that it requires no great depth of sagacity to discover) ; and in the next place, most likely, indulge in some criticisms scarce flattering on his birth,[1] the more likely if their own birth happened to be mean or doubtful ; and if they happened to be vulgar fine people with disputed pretensions to good looks, they would to a certainty set him down as unpolished and ill-looking. But a hundred chances to one they would not tell you he is among the cleverest men of his day—and not the cleverest only, but the most

---

[1] ' Gracie, of Dumfries, kind of "genealogist by trade," had marked long since (of his own accord, not knowing me) my grandfather to be lineally descended from the "first Lord Carlyle," and brings us down from the brother of the murdered Duncan. What laughing my darling and I had when that document arrived.—T. C.'

enlightened ; that he possesses all the qualities I deem essential in my husband—a warm, true heart to love me, a towering intellect to command me, and a spirit of fire to be the guiding star of my life.[1] Excellence of this sort always requires some degree of superiority in those who duly appreciate it. In the eyes of the *canaille*, poor soulless wretches, it is mere *foolishness ;* and it is only the *canaille* who babble about other people's affairs.

Such, then, is this future husband of mine—not a great man according to the most common sense of the word, but truly great in its natural proper sense : a scholar, a poet, a philosopher, a wise and noble man, one ' who holds his patent of nobility from Almighty God,' and whose high stature of manhood is not to be measured by the inch rule of Lilliputs. Will you like him ? No matter whether you do or not, since I like him in the deepest part of my soul.[2]

I would invite you to my wedding if I meant to invite anyone ; but to my taste such ceremonies cannot be *too* private. Besides by making distinctions amongst my relations on the occasion, I should be sure to give offence ; and by God's blessing I will have no one there who does not feel kindly both towards *him* and *me.*

My affectionate regards to my uncle ; a kiss to wee John ; and believe me always,

Your sincere friend and dutiful niece,

JANE WELSH.[3]

The wedding day drew on ; not without (as was

---

[1] ' Alas ! alas !—T. C.'

[2] ' God bless thee, dear one !—T. C.'

[3] ' Letter read now—January 24, 1868—after a sleepless night withal such as has too often befallen latterly, cuts me through the soul with inexpressible feelings—*remorse* no small portion of them. Oh ! my ever dear one ! How was all this fulfilled for thee——fulfilled !!—T. C.'

21—2

natural) more than the usual nervousness on both sides
at the irrevocable step which was about to be ventured.
Carlyle knew too well 'that he was a perverse mortal
to deal with,' 'that the best resolutions made shipwreck
in practice,' and that ' it was a chance if any woman
could be happy with him.' 'The brightest moment
of his existence,' as in anticipation he had regarded
his marriage, was within three weeks of him, yet he
found himself 'splenetic, sick, sleepless, void of faith,
hope, and charity—in short, altogether bad and worthless.' 'I trust Heaven I shall be better soon,' he said;
' a certain incident otherwise will wear a quite original
aspect.' Clothes had to be provided, gloves thought
of. Scotch custom not recognising licences in such
cases, required that the names of the intended pair
should be proclaimed in their respective churches; and
this to both of them was intolerable. They were to be
married in the morning at Templand, and to go the
same day to Comely Bank.

Carlyle, thrifty always, considered it might be expedient 'to take seats in the coach from Dumfries.'
The coach would be safer than a carriage, more certain
of arriving, &c. So nervous was he, too, that he wished
his brother John to accompany them on their journey—
at least part of the way. In her mind the aspect of
the affair varied between tragic and comic, Carlyle's
troubles over the details being ludicrous enough.

I am resolved in spirit (she said), and even joyful—joyful
in the face of the dreaded ceremony, of starvation, and of
every horrible fate. Oh, my dearest friend, be always so
good to me, and I shall make the best and happiest wife.

When I read in your looks and words that you love me, then I care not one straw for the whole universe besides. But when you fly from me to smoke tobacco, or speak of me as a mere circumstance of your lot, then indeed my heart is troubled about many things.

Miss Welsh, too, as well as Carlyle, had a fiery temper. When provoked she was as hard as flint, with possibilities of dangerous sparks of fire. She knew her tendencies and made the best resolutions :—

I am going really to be a very meek-tempered wife (she wrote to him). Indeed, I am begun to be meek-tempered already. My aunt tells me she could live for ever with me without quarrelling, I am so reasonable and equable in my humour. There is something to gladden your heart withal. And more than this, my grandfather observed, while I was supping my porridge last night, that 'she was really a douce peaceable body that Pen.' Do you perceive, my good sir, the fault will be wholly your own if we do not get on most harmoniously together.

The grandfather, as Carlyle was coming into his family, was studying what he had already written.

My grandfather (she added) has been particularly picturesque these two days. On coming down stairs on Sunday evening I found him poring over 'Wilhelm Meister.' 'A strange choice,' I observed, by way of taking the first word with him, 'for Sunday reading.' He answered me quite sharply, 'Not at all, miss ; the book is a very good book ; it is all about David and Goliah.'

Jest as she would, however, Miss Welsh was

frightened and Carlyle was frightened.   The coach
suggestion had sent a shiver through her.   They comforted one another as if they were going to be executed.

To Thomas Carlyle.

Templand : October 10.
You desired me to answer your letter on Thursday, but I
have waited another post that I might do it better, if indeed
any good thing is to be said under such horrid circumstances.
Oh do, for Heaven's sake, get into a more benignant humour,
or the incident will not only wear a very original aspect, but
likewise a very heart-breaking one.   I see not how I am to
go through with it.   I turn quite sick at the thought.   But
it were Job's comfort to vex you with my anxieties and
'severe affection.'   I will rather set before you, by way of
encouragement, that the purgatory will soon be past, and
would speak peace where there is no peace, only that you
would easily see through such affected philosophy.   There is
nothing for us then but, like the Annan congregation, to
pray to the Lord.

I have said that I delayed writing that I might do it more
satisfactorily for this reason.   I expected to know last night
when my mother is to come from Edinburgh, in which case
I should have been able to name some day, though not so
early a one as that proposed ; but alas ! alas ! my mother is
dilatory and uncertain as ever, and the only satisfaction I can
give you at this time is to promise I will soon write again.
What has taken her to Edinburgh so inopportunely ! to set
some fractions of women cutting out white gowns, a thing
which might have been done with all convenience when we
were there last month.   But some people are wise, and some
are otherwise, and I shall be glad to get the gowns any way,
for I should like ill to put you to charge in that article for a

very great while. Besides, you know it would be a bad omen
to marry in mourning. When I first put it on, six years
ago,[1] I thought to wear it for ever ; but I have found a
second father, and it were ungrateful not to show, even
externally, how much I rejoice in him.

I fear you must be proclaimed to your own parish. Pity,
since you are so ashamed of me ! but I will enlighten you
on that head also in my next.

With respect to the journey part of the business, I loudly
declare for running the risk of being stuck up part of the
way (which at this season of the year is next to none) rather
than undergo the unheard-of horror of being thrown into the
company of strangers in such severe circumstances, or possibly,
which would be still worse, of some acquaintance in the stage
coach. For the same reason I prohibit John from going
with us an inch of the road ; and he must not think there is
any unkindness in this. I hope your mother is praying for
me. Give her my affectionate regards.

JANE WELSH.

Carlyle, on his side, tried to allay his fears of what
Miss Welsh called 'the odious ceremony' by reading
Kant, and had reached the hundred and fiftieth page of
the 'Kritik der reinen Vernunft,' when he found that it
was too abstruse for his condition, and that Scott's
novels would answer better. With this assistance he
tried to look more cheerfully on the adventure.

After all (he said) I believe we take this impending ceremony far too much to heart. Bless me ! Have not many
people been married before now ? and were they not all carried
through with some measure of Christian *comfoart*, and taught

---

[1] For her father. She had worn mourning ever since.

to see that marriage was simply nothing—but marriage?
Take courage, then, and let no 'cold shudder' come over
you; and call not this an odious ceremony, but rather a
blessed ordinance sanctioning by earthly laws what is already
sanctioned in heaven; uniting two souls for worldly joy and
woe which in God's sight have chosen one another from
amongst all men.   Can any road be dark which is leading
thither?   You will see it will be all 'smooth as oil,' notwithstanding our forebodings.   Consider Goethe's saying, 'We
look on our scholars as so many swimmers, each of whom in
the element that threatened to devour him, unexpectedly feels
himself borne up and able to make progress; and so it is
with all that man undertakes '—with marriage as with other
things.   By all reasons, therefore, German and English, I
call on you to be composed in spirit, and to fear no evil in
this really blessed matter.

To your arrangements about the journey and the other
items of the how and when, I can only answer as becomes me.
Be it as thou hast said.   Let me know your will and it shall
be my pleasure.   And so by the blessing of Heaven we shall
roll along side by side with the speed of post-horses till we
arrive at Comely Bank.   I shall only stipulate that you will
let me, by the road, as occasion serves, *smoke three cigars*
without criticism or reluctance, as things essential to my
perfect contentment.   Yet if you object to this article, think
not that I will break off the match on that account, but
rather, like a dutiful husband, submit to the everlasting
ordinance of Providence, and let my wife have her way.

You are very kind, and more just than I have reason to
expect, in imputing my ill-natured speeches (for which
Heaven forgive me) to their true cause—a disordered nervous system.   Believe me, Jane, it is not I, but the Devil
speaking out of me, which could utter one harsh word to a
heart that so little deserves it.   Oh, I were blind and

wretched if I could make thee unhappy. But it will not and shall not be, for I am not naturally a villain ; and at bottom I do love you well. And so when we have learnt to know each other as we are, and got all our arrangements accomplished and our household set in order, I dare promise you that it will all be well, and we shall live far happier than we have ever hoped. Sickness is the origin, but no good cause, of indiscriminating spleen ; if we are wise we must learn, if not to resist, at least to evade its influences—a science in which even I in the midst of my own establishment fancy I have made some progress, and despair not of making more.

As to the proclamation, on which I expect your advice, I protest I had rather be proclaimed in all the parish churches of the empire than miss the little bride I have in my eye, whom I see not how I am to do without. So get the gowns made ready and loiter not, and tell me, and in a twinkling *me voilà !* Thank your aunt for her kind invitation, which I do not refuse or accept till the next letter, waiting to see how matters turn. I was surely born to be a Bedouin. Without freedom ' I should soon die and do nocht ava.' My chosen abode is in my own house in preference to the palace of Windsor ; and next to this shall I not, with the man in the play, take my ease at mine inn ?

My mother's prayers (to speak with all seriousness) are, I do believe, not wanting either to you or to me, and if the sincere wishes of a true soul can have any virtue, we shall not want a blessing. She bids me send you the kindest message I can contrive, which I send by itself without contrivance. She says she will have one good *greet* when we set off, and then be at peace. Now then what remains but that you appoint the date, that you look forward to it with trust in me and trust in yourself, and come with trust to your husband's arms and heart, there to abide through all chances for ever ? Oh, we are two ungrateful wretches, or we should be happy. Write soon, and love me for ever; and so goodnight, *mein Herzenskind.* Thine *auf ewig,*

T. CARLYLE.

So the long drama came to its conclusion. The banns were published, the clothes made, the gloves duly provided. The day was the 17th of October, 1826. Miss Welsh's final letter, informing Carlyle of the details to be observed was humorously headed, '*The last Speech and marrying Words of that unfortunate young woman, Jane Baillie Welsh.*'

Truly (answered Carlyle), a most delightful and swanlike melody is in them—a tenderness and warm devoted trust worthy of such a maiden bidding farewell to the unmarried earth of which she was the fairest ornament. Let us pray to God that our holy purpose is not frustrated. Let us trust in Him and in each other, and fear no evil that can befall us.

They were married at Templand in the quietest fashion, John Carlyle the only other person present except Miss Welsh's family. Breakfast over, they drove off, *not* in the coach, but in a post-chaise, and without the brother. No delays or difficulties befell them on the road. Whether Carlyle did or did not smoke his three cigars remains unrecorded. In the evening they arrived safely at Comely Bank.

Regrets and speculations on 'the might have beens' of life are proverbially vain. Nor is it certain that there is anything to regret. The married life of Carlyle and Jane Welsh was not happy in the roseate sense of happiness. In the fret and chafe of daily life the sharp edges of the facets of two diamonds remain keen, and they never wear into surfaces which harmoniously correspond. A man and a woman of exceptional originality and genius are proper mates for one another only if they have some other object before them besides happiness, and are content to do without it. For the forty years which these two extraordinary persons lived together, their essential conduct to the world and to each other was sternly upright. They had to encounter poverty in its most threatening aspect—poverty which they might at any moment have escaped if Carlyle would have sacrificed his intellectual integrity, would have carried his talents to the market, and written down to the level of the multitude. If he flagged, it was his wife who spurred him on; nor would she ever allow him to do less than his very best. She never flattered anyone, least of all her husband; and when she saw cause for it the sarcasms flashed out from her as the sparks fly from lacerated steel. Carlyle, on his side, did not find in his marriage the miraculous transformation of nature which he had promised himself. He remained lonely and dyspeptic, possessed by thoughts and convictions which struggled in him for utterance, and which could be fused and cast into form only (as I have heard him say) when his whole mind was like a furnace at white heat. The work which he has done is before the world, and the world has long acknowledged what it owes to him. It would not have been done as well, perhaps it would never have been done at all, if he had not had a woman at his side who would bear, without resenting it, the outbreaks of his dyspeptic humour, and would shield him from the petty troubles of a poor man's life—from vexations which would have irritated him to madness—by her own incessant toil.

The victory was won, but, as of old in Aulis, not without a victim. Miss Welsh had looked forward to being Carlyle's intellectual companion, to sharing his thoughts and helping him with his writings. She was not overrating her natural powers when she felt herself equal to such a position and deserving it. The reality was not like the dream. Poor as they were, she had to work as a menial servant. She, who had never known a wish ungratified for any object which money could buy; she, who had seen the rich of the land at her feet, and might have chosen among them at pleasure, with a weak frame withal which had never recovered the shock of her father's death—she after all was obliged to slave like the wife of her husband's friend Wightman the hedger, and cook and wash and scour and mend shoes and clothes for many a weary year. Bravely she went through it all; and she would have gone through it cheerfully if she had been rewarded with ordinary gratitude. But if things were done rightly, Carlyle did not inquire who did them. Partly he was occupied, partly he was naturally undemonstrative, and partly she in generosity concealed from him the worst which she had to bear. The hardest part of all was that he did not see that there was occasion for any special acknowledgment. Poor men's wives had to work. She was a poor man's wife, and it was fit and natural that she should work. He had seen his mother and his sisters doing the drudgery of his father's household without expecting to be admired for doing it. Mrs. Carlyle's life was entirely lonely, save so far as she had other friends. He consulted her judgment about his writings, for he knew the value of it, but in his conceptions and elaborations he chose to be always by himself. He said truly that he was a Bedouin. When he was at work he could bear no one in the room; and at least through middle life, he rode and walked alone, not choosing to have his thoughts interrupted. The slightest noise or movement at night shattered his nervous system; therefore he required a bedroom to himself; thus from the first she saw little of him, and as time went on less and less; and she, too, was human and irritable. Carlyle proved, as his mother had known him, 'ill to deal wi'.' Generous and kind as he was at heart, and as he always showed himself when he had leisure to reflect, 'the Devil,' as he had said, 'continued to speak out of him in distempered sentences,' and the bitter arrow was occasionally shot back.

Miss Welsh, it is probable, would have passed through life more pleasantly had she married someone in her own rank of life; Carlyle might have gone through it successfully with his mother or a sister to look after him. But, after all is said, trials and sufferings are only to be regretted when they have proved too severe to be borne. Though the lives of the Carlyles were not happy, yet if we look at them from the beginning to the end they were grandly beautiful. Neither of them probably under other conditions would have risen to as high an excellence as in fact they each achieved; and the main question is not how happy men and women have been in this world, but what they have made of themselves. I well remember the bright assenting laugh with which she once responded to some words of mine when the propriety was being discussed of relaxing the marriage laws.   I had said that the true way to look at marriage was as a discipline of character.

CHAPTER XX.

A.D. 1826.   ÆT. 31.

MARRIED life had begun; and the first eighteen months of his new existence Carlyle afterwards looked back upon as the happiest that he had ever known. Yet the rest which he had expected did not come immediately. He could not rest without work, and work was yet to be found. Men think to mend their condition by a change of circumstances. They might as well hope to escape from their shadows. His wife was tender, careful, thoughtful, patient, but the spirit which possessed her husband, whether devil or angel he could hardly tell, still left him without peace.

I am still dreadfully confused (he wrote to his mother a few days after his arrival at Comely Bank), I am still far from being at home in my new situation, but . . . . I have reason to say that I have been mercifully dealt with; and if an outward man worn with continual harassments and spirits wasted with so many agitations would let me see it, that I may fairly calculate on being far happier than I have ever been. The house is a perfect model, furnished with every accommodation that heart could desire, and for my wife, I may say in my heart that she is far better than any other wife, and loves me with a devotedness which it is a mystery to me how I have ever deserved. She is gay and happy as a lark, and looks with such soft cheerfulness into my gloomy countenance, that new hope passes over into me every time I meet her eye. In truth I was very sullen yesterday, sick with sleeplessness, nervous, bilious, splenetic, and all the rest of it.

His days were spent in solitary wanderings by the sad autumnal sea. He begged his brother John to come to him.

I am all in a maze (he said), scarce knowing the right hand from the left in the path I have to walk. I am still imperfectly supplied with sleep ; no wonder therefore that my sky should be tinged with gloom. Meanwhile, tell my mother that I do believe I shall get hefted to my new situation, and then be one of the happiest men alive. Tell her also that by Jane's express request I am to read a sermon and a chapter with commentary, at least every Sabbath morning, to my household, also that we are taking seats in church, and design to live soberly and devoutly as beseems us. On the whole this wife of mine surpasses my hopes. She is so tolerant, so kind, so cheerful, so devoted to me : oh that I were worthy of her ! Why am I not happy then ? Alas ! Jack, I am bilious. I have to swallow salts and oil ; the physic leaves me pensive yet quiet in heart, and on the whole happy enough ; but the next day comes a burning stomach and a heart full of bitterness and gloom.

The entries in his dairy are still more desponding.

December 7, 1826.—My whole life has been a continual nightmare, and my awakening will be in hell.—TIECK.

There is just one man unhappy : he who is possessed by some idea which he cannot convert into action, or still more which restrains or withdraws him from action.—GOETHE.

The end of man is an action, not a thought.—ARISTOTLE.

Adam is fabled by the Talmudists to have had a wife before Eve : she was called Lilith, and their progeny was all manner of aquatic and aerial—devils.—BURTON.

As he grew more composed, Carlyle thought of writing some kind of didactic novel. He could not write a novel, any more than he could write poetry. He had no *invention*. His genius was for fact ; to lay hold on truth, with all his intellect and all his imagination. He could no more invent than he could lie. Still he laboured at it in his thoughts, and in the intervals he threw himself into a course of wide and miscellaneous reading. Sir Thomas Browne, Raleigh, Shaftesbury, Herder, Tieck, Hans Sachs, Werner, Sir William Temple, Scaliger, Burton, Alison, Mendelssohn, Fichte, Schelling, Kant, Heyne, Italian books, Spanish books, French books, occupied or at least distracted him, and short extracts or observations mark his steps as he went along.

December 3, 1826.—The conclusion of the essay on Urn-burial (Sir Thomas Browne) is absolutely beautiful : a still elegiac mood, so soft, so deep, so solemn and tender, like the song of some departed saint flitting faint under the everlasting canopy of night ; an echo of deepest meaning ' from the great and famous nations of the dead.' Browne must have been a good man. What was his history ? What the real form of his character ? *Abiit ad plures.* ' He hath gone to the greater number.' Two infants reasoning in the womb about the nature of this life might be no unhandsome type of two men reasoning here about the life that is to come. I should like to know more of Browne ; but I ought to understand his time better also. What are we to make of this old

English literature ?　Touches of true beauty are thickly scattered over these works ; great learning, solidity of thought ; but much, much that now cannot avail any longer. Certainly the *spirit* of that age was far better than that of ours.　Is the form of our literature an improvement intrinsically, or only a form better adapted to our actual condition ?　I often think the latter.　Difficulty of speaking on these points without affectation.　We know not what to think, and would gladly think something very striking and pretty.

Sir Walter Raleigh's 'Advice to his Son,' worldly wise, sharp, far-seeing.　The motto, 'Nothing like getting on.'　Of Burghley's ' Advice' the motto is the same ; the execution, if I rightly remember, is in a gentler and more loving spirit. Walsingham's ' Manual ' I did not read.　These men of Elizabeth's are like so many Romans or Greeks.　Were we to seek for the Cæsars, the Ciceros, Pericles, Alcibiades of England, we should find them nowhere if not in that era. Wherefore are these things hid, or worse than hid, presented in false tinsel colours, originating in affected ignorance and producing affected ignorance ?　Would I knew rightly about it and could present it rightly to others.　For 'hear, alas ! this mournful truth, nor hear it with a frown.'　There in that old age lies the *only* true *poetical* literature of England. The poets of the last age took to pedagogy (Pope and his school), and shrewd men they were ; those of the present age to ground and lofty tumbling, and it will do your heart good to see how they vault.

It is a damnable heresy in criticism to maintain either expressly or implicitly that the ultimate object of poetry is sensation.　That of cookery is such, but not that of poetry. Sir Walter Scott is the great intellectual *restaurateur* of Europe.　He might have been numbered among the Conscript Fathers.　He has chosen the worser part, and is only a huge Publicanus.　What are his novels—any one of them ?

A bout of champagne, claret, port, or even ale drinking. Are we wiser, better, holier, stronger? No. We have been amused. Oh, Sir Walter, thou knowest so well that *Virtus laudatur et alget!* Byron—good generous hapless Byron! And yet when he died he was only a *Kraftmann* (*Power-man* as the Germans call them). Had he lived he would have been a poet.

What shall I say of Herder's 'Ideen zur Philosophie der Geschichte der Menschheit'? An extraordinary book, yet one which by no means wholly pleaseth me. If Herder were not known as a devout man and clerk, his book would be reckoned atheistical. Everything is the effect of circumstances or organisation. *Er war was er seyn konnte.* The breath of life is but a higher intensation of light and electricity. This is surely very dubious, to say no worse of it. Theories of this and kindred sorts deform his whole work— immortality not shown us, but left us to be hoped for and to be believed by faith. This world sufficiently explainable without reference to another. Strange ideas about the Bible and religion; passing strange we think them for a clergyman. Must see more of Herder. He is a new species in some degree.

December 7.—Chateaubriand, Friedrich Schlegel, Werner, and that class of man among ourselves, are one of the distinctive features of the time. When Babylon the Great is about to be destroyed, her doom is already appointed by infidelity; and religion, too much interwoven with that same Babylon, has not yet risen on her mind, but seems rather, only seems, as if about to perish with her. A curious essay might be written on the customary grounds of human belief. Yes, it is true. The decisions of reason (*Vernunft*) are superior to those of understanding (*Verstand*). The latter vary in every age (by what law?), while the former last for ever, and are the same in all forms of manhood.

Oh Parson Alison, what an essay 'On Taste' is that of thine! Oh most intellectual Athenian, what accounts are those you give us of Morality and Faith, and all that really makes a man a man? Can you believe that the 'Beautiful' and 'Good' have no deeper root in us than 'association,' 'sympathy,' 'calculation'? Then, if so, whence, in Heaven's name, comes this sympathy, the pleasure of this association, the *obligancy* of this utility? You strive, like the witch in Hoffmann to work from the outside inwards, and two inches below the surface you will never get.

The philosophy of Voltaire and his tribe exhilarates and fills us with glorying for a season—the comfort of the Indian who warmed himself at the flames of his bed.

A clown that killed his ass for drinking up the moon, *ut lunam mundo redderet. In Lud. Vives.* True of many critics of sceptics. The sceptics have not drank up the moon, but the reflection of it in their own dirty puddles; therefore need not be slain.

January, 1827.—Read Mendelssohn's 'Phædon,' a half translation, half imitation of Plato's 'Phædon,' or last thoughts of Socrates on the immortality of the soul. On the whole a good book—and convincing? *Ay de mi!* These things, I fear, are not to be proved but believed; not seized by the understanding, but by faith. However, it is something to remove errors if not introduce truths; and to show us that our analogies drawn from corporeal things are entirely inapplicable to the case. For the present, I will confess it, I scarce see how we can reason with absolute certainty on the nature or fate of anything, for it seems to me we only see our own perceptions and their relations; that is to say, our soul sees only its own partial reflex and manner of existing and conceiving.

Sapientia prima est stultitiâ caruisse. Fully as well thus, *Stultitia prima est sapientiâ caruisse :* the case of all materialist metaphysicians, most utilitarians, moralists, and generally all negative philosophers, by whatever name they call themselves. It was God that said Yes. It is the Devil that for ever says No.

Leibnitz and Descartes found all truth to rest on our seeing and believing in God. We English have found our seeing and believing in God to rest on all truth, and pretty work we have made of it.

Is not political economy useful? and ought not Joseph Hume and Macculloch to be honoured of all men? My cow is useful, and I keep her in the stable, and feed her with oilcake and ' chaff and dregs,' and esteem her truly. But shall she live in my parlour? No; by the Fates, she shall live in the stall.

Virtue *is* its own reward, but in a very different sense than you suppose, Dr. Gowkthrapple. The *pleasure* it brings! Had you ever a diseased liver? I will maintain, and appeal to all competent judges, that no evil conscience with a good nervous system ever caused a tenth part of the misery that a bad nervous system, conjoined with the best conscience in nature, will always produce. What follows, then? Pay off your moralist, and hire two apothecaries and two cooks. Socrates is inferior to Captain Barclay; and the ' Enchiridion ' of Epictetus must hide its head before Kitchener's ' Peptic Precepts.' Heed not the immortality of the soul so long as you have beefsteaks, porter, and—blue pills. *Das hole der Teufel!* Virtue is its own reward, because it needs no reward.

To prove the existence of God, as Paley has attempted to do, is like lighting a lantern to seek for the sun. If you look hard by your lantern, you may miss your search.

An historian must write, so to speak, in *lines;* but every event is a *superficies.* Nay, if we search out its causes, a *solid.* Hence a primary and almost incurable defect in the

art of narration, which only the very best can so much as
approximately remedy. N.B. I understand this myself. I
have known it for years, and have written it now, with the
purpose, perhaps, of writing it at large elsewhere.

The courtesies of political life too often amount to little
more than this, ' Sir, you and I care not two brass farthings
the one for the other. We have and can have no friendship
for each other. Nevertheless, let us enact it if we cannot
practise it. Do you tell so many lies, and I shall tell so
many ; and depend on it, the result will be of great service
to both. For is not this December weather very cold ?
And though our grates are full of ice, yet if you keep a
picture of fire before yours, and I another before mine, will
not this be next to a real coal and wood affair ? '

Goethe ('Dichtung und Wahrheit,' ii. 14) asserts that
the sublime is natural to all young persons and peoples ;
but that daylight (of reason) destroys it unless it can unite
itself with the Beautiful ; in which case it remains indestructible—a fine observation.

The economics, all this time, had to be attended to,
and the prospect refused to brighten ; and this did not
mend Carlyle's spirits.

No talent for the market, thought I—none ; the reverse
rather (so he says of himself, looking back in later years).
Indeed, I was conscious of no considerable talent whatever,
only of infinite shyness and abstruse humour, veiled pride,
&c., and looked out oftenest on a scene that was abundantly
menacing to me. What folly was in all this, what pusil-
lanimity and beggarly want of hope. Nothing in it now
seems respectable except that of 'unfitness for the market,'
&c., namely, the faith I had in me, and never would let go,
that it was better to perish than do dishonest work, or do

one's honest work otherwise than well. All the rest I may now blush for, and perhaps pity ; blush for especially.

One piece of good fortune the Carlyles had. He had some friends in Edinburgh and she many ; and he was thus forced out of himself. He was not allowed after all to treat visitors as 'nauseous intruders.' His wife had a genius for small evening entertainments ; little tea parties such as in after days the survivors of us remember in Cheyne Row, over which she presided with a grace all her own, and where wit and humour were to be heard flashing as in no other house we ever found or hoped to find. These began in Edinburgh ; and no one who had been once at Comely Bank refused a second invitation. Brewster came and De Quincey, penitent for his article on 'Meister,' and Sir William Hamilton and Wilson (though Wilson for some reason was shy of Carlyle), and many more.

Carlyle, finding no employment offered him, was trying to make it. He sketched a prospectus for a literary Annual Register, 'a work which should perform for the intelligent part of the reading world such services as " Forget-me-Nots," "Souvenirs," &c. seemed to perform for the idle part of it.' 'It was to exhibit a compressed view of the actual progress of *mind* in its various manifestations during the past year.' The subjects were to be ' biographical portraits of distinguished persons lately deceased,' ' essays, sketches, miscellanies of various sorts, illustrating the existing state of literature, morals, and manners—on which points,' Carlyle thought, ' several things might be adduced not a little surprising to the optimists and the mob of gentlemen that wrote with ease.' 'Thirdly, critiques with extracts from the few really good books produced in England, Germany, and France, an essence of reviewing, a spirit of the literary produce of the year.' 'Fourthly, a similar account might be given of works of art and discoveries of science.' 'Fifthly, though politics were to be excluded, any incidents, misfortunes, delusions, crimes, or heroic actions illustrative of the existing spiritual condition of man, might be collected and pre- served.' Poetry was to be admitted if it could be had good of its kind, only 'with rigid exclusion of Odes written at ——, Verses to ——, and the whole genus of Songs by a Person of Quality.'

Pity that no Edinburgh or London publisher could see his way to assisting Carlyle in this enterprise ; for he would have written most of it himself, and such a record would now be of priceless value. But he was unknown and unprepossessing. Neither the Meister nor the Schiller were selling as well as had been ex- pected. The booksellers hung back, and they judged rightly, perhaps, for their own interests. Carlyle, like all really original writers, had to create the taste which could appreciate him. The scheme came to nothing, and his small capital was slowly melting away.

The picture of the Comely Bank life given in the 'Reminiscences' may be supplemented from the family letters.

Jane Welsh Carlyle to Mrs. Carlyle, Scotsbrig.[1]

Comely Bank : December 9, 1826.

My dear Mother,—I must not let the letter go without

---

[1] Being a postscript to a letter of Carlyle's own.

adding my ' Be of good cheer.' You would rejoice to see
how much better my husband is since we came hither. And
we are really very happy. When he falls on some work we
shall be still happier. Indeed I should be very stupid or
very thankless if I did not congratulate myself every hour of
the day on the lot which it has pleased Providence to assign
me. My husband is so kind, so in all respects after my own
heart. I was sick one day, and he nursed me as well as my
own mother could have done, and he never says a hard word
to me unless I richly deserve it. We see great numbers of
people, but are always most content alone. My husband
reads then, and I read or work, or just sit and look at him,
which I really find as profitable an employment as any other.
God bless you and my little Jean, whom I hope to see at no
very distant date.

Thomas Carlyle to Mrs. Carlyle, Scotsbrig.

Comely Bank : January 2, 1827.

My dear Mother,—At length Tait (the publisher) has
given me an opportunity of sending off the weary book,[1] and
along with it a word or two to enquire after your welfare and
assure you of my own. The German Romance I have
inscribed to my father, though I know he will not read a line
of it. From you, however, I hope better things ; and at any
rate I have sent you a book which I am sure you *will* read,
because it relates to a really good man, and one engaged in a
cause which all men must reckon good. You must accept
this ' Life of Henry Martyn ' as a new year's gift from me ;
and while reading it believe that *your* son is a kind of
missionary in his way—not to the heathen of India, but to
the British heathen, an innumerable class whom he would
gladly do something to convert if his perplexities and mani-

---

[1] German Romance.

fold infirmities would give him leave. . . . We must wait patiently and study to do what service we can, not despising the day of small things, but meekly trusting that hereafter it may be the day of greater.

I am beginning to be very instant for some sort of occupation, which, indeed, is my chief want at present. I must stir the waters and see what is to be done. Many many plans I have, but few of them, I doubt, are likely to prove acceptable at present ; the times are so bad, and bookselling trade so dull. Something, however, I will fix upon, for work is as essential to me as meat and drink. Of money we are not in want. The other morning Mrs. Welsh sent us a letter with sixty pounds enclosed, fearing lest cleanness of teeth might be ready to overtake us. I thought it extremely kind and handsome ; but we returned the cash with many thanks, wishing to fight our own battle at least till the season of need arrive.

I have not said a word yet about your kind Scotsbrig package. It was all right and in order, only that a few of the eggs (the box not being completely stuffed and firm) had suffered by the carriage. Most part of these Jane has already converted into custards, pancakes, or the other like ware ; the others I am eating and find excellent. A woman comes here weekly with a fresh stock to us, and I eat just one daily, the price being 15*d.* per dozen. Now, my dear mother, you must make Alick write to me, and tell me all that is going on with himself or you. Wish all hands a happy new year in my name, and assure them all, one by one, that I will love them truly all my days.

Thomas Carlyle to Alexander Carlyle.

Comely Bank: February 3.

Our situation at Comely Bank continues to be unexcep-

tionable—nay, in many points truly enviable. Ill health is
not harder on us than usual, and all other things are about
as one could wish them. It is strange, too, how one gets
habituated to sickness. I bear my pain as Christian did his
pack in the ' Pilgrim's Progress,' strapped on too tightly for
throwing off ; but the straps do not gall me as they once did ;
in fact, I believe I am rather better, and certainly I have not
been happier for many a year. Last week, too, I fairly began
—a book.[1] Heaven only knows what it will turn to, but I
have sworn to finish it. You shall hear about it as it pro-
ceeds, but as yet we are only got through the first chapter.
You would wonder how much happier steady occupation
makes us, and how smoothly we all get along. Directly
after breakfast the good wife and the Doctor[2] retire upstairs
to the drawing-room, a little place all fitted up like a lady's
workbox, where a spunk of fire is lit for the forenoon ; and
I meanwhile sit scribbling and meditating and wrestling
with the powers of dullness, till one or two o'clock, when I
sally forth into the city or towards the seashore, taking care
only to be home for the important purpose of consuming
my mutton chop at four. After dinner we all read learned
languages till coffee (which we now often take at night instead of tea), and so on till bedtime ; only that Jane often
sews ; and the Doctor goes up to the celestial globe, studying
the fixed stars through an upshoved window, and generally
comes down to his porridge about ten with a nose dropping
at the extremity. Thus pass our days in our trim little
cottage, far from all the uproar and putrescence (material
and spiritual) of the reeky town, the sound of which we hear
not, and only see over the knowe the reflection of its gaslights
against the dusky sky, and bless ourselves that we have

[1] The novel.
[2] John Carlyle, now staying with them.

neither part nor lot in the matter. Many a time on a soft
mild night I smoke my pipe in our little flower garden, and
look upon all this and think of all absent and present friends,
and feel that I have good reason 'to be thankful I am not
in Purgatory.'

Of society we might have abundance. People come on
foot, on horseback, and even in wheeled carriages to see us,
most of whom Jane receives upstairs, and despatches with
assurances that the weather is good, bad, or indifferent, and
hints that their friendship passes the love of women. We
receive invitations to dinner also ; but Jane has a circular—or rather two circulars—one for those she values, and
one for those she does not value ; and one or other of these
she sends in excuse. Thus we give no dinners and take none,
and by the blessing of heaven design to persist in this course
so long as we shall see it to be best. Only to some three or
four chosen people we give notice that on Wednesday nights
we shall *always* be at home, and glad if they will call and
talk for two hours with no other entertainment but a cordial
welcome and a cup of innocent tea. Few Wednesday evenings
(pass) accordingly when some decent soul or other does not
step in and take his place among us ; and we converse and
really, I think, enjoy ourselves more than I have witnessed at
any beef-eating and wine-bibbing convention which I have
been trysted with attending.

I had almost forgot to tell you that I have in my pocket a
letter of introduction to Jeffrey of the 'Edinburgh Review.'
It was sent to me from Procter of London. One of these
days I design presenting it, and you shall hear the result.

Jane Welsh Carlyle to Mrs. Carlyle, Scotsbrig.

21 Comely Bank : February 17.

My husband is busy below stairs, and I, it seems, am

this time to be the writer—with greater willingness than
ability, indeed, for I have been very stupid these some days
with cold. But you must not be left in the idea that we
are so neglectful as we have seemed. A little packet was
actually written to go by the carrier on Wednesday ; when
the rain fell and the wind blew, so that no living creature
dared venture to his quarters. The Doctor proceeded thither
as early as was good for his health, in case fortune in the
shape of bad weather, or whisky, had interposed delay. By
that time, however, carrier, boxes, and Bobby were all far on
the road ; so you see there was nothing for it but to write
by post, which I lose no time in doing.

And now let me thank you for the nice eggs and butter,
which arrived in best preservation and so opportunely—just
as I was lamenting over the emptied cans as one who had
no hope. Really it is most kind in you to be so mindful
and helpful of our town wants, and most gratifying to us to
see ourselves so cared for.

The new book is going on at a regular rate, and I would
fain persuade myself that his health and spirits are at the
same regular rate improving. More contented he certainly
is since he applied himself to this task, for he was not born
to be anything but miserable in idleness. Oh that he were
indeed well, well beside *me*, and occupied as he ought.
How plain and clear life would then lie before us ! I verily
believe there would not be such a happy pair of people on
the face of the whole earth. Yet we must not wish this too
earnestly. How many precious things do we not already
possess which others have not, have hardly an idea of ! Let
us enjoy them then, and bless God that we are permitted
to enjoy them rather than importune his goodness with
vain longing for more. Indeed we have a most quiet and
even happy life here. Within doors all is warm, is swept
and garnished, and without the country is no longer winter

like, but beginning to be gay and green. Many pleasant people come to see us; and such of our visitors as are *not* pleasant people have at least the good effect of enhancing the pleasures to us of being alone. *Alone* we are never weary. If I have not Jean's enviable gift of talking, I am at least among the best listeners in the kingdom, and my husband has always something interesting and instructive to say. Then we have books to read—all sorts of them, from Scott's Bible down to novels—and I have sewing-needles, and purse-needles, and all conceivable implements for ladies' work. There is a piano, too, for 'soothing the savage breast' when one cares for its charms; but I am sorry to say neither my playing nor my singing seems to give Mr. C. much delight. I console myself, however, with imputing the blame to his want of taste rather than to my want of skill.

So Jean is not coming yet. Well, I am sorry for it; but I hope the time is coming. In the mean time she must be a good girl, and read as much as she has time for, and above all things cultivate this talent of speech. It is my husband's worst fault to me that I will not or cannot speak. Often when he has talked for an hour without answer, he will beg for some signs of life on my part and the only sign I can give is a little kiss. Well, that is better than nothing; don't you think so?

She might well say, 'He has talked for an hour without answer.' It was not easy to answer Carlyle. Already it seems his power of speech, unequalled so far as my experience goes by that of any other man, had begun to open itself. 'Carlyle first, and all the rest nowhere,' was the description of him by one of the best judges in London, when speaking of the great talkers of the day. His vast reading, his minute observation, his miraculously retentive memory, gave him something valuable to say on every subject which could be raised. What he took into his mind was dissolved and recrystallised into original combinations of his own. His writing, too, was as fluent as his speech. His early letters—even the most exquisitely finished sentences of them—are in an even and beautiful hand without erasure or alteration of a phrase. Words flowed from him with a completeness of form which no effort could improve. When he was excited it was like the eruption of a volcano, thunder and lightning, hot stones and smoke and ashes. He had a natural tendency to exaggeration, and although at such times his extraordinary metaphors and flashes of Titanesque humour made him always worth listening to, he was at his best when talking of history or poetry or biography, or of some contemporary person or incident which had either touched his sympathy or amused his delicate sense of absurdity. His laugh was from his whole nature, voice, eyes, and even his body. And there was never any malice in it. His own definition of humour, 'a genial sympathy with the under side,' was the definition also of his own feeling about all things and all persons, when it was himself that was speaking, and not what he called the devil that was occasionally in possession. In the long years that I was intimate with him I never heard him tell a malicious story or say a malicious word of any human being. His language was sometimes like the rolling of a great cathedral organ, sometimes like the softest flute-notes, sad or playful as the mood or the subject might be; and you listened—threw in, perhaps, an occasional word to show that you went along with him, but you were simply charmed, and listened on without caring to interrupt. Interruption, indeed, would answer little purpose, for Carlyle did not bear contradiction any better than Johnson. Contradiction would make him angry and unreasonable. He gave you a full picture of what was in his own mind, and you took it away with you and reflected on it.

This singular faculty—which, from Mrs. Carlyle's language, appears to have been shared in some degree by his sister Jean—had been the spell which had won his wife, as Othello's tales of his adventures won the heart of Desdemona; and it was already brightening the evenings at Comely Bank. She on her side gives an imperfect idea of her own occupations when she describes herself as busy with needlework and books and the piano. They kept but one servant, and neither she nor her husband could endure either dirt or disorder, while Carlyle's sensitive stomach required a more delicate hand in the kitchen than belonged to a maid of all work. The days of the loaf—her first baking adventure, which she watched as Benvenuto Cellini watched his Perseus—were not yet. Edinburgh bread was eatable, and it was not till they were at Craigenputtock that she took charge of the oven. But Carlyle himself has already described her as making the damaged Scotsbrig eggs into custards and puddings. 'When they married,' Miss Jewsbury says, 'she had determined that he should never write for money, but only when he had something to say, and that she would make whatever money he gave her answer for all needful purposes. She managed so well that comfort was never absent from her house, and no one looking on could have guessed whether they were rich or poor. Whatever she had to do she did with a peculiar personal grace that gave a charm to the most prosaic details. But she had to put her hand to tasks of the rudest kind. No one who in later years saw her lying on the sofa in broken health and languor would guess the amount of energetic hard work she had done in her life. Her insight was like witchcraft. When she was to make her first pudding she went into the kitchen and locked the door on herself, having got the servant out of the road. It was to be *such* a pudding—not just a common pudding but something special, and it was good, being made with care by weight and measure.'

Thus prettily Carlyle's married life began, the kind friends at Scotsbrig sending weekly supplies by the carrier. But even with Mrs. Carlyle to husband them the visible financial resources were ebbing and must soon come to low water; and on this side the prospect resolutely refused to mend. The novel was a failure and eventually had to be burnt. The hope which had vaguely lingered of some regular and salaried appointment faded away. Overtures of various kinds to London publishers had met with no acceptance. German Romance was financially a failure also, and the Edinburgh publishers would make no future ventures. Under these conditions it is not wonderful that (resolved as he was never to get into money difficulties) Carlyle's mind reverted before long to his old scheme of settling at Craigenputtock. He no longer thought of turning farmer himself. His wife's ridicule would have saved him from any rash enterprise of that kind. But his brother Alick was still willing to undertake the farm and to make a rent out of it. For himself he looked to it only as a cheap and quiet residence. His Hoddam experience had taught him the superior economy of a country life. At Craigenputtock he could have his horse, pure air, milk diet, all really or theoretically essential to his health. Edinburgh society he considered was of no use to him ; practical Edinburgh, he was equally sure, would do nothing for him ; and away on the moors ' he could go on with his literature and with his life-task generally in the absolute solitude and pure silence of nature, with nothing but loving and helpful faces round him under clearly improved omens.' To his wife he did recognise that the experiment would be unwelcome. She had told him before her marriage that she could not live a month at Craigenputtock with an angel, while at Comely Bank she had little to suffer and something to enjoy.

Her modest days (he says), which never demanded much to make them happy, were beginning to have many little joys and amusements of their own in that bright scene, and she would have to change it for one of the loneliest, mooriest, and dullest in nature. To her it was a great sacrifice, if to me it was the reverse ; but at no moment, even by a look, did she ever say so. Indeed I think she never felt so at all. She would have gone to Nova Zembla with me, and found *it* the right place had benefit to me or set purpose of mine lain there.

Only one recommendation Craigenputtock could have

had to Mrs. Carlyle—that it was her own ancestral property, and that her father had been born there. Happily her mother, when the scheme was mentioned to her, approved heartily. Templand was but fifteen miles from Craigenputtock gate, not more than a morning's ride, and frequent meetings could be looked forward to. The present tenant of Craigenputtock was in arrears with his rent, and was allowing house and fences to go to ruin. Some change or other had become indispensable, and Mrs. Welsh was so anxious to have the Carlyles there that she undertook to put the rooms in repair and to pay the expenses of the move.

After a week or two of consideration Carlyle joined his brother Alick in the middle of April at Dumfries, Mrs. Welsh paying her daughter a visit during his absence. They drove out together and examined the place, and the result was that the tenant was to go, while Carlyle was to enter into possession at Whitsuntide; the house was to be made habitable, and, unless some unforeseen good luck should befall Carlyle meanwhile, he and his wife were to follow when it was ready to receive them. One pretty letter from her has been preserved, which was written to her husband when he was absent on this expedition.

To Thomas Carlyle.

Comely Bank: April, 1827.

Dear, Dear—Cheap, Cheap,[1]—I met the postman yesterday

---

[1] ' Cheap ! cheap ! ' was an answer with which Carlyle had replied once to some endearment of hers.

morning, and something bade me ask if there were any letters. Imagine my agitation when he gave me yours four and twenty hours before the appointed time. I was so glad and so frightened, so eager to know the *whole* contents that I could hardly make out any part. In the little tobacconist's, where I was fain to seek a quiet place, I did at length, with much heart-beating, get through the precious paper, and found that you still loved me pretty well, and that the 'Craig o' Putto' was still a hope ; as also that if you come not back to poor Goody on Saturday it will not be for want of will.[1] Ah ! nor yet will it be for want of the most fervent prayers to Heaven that a longing Goody can put up ; for I am sick—sick to the heart—of this absence, which indeed I can only bear in the faith of its being brief. . . .

Alas, the poor Craig o' Putto ! What a way it is in with these good-for-nothing sluggards ! I need not recommend to you to do all that is possible—nay, 'to do the impossible' —to get them out. Even suppose we did not wish the place for ourselves, it would be miserable to consign it to such hands. You will use all fair means, therefore, to recover it from them—that is, all honest means ; for, as to the tenderness and delicacy which would have been becoming towards a worthy tenant, it were here out of place. I shall be very anxious until I hear from you again. Would to heaven the business was settled, and in the way we wish ! These perplexities and suspenses are not good for bilious people : indeed, they are making *me* positively ill. How often since you went have I been reminded of your figure about the *hot ashes* (?), and my head has ached more continuously than at any time these six months. But health and spirits will come back when my husband comes back with good news—or, rather, when he comes back at all, whether his news be good

---

[1] Goody was Carlyle's name for his wife at this time.

or bad. . . . To be separated from you one week is frightful
as a foretaste of what it *might* be, but I will not think of this
if I can help it ; and after all why should I think of life
without you ? Is not my being interwoven with yours so
close that it can have no separate existence ? Yes, surely,
we will live together and die together and be together through
all eternity. But you will be calling this 'French senti-
mentality,' I fear ; and even 'the style of mockery is better
than that.'

I have not been altogether idle since we parted, though
I threatened I would take to bed. I have finished my review,
the representation of female character in the Greek poets, and
the comparison between Cæsar and Alexander, with all that
I could understand of the 'Friend ;' over and above which I
have transacted a good deal of shaping and sewing, the result
of which will be complete, I hope, by the day of your return,
and fill you with 'weender and amazement.'[1] Gilbert Burns
is gone. Mr. Brodie told us of his death last week. Besides
him, Mrs. Binnie, the Bruce people, and Mrs. Aitken, we
have had no visitors, and I have paid no visits. Last night
I was engaged to Mrs. Bruce, but I wrapped a piece of
flannel about my throat and made my mother carry an
apology of *cold*. But I may cut short these insipidities.
My kindest love to all, from the wee'est up to Lord Moon.[2]

Here is Carlyle's answer, coming from his best, his
real self—the true Carlyle, which always lay below,
however irritable or moody the surface.

[1] 'Report of little Jean's of some preacher who had profusely employed that locution, pronounced as here.—T. C.' This is one of the
letters specially annotated by Carlyle for publication.

[2] 'The Lord Moon is brother John = the Lord Mohun of Hamilton's
tragic ballad, which is still sung in those parts. Epithet from brother
Alick indicating breadth of face.—T. C.'

To the *Wife.*

Scotsbrig : April 17, 1827.

Not unlike what the drop of water from Lazarus's finger might have been to Dives in the flame was my dearest Goody's letter to her husband yesterday afternoon. Blacklock [1] had retired to the bank for fifteen minutes ; the whirlwind was sleeping for that brief season, and I smoking my pipe in grim repose, when Alick came back with your messenger. No ; I do not love you in the least—only a little *sympathy* and *admiration*, and a certain *esteem.* Nothing more ! oh my dear best wee woman—but not a word of all this.

Such a day I never had in my life, but it is all over and well, and now ' Home, brothers, home ! '

Oh, Jeannie, how happy shall we be in this Craig o' Putto ! Not that I look for an Arcadia or a Lubberland there ; but we shall sit under our bramble and our saugh tree, and none to make us afraid ; and my little wife will be there for ever beside me, and I shall be well and blest, and ' the latter end of that man will be better than the beginning.'

Surely I shall learn at length to prize the pearl of great price which God has given to me unworthy. Surely I already know that to me the richest treasure of this sublunary life has been awarded—the heart of my own noble Jane. Shame on me for complaining, sick and wretched though I be. Bourbon and Braganza, when I think of it, are but poor men to me. Oh Jeannie ! oh my wife ! we will never part, never through eternity itself ; but I will love thee and keep thee in my heart of hearts ! that is, unless I grew a very great fool—which, indeed, this talk doth somewhat betoken.

God bless thee ! Ever thine,

T. CARLYLE.

[1] The outgoing tenant of Craigenputtock.

CHAPTER XXI.

A.D. 1827.   ÆT. 32.

ALEXANDER CARLYLE, with his sister Mary, went into occupation of Craigenputtock at Whitsuntide 1827. His brother had intended to join him before the end of the summer, but at this moment affairs in Edinburgh began to brighten and took a turn which seemed at one time likely to lead into an entirely new set of conditions.   Carlyle had mentioned that he had a letter of introduction to Jeffrey. He had delayed presenting it, partly, perhaps, on account of the absolute silence with which some years before Jeffrey had received a volunteered contribution from him for the 'Edinburgh Review.' Irving had urged the experiment, and it had been made. The MS. was not only not accepted, but was neither acknowledged nor returned. Carlyle naturally hesitated before making another advance where he had been repulsed so absolutely. He determined, however, shortly after his return from his Craigenputtock visit, to try again. He called on the great man and was kindly received.   Jeffrey was struck with him; did not take particularly to his opinions; but perceived at once, as he frankly said to him, that 'he was a man of original character and right heart,' and that he would 'be proud and happy to know more of him.'   A day or two after he called with Mrs. Jeffrey at Comely Bank, and

was as much—perhaps even more—attracted by the
lady whom he found there, and whom he discovered
to be some remote Scotch kinswoman.   It was the
beginning of a close and interesting intimacy, entered
upon, on Jeffrey's part, with a genuine recognition of
Carlyle's qualities and a desire to be useful to him,
which, no doubt, would have assumed a practical form
had he found his new friend amenable to influence or
inclined to work in harness with the party to which
Jeffrey belonged.   But Jeffrey was a Benthamite on
the surface, and underneath an Epicurean, with a
good-humoured contempt for enthusiasm and high
aspirations.   Between him and a man so 'dreadfully
in earnest' as Carlyle, there could be little effective
communion, and Carlyle soon ceased to hope, what
at first he had allowed himself to expect, that Jeffrey
might be the means of assisting him into some independent situation.

The immediate effect of the acquaintance, however,
was Carlyle's admission, freely offered by the editor,
into the 'Edinburgh Review,' a matter just then of
infinite benefit to him, drawing him off from didactic
novels into writing the series of Essays, now so well
known as the Miscellanies, in which he tried his wings
for his higher flights, and which in themselves contain
some of his finest thoughts and most brilliant pictures.
His first contribution was to be for the number
immediately to appear, and Jeffrey was eager to
receive it.

Carlyle was not particularly elated, and mentions the
subject slightly in a letter to his brother Alick about
the establishment at Craigenputtock.

To Alexander Carlyle.

Comely Bank: June 3.

It gave us real pleasure to find that you had in very deed made a settlement in your new abode, and were actually boiling your pot at the Craig o' Putto under circumstances however unpropitious. Your tears for parting (from Scotsbrig) will scarcely be dried yet, but in a little while you will look upon this movement in its real light, not as a parting, but as a truly blessed reunion for us all, where, I hope and believe, many good days are in store for every one of us. It will not be long till you have scrubbed up the old Craig, put in the broken slates, and burnt or buried the rotten rags of the late housewife, who, I am told, is indeed a slattern, and not only so, but a drunkard, which is far worse. Mary's nimble fingers and an orderly head will have introduced new arrangements into the mansion; things will begin to go their usual course, and the mavis and tomtit will no longer sing to sad hearts. Poor Mary! Be good to her in this her first removal from home, and remember that you are not only a brother to her, but, as it were, a husband and father.

As to the house, I think with you it were better if we all saw it before the plans were settled. Jane and I are both for coming down shortly. We shall not be long in seeing you. The only thing that absolutely detains me is a little article which I have to write before the end of this month for the 'Edinburgh Review'—a very brief one—which I begin to-morrow.

To his brother John he was more explicit.

To John Carlyle.

Comely Bank: June 4.

Of my own history since I wrote last I need mention only

one or two particulars. Everything goes its course. I fight
with dullness and bile in the forenoons as of old ; I still walk
diligently, talk *de omni scibili* when I can find fit or unfit
audience, and so live on in the old light and shadow fashion
much as you knew me before, only with rather more comfort
and hope than with less. Our evening parties continue their
modest existence. Last Wednesday we had Malcolm[1]
and one Paterson, said to be 'the hope of the Scottish
Church,' a very feckless young man so far as externals go,
for his voice is the shrillest treble, he wears spectacles, and
would scarcely weigh six stone avoirdupois ; but evidently
shrewd, vehement, modest, and, on the whole, well gifted
and conditioned. . . .

One day I resolutely buckled myself up and set forth to
the Parliament House for the purpose of seeing our Reviewer
(Jeffrey). The little Jewel of Advocates was at his post. I
accosted him, and, with a little explanation, was cheerfully
recognised. 'The Article—where is the Article ? ' seemed
to be the gist of his talk to me : for he was to all appearance
anxious that I would undertake the task of Germanising the
public, and ready even to let me do it *con amore*, so I did
not treat the whole earth not yet Germanised as 'a parcel of
blockheads,' which surely seemed a fair enough request. We
walked to his lodgings discussing these matters. Two days
after, having revolved the thing, I met him again with
notice that I would 'undertake.' The next number of the
' Review,' it appeared, was actually in the press, and to be
printed off before the end of June, so that no large article
could find place there till the succeeding quarter. However,
I engaged, as it were for paving the way, to give him in this
present publication some little short paper, I think on the
subject of Jean Paul, though that is not quite settled with

---

[1] See *Reminiscences,* vol. i. p. 266.

myself yet. And thus, oh Jack, thou see'st me occupied with a new trade! On the whole I am rather glad of this adventure, for I think it promises to be the means of a pleasant connection. Certainly Jeffrey is by much the most lovable of all the literary men I have seen, and he seemed ready, nay desirous, if time would but permit, to cultivate a further intimacy.

Jean Paul was decided on, to be followed in the autumn by a more elaborate article on the general state of German literature. This paper was written at once, and forms the first of the Miscellaneous Essays in the collected edition of Carlyle's works. Carlyle's 'style,' which has been a rock of offence to so many people, has been attributed to his study of Jean Paul. No criticism could be worse founded. His style shaped itself as he gathered confidence in his own powers, and had its origin in his father's house in Annandale. His mode of expressing himself remained undistinguished by its special characteristics till he had ceased to occupy himself with the German poets. Of his present undertaking Carlyle says:—

Perhaps it was little De Quincey's reported admiration of Jean Paul—Goethe a mere corrupted pigmy to him—that first put me upon trying to be orthodox and admire. I dimly felt poor De Quincey, who passed for a mighty seer in such things, to have exaggerated, and to know, perhaps, but little of either Jean Paul or Goethe. However, I held on reading and considerably admiring Jean Paul on my own score, though always with something of secret disappointment. I could now wish, perhaps, that I hadn't. My first favourite books had been Hudibras and Tristram Shandy. Everybody was proclaiming it such a feat for a man to have wit, to have humour above all. There was always a small secret something of affectation, which is not now secret to me, in that part of my affairs. As to my poor style, Edward Irving and his admiration of the old Puritans and Elizabethans—whom at heart I never could entirely adore, though trying hard—his and everybody's doctrine on that head played a much more important part than Jean Paul upon it. And the most important by far was that of nature, you would perhaps say, if you had ever heard my father speak, or my mother, and her inward melodies of heart and voice.

Carlyle's acquaintance with Wilson—Christopher North—had been slight, Wilson, perhaps, dreading his radicalism. In the course of the summer, however, accident threw them more closely together, and one of their meetings is thus described.

To John Carlyle.

21 Comely Bank.

Last night I supped with John Wilson, Professor of Moral Philosophy here, author of the 'Isle of Palms,' &c., a man of the most fervid temperament, fond of all stimulating things, from tragic poetry down to whisky punch. He snuffed and smoked cigars and drank liquors, and talked in the most indescribable style. It was at the lodging of one John Gordon, a young very good man from Kirkcudbright, who sometimes comes here. Daylight came on us before we parted; indeed, it was towards three o'clock as the Professor and I walked home, smoking as we went. I had scarcely either eaten or drunk, being a privileged person, but merely enjoyed the strange volcanic eruptions of our poet's convivial genius. He is a broad sincere man of six feet, with long

dishevelled flax-coloured hair, and two blue eyes keen as an
eagle's. Now and then he sank into a brown study, and
seemed dead in the eye of law. About two o'clock he was
sitting in this state smoking languidly, his nose begrimed
with snuff, his face hazy and inert ; when all at once flashing
into existence, he inquired of John Gordon, with an irresist-
ible air, ' I hope, Mr. Gordon, you don't believe in universal
damnation ?' It was wicked, but all hands burst into in-
extinguishable laughter. But I expect to see Wilson in a more
philosophic key ere long ; he has promised to call on me,
and is, on the whole, a man I should like to know better.
Geniuses of any sort, especially of so kindly a sort, are so very
rare in this world.

Another and yet brighter episode of this summer
was a further and far more remarkable letter from
Goethe. Carlyle had sent the ' Life of Schiller ' to
Weimar, and afterwards the volumes of German
Romance. They were acknowledged with a gracious
interest which went infinitely beyond his warmest
hopes. There was not a letter only, but little remembrances for himself and his wife ; and better even than
the presents, a few lines of verse addressed to each of
them.

Carlyle sends the account to his mother.

Comely Bank : August 11.

News came directly after breakfast that a packet from
Goethe had arrived in Leith. Without delay I proceeded
thither, and found a little box carefully overlapped in wax
cloth, and directed to me. After infinite wranglings and
perplexed misdirected higglings I succeeded in rescuing the
precious packet from the fangs of the Custom House sharks,
and in the afternoon it was safely deposited in our little

parlour—the daintiest boxie you ever saw—so carefully packed, so neatly and tastefully contrived was everything. There was a copy of Goethe's poems in five beautiful little volumes for ' the valued marriage pair Carlyle ;' two other little books for myself, then two medals, one of Goethe himself and another of his father and mother ; and, lastly, the prettiest wrought-iron necklace with a little figure of the poet's face set in gold for ' my dear spouse,' and a most dashing pocket-book for me. In the box containing the necklace, and in each pocket of the pocket-book were cards, each with a verse of poetry on it in the old master's own hand. All these I will translate to you by-and-by, as well as the long letter which lay at the bottom of all, one of the kindest and gravest epistles I ever read. He praises me for the ' Life of Schiller ' and the others ; asks me to send him some account of my own previous history, &c. In short, it was all extremely graceful, affectionate and patriarchal. You may conceive how much it pleased us. I believe a ribbon with the order of the Garter would scarcely have flattered either of us more.

The letter from Goethe was this :[1]—

To Thomas Carlyle.

Weimar : July 20, 1827.

In a letter of the 15th of March which I sent by the post, and which I trust has reached you safely, I mentioned the great pleasure which your present had given me. It found me in the country where I could study and enjoy it with

---

[1] In einem Schreiben vom 15. März, welches ich mit der Post absendete und Sie hoffentlich zu rechter Zeit werden erhalten haben, vermeldete ich wie viel Vergnügen mir Ihre Sendung gebracht. Sie fand mich auf dem Lande, wo ich sie mit mehrerer Ruhe betrachten

greater leisure. I now am enabled to send a packet to you likewise, which I hope that you will be kind enough to accept from me.

Let me, in the first place, tell you, my dear sir, how very highly I esteem your '*Biography* of Schiller.' It is remarkable for the careful study which it displays of the incidents of Schiller's life, and one clearly perceives in it a study of his works and a hearty sympathy with them. The complete insight which you have thus obtained into the character and high merits of this man is really admirable, so clear it is, and so appropriate, so far beyond what might have been looked for in a writer in a distant country.

Here the old saying is verified, 'a good will helps to a full understanding.' It is just because the Scot can look with affection on a German and can honour and love him, that he acquires a sure eye for that German's finest qualities. He raises himself into a clearness of vision which Schiller's own countrymen could not arrive at in earlier days. For those who live with superior men are easily mistaken in their

und geniessen konnte. Gegenwärtig sehe ich mich in dem Stande, auch ein Packet an Sie abzuschicken mit dem Wunsche freundlicher Aufnahme.

Lassen Sie mich vorerst, mein Theuerster, von Ihrer Biographie Schillers das Beste sagen. Sie ist merkwürdig, indem sie ein genaues Studium der Vorfälle seines Lebens beweist, so wie denn auch das Studium seiner Werke und eine innige Theilnahme an denselben daraus hervorgeht. Bewundernswürdig ist es wie Sie sich auf diese Weise eine genügende Einsicht in den Character und das hohe Verdienstliche dieses Mannes verschafft, so klar und so gehörig als es kaum aus der Ferne zu erwarten gewesen.

Hier bewahrheitet sich jedoch ein altes Wort: 'Der gute Wille hilft zu vollkommener Kenntniss.' Denn gerade dass der Schottländer den deutschen Mann mit Wohlwollen anerkennt, ihn verehrt und liebt, dadurch wird er dessen treffliche Eigenschaften am sichersten gewahr, dadurch erhebt er sich zu einer Klarheit zu der sogar Landsleute des Trefflichen in früheren Tagen nicht gelangen konnten; denn die Mitle-

judgment. Personal peculiarities irritate them. The swift changing current of life displaces their points of view, and hinders them from perceiving and recognising the true worth of such men.

Schiller's character, however, was so extraordinary that his biographer could start with the idea of an excellent man before him. He could carry that idea through all individual destinies and achievements, and thus see his task accomplished.

The notices, prefixed to 'German Romance,' of the lives of Musæus, Hoffmann, Richter, &c., can be approved of equally in their several kinds. They are compiled with care, are briefly set out, and provide an adequate notion of each author's personal character, and of the effect of it upon his writings.

Mr. Carlyle displays throughout a calm, clear sympathy with poetical literary activity in Germany. He throws himself into the especial national tendency, and gives individuals their credit each in his place.

benden werden an vorzüglichen Menschen gar leicht irre: das Besondere der Person stört sie, das laufende bewegliche Leben verrückt ihre Standpunkte und hindert das Kennen und Anerkennen eines solchen Mannes.

Dieser aber war von so ausserordentlicher Art, dass der Biograph die Idee eines vorzüglichen Mannes vor Augen halten und sie durch individuelle Schicksale und Leistungen durchführen konnte, und sein Tagewerk dergestalt vollbracht sah.

Die vor den *German Romances* mitgetheilten Notizen über das Leben Musäus, Hoffmanns, Richters &c. kann man in ihrer Art gleichfalls mit Beyfall aufnehmen; sie sind mit Sorgfalt gesammelt, kürzlich dargestellt und geben von eines jeden Autors individuellem Character und der Einwirkung desselben auf seine Schriften genugsame Vorkenntniss.

Durchaus beweist Herr Carlyle eine ruhige, klare Theilnahme an den deutschen poetisch-literarischen Beginnen: er giebt sich hin an das eigenthümliche Bestreben der Nation, er lässt den Einzelnen gelten, jeden an seiner Stelle.

Let me add a few general observations which I have long harboured in silence, and which have been stirred up by these present works.

It is obvious that for a considerable time the efforts of the best poets and æsthetic writers throughout the world have been directed towards the general characteristics of humanity. In each particular sphere, be it history, mythology, fiction, more or less arbitrarily conceived, the universal is made to show and shine through what is merely individual or national.

In practical life we perceive the same tendency, which pervades all that is of the earth earthy, crude, wild, cruel, false, selfish, and treacherous, and tries everywhere to spread a certain sereneness. We may not, indeed, hope from this the approach of an era of universal peace ; but yet that strifes which are unavoidable may grow less extreme, wars less savage, and victory less overbearing.

Whatever in the poetry of all nations aims and tends towards this, is what the others should appropriate. And one must study and make allowances for the peculiarities of

Sey mir nun erlaubt allgemeine Betrachtungen hinzuzufügen, welche ich längst bey mir im Stillen hege und die mir bey den vorliegenden Arbeiten abermals frisch aufgeregt worden.

Offenbar ist das Bestreben der besten Dichter und ästhetischen Schriftsteller aller Nationen schon seit geraumer Zeit auf das allgemein Menschliche gerichtet. In jedem Besondern, es sey nun historisch, mythologisch, fabelhaft, mehr oder weniger willkührlich ersonnen, wird man durch Nationalität und Persönlichkeit hindurch jenes Allgemeine immer mehr durchleuchten und durchschimmern sehn.

Da nun auch im practischen Lebensgange ein gleiches obwaltet und durch alles Irdisch-Rohe, Wilde, Grausame, Falsche, Eigennützige, Lügenhafte sich durchschlingt, und überall einige Milde zu verbreiten trachtet, so ist zwar nicht zu hoffen dass ein allgemeiner Friede dadurch sich einleite, aber doch dass der unvermeidliche Streit nach und nach lässlicher werde, der Krieg weniger grausam, der Sieg weniger übermüthig.

Was nun in den Dichtungen aller Nationen hierauf hindeutet und

each nation, in order to have real intercourse with it. The special characteristics of a people are like its language and its currency. They facilitate exchange ; indeed, they first make exchange possible.

Pardon me, my dear sir, for these remarks, which perhaps are not quite coherent, nor to be scanned all at once ; they are drawn from the great ocean of observations, which, as life passes on, swells up more and more round every thinking person. Let me add some more observations which I wrote down on another occasion, but which apply specially to the business on which you are now engaged.

We arrive best at a true general toleration when we can let pass individual peculiarities, whether of persons or peoples, without quarrelling with them ; holding fast nevertheless to the conviction that genuine excellence is distinguished by this mark, that it belongs to all mankind. To such intercourse and mutual recognition the Germans have long contributed.

hinwirkt, diess ist es was die übrigen sich anzueignen haben. Die Besonderheiten einer jeden muss man kennen lernen, und sie ihr zu lassen, um gerade dadurch mit ihr zu verkehren ; denn die Eigenheiten einer Nation sind wie ihre Sprache und ihre Münzsorten, sie erleichtern den Verkehr, ja, sie machen ihn erst vollkommen möglich.

Verzeihen Sie mir, mein Werthester, diese vielleicht nicht ganz zusammenhängenden noch alsbald zu überschauenden Aeusserungen ; sie sind geschöpft aus dem Ocean der Betrachtungen, der um einen jeden Denkenden mit den Jahren immer mehr anschwillt. Lassen Sie mich noch Einiges hinzufügen, welches ich bey einer andern Gelegenheit niederschrieb, das sich jedoch hauptsächlich auf Ihr Geschäft unmittelbar beziehen lässt.

Eine wahrhaft allgemeine Duldung wird am sichersten erreicht, wenn man das Besondere der einzelnen Menschen und Völkerschaften auf sich beruhen lässt, bey der Ueberzeugung jedoch festhält, dass das wahrhaft Verdienstliche sich dadurch auszeichnet dass es der ganzen Menschheit angehört. Zu einer solchen Vermittlung und wechselseitigen Anerkennung tragen die Deutschen seit langer Zeit schon bey.

He who knows and studies German finds himself in the market where the wares of all countries are offered for sale ; while he enriches himself, he is officiating as interpreter.

A translator therefore should be regarded as a trader in this great spiritual commerce, and as one who makes it his business to advance the exchange of commodities. For say what we will of the inadequacy of translation, it always will be among the weightest and worthiest factors in the world's affairs.

The Koran says that God has given each people a prophet in its own tongue. Each translator is also a prophet to his people. The effects of Luther's translation of the Bible have been immeasurable, though criticism has been at work picking holes in it to the present day. What is the enormous business of the Bible Society but to make known the Gospel to every nation in its own tongue ?

But from this point we might be led into endless speculations. Let me conclude.

Wer die deutsche Sprache versteht und studirt befindet sich auf dem Markte wo alle Nationen ihre Waaren anbieten. Er spielt den Dolmetscher indem er sich selbst bereichert.

Und so ist jeder Uebersetzer anzusehen, dass er sich als Vermittler dieses allgemein geistigen Handels bemüht, und den Wechseltausch zu befördern sich zum Geschäfft macht. Denn was man auch von der Unzulänglichkeit des Uebersetzens sagen mag, so ist und bleibt es doch eines der wichtigsten und würdigsten Geschäffte in dem allgemeinen Weltwesen.

Der Koran sagt : 'Gott hat jedem Volke einen Propheten gegeben in seiner eignen Sprache.' So ist jeder Uebersetzer ein Prophet seinem Volke. Luthers Bibelübersetzung hat die grössten Wirkungen hervorgebracht, wenn schon die Kritik daran bis auf den heutigen Tag immerfort bedingt und mäkelt. Und was ist denn das ganze ungeheure Geschäfft der Bibelgesellschaft als das Evangelium einem jeden Volke in seiner eignen Sprache zu verkündigen ?

Hier lassen Sie mich schliessen, wo man ins Unendliche fortfahren

Oblige me with an early reply, that I may know that my
packet has reached your hands.

Commend me to your excellent wife, for whom I send
a few trifles. Give me pleasure by accepting them in return
for her charming present. May your life together be happy,
and may many years be your portion.

I have yet something to add. May Mr. Carlyle take in
friendly part what I have said above. May he consider it well,
and throw it into dialogue, as if he and I had been conversing
in person together.

I have now to thank him for the pains which he has taken
with my own writings, and for the good and affectionate
tone in which he has been pleased to speak of myself and
of my history. I may thus gratify myself with a belief that
hereafter, on more complete acquaintance with my works,
and after the publication especially of my correspondence
with Schiller, he will not alter his opinion either of my
friend or of me, but will find it confirmed by fresh particulars.

könnte, und erfreuen Sie mich bald mit einiger Erwiederung, wodurch
ich Nachricht erhalte, dass gegenwärtige Sendung zu Ihnen gekommen
ist.

  Zum Schlusse lassen Sie mich denn auch Ihre liebe Gattin begrüssen,
für die ich einige Kleinigkeiten, als Erwiederung ihrer anmuthigen
Gabe, beyzulegen mir die Freude mache. Möge Ihnen ein glückliches
Zusammenleben viele Jahre bescheert seyn.

  Nach allem diesem finde ich mich angeregt Einiges hinzuzufügen :
Möge Herr Carlyle alles obige freundlich aufnehmen und durch anhal-
tende Betrachtung in ein Gespräch verwandeln, damit es ihm zu Muthe
werde als wenn wir persönlich einander gegenüber ständen.

  Habe ich ihm ja sogar noch für die Bemühung zu danken, die er an
meine Arbeiten gewendet hat, für den guten und wohlwollenden Sinn
mit dem er von meiner Persönlichkeit und meinen Lebenereignissen zu
sprechen geneigt war. In dieser Ueberzeugung darf ich mich denn
auch zum voraus freuen, dass künftighin, wenn noch mehrere von
meinen Arbeiten ihm bekannt werden, besonders auch wenn meine
Correspondenz mit Schiller erscheinen wird, er weder von diesem

Wishing him from my heart all good things and with genuine sympathy with him,

J. W. GOETHE.

Such was Goethe's letter, which so much and so justly delighted Carlyle. On a card in a pocket-book sent with it was written, 'Mr. Carlyle will give me especial pleasure by some account of his past life.'
On another card were the lines—

> Augenblicklich aufzuwarten
> Schicken Freunde solche Karten ;
> Diesmal aber heissts nicht gern,
> Euer Freund ist weit und fern.—GOETHE.

Weimar, 20. Juli, 1827.

A third card was in a box with the wrought iron necklace which was intended for Mrs. Carlyle. On this was written—

> Wirst du in den Spiegel blicken
> Und vor deinen heitern Blicken
> Dich die ernste Zierde schmücken :
> Denke dass nichts besser schmückt
> Als wenn man den Freund beglückt.—G.

The ' books ' were ' Faust,' the first five volumes of the

Freunde noch von mir seine Meinung ändern, sondern sie vielmehr durch manches Besondere noch mehr bestätigt finden wird.

Das Beste herzlich wünschend
Treu theilnehmend,
J. W. GOETHE.

Weimar, a. 20. Jul. 1827.

latest edition of Goethe's works, and the last published number of 'Kunst und Alterthum.' There were two medallions, as Carlyle had told his mother—one of them of Goethe with an eagle on the reverse; the other of himself also, with his father and mother on the reverse. The whole present, Carlyle said, was most tasteful, and to him as precious as *any* such present could possibly be.

A still more charming, because unintended, compliment was to follow from the same quarter. When the purposed removal to Craigenputtock came to be talked of among Carlyle's Edinburgh friends, it seemed to them 'considerably fantastic and unreasonable.'

Prospects in Edinburgh (he says) had begun to brighten economically and otherwise; the main origin of this was our acquaintance with the brilliant Jeffrey, a happy accident rather than a matter of forethought on either side. My poor article on Jean Paul, willingly enough admitted into his 'Review,' excited a considerable, though questionable, sensation in Edinburgh, as did the next still weightier discharge of 'German Literature,' in that unexpected vehicle, and at all events denoted me as a fit head for that kind of adventure. In London, shortly after, had arisen a 'Foreign Quarterly Review,' and then in a month or two, on some booksellers' quarrel, a 'Foreign Review,' on both of which I was employed, courted, &c., till their brabble healed itself. This and the like of this formed our principal finance fund during all the Craigenputtock time. For nothing had shaken our determination to the new home. Very well, very well, I said to all this. It will go much further there instead of straitened as here.

The article on German literature reached Weimar.

It was of course anonymous. Goethe read it, and, curious to know the authorship of such an unexpected appearance, wrote to Carlyle for information. 'Can you tell me,' he said, 'who has written the paper on the state of German literature in the "Edinburgh Review"? It is believed here to be by Mr. Lockhart, Sir Walter Scott's stepson. They are both serious, well-disposed men, and equally deserving of honour.'[1] Goethe could not be suspected of insincere politeness, and every sentence of the previous letter was a genuine expression of true feeling; but this indirect praise was so clearly undesigned, that it was doubly encouraging.

Carlyle was still determined on Craigenputtock, but various causes continued to detain him in Edinburgh. The acquaintance with Jeffrey ripened into a warm intimacy. Jeffrey was a frequent visitor in Comely Bank; the Carlyles were as often his guests at Craigcrook. They met interesting persons there, whose society was pleasant and valuable. Jeffrey was himself influential in the great world of politics, and hopes revived—never, perhaps, very ardently in Carlyle himself, but distinctly in his wife and among his friends—that he would be rescued by some fitting appointment from banishment to the Dumfriesshire moors. Carlyle was now famous in a limited circle, and might reasonably be selected for a professorship or some similar

---

[1] I am sorry that of this letter from Goethe only this single passage is preserved. Indeed, as I have already said, the originals of all Goethe's letters to Carlyle have disappeared, and there remain only the copies of some of them which he sent to his brother. *Note 2nd Edition.*—The letters of Goethe have been since found and have been edited by Professor Norton. The full text of this letter is given by Mr. Norton. *Correspondence between Goethe and Carlyle*, p. 40, &c.

situation; while other possibilities opened on various sides to which it was at least his duty to attend. Meanwhile demands came in thick for fresh articles: Jeffrey wanted one on Tasso; the 'Foreign Quarterly' wanted anything that he pleased to send, with liberal offers of pay. He could not afford at such a moment to be out of the reach of libraries, and therefore for the present he left his brother alone in the moorland home.

In the summer he and his wife had run down for a short holiday to Scotsbrig, giving a few brief days to Templand, and a glance at Craigenputtock. By August they were again settled in Comely Bank. The Carlyles, as he said long before, were a clannish set, and clung tenaciously together. The partings after ever so brief a visit were always sorrowful.

To Mrs. Carlyle, Scotsbrig.

21 Comely Bank: August 11.

My dear Mother,—It was pity that we were all so *wae* that day we went off; but one cannot well help it. This life is but a series of meetings and partings, and many a tear one might shed, while these 'few and evil days' pass over us. But we hope there is another scene to which this is but the passage, where good and holy affections shall live as in their home, and for true friends there shall be no more partings appointed. God grant we may all have our lot made sure in that earnest and enduring country; for surely this world, the more one thinks of it, seems the more fluctuating, hollow, and unstable. What are its proudest hopes but bubbles on the stream of time, which the next rushing wave will scatter into air? You have heard of Canning's death—the Prime Minister of Britain, the skilful

statesman on whom all eyes in England and Europe were
expectingly fixed.

> What is life? a thawing ice board
>   On a sea with sunny shore;
> Gay we sail, it melts beneath us;
>   We are sunk and seen no more.

But I must leave these moralities, in which, perhaps, I am
too apt to indulge. Before this time Mary will be with you
and have reported progress up to Monday last, the day when
I left Craigenputtock. She will have told you how Jane and
I were overtaken by rain at Dumfries, and how we spent the
night with the hospital man in Academy Street, and how
his daft maid came bouncing into the room after we were in
bed, to the astonishment of Goody, altogether unaccustomed
to such familiarity. For the rest, however, we did as well
as might be, and the order of 'Mary Stuart's' apartment
was considerably admired. On Monday evening, after
parting with the Doctor, I cantered along without adventure
to Templand; was met two bow-shots from the house by a
young wife well known to me and glad to get me back, and
next morning by ten o'clock both she and I were safely
mounted *on the roof* of the Edinburgh coach, where, the day
being fine, we continued comfortably enough seated, till
about half-past eight the natural progress of the vehicle
landed us safe and sound in our own neighbourhood. The
house was standing quiet and almost overgrown with flowers.
Next day everything returned to its old routine, and we were
sitting in our bright still little cottage as if we had never
stirred out of it. I set to work to trim the garden till my
mind should settle after its wanderings, but as yet I am not
half through with it.

You *must come hither in winter*, that is a settled point.
My father and you may journey together by Hawick, or many

ways. Alick was even calculating the relative costs and profits of coming to Edinburgh himself with a cartload of potatoes and other necessaries. In case of his visiting us, you might all then come together. But *any way you* MUST come. It would be a grievous disappointment if I could not have the pleasure of showing you this city and its wonders, and if we missed this opportunity there is no saying when another might occur. So settle it with yourself that you *are* to come, and in the meantime consider when you can do it best, and we will study to conform.

I went on Saturday to see Jeffrey, but found him from home for a week. So soon as I have got Goethe a letter written, and various other little odd things transacted, I design sitting down to my *large* article for his ‘ Review ; ’ after which I shall be ready for the *poor book*,[1] which, alas ! has been dreadfully overlooked of late. It is a pity one had not twenty minds and hands ; double pity one did not faithfully employ the mind and hands one has ; but I will turn a new leaf shortly, for idle I cannot and must not be. *The sweat of the brow* is not a curse but the wholesomest blessing in life. Remember me in warmest affection to everyone at Scotsbrig. I would give a shilling for a long letter. Surely you may club one up amongst you.

I am ever, my dear mother's son,

T. CARLYLE.

With reputation growing, and economics less unsatisfactory, Carlyle's spirits were evidently rising. We hear no more of pain and sickness and bilious lamentations, and he looked about him in hope and comfort. The London University was getting itself established, offering opportunities for Nonconformist genius such as

---

[1] Not yet consciously abandoned, but never again taken up.

England had never before provided. Professors were wanted there in various departments of knowledge. He was advised to offer himself to be one of them, and he wrote to Irving to inquire, with no particular result:—

To John Carlyle.

Comely Bank: September 5.

I had a letter from Edward Irving the other day about the Æsthetical Professorship in the London University.[1] In a strange, austere, puritanical, yet on the whole honest and friendly looking style, he advises me to proceed and make the attempt. 'The Lord,' he says, blesses him ; his Church rejoices in 'the Lord ;' in fact, the Lord and he seem to be quite hand and glove. He looks unhappy, for his tone sounds hollow, like some voice from a sepulchral aisle ; yet I do honestly believe there is much worth among his failings, much precious truth among all this *cant*. I must even regret that he goes into those matters with so very disunited a heart ; but there where he stands, I wish I and every one of us were half as good men. As to this 'projection,' as he calls it, I have not yet taken any steps, being indeed too busy for doing anything. I was to write to him again, but have not. I wait for counsel from Jeffrey, whom I have not since seen.

In appointments to the London University, the great Brougham, not yet Chancellor or peer, but member for Yorkshire, and greatest orator in the House of Commons, was likely to be omnipotent. Jeffrey, it was equally probable, would carry weight with Brougham ; and Jeffrey, when Carlyle consulted him, expressed the

[1] It was not yet decided what the chair was to be—Rhetoric, Taste, Moral Philosophy, English Literature, or what.

utmost personal willingness to be of use to Carlyle.
But his reply illustrates what Goethe had just observed
about Schiller, that genius rarely finds recognition from
contemporaries as long as it can possibly be withheld.
At all times, Jeffrey said, he would be willing to recommend Carlyle as a man of genius and learning; he did
not conceal, however, that difficulties would lie in the
way of his success in this especial enterprise. Carlyle,
he said, was a sectary in taste and literature, and was
inspired with the zeal by which sectaries were distinguished; nay, was inclined to magnify the special
doctrines of his sect, and rather to aggravate than
reconcile the differences which divided them from
others. He confessed, therefore, that he doubted
whether the patrons either would or ought to appoint
such a person to such a charge. The sincerity and
frankness of Carlyle's character increased the objection;
the more honest he was the more peremptorily he
would insist on the articles of his philosophic creed—a
creed which no one of the patrons adopted, and most of
them regarded as damnable heresy. It was therefore
but too likely that this would prove an insuperable
obstacle. In all other respects Jeffrey considered
Carlyle fully qualified, and likely, if appointed, to do
great credit to the establishment. But he was afraid
that Carlyle would not wish to disguise those singulari-
ties of opinion from which he foresaw the obstructions
to his success; and as a further difficulty he added that
the chair at which Carlyle was aiming had long been
designed for Thomas Campbell, and would probably be
given to him.

Jeffrey invited Carlyle and his wife to dinner, however, to talk the chances over. Carlyle assured Jeffrey 'that there was no sectarianism or heresy in the matter. He was more open to light,' he said, 'than others of his craft; and he was satisfied for himself that the patrons of the University would do excellently well to make him professor.' 'Jeffrey,' Mrs. Carlyle thought, 'was in his heart of the same opinion.' She was herself uncertain whether she wished her husband to succeed or not; but London would at all events be an escape from Craigenputtock. Reflection had not tended to make the moor more palatable to her. Her little sister-in-law Jean had just been sent out thither to keep her brother company.

'Poor Jean!' Mrs. Carlyle wrote about this. 'She is seeing the world all on a sudden. What will the creature make of herself at Craigenputtock? I hope they took her garters from her, and everything in the shape of hemp or steel.'

Jeffrey did what he could, perhaps not with very great ardour, but with vigour enough to save him from the charge of neglecting his friend. He went on a visit to Brougham in the autumn. He mentioned Carlyle, and in high terms of praise. He 'found Brougham, however, singularly shy on the subject, and though the subject was introduced half a dozen times during Jeffrey's stay, Brougham was careful to evade it, in a way that showed that he did not wish to be pressed for an answer even by an intimate friend.'

'I may add in confidence,' Jeffrey said, 'that he made very light of Irving's recommendation, and it was not likely to be of much weight with any of the other directors either.'

Notwithstanding these discouragements, Carlyle silently nourished some hope of success.

I believe (he wrote to his brother in October) that no appointment to the London chair will take place for a considerable time, and in the meanwhile Brougham will keep his eye on me, and if he finds that I prosper may apply to me; if not, will leave me standing. At all events the thing is right. I am before these people in some shape, perhaps as near my real one as I could expect; and if they want nothing with me, 'the Devil b' in me,' as daft Wull said, if I want anything with them either. I am still as undetermined as ever whether their acceptance of me would be for my good or not.

He came to know Brougham better in after years. There was probably no person in England less likely to recognise Carlyle's qualities; and the more distinguished Carlyle became, the more Brougham was sure to have congratulated himself on having kept his new University clear of such an influence. It must be admitted that the '*disesteem*' was equally marked on both sides.

Carlyle meanwhile did not rest on the vain imagination of help from others. He worked with all his might on the new line which had been opened to him, and here I have to mention one of those peculiarly honourable characteristics which meet us suddenly at all turns of his career. He had paid his brother's expenses at the University out of his salary as the Bullers' tutor. He was now poor himself with increased demands upon him, but the first use which he made of his slightly improved finances was to send John Carlyle to complete his education in the medical schools in Germany. He estimated John's talents with a brother's affection, and he was resolved to give him the best chances of distinguishing himself. The cost was greater than he had calculated on, but he was not discouraged.

To John Carlyle.

Comely Bank: November 29, 1827.

Do not, good brother, let thy heart be cast down for the Mammon of this world. A few more hard sovereigns we are yet, thank Heaven, in a condition to furnish. Write for what is necessary and it will be sent. Above all do not neglect dissection and surgery for the sake of any poor thrift there might be in the omission of it. Go on and prosper. Learn all and everything that is to be learned ; and if you come home to us a good well-appointed man and physician, we will not think the money ill-bestowed.

The remainder of the same letter carries on the picture of daily life at Comely Bank.

The 'Edinburgh Review' is out some time ago, and the 'State of German Literature' has been received with considerable surprise and approbation by the Universe. Thus, for instance, De Quincey praises it in his 'Saturday Post.' Sir William Hamilton tells me it is 'cap-tal,' and Wilson informs John Gordon that it 'has done me a deil o' good.' De Quincey was here last Wednesday and sate till midnight. He is one of the smallest men you ever in your life beheld ; but with a most gentle and sensible face, only that the teeth are destroyed by opium, and the little bit of an under lip projects like a shelf. He speaks with a slow, sad, and soft voice in the politest manner I have almost ever witnessed, and with great gracefulness and sense, were it not that he seems decidedly given to prosing. Poor little fellow ! It might soften a very hard heart to see him so courteous, yet so weak and poor ; retiring *home* with his two children to a miserable lodging-house, and writing all day for the king of donkeys, the proprietor of the 'Saturday Post.' I lent him Jean Paul's autobiography, which I got lately from Hamburgh, and advised him to translate it for Blackwood, that so he might raise a few pounds, and fence off the Genius of Hunger yet a little while. Poor little De Quincey ! He is an innocent man, and, as you said, extremely *washable* away.

CHAPTER XXII.

A.D 1827. ÆT. 32.

WHILE Carlyle was taking care of his brother, an active interest was rising in Edinburgh about himself. Scotch people were beginning to see that a remarkable man had appeared among them, and that they ought not to let him slip through their hands. A new opening presented itself which he thus describes to his father.

To Mr. James Carlyle, Scotsbrig.

Comely Bank : December 22.

There has been a fresh enterprise started for me, no less than the attempt to be successor to Dr. Chalmers in the St. Andrew's University. He, Chalmers, is at present Professor of Moral Philosophy there, but is just removing to Edinburgh to be Professor of Divinity, and I have been consulting with my friends whether it would be prudent in me to offer myself as a candidate for the vacant office. They all seem to think sincerely that if the election proceeded on fair principles I might have a chance of rather a good sort ; but this proviso is only a doubtful one, the custom having long been to decide such things by very *un*fair principles. As yet nothing is determined ; but my patrons are making inquiry to see how the land lies ; and some time next week we shall know what to do. Most part are inclined to think I ought to try.

Among those who encouraged Carlyle in this

ambition, and lent active help, Jeffrey was now the first, and, besides general recommendations, wrote most strongly in his favour to Dr. Nicol, the Principal of the University. Equal testimonials, viewed by the intrinsic quality of the givers, to those which were collected or spontaneously offered on this occasion, were perhaps never presented by any candidate for a Scotch professorship. Goethe himself wrote one, which in these times might have carried the day; but Goethe was then only known in Scotland as a German dreamer. Carlyle, though again personally pretending indifference, exerted himself to the utmost, and was, perhaps, more anxious than he was aware of being.

To Mrs. Carlyle, Scotsbrig.

Comely Bank : January, 1828.

I am as diligent as possible storming the battlements of St. Andrew's University for *the* professorship for which I have actually eight days ago declared myself formally a candidate ! This was after all due investigation, conducted by Jeffrey and others, from which, if I could gather no fixed hope of my succeeding, it seemed at least that there was no fixed determination against me ; that I might try without censure—nay, in my circumstances, ought to try. I accordingly wrote off to St. Andrews, and next day to all the four winds, in quest of recommendations—to Goethe, to Irving, to Buller, to Brewster, &c. These same recommendations are now beginning to come in upon me. I had one from Brewster two days ago (with the offer of further help), and this morning came a decent testificatory letter from Buller, and a most majestic certificate in three pages from Edward Irving. The good orator speaks as from the heart, and truly says, as he has ever done, that he thinks me a most worthy man—not forgetting to mention among my other advantages the 'prayers of religious parents,' a blessing which, if I speak less of it, I hope I do not feel less than he. On the whole it is a splendid affair this of his ; and being tempered by the recommendation of John Leslie,[1] may do me much good. Before the end of next week I expect to have all my testimonials sent off ; and there the matter may for a long time rest, the period of election being still unfixed. Of my hopes and calculations as to success I can say nothing, being myself able to form no judgment. I am taught to believe that if merit gain it, I shall gain ; which is a proud belief and ought to render failure a matter of comparative indifference to me ; more especially as, like the weather in Cowthwaites' calculations, I can do 'owther way.' I often care not sixpence whether I get it or no ; but we shall see. If it is laid out for me it *will* come ; if not, not.

Jeffrey had been alert making inquiries. The nomination he had found to rest in substance with the Principal, Dr. Nicol, an active, jobbing, popular man, who had placed most of the present professors and conferred obligations on all, and who, through his influence in earlier days with Lord Melville, had acquired an absolute ascendency in the St. Andrew's Senate. Nicol secured, the rest of the votes might be counted on ; without Nicol they could not. The Principal was described by Jeffrey as good-natured, sensible, and worldly, not without some sense of the propriety of attracting men of talent and reputation into the University staff ; but cautious and prudent,

[1] Sir John Leslie, Professor of Mathematics in Edinburgh, who had been Carlyle's teacher.

possessing neither genius nor learning, and without reverence for them. In Church matters Nicol was moderate, with distrust and contempt for every kind of enthusiasm. It was not unlikely, therefore, that he had already cast his eyes on some decent, manageable, and judicious priest for the office. With such a man testimonials from Irving would be rather injurious than useful. Men of rank would weigh most, and next to them men of repute for learning.

There is a certain humour in the claims of Thomas Carlyle, supported by the most famous man of letters in Europe, being submitted to be tried in the scales by such a person as this. But so it was, and is, and perhaps must be, in constitutional countries, where high office may fall on the worthy, but rarely or never on the most worthy. It is difficult everywhere for the highest order of merit to find recognition. Under a system of popular election it is almost impossible.

My testimonials (Carlyle wrote to his brother John) [1] are in such terms that if I cannot carry the place I think it may seem vain to attempt to carry *any* such place by means of testimonials to *merit* alone. The dear little Duke [2]— Jane says she could kiss him—has written me a paper which might of itself bring me any professorship in the island. Irving also spends five heroical pages on my merits, and Wilson says there is no man known to him fitter for the office ; so what more can I do but let the matter take its course and await the issue ' with indescribable composure.' The truth is, I hardly care which way it go. A man, if you

---

[1] Feb. 1, 1828.

[2] Duke of Craigcrook, the name by which Jeffrey went.

give him meat and clothes, is, or ought to be, sufficient for
himself in this world ; and his culture is but beginning if
he think that any outward influence of person or thing can
either make him or mar him. If I do not go thither (which,
after all, is very likely ; for ——, an old stager, talks of
applying), why then *I* shall not go, and *they* will not get
me ; and the sun will rise and set, and the grass will grow,
and I shall have eyes to see and ears to hear notwithstanding.
Do all that you can in honesty, and reckon the result indubitable ; for the *inward* result will not fail if rightly
endeavoured : and for the *outward*, 'non flocci facias,' do
not value it a rush.

After a few weeks the suspense was over. Carlyle
was not appointed ; someone else was ; and someone
else's church was made over to another someone else
whom it was desirable to oblige ; 'and so the whole
matter was rounded off in the neatest manner possible.'
Such at least was Carlyle's account of what he understood to be the arrangement. Perhaps the 'someone
else' was a fitter person after all. Education in
countries so jealous of novelty as Great Britain is, or
at least was sixty years ago, follows naturally upon lines
traced out by custom, and the conduct of it falls as a
matter of course to persons who have never deviated
from those lines. New truths are the nutriment of the
world's progress. Men of genius discover them, insist
upon them, prove them in the face of opposition, and
if the genius is not merely a phosphorescent glitter,
but an abiding light, their teaching enters in time into
the University curriculum. But out of new ideas time
alone can distinguish the sound and real from the
illusive and imaginary ; and it was enough that

Carlyle was described as a man of original and extra-ordinary gifts to make college patrons shrink from contact with him.

Carlyle himself dimly felt that St. Andrew's might not be the best place for him. It seemed hard to refuse promotion to a man because he was too good for it, and no doubt he would have been pleased to be appointed. But for the work which Carlyle had to do a position of intellectual independence was indispens-able, and his apprenticeship to poverty and hardship had to be prolonged still further to harden his nerves and perhaps to test his sincerity. The loss of this professorship may be regretted for Mrs. Carlyle's sake, who did not need the trials which lay before her. Carlyle himself in a University chair would have been famous in his day, and have risen to wealth and conse-quence, but he might not have been the Carlyle who has conquered a place for himself among the Im-mortals.

So ended the only fair prospect which ever was opened to him of entering any of the beaten roads of life; and fate having thus decided in spite of the loud remonstrance of all friends, of Jeffrey especially, Carlyle became once more bent on removing to Craigenputtock.

The certificate of the angel Gabriel (he said) would not have availed me a pin's worth. The Devil may care ; I can still live independent of all persons whatever. At the Craig, if we stick together as we have done, we may fairly bid defiance to the constable. Praised be heaven ! for of all curses that of being baited for debt, or even frightened of falling into it, is surely the bitterest.

The repairs in the old house were hastened forward, that it might be ready for them in the spring.

The domestic scene in Comely Bank had been meantime brightened by the long-talked-of event of the visit of old Mrs. Carlyle to Edinburgh. In all her long life she had never yet been beyond Annandale, had never seen the interior of any better residence than a Scottish farmhouse. To the infinite heaven spread above the narrow circle of her horizon she had perhaps risen as near on wings of prayer and piety as any human being who was upon the earth beside her; but of the earth itself, of her own Scotland, she knew no more than could be descried from Burnswark Hill. She was to spend Christmas week at Comely Bank. She arrived at the beginning of December.

To James Carlyle, Scotsbrig.

Comely Bank: December 22, 1827.

My dear Father,—My mother will not let me rest any longer till I write to you; she says it was promised that a letter should go off the very night Jean and she arrived; and nevertheless it is a melancholy fact that above two weeks have elapsed since that event, and no better tidings been sent you than a word or two in the blank line of the ' Courier.' I would have written sooner had I been in right case, or indeed had there been anything more to communicate than what so brief an announcement might convey as well as a much larger one.

The two wayfarers did *not* find me waiting for them at the coach that Wednesday evening. Unhappily it was quite out of my power to keep that or any other appointment. I had been seized about a week before with a most

virulent sore-throat, which detained me close prisoner in the
house.   All that I could do in these circumstances was
to send out a trusty substitute, a Mr. Gordon, who kindly
undertook the office.   But he, mistaking one coach for
another, went and waited at the *wrong* inn ; so that our
beloved pilgrims were left to their own resources, and had to
pilot their way hither under the guidance of the porter who
carried their box.   This, however, they accomplished without
difficulty or accident, and rejoiced us all by their safe and, in
part at least, unexpected arrival.

Since then all things have gone on prosperously.   Jane
has been busy, and still is so, getting ready suitable apparel
of bonnets and frocks.   My mother has heard Andrew
Thomson in his 'braw kirk,' not much to her satisfaction,
since 'he had to light *four* candles before ever he could
strike.'   She has also seen old Mrs. Hope, the Castle of
Edinburgh, the Martyrs' Graves, John Knox's house, and
who knows how many other wonders, of which I doubt not
she will give you a true and full description when she returns.
As yet, however, the half has not been seen.   The weather
has been so stormy that travelling out was difficult, and I
have been in no high condition for officiating as guide.   In
stormy days she *smokes* along with me, or sews wearing
raiment, or reads the wonderful articles of my writing in the
'Edinburgh Review.'   She has also had a glimpse of Francis
Jeffrey, the great critic and advocate, and a shake of the
hand from a true German doctor.

Nevertheless she is extremely anxious about getting
home, and indeed fails no day to tell us several times that
she ought to be off.   'She is doing nothing,' she says ;
'and they'll a' be in a hubble of work ' at home.   I tell her
she was never idle for two weeks in her life before, and
ought therefore to give it a fair trial ; that 'the hubble at
home' will all go on rightly enough in her absence ; that,

in short, she should not go this year but the next. So I am in hopes we shall get her persuaded to stay where she is till after New Year's Day, which is now only nine or ten days distant, and then we will let her go in peace. The two Janes and she are all out in the town at present buying muslin for sundry necessary articles of dress which we have persuaded the mother to undertake the wearing of. These may keep her, I hope, in some sort of occupation ; for idle, I see, she cannot and will not be. We will warn you duly when to expect her.

I trust *you* will soon be well enough for a journey hither ; for you too, my dear father, *must* see Edinburgh before we leave it. I have thoughts of *compelling* you to come with me when I come down.

I am ever, your affectionate son,

T. CARLYLE.

James Carlyle did not come. He was with his son once afterwards at Craigenputtock, but he never saw Edinburgh.

My mother (Carlyle wrote to his brother on the 1st of February) stayed about four weeks, then went home by Hawick, pausing a few days there. She was in her usual health, wondered much at Edinburgh, but did not seem to relish it excessively. I had her at the pier of Leith and showed her where your ship vanished, and she looked over the blue waters eastward with wettish eyes, and asked the dumb waters 'when he would be back again.' Good mother ! but the time of her departure came on, and she left us stupefied by the magnitude of such an enterprise as riding over eighty miles in the ' Sir Walter Scott ' without jumping out of the window, which I told her was the problem. Dear mother ! let us thank God that she is still here in the earth spared for us, and, I hope, to see good. I would not exchange her for any ten mothers I have ever seen. Jane (Jean) the less she left behind her, ' to improve her mind.' The creature seems to be doing very fairly, and is well and contented. *My* Jane, I grieve to say, is yet far enough from well, but I hope much from summer weather and a smart pony in the south. She is not by any means an established *valetudinarian*, yet she seldom has a day of true health, and has not gained strength entirely since you left her.

I give a few more extracts from letters written to his brother during the remainder of the Comely Bank time.

To John Carlyle.

Comely Bank : March 7.

Explain to me how I may send you a matter of twenty pounds, or such other sum as you may require, to bring you home to us again. I have no want of money for all needful purposes at present ; and (I thank God for it) I am able to earn more ; neither is there any investment for it half so good as these in the bank of affection, where perishable silver and gold is converted into imperishable remembrances of kind feelings. Speak, therefore, plainly and speedily and it shall be done. . . .

I am glad to find that you admire Schelling, and know that you do not understand him. That is right, my dear Greatheart. Look into the deeply significant regions of Transcendental philosophy (as all philosophy *must* be) and feel that there are wonders and mighty truths hidden in them ; but look with your clear grey Scottish eyes and shrewd Scottish understanding, and refuse to be mystified even by your admiration. Meanwhile, Diligence, Truth ; Truth, Diligence. These are our watchwords, whether we have ten talents or only a decimal fraction of one.

I have not a syllable to tell you about the London University except that according to all human probability the people neither now nor at any other time will have the least to do with me. I heard the other day from Charles Buller the younger. He says that, hearing of my purpose, he went to Mill (the British India Philister), who is one of the directors, and spoke with him ; but found that my German metaphysics were an unspeakable stone of stumbling to that great thinker, whereby Buller began to perceive that my chances had diminished to the neighbourhood of zero. It appears, however, that I am become a sort of newspaper *Literatus* in London on the strength of these articles (bless them), and that certain persons wonder what manner of man I am. A critic in the ' Courier ' (apparently the worst in nature from the one sentence that I read of him) says I am ' the supremest German scholar in the British Empire.' *Das hole der Teufel !* However, I am rather amused at the *naïveté* with which Crabbe Robinson talks to me on this subject. He characterises the papers as a splendid instance of literary *ratting* on the part of the editor, and imputing the whole composition to a Sir — Hamilton, advocate, says it has some eloquence, and though it cuts its own throat (to speak as a figure), will do GOOD.

The ' Foreign Review ' gave me 47*l*. for my trash on Werner.[1] I have sent them a far better paper on Goethe's ' Helena,'[2] for which I shall not get so much. I have engaged to send in a long paper on Goethe's character, generally, this of ' Helena ' being a sort of introduction.

---

[1] *Miscellanies*, vol. i. p. 101.

[2] *Ibid.* p. 171.

How matters stand at Craigenputtock I can only guess, but am going down to see. I am in no small uncertainty. This Edinburgh is getting more agreeable to me, more and more a sort of home ; and I *can* live in it, if I like to live perpetually unhealthy, and strive for ever against becoming a *hack ;* for that I cannot be. On the other hand, I should have liberty and solitude for aught I like best among the moors—only Jane, though like a good wife she says nothing, seems evidently getting more and more afraid of the whole enterprise. She is not at all stout in health. But I must go and look at things with my own eyes, and now as ever there is need of mature resolve, and steadfast when mature.

March 12.

Jeffrey and I continue to love one another like a new Pylades and Orestes. At least, such is often my feeling towards him. Good little Duke ! There are few men like thee in this world, Epicurean in creed though thou be, and living all thy days among Turks in grain.

Wilson I can get little good of, though we are as great as ever. Poor Wilson ! It seems as if he shrunk from too close a union with anyone. His whole being seems hollowed out, as it were, and false and counterfeit in his own eyes. So he encircles himself with wild cloudy sportfulness, which to me often seems reckless and at bottom full of sharp sorrow. Oh that a man would not halt between two opinions. How can anyone love poetry and rizzered haddocks with whisky toddy, outwatch the Bear with Peter Robinson, and at the same time with William Wordsworth ? For the last four weeks he has been very unwell, and his friends are not without apprehension for him. He purposes to visit Switzerland in summer and take De Quincey with him. I called yesterday on De Quincey about two o'clock and found him invisible in bed. His landlady, a dirty, very wicked looking woman, said, if he rose at all, it was usually about five o'clock. Unhappy little opium eater, and a quicker little fellow, or of meeker soul (if he had but lived in Paradise or Lubberland) is not to be found in these parts.

The intellectual city is at present entertaining itself not a little with the Apocrypha controversy, in which Grey the minister and Thomson the minister are exhibiting the various manner of offence and defence, to the edification of all parties interested. Translated into the language of the shambles, where their spirit clearly enough originates, these pamphlets of theirs mean simply, 'Sir, you are a d—d rascal,' and 'No, sir, *you* are a d—d rascal.' Happily I have read next to nothing of the whole, and heard as little of it as I possibly could. But now some private wag has taken up the task of caricaturing in pictorial wise these reverend persons ; and a crowd shoving and shouldering for a clear and clearer view may be seen at all printshop windows contemplating the distorted figures of their *pawstors* depicted as bulldogs and greyhounds, as preachers and prizefighters climbing the steeple like orthodox men, or throttling one another like exasperated fishwomen ; for there are said to be twelve caricatures in the course of publication, and a fresh one comes out every now and then. What Thomson and Grey say to it I know not. For myself I should only say in the words of the old poem—

> May the Lord put an end unto all cruel wars,
> And send peace and contentment unto all British tars.

Eager as Carlyle was to be gone from Edinburgh, he confessed that in his wife's manner he had detected an unwillingness to bury herself in the moors. The evident weakness of her health alarmed him, and he could scarcely have forgotten the aversion with which

she had received his first suggestion of making Craigenputtock their home. For himself his mind was
made up; and usually when Carlyle wished anything
he was not easily impressed with objections to it.
In this instance, however, he was evidently hesitating.
Craigenputtock, sixteen miles from the nearest town
and the nearest doctor, cut off from the outer world
through the winter months by snow and flood, in
itself gaunt, grim, comfortless, and utterly solitary,
was not a spot exactly suited to a delicate and daintily
nurtured woman. In the counter scale was her
mother, living a few miles below in Nithsdale. But
for this attraction Mrs. Carlyle would have declined
the adventure altogether; as it was she trembled at
the thought of it.

The house in Comely Bank was held only by the
year. They were called on to determine whether they
would take it for another twelve months or not. Before deciding they resolved to see Craigenputtock together once more. Little Jean was left in charge at
Edinburgh, and Carlyle and Mrs. Carlyle went down
to Dumfriesshire. 'I still remember,' he said in the
'Reminiscences,' 'two grey blusterous March days at
Craigenputtock with the proof-sheets of Goethe's
"Helena" in my hand, and Dumfries architects chao-
tically joined therewith.'

On a blusterous March day Craigenputtock could
not look to advantage. They left it still irresolute,
and perhaps inclining to remain among their friends.
But the question had been settled for them in their
absence; on returning to Comely Bank they found
that their landlord, not caring to wait longer till they

had made up their minds, had let the house to another tenant, and that at all events they would have to leave it at Whitsuntide. This ended the uncertainty.

We found all well at Comely Bank (Carlyle wrote to his mother, when he came back), only the fire a little low, and the maid gone out seeking places, so that it was some space before tea could be raised. The wise young stewardess [1] had sunk considerably into pecuniary embarrassments, but in all other points was well and happy, and had managed herself throughout with a degree of prudence and *gumption* far beyond her years. Indeed both Jane and I were surprised at the acuteness the little crow had displayed in all emergencies, and perhaps still more at the strange growth she had made in manner and bearing during our absence, for she seemed to have enlarged into a sort of woman during that period of self-direction. The best of our news is that we *are* coming down to the Craig this Whitsunday to take up our abode there. This house was found to have been *let* during our absence. Since we had to flit any way, whither should we flit but to our own house on the moor? We are coming down then against the term, to *neighbour* you. Will you be good neighbours or bad? I cannot say, Mrs. Carlyle, but I jealouse you, I jealouse you. However, we are to try; for Jane and I were out this very day, buying paper for the two rooms, which is already on its way to Dumfries; and the painters we trust are busy, and Aliek and Uncle John doing great things, that the mansion house may be swept and smooth by the 26th of May, when we will visit it with bag and baggage, we hope as a permanent home.

I anticipate with confidence (he wrote at the same time to his brother) a friendly and rather comfortable arrangement

---

[1] Jean, his sister.

at the Craig, in which, not in idleness, yet in peace and more self-selected occupations, I may find more health, and, what I reckon weightier, more scope to improve and worthily employ myself, which either here or there I reckon to be the great end of existence and the only happiness.

So ended the life at 21 Comely Bank—the first married home of the Carlyles; which began ominously, as a vessel rolls when first launched, threatening an overturn, and closed with improved health and spirits on Carlyle's part, and prospects which, if not brilliant, were encouraging and improving. He had been fairly introduced into the higher walks of his profession, and was noticed and talked about. Besides the two articles on Jean Paul and on German literature, he had written the paper on Werner, the essay on Goethe's ' Helena,' and the more elaborate and remarkable essay on Goethe himself, which now stand among the ' Miscellanies.' [1]   Goethe personally remained kind and attentive.   He had studied Carlyle's intellectual temperament, and had used an expression about him in the St. Andrews testimonial which showed how clear an insight he had gained into the character of it. Carlyle was resting, he said, on an *original foundation*, and was so happily constituted that he could develop out of himself the requirements of what was good and beautiful [2]—*out of himself*, not out of contact with others.   The work could be done, therefore, as well,

---

[1] Vol. i. p. 233.

[2] ' Wodurch an den Tag gelegt wird, dass er auf einem originalen Grund beruhe, und die Erfordernisse des Guten und Schönen aus sich selbst zu entwickeln das Vergnügen habe.'   *Note 2nd Edition.*—Testimonial given in full by Norton, p. 71.

or perhaps better, in solitude. Along with the testimonial had come a fresh set of presents, with more cards and verses and books, and with a remembrance of himself which Carlyle was to deliver to Sir Walter Scott. It was a proud tribute, and proud he was to report of it to Scotsbrig.

I must tell you (he wrote) of the arrival of Goethe's box, with such a catalogue of rarities as would astonish you. There was a bracelet and gold breast-pin (with the poet's bust on a ground of steel), besides two gilt books for Jane, and for the husband I know not how many verses and cards and beautiful volumes, the whole wrapped in about half a quire of German newspapers. Sir Walter Scott's medals are not yet delivered, the baronet being at present in London ; but I have written to him announcing what lies here for his acceptance, and in some week or two I cannot but expect that I shall speak with the great man and, having delivered my commission, wish him good morning. To Goethe I have already written to thank him for such kindness.

This was the last of Comely Bank. A few days later the Carlyles were gone to the Dumfriesshire moorland where for seven years was now to be their dwelling-place. Carlyle never spoke to Scott, as he hoped to do ; nor did Sir Walter even acknowledge his letter. It seems that the medals and the letter to Scott from Goethe were entrusted to Wilson, by whom, or by Jeffrey, they were delivered to Scott on the arrival of the latter soon after in Edinburgh. Carlyle's letter, of which Wilson had also taken charge, was perhaps forgotten by him.

A CATALOGUE OF WORKS

IN

GENERAL LITERATURE

PUBLISHED BY

MESSRS. LONGMANS, GREEN, & CO.,

39 PATERNOSTER ROW, LONDON, E.C.

MESSRS. LONGMANS, GREEN, & CO.

Issue the undermentioned Lists of their Publications, which may be had post free on application :—

1. MONTHLY LIST OF NEW WORKS AND NEW EDITIONS.
2. QUARTERLY LIST OF ANNOUNCEMENTS AND NEW WORKS.
3. NOTES ON BOOKS; BEING AN ANALYSIS OF THE WORKS PUBLISHED DURING EACH QUARTER.
4. CATALOGUE OF SCIENTIFIC WORKS.
5. CATALOGUE OF MEDICAL AND SURGICAL WORKS.
6. CATALOGUE OF SCHOOL BOOKS AND EDUCATIONAL WORKS.
7. CATALOGUE OF BOOKS FOR ELEMENTARY SCHOOLS AND PUPIL TEACHERS.
8. CATALOGUE OF THEOLOGICAL WORKS BY DIVINES AND MEMBERS OF THE CHURCH OF ENGLAND.
9. CATALOGUE OF WORKS IN GENERAL LITERATURE.

ABBEY (Rev. C. J.) and OVERTON (Rev. J. H.).—THE ENGLISH CHURCH IN THE EIGHTEENTH CENTURY. Cr. 8vo. 7s. 6d.

ABBOTT (Evelyn).—A HISTORY OF GREECE. In Two Parts.
Part I.—From the Earliest Times to the Ionian Revolt. Cr. 8vo. 10s. 6d.
Part II. Vol. I.—500-445 B.C. [*In the Press.*] Vol. II.—[*In Preparation.*]

———— HELLENICA. A Collection of Essays on Greek Poetry, Philosophy, History, and Religion. Edited by EVELYN ABBOTT. 8vo. 16s.

ACLAND (A. H. Dyke) and RANSOME (Cyril).—A HANDBOOK IN OUTLINE OF THE POLITICAL HISTORY OF ENGLAND TO 1890. Chronologically Arranged. Crown 8vo. 6s.

ACTON (Eliza).—MODERN COOKERY. With 150 Woodcuts. Fcp. 8vo. 4s. 6d.

A. K. H. B.—THE ESSAYS AND CONTRIBUTIONS OF. Crown 8vo. 3s. 6d. each.

Autumn Holidays of a Country Parson.

Changed Aspects of Unchanged Truths.

Commonplace Philosopher.

Counsel and Comfort from a City Pulpit.

Critical Essays of a Country Parson.

East Coast Days and Memories.

Graver Thoughts of a Country Parson. Three Series.

Landscapes, Churches, and Moralities.

Leisure Hours in Town.

Lessons of Middle Age.

Our Little Life. Two Series.

Our Homely Comedy and Tragedy.

Present Day Thoughts.

Recreations of a Country Parson. Three Series.

Seaside Musings.

Sunday Afternoons in the Parish Church of a Scottish University City.

———— 'To Meet the Day' through the Christian Year; being a Text of Scripture, with an Original Meditation and a Short Selection in Verse for Every Day. Crown 8vo. 4s. 6d.

AMERICAN WHIST, Illustrated: containing the Laws and Principles of the Game, the Analysis of the New Play. By G. W. P. Fcp. 8vo. 6s. 6d.

AMOS (Sheldon).—A PRIMER OF THE ENGLISH CONSTITUTION AND GOVERNMENT. Crown 8vo. 6s.

ANNUAL REGISTER (The). A Review of Public Events at Home and Abroad, for the year 1800. 8vo. 18s.

. Volumes of the 'Annual Register' for the years 1863-1889 can still be had.

ANSTEY (F.).—THE BLACK POODLE, and other Stories. Crown 8vo. 2s. boards.; 2s. 6d. cloth.

———— VOCES POPULI. Reprinted from *Punch*. First Series, with 20 Illustrations by J. BERNARD PARTRIDGE. Fcp. 4to. 5s.

ARISTOTLE—The Works of.

———— THE POLITICS, G. Bekker's Greek Text of Books I. III. IV. (VII.), with an English Translation by W. E. BOLLAND, and short Introductory Essays by ANDREW LANG. Crown 8vo. 7s. 6d.

———— THE POLITICS, Introductory Essays. By ANDREW LANG. (From Bolland and Lang's 'Politics'.) Crown 8vo. 2s. 6d.

———— THE ETHICS, Greek Text, illustrated with Essays and Notes. By Sir ALEXANDER GRANT, Bart. 2 vols. 8vo. 32s.

———— THE NICOMACHEAN ETHICS, newly translated into English. By ROBERT WILLIAMS. Crown 8vo. 7s. 6d.

ARMSTRONG (G. F. Savage-).—POEMS: Lyrical and Dramatic. Fcp. 8vo. 6s.

BY THE SAME AUTHOR. Fcp. 8vo.

King Saul. 5s.

King David. 5s.

King Solomon. 6s.

Ugone; a Tragedy. 6s.

A Garland from Greece. Poems. 9s.

Stories of Wicklow. Poems. 9s.

Mephistopheles in Broadcloth; a Satire. 4s.

The Life and Letters of Edmond J. Armstrong. 7s. 6d.

ARMSTRONG (E. J.).—POETICAL WORKS. Fcp. 8vo. 5s.

———— ESSAYS AND SKETCHES. Fcp. 8vo. 5s.

ARNOLD (Sir Edwin).—THE LIGHT OF THE WORLD, or the Great Consummation. A Poem. Crown 8vo. 7s. 6d. net.

ARNOLD (Dr. T.).—INTRODUCTORY LECTURES ON MODERN HISTORY. 8vo. 7s. 6d.

———— SERMONS PREACHED MOSTLY IN THE CHAPEL OF RUGBY SCHOOL. 6 vols. crown 8vo. 30s., or separately, 5s. each.

———— MISCELLANEOUS WORKS. 8vo. 7s. 6d.

ASHLEY (J. W.).—ENGLISH ECONOMIC HISTORY AND THEORY. Part I.—The Middle Ages. Crown 8vo. 5s.

ATELIER (The) du Lys; or, An Art Student in the Reign of Terror. By the Author of ' Mademoiselle Mori '. Crown 8vo. 2s. 6d.

BY THE SAME AUTHOR. Crown 2s. 6d. each.

MADEMOISELLE MORI.
THAT CHILD.
UNDER A CLOUD.
THE FIDDLER OF LUGAU.
A CHILD OF THE REVOLU-TION.
HESTER'S VENTURE.
IN THE OLDEN TIME.

BACON.—COMPLETE WORKS. Edited by R. L. ELLIS, J. SPEDDING, and D. D. HEATH. 7 vols. 8vo. £3 13s. 6d.

———— LETTERS AND LIFE, INCLUDING ALL HIS OCCASIONAL WORKS. Edited by J. SPEDDING. 7 vols. 8vo. £4 4s.

———— THE ESSAYS; with Annotations. By Archbishop WHATELY. 8vo. 10s. 6d.

———— THE ESSAYS; with Introduction, Notes, and Index. By E. A. ABBOTT. 2 vols. Fcp. 8vo. 6s. Text and Index only. Fcp. 8vo. 2s. 6d.

BADMINTON LIBRARY (The), edited by the DUKE OF BEAUFORT, assisted by ALFRED E. T. WATSON.

HUNTING. By the DUKE OF BEAUFORT, and MOWBRAY MORRIS. With 53 Illustrations. Crown 8vo. 10s. 6d.

FISHING. By H. CHOLMONDELEY-PENNELL.
Vol. I. Salmon, Trout, and Grayling. 158 Illustrations. Crown 8vo. 10s. 6d.
Vol. II. Pike and other Coarse Fish. 132 Illustrations. Crown 8vo. 10s. 6d.

RACING AND STEEPLECHASING. By the EARL OF SUFFOLK AND BERKSHIRE, W. G. CRAVEN, &c. 56 Illustrations. Crown 8vo. 10s. 6d.

SHOOTING. By LORD WALSINGHAM, and Sir RALPH PAYNE-GALLWEY, Bart.
Vol. I. Field and Covert. With 105 Illustrations. Crown 8vo. 10s. 6d.
Vol. II. Moor and Marsh. With 65 Illustrations. Crown 8vo. 10s. 6d.

CYCLING. By VISCOUNT BURY (Earl of Albemarle) and G. LACY HILLIER. With 89 Illustrations. Crown 8vo. 10s. 6d.

ATHLETICS AND FOOTBALL. By MONTAGUE SHEARMAN. With 41 Illustrations. Crown 8vo. 10s. 6d.

BOATING. By W. B. WOODGATE. With 49 Illustrations. Crown 8vo. 10s. 6d.

CRICKET. By A. G. STEEL and the Hon. R. H. LYTTELTON. With 63 Illustrations. Crown 8vo. 10s. 6d.

DRIVING. By the DUKE OF BEAUFORT. With 65 Illustrations. Crown 8vo. 10s. 6d.

BADMINTON LIBRARY (The)—(continued).

FENCING, BOXING, AND WRESTLING. By WALTER H. POLLOCK, F. C. GROVE, C. PREVOST, E. B. MICHELL, and WALTER ARMSTRONG. With 42 Illustrations. Crown 8vo. 10s. 6d.

GOLF. By HORACE HUTCHINSON, the Rt. Hon. A. J. BALFOUR, M.P., ANDREW LANG, Sir W. G. SIMPSON, Bart., &c. With 88 Illustrations. Crown 8vo. 10s. 6d.

TENNIS, LAWN TENNIS, RACKETS, AND FIVES. By J. M. and C. G. HEATHCOTE, E. O. PLEYDELL-BOUVERIE, and A. C. AINGER. With 79 Illustrations. Crown 8vo. 10s. 6d.

RIDING AND POLO. By Captain ROBERT WEIR, Riding-Master, R.H.G., J. MORAY BROWN, &c. With 59 Illustrations. Cr. 8vo.

BAGEHOT (Walter).—BIOGRAPHICAL STUDIES. 8vo. 12s.

———— ECONOMIC STUDIES. 8vo. 10s. 6d.

———— LITERARY STUDIES. 2 vols. 8vo. 28s.

———— THE POSTULATES OF ENGLISH POLITICAL ECONOMY. Crown 8vo. 2s. 6d.

———— A PRACTICAL PLAN FOR ASSIMILATING THE ENGLISH AND AMERICAN MONEY AS A STEP TOWARDS A UNIVERSAL MONEY. Crown 8vo. 2s. 6d.

BAGWELL (Richard).—IRELAND UNDER THE TUDORS. (3 vols.) Vols. I. and II. From the first invasion of the Northmen to the year 1578. 8vo. 32s. Vol. III. 1578-1603. 8vo. 18s.

BAIN (Alex.).—MENTAL AND MORAL SCIENCE. Crown 8vo. 10s. 6d.

———— SENSES AND THE INTELLECT. 8vo. 15s.

———— EMOTIONS AND THE WILL. 8vo. 15s.

———— LOGIC, DEDUCTIVE AND INDUCTIVE. Part I., *Deduction*, 4s. Part II., *Induction*, 6s. 6d.

———— PRACTICAL ESSAYS. Crown 8vo. 2s.

BAKER (James).—BY THE WESTERN SEA: a Novel. Cr. 8vo. 3s. 6d.

BAKER.—EIGHT YEARS IN CEYLON. With 6 Illustrations. Crown 8vo. 3s. 6d.

———— THE RIFLE AND THE HOUND IN CEYLON. With 6 Illustrations. Crown 8vo. 3s. 6d.

BALL (The Rt. Hon. T. J.).—THE REFORMED CHURCH OF IRELAND (1537-1889). 8vo. 7s. 6d.

———— HISTORICAL REVIEW OF THE LEGISLATIVE SYSTEMS OPERATIVE IN IRELAND (1172-1800). 8vo. 6s.

BEACONSFIELD (The Earl of).—NOVELS AND TALES. The Hughenden Edition. With 2 Portraits and 11 Vignettes. 11 vols. Crown 8vo. 42s.

Endymion.	Venetia.	Alroy, Ixion, &c.
Lothair.	Henrietta Temple.	The Young Duke, &c.
Coningsby.	Contarini Fleming, &c.	Vivian Grey.
Tancred. Sybil.		

NOVELS AND TALES. Cheap Edition. 11 vols. Crown 8vo. 1s. each, boards; 1s. 6d. each, cloth.

BECKER (Professor).—GALLUS; or, Roman Scenes in the Time of Augustus. Post 8vo. 7s. 6d.

———— CHARICLES; or, Illustrations of the Private Life of the Ancient Greeks. Post 8vo. 7s. 6d.

BELL (Mrs. Hugh).—WILL O' THE WISP: a Story. Crown 8vo. 3s. 6d.

———— CHAMBER COMEDIES. Crown 8vo. 6s.

BLAKE (J.).—TABLES FOR THE CONVERSION OF 5 PER CENT. INTEREST FROM $\frac{1}{8}$ TO 7 PER CENT. 8vo. 12s. 6d.

BOOK (THE) OF WEDDING DAYS. Arranged on the Plan of a Birthday Book. With 96 Illustrated Borders, Frontispiece, and Title-page by Walter Crane; and Quotations for each Day. Compiled and Arranged by K. E. J. REID, MAY ROSS, and MABEL BAMFIELD. 4to. 21s.

BRASSEY (Lady).—A VOYAGE IN THE 'SUNBEAM,' OUR HOME ON THE OCEAN FOR ELEVEN MONTHS.

Library Edition. With 8 Maps and Charts, and 118 Illustrations, 8vo. 21s.
Cabinet Edition. With Map and 66 Illustrations, Crown 8vo. 7s. 6d.
Cheap Edition. With 66 Illustrations, Crown 8vo. 3s. 6d.
School Edition. With 37 Illustrations, Fcp. 2s. cloth, or 3s. white parchment.
Popular Edition. With 60 Illustrations, 4to. 6d. sewed, 1s. cloth.

———— SUNSHINE AND STORM IN THE EAST.

Library Edition. With 2 Maps and 114 Illustrations, 8vo. 21s.
Cabinet Edition. With 2 Maps and 114 Illustrations, Crown 8vo. 7s. 6d.
Popular Edition. With 103 Illustrations, 4to. 6d. sewed, 1s. cloth.

———— IN THE TRADES, THE TROPICS, AND THE 'ROARING FORTIES'.

Cabinet Edition. With Map and 220 Illustrations, Crown 8vo. 7s. 6d.
Popular Edition. With 183 Illustrations, 4to. 6d. sewed, 1s. cloth.

———— THE LAST VOYAGE TO INDIA AND AUSTRALIA IN THE 'SUNBEAM'. With Charts and Maps, and 40 Illustrations in Monotone (20 full-page), and nearly 200 Illustrations in the Text. 8vo. 21s.

———— THREE VOYAGES IN THE 'SUNBEAM'. Popular Edition. With 346 Illustrations, 4to. 2s. 6d.

BRAY (Charles).—THE PHILOSOPHY OF NECESSITY; or, Law in Mind as in Matter. Crown 8vo. 5s.

BRIGHT (Rev. J. Franck).—A HISTORY OF ENGLAND. 4 vols. Cr. 8vo.

Period I.—Mediaeval Monarchy: The Departure of the Romans to Richard III. From A.D. 449 to 1485. 4s. 6d.
Period II.—Personal Monarchy: Henry VII. to James II. From 1485 to 1688. 5s.
Period III.—Constitutional Monarchy: William and Mary to William IV. From 1689 to 1837. 7s. 6d.
Period IV.—The Growth of Democracy: Victoria. From 1837 to 1880. 6s.

BRYDEN (H. A.).—KLOOF AND KARROO: Sport, Legend, and Natural History in Cape Colony. With 17 Illustrations. 8vo. 10s. 6d.

BUCKLE (Henry Thomas).—HISTORY OF CIVILISATION IN ENGLAND AND FRANCE, SPAIN AND SCOTLAND. 3 vols. Cr. 8vo. 24s.

BULL (Thomas).—HINTS TO MOTHERS ON THE MANAGEMENT OF THEIR HEALTH during the Period of Pregnancy. Fcp. 8vo. 1s. 6d.
———— THE MATERNAL MANAGEMENT OF CHILDREN IN HEALTH AND DISEASE. Fcp. 8vo. 1s. 6d.

BUTLER (Samuel).—EREWHON. Crown 8vo. 5s.
———— THE FAIR HAVEN. A Work in Defence of the Miraculous Element in our Lord's Ministry. Crown 8vo. 7s. 6d.
———— LIFE AND HABIT. An Essay after a Completer View of Evolution. Cr. 8vo. 7s. 6d.
———— EVOLUTION, OLD AND NEW. Crown 8vo. 10s. 6d.
———— UNCONSCIOUS MEMORY. Crown 8vo. 7s. 6d.
———— ALPS AND SANCTUARIES OF PIEDMONT AND THE CANTON TICINO. Illustrated. Pott 4to. 10s. 6d.
———— SELECTIONS FROM WORKS. Crown 8vo. 7s. 6d.
———— LUCK, OR CUNNING, AS THE MAIN MEANS OF ORGANIC MODIFICATION? Crown 8vo. 7s. 6d.
———— EX VOTO. An Account of the Sacro Monte or New Jerusalem at Varallo-Sesia. Crown 8vo. 10s. 6d.
———— HOLBEIN'S 'LA DANSE'. 3s.

CARLYLE (Thomas).—THOMAS CARLYLE: a History of his Life. By J. A. FROUDE. 1795-1835, 2 vols. Cr. 8vo. 7s. 1834-1881, 2 vols. Cr. 8vo. 7s.

CASE (Thomas).—PHYSICAL REALISM: being an Analytical Philosophy from the Physical Objects of Science to the Physical Data of Sense. 8vo. 15s.

CHETWYND (Sir George).—RACING REMINISCENCES AND EXPERIENCES OF THE TURF. 2 vols. 8vo. 21s.

CHILD (Gilbert W.).—CHURCH AND STATE UNDER THE TUDORS. 8vo. 15s.

CHISHOLM (G. G.).—HANDBOOK OF COMMERCIAL GEOGRAPHY. With 29 Maps. 8vo. 16s.

CHURCH (Sir Richard).—Commander-in-Chief of the Greeks in the War of Independence: a Memoir. By STANLEY LANE-POOLE. 8vo. 5s.

CLIVE (Mrs. Archer).—POEMS. Including the IX. Poems. Fcp. 8vo. 6s.

CLODD (Edward).—THE STORY OF CREATION: a Plain Account of Evolution. With 77 Illustrations. Crown 8vo. 3s. 6d.

CLUTTERBUCK (W. J.).—THE SKIPPER IN ARCTIC SEAS. With 39 Illustrations. Crown 8vo. 10s. 6d.

COLENSO (J. W.).—THE PENTATEUCH AND BOOK OF JOSHUA CRITICALLY EXAMINED. Crown 8vo. 6s.

COLMORE (G.).—A LIVING EPITAPH: a Novel. Crown 8vo. 6s.

COMYN (L. N.).—ATHERSTONE PRIORY: a Tale. Crown 8vo. 2s. 6d.

CONINGTON (John).—THE ÆNEID OF VIRGIL. Translated into English Verse. Crown 8vo. 6s.
———— THE POEMS OF VIRGIL. Translated into English Prose. Cr. 8vo. 6s.

COX (Rev. Sir G. W.).—A HISTORY OF GREECE, from the Earliest Period to the Death of Alexander the Great. With 11 Maps. Cr. 8vo. 7s. 6d.

CRAKE (Rev. A. D.).—HISTORICAL TALES. Cr. 8vo. 5 vols. 2s. 6d. each.

Edwy the Fair; or, The First Chronicle of Æscendune.

Alfgar the Dane; or, The Second Chronicle of Æscendune.

The Rival Heirs; being the Third and Last Chronicle of Æscendune.

The House of Walderne. A Tale of the Cloister and the Forest in the Days of the Barons' Wars.

Brian Fitz-Count. A Story of Wallingford Castle and Dorchester Abbey.

———— HISTORY OF THE CHURCH UNDER THE ROMAN EMPIRE, A.D. 30-476. Crown 8vo. 7s. 6d.

CREIGHTON (Mandell, D.D.)—HISTORY OF THE PAPACY DURING THE REFORMATION. 8vo. Vols. I. and II., 1378-1464, 32s.; Vols. III. and IV., 1464-1518, 24s.

CRUMP (A.).—A SHORT ENQUIRY INTO THE FORMATION OF POLITICAL OPINION, from the Reign of the Great Families to the Advent of Democracy. 8vo. 7s. 6d.

———— AN INVESTIGATION INTO THE CAUSES OF THE GREAT FALL IN PRICES which took place coincidently with the Demonetisation of Silver by Germany. 8vo. 6s.

CURZON (Hon. George N.).—RUSSIA IN CENTRAL ASIA IN 1889 AND THE ANGLO-RUSSIAN QUESTION. 8vo. 21s.

DANTE.—LA COMMEDIA DI DANTE. A New Text, carefully Revised with the aid of the most recent Editions and Collations. Small 8vo. 6s.

DELAND (Mrs.).—JOHN WARD, PREACHER. Cr. 8vo. 2s. bds., 2s. 6d. cl.

———— SIDNEY: a Novel. Crown 8vo. 6s.

———— THE OLD GARDEN, and other Verses. Fcp. 8vo. 5s.

DE REDCLIFFE.—THE LIFE OF THE RIGHT HON. STRATFORD CANNING: VISCOUNT STRATFORD DE REDCLIFFE. By STANLEY LANE-POOLE. With 3 Portraits. Crown 8vo. 7s. 6d.

DE SALIS (Mrs.).—Works by :—

Savouries à la Mode. Fcp. 8vo. 1s. 6d.

Entrées à la Mode. Fcp. 8vo. 1s. 6d.

Soups and Dressed Fish à la Mode. Fcp. 8vo. 1s. 6d.

Oysters à la Mode. Fcp. 8vo. 1s. 6d.

Sweets and Supper Dishes à la Mode. Fcp. 8vo. 1s. 6d.

Dressed Vegetables à la Mode. Fcp. 8vo. 1s. 6d.

Dressed Game and Poultry à la Mode. Fcp. 8vo. 1s. 6d.

Puddings and Pastry à la Mode. Fcp. 8vo. 1s. 6d.

Cakes and Confections à la Mode. Fcp. 8vo. 1s. 6d.

Drinks à la Mode. Fcp. 8vo. 1s. 6d.

Tempting Dishes for Small Incomes. Fcp. 8vo. 1s. 6d.

Floral Decorations. Fcp. 8vo. 1s. 6d.

Wrinkles and Notions for every Household. Crown 8vo. 2s. 6d.

DE TOCQUEVILLE (Alexis).—DEMOCRACY IN AMERICA. Translated by HENRY REEVE, C.B. 2 vols. Crown 8vo. 16s.

DOWELL (Stephen).—A HISTORY OF TAXATION AND TAXES IN ENGLAND. 4 vols. 8vo. Vols. I. and II., The History of Taxation, 21s. Vols. III. and IV., The History of Taxes, 21s.

DOYLE (A. Conan).—MICAH CLARKE: a Tale of Monmouth's Rebellion. With Frontispiece and Vignette. Crown 8vo. 3s. 6d.

———— THE CAPTAIN OF THE POLESTAR; and other Tales. Cr. 8vo. 6s.

DRANE (Augusta T.).—THE HISTORY OF ST. DOMINIC, FOUNDER OF THE FRIAR PREACHERS. With 32 Illustrations. 8vo. 15s.

DUBLIN UNIVERSITY PRESS SERIES (The): a Series of Works undertaken by the Provost and Senior Fellows of Trinity College, Dublin.

Abbot's (T. K.) Codex Rescriptus Dublinensis of St. Matthew. 4to. 21s.
—————— Evangeliorum Versio Antehieronymiana ex Codice Usseriano (Dublinensi). 2 vols. Cr. 8vo. 21s.

Allman's (G. J.) Greek Geometry from Thales to Euclid. 8vo. 10s. 6d.

Burnside (W. S.) and Panton's (A. W.) Theory of Equations. 8vo. 12s. 6d.

Casey's (John) Sequel to Euclid's Elements. Crown 8vo. 3s. 6d.
—————— Analytical Geometry of the Conic Sections. Crown 8vo. 7s. 6d.

Davies' (J. F.) Eumenides of Æschylus, With Metrical English Translation. 8vo. 7s.

Dublin Translations into Greek and Latin Verse. Edited by R. Y. Tyrrell. 8vo. 6s.

Graves' (R. P.) Life of Sir William Hamilton. 3 vols. 15s. each.

Griffin (R. W.) on Parabola, Ellipse, and Hyperbola. Crown 8vo. 6s.

Hobart's (W. K.) Medical Language of St. Luke. 8vo. 16s.

Leslie's (T. E. Cliffe) Essays in Political Economy. 8vo. 10s. 6d.

Macalister's (A.) Zoology and Morphology of Vertebrata. 8vo. 10s. 6d.

MacCullagh's (James) Mathematical and other Tracts. 8vo. 15s.

Maguire's (T.) Parmenides of Plato, Text with Introduction, Analysis, &c. 8vo. 7s. 6d.

Monck's (W. H. S.) Introduction to Logic. Crown 8vo. 5s.

Robert's (R. A.) Examples on the Analytic Geometry of Plane Conics. Crown 8vo. 5s.

Southey's (R.) Correspondence with Caroline Bowles. Edited by E. Dowden. 8vo. 14s.

Stubbs' (J. W.) History of the University of Dublin, from its Foundation to the End of the Eighteenth Century. 8vo. 12s. 6d.

Thornhill's (W. J.) The Æneid of Virgil, freely translated into English Blank Verse. Crown 8vo. 7s. 6d.

Tyrrell's (R. Y.) Cicero's Correspondence. Vols. I., II. and III. 8vo. each 12s.
—————— The Acharnians of Aristophanes, translated into English Verse. Crown 8vo. 1s.

Webb's (T. E.) Goethe's Faust, Translation and Notes. 8vo. 12s. 6d.
—————— The Veil of Isis; a Series of Essays on Idealism. 8vo. 10s. 6d.

Wilkin's (G.) The Growth of the Homeric Poems. 8vo. 6s.

EWALD (Heinrich).—THE ANTIQUITIES OF ISRAEL. 8vo. 12s. 6d.
—————— THE HISTORY OF ISRAEL. 8vo. Vols. I. and II. 24s. Vols. III. and IV. 21s. Vol. V. 18s. Vol. VI. 16s. Vol. VII. 21s. Vol. VIII. 18s.

FARNELL (G. S.).—THE GREEK LYRIC POETS. 8vo. 16s.

FARRAR (F. W.).—LANGUAGE AND LANGUAGES. Crown 8vo. 6s.

FIRTH (J. C.).—NATION MAKING: a Story of New Zealand Savageism and Civilisation. Crown 8vo. 6s.

FITZWYGRAM (Major-General Sir F.).—HORSES AND STABLES. With 19 pages of Illustrations. 8vo. 5s.

FORD (Horace).—THE THEORY AND PRACTICE OF ARCHERY. New Edition, thoroughly Revised and Re-written by W. BUTT. 8vo. 14s.

FOUARD (Abbé Constant).—THE CHRIST THE SON OF GOD. With Introduction by Cardinal Manning. 2 vols. Crown 8vo. 14s.

FOX (C. J.).—THE EARLY HISTORY OF CHARLES JAMES FOX. By the Right Hon. Sir. G. O. TREVELYAN, Bart.
Library Edition. 8vo. 18s. | Cabinet Edition. Crown 8vo. 6s.

FRANCIS (Francis).—A BOOK ON ANGLING : including full Illustrated Lists of Salmon Flies. Post 8vo. 15s.

FREEMAN (E. A.).—THE HISTORICAL GEOGRAPHY OF EUROPE. With 65 Maps. 2 vols. 8vo. 31s. 6d.

FROUDE (James A.).—THE HISTORY OF ENGLAND, from the Fall of Wolsey to the Defeat of the Spanish Armada. 12 vols. Crown 8vo. £2 2s.
———— THE ENGLISH IN IRELAND IN THE EIGHTEENTH CENTURY. 3 vols. Crown 8vo. 18s.
———— SHORT STUDIES ON GREAT SUBJECTS.
Cabinet Edition. 4 vols. Cr. 8vo. 24s. | Cheap Edit. 4 vols. Cr. 8vo. 3s. 6d. ea.
———— CÆSAR : a Sketch. Crown 8vo. 3s. 6d.
———— OCEANA ; OR, ENGLAND AND HER COLONIES. With 9 Illustrations. Crown 8vo. 2s. boards, 2s. 6d. cloth.
———— THE ENGLISH IN THE WEST INDIES; or, the Bow of Ulysses. With 9 Illustrations. Crown 8vo. 2s. boards, 2s. 6d. cloth.
———— THE TWO CHIEFS OF DUNBOY; an Irish Romance of the Last Century. Crown 8vo. 3s. 6d.
———— THOMAS CARLYLE, a History of his Life. 1795 to 1835. 2 vols. Crown 8vo. 7s. 1834 to 1881. 2 vols. Crown 8vo. 7s.

GALLWEY (Sir Ralph Payne-).—LETTERS TO YOUNG SHOOTERS. (First Series.) On the Choice and Use of a Gun. Crown 8vo. 7s. 6d.

GARDINER (Samuel Rawson).—HISTORY OF ENGLAND, 1603-1642. 10 vols. Crown 8vo. price 6s. each.
———— A HISTORY OF THE GREAT CIVIL WAR, 1642-1649. (3 vols.) Vol. I. 1642-1644. With 24 Maps. 8vo. 21s. (*out of print*). Vol. II. 1644-1647. With 21 Maps. 8vo. 24s. Vol. III. 1647-1649.   [*In the Press.*
———— THE STUDENT'S HISTORY OF ENGLAND. Vol. I. B.C. 55-A.D. 1509, with 173 Illustrations, Crown 8vo. 4s. Vol. II. 1509-1689, with 96 Illustrations. Crown 8vo. 4s. Vol. III. 1689-1885, with Illustrations. Crown 8vo. 4s. Complete in 1 vol. Crown 8vo.

GIBERNE (Agnes).—MISS DEVEREUX, SPINSTER. 2 vols. Crown 8vo. 17s.
———— RALPH HARDCASTLE'S WILL. With Frontispiece. Cr. 8vo. 5s.
———— NIGEL BROWNING. Crown 8vo. 5s.

GOETHE.—FAUST. A New Translation chiefly in Blank Verse ; with Introduction and Notes. By JAMES ADEY BIRDS. Crown 8vo. 6s.
———— FAUST. The Second Part. A New Translation in Verse. By JAMES ADEY BIRDS. Crown 8vo. 6s.

GREEN (T. H.)—THE WORKS OF THOMAS HILL GREEN. (3 Vols.) Vols. I. and II. 8vo. 16s. each. Vol. III. 8vo. 21s.
———— THE WITNESS OF GOD AND FAITH : Two Lay Sermons. Fcp. 8vo. 2s.

GREVILLE (C. C. F.).—A JOURNAL OF THE REIGNS OF KING GEORGE IV., KING WILLIAM IV., AND QUEEN VICTORIA. Edited by H. REEVE. 8 vols. Crown 8vo. 6s. each.

GWILT (Joseph).—AN ENCYCLOPÆDIA OF ARCHITECTURE. With more than 1700 Engravings on Wood. 8vo. 52s. 6d.

HAGGARD (Ella).—LIFE AND ITS AUTHOR: an Essay in Verse. With a Memoir by H. Rider Haggard, and Portrait. Fcp. 8vo. 3s. 6d.

HAGGARD (H. Rider).—SHE. With 32 Illustrations. Crown 8vo. 3s. 6d.
——— ALLAN QUATERMAIN. With 31 Illustrations. Crown 8vo. 3s. 6d.
——— MAIWA'S REVENGE. Crown 8vo. 2s. boards, 2s. 6d. cloth.
——— COLONEL QUARITCH, V.C. Crown 8vo. 3s. 6d.
——— CLEOPATRA: With 29 Illustrations. Crown 8vo. 3s. 6d.
——— BEATRICE. Crown 8vo. 6s.
——— ERIC BRIGHTEYES. With 51 Illustrations. Crown 8vo. 6s.

HAGGARD (H. Rider) and LANG (Andrew).—THE WORLD'S DESIRE. Crown 8vo. 6s.

HALLIWELL-PHILLIPPS (J. O.)—A CALENDAR OF THE HALLI-WELL-PHILLIPPS COLLECTION OF SHAKESPEAREAN RARITIES. Second Edition. Enlarged by Ernest E. Baker. 8vo. 10s. 6d.
——— OUTLINE OF THE LIFE OF SHAKESPEARE. 2 vols. Royal 8vo. 21s.

HARRISON (Jane E.).—MYTHS OF THE ODYSSEY IN ART AND LITERATURE. Illustrated with Outline Drawings. 8vo. 18s.

HARRISON (F. Bayford).—THE CONTEMPORARY HISTORY OF THE FRENCH REVOLUTION. Crown 8vo. 3s. 6d.

HARTE (Bret).—IN THE CARQUINEZ WOODS. Fcp. 8vo. 1s. bds., 1s. 6d. cloth.
——— BY SHORE AND SEDGE. 16mo. 1s.
——— ON THE FRONTIER. 16mo. 1s.

HARTWIG (Dr.).—THE SEA AND ITS LIVING WONDERS. With 12 Plates and 303 Woodcuts. 8vo. 10s. 6d.
THE TROPICAL WORLD. With 8 Plates and 172 Woodcuts. 8vo. 10s. 6d.
THE POLAR WORLD. With 3 Maps, 8 Plates and 85 Woodcuts. 8vo. 10s. 6d.
THE SUBTERRANEAN WORLD. With 3 Maps and 80 Woodcuts. 8vo. 10s. 6d.
THE AERIAL WORLD. With Map, 8 Plates and 60 Woodcuts. 8vo. 10s. 6d.

HAVELOCK.—MEMOIRS OF SIR HENRY HAVELOCK, K.C.B. By JOHN CLARK MARSHMAN. Crown 8vo. 3s. 6d.

HEARN (W. Edward).—THE GOVERNMENT OF ENGLAND: its Structure and its Development. 8vo. 16s.
——— THE ARYAN HOUSEHOLD: its Structure and its Development. An Introduction to Comparative Jurisprudence. 8vo. 16s.

HISTORIC TOWNS. Edited by E. A. FREEMAN and Rev. WILLIAM HUNT. With Maps and Plans. Crown 8vo. 3s. 6d. each.

Bristol. By Rev. W. Hunt.	**Winchester.** By Rev. G. W. Kitchin.
Carlisle. By Dr. Mandell Creighton.	**New York.** By Theodore Roosevelt.
Cinque Ports. By Montagu Burrows.	**Boston (U.S.).** By Henry Cabot
Colchester. By Rev. E. L. Cutts.	Lodge.
Exeter. By E. A. Freeman.	**York.** By Rev. James Raine.
London. By Rev. W. J. Loftie.	[In preparation.
Oxford. By Rev. C. W. Boase.	

HODGSON (Shadworth H.).—TIME AND SPACE: a Metaphysical Essay. 8vo. 16s.
——— THE THEORY OF PRACTICE: an Ethical Enquiry. 2 vols. 8vo. 24s.
——— THE PHILOSOPHY OF REFLECTION. 2 vols. 8vo. 21s.
——— OUTCAST ESSAYS AND VERSE TRANSLATIONS. Crown 8vo. 8s. 6d.

HOWITT (William).—VISITS TO REMARKABLE PLACES. 80 Illustrations. Crown 8vo. 3s. 6d.

HULLAH (John).—COURSE OF LECTURES ON THE HISTORY OF MODERN MUSIC. 8vo. 8s. 6d.
——— COURSE OF LECTURES ON THE TRANSITION PERIOD OF MUSICAL HISTORY. 8vo. 10s. 6d.

HUME.—THE PHILOSOPHICAL WORKS OF DAVID HUME. Edited by T. H. GREEN and T. H. GROSE. 4 vols. 8vo. 56s.

HUTCHINSON (Horace).—CREATURES OF CIRCUMSTANCE: a Novel. 3 vols. Crown 8vo. 25s. 6d.
——— CRICKETING SAWS AND STORIES. With rectilinear Illustrations by the Author. 16mo. 1s.
——— FAMOUS GOLF LINKS. By HORACE G. HUTCHINSON, ANDREW LANG, H. S. C. EVERARD, T. RUTHERFORD CLARK, &c. With numerous Illustrations by F. P. Hopkins, T. Hodges, H. S. King, &c. Crown 8vo. 6s.

HUTH (Alfred H.).—THE MARRIAGE OF NEAR KIN. Royal 8vo. 21s.

INGELOW (Jean).—POETICAL WORKS. Vols. I. and II. Fcp. 8vo. 12s. Vol. III. Fcp. 8vo. 5s.
——— LYRICAL AND OTHER POEMS. Selected from the Writings of JEAN INGELOW. Fcp. 8vo. 2s. 6d. cloth plain, 3s. cloth gilt.
——— VERY YOUNG and QUITE ANOTHER STORY: Two Stories. Crown 8vo. 6s.

JAMESON (Mrs.).—SACRED AND LEGENDARY ART. With 19 Etchings and 187 Woodcuts. 2 vols. 8vo. 20s. net.
——— LEGENDS OF THE MADONNA, the Virgin Mary as represented in Sacred and Legendary Art. With 27 Etchings and 165 Woodcuts. 8vo. 10s. net.
——— LEGENDS OF THE MONASTIC ORDERS. With 11 Etchings and 88 Woodcuts. 8vo. 10s. net.
——— HISTORY OF OUR LORD. His Types and Precursors. Completed by LADY EASTLAKE. With 31 Etchings and 281 Woodcuts. 2 vols. 8vo. 20s. net.

JEFFERIES (Richard).—FIELD AND HEDGEROW. Last Essays. Crown 8vo. 3s. 6d.
——— THE STORY OF MY HEART: My Autobiography. Crown 8vo. 3s. 6d.

JENNINGS (Rev. A. C.).—ECCLESIA ANGLICANA. A History of the Church of Christ in England. Crown 8vo. 7s. 6d.

JESSOP (G. H.).—JUDGE LYNCH: a Tale of the California Vineyards. Crown 8vo. 6s.

———— GERALD FFRENCH'S FRIENDS. Crown 8vo. 6s.

JOHNSON (J. & J. H.).—THE PATENTEE'S MANUAL; a Treatise on the Law and Practice of Letters Patent. 8vo. 10s. 6d.

JORDAN (William Leighton).—THE STANDARD OF VALUE. 8vo. 6s.

JUSTINIAN.—THE INSTITUTES OF JUSTINIAN; Latin Text, with English Introduction, &c. By THOMAS C. SANDARS. 8vo. 18s.

KALISCH (M. M.).—BIBLE STUDIES. Part I. The Prophecies of Balaam. 8vo. 10s. 6d. Part II. The Book of Jonah. 8vo. 10s. 6d.

KALISCH (M. M.).—COMMENTARY ON THE OLD TESTAMENT; with a New Translation. Vol. I. Genesis, 8vo. 18s., or adapted for the General Reader, 12s. Vol. II. Exodus, 15s., or adapted for the General Reader, 12s. Vol. III. Leviticus, Part I. 15s., or adapted for the General Reader, 8s. Vol. IV. Leviticus, Part II. 15s., or adapted for the General Reader, 8s.

KANT (Immanuel).—CRITIQUE OF PRACTICAL REASON, AND OTHER WORKS ON THE THEORY OF ETHICS. 8vo. 12s. 6d.

———— INTRODUCTION TO LOGIC. Translated by T. K. Abbott. Notes by S. T. Coleridge. 8vo. 6s.

KENDALL (May).—FROM A GARRET. Crown 8vo. 6s.

———— DREAMS TO SELL; Poems. Fcp. 8vo. 6s.

———— 'SUCH IS LIFE': a Novel. Crown 8vo. 6s.

KENNEDY (Arthur Clark).—PICTURES IN RHYME. With 4 Illustrations by Maurice Greiffenhagen. Crown 8vo. 6s.

KILLICK (Rev. A. H.).—HANDBOOK TO MILL'S SYSTEM OF LOGIC. Crown 8vo. 3s. 6d.

KNIGHT (E. F.).—THE CRUISE OF THE 'ALERTE'; the Narrative of a Search for Treasure on the Desert Island of Trinidad. With 2 Maps and 23 Illustrations. Crown 8vo. 10s. 6d.

———— SAVE ME FROM MY FRIENDS: a Novel. Crown 8vo. 6s.

LADD (George T.).—ELEMENTS OF PHYSIOLOGICAL PSYCHOLOGY. 8vo. 21s.

———— OUTLINES OF PHYSIOLOGICAL PSYCHOLOGY. A Text-Book of Mental Science for Academies and Colleges. 8vo. 12s.

LANG (Andrew).—CUSTOM AND MYTH: Studies of Early Usage and Belief. With 15 Illustrations. Crown 8vo. 7s. 6d.

———— BOOKS AND BOOKMEN. With 2 Coloured Plates and 17 Illustrations. Crown 8vo. 6s. 6d.

———— GRASS OF PARNASSUS. A Volume of Selected Verses. Fcp. 8vo. 6s.

———— BALLADS OF BOOKS. Edited by ANDREW LANG. Fcp. 8vo. 6s.

———— THE BLUE FAIRY BOOK. Edited by ANDREW LANG. With 8 Plates and 130 Illustrations in the Text. Crown 8vo. 6s.

———— THE RED FAIRY BOOK. Edited by ANDREW LANG. With 4 Plates and 96 Illustrations in the Text. Crown 8vo. 6s.

LAVIGERIE.—CARDINAL LAVIGERIE AND THE AFRICAN SLAVE TRADE. 8vo. 14s.

LAYARD (Nina F.).—POEMS. Crown 8vo. 6s.

LECKY (W. E. H.).—HISTORY OF ENGLAND IN THE EIGHTEENTH CENTURY. 8vo. Vols. I. and II. 1700-1760. 36s. Vols. III. and IV. 1760-1784. 36s. Vols. V. and VI. 1784-1793. 36s. Vols. VII. and VIII. 1793-1800. 36s.

——— THE HISTORY OF EUROPEAN MORALS FROM AUGUSTUS TO CHARLEMAGNE. 2 vols. Crown 8vo. 16s.

——— HISTORY OF THE RISE AND INFLUENCE OF THE SPIRIT OF RATIONALISM IN EUROPE. 2 vols. Crown 8vo. 16s.

LEES (J. A.) and CLUTTERBUCK (W. J.).—B.C. 1887, A RAMBLE IN BRITISH COLUMBIA. With Map and 75 Illustrations. Cr. 8vo. 6s.

LEGER (Louis).—A HISTORY OF AUSTRO-HUNGARY. From the Earliest Time to the year 1889. With Preface by E. A. Freeman. Cr. 8vo. 10s. 6d.

LEWES (George Henry).—THE HISTORY OF PHILOSOPHY, from Thales to Comte. 2 vols. 8vo. 32s.

LIDDELL (Colonel R. T.).—MEMOIRS OF THE TENTH ROYAL HUSSARS. With Numerous Illustrations. 2 vols. Imperial 8vo. 63s.

LONGMAN (Frederick W.).—CHESS OPENINGS. Fcp. 8vo. 2s. 6d.

——— FREDERICK THE GREAT AND THE SEVEN YEARS' WAR. Fcp. 8vo. 2s. 6d.

LOUDON (J. C.).—ENCYCLOPÆDIA OF GARDENING. With 1000 Woodcuts. 8vo. 21s.

——— ENCYCLOPÆDIA OF AGRICULTURE; the Laying-out, Improvement, and Management of Landed Property. With 1100 Woodcuts. 8vo. 21s.

——— ENCYCLOPÆDIA OF PLANTS; the Specific Character, &c., of all Plants found in Great Britain. With 12,000 Woodcuts. 8vo. 42s.

LUBBOCK (Sir J.).—THE ORIGIN OF CIVILISATION and the Primitive Condition of Man. With 5 Plates and 20 Illustrations in the Text. 8vo. 18s.

LYALL (Edna).—THE AUTOBIOGRAPHY OF A SLANDER. Fcp. 8vo. 1s. sewed.

LYDE (Lionel W.).—AN INTRODUCTION TO ANCIENT HISTORY. With 3 Coloured Maps. Crown 8vo. 3s.

MACAULAY (Lord).—COMPLETE WORKS OF LORD MACAULAY. Library Edition, 8 vols. 8vo. £5 5s. | Cabinet Edition, 16 vols. post 8vo. £4 16s.

——— HISTORY OF ENGLAND FROM THE ACCESSION OF JAMES THE SECOND.
Popular Edition, 2 vols. Crown 8vo. 5s. | People's Edition, 4 vols. Crown 8vo. 16s.
Student's Edition, 2 vols. Crown 8vo. | Cabinet Edition, 8 vols. Post 8vo. 48s.
12s. | Library Edition, 5 vols. 8vo. £4.

——— CRITICAL AND HISTORICAL ESSAYS, WITH LAYS OF ANCIENT ROME, in 1 volume.
Popular Edition, Crown 8vo. 2s. 6d. | Authorised Edition, Crown 8vo. 2s. 6d., or 3s. 6d. gilt edges.

MACAULAY (Lord).—ESSAYS (continued).

———— CRITICAL AND HISTORICAL ESSAYS.

Student's Edition.   Crown 8vo. 6s.

People's Edition, 2 vols. Crown 8vo. 8s.

Trevelyan Edition, 2 vols. Crown 8vo. 9s.

Cabinet Edition, 4 vols. Post 8vo. 24s.

Library Edition, 3 vols. 8vo. 36s.

———— ESSAYS which may be had separately, price 6d. each sewed, 1s. each cloth.

Addison and Walpole.

Frederic the Great.

Croker's Boswell's Johnson.

Hallam's Constitutional History.

Warren Hastings (3d. sewed, 6d. cloth).

The Earl of Chatham (Two Essays).

Ranke and Gladstone.

Milton and Machiavelli.

Lord Bacon.

Lord Clive.

Lord Byron, and the Comic Drama-tists of the Restoration.

The Essay on Warren Hastings, anno-tated by S. Hales. Fcp. 8vo. 1s. 6d.

The Essay on Lord Clive, annotated by H. Courthope Bowen. Fcp. 8vo. 2s. 6d.

———— SPEECHES.   People's Edition, Crown 8vo. 3s. 6d.

———— LAYS OF ANCIENT ROME, &c.   Illustrated by G. Scharf.   Library Edition. Fcp. 4to. 10s. 6d.

Bijou Edition, 18mo. 2s. 6d. gilt top.

Popular Edition, Fcp. 4to. 6d. sewed, 1s. cloth.

——————————————————— 8vo. 3s. 6d. gilt edges.

Illustrated by J. R. Weguelin.   Crown 8vo. 3s. 6d. gilt edges.

Cabinet Edition, Post 8vo. 3s. 6d.

Annotated Edition, Fcp. 8vo. 1s. sewed, 1s. 6d. cloth.

———— MISCELLANEOUS WRITINGS.

People's Edition.   Crown 8vo. 4s. 6d.

Library Edition, 2 vols. 8vo. 21s.

———— MISCELLANEOUS WRITINGS AND SPEECHES.

Popular Edition.   Crown 8vo. 2s. 6d.

Student's Edition.   Crown 8vo. 6s.

Cabinet Edition, Post 8vo. 24s.

———— SELECTIONS FROM THE WRITINGS OF LORD MACAULAY. Edited, with Notes, by the Right Hon. Sir G. O. TREVELYAN.   Crown 8vo. 6s.

———— THE LIFE AND LETTERS OF LORD MACAULAY.   By the Right Hon. Sir G. O. TREVELYAN.

Popular Edition.   Crown. 8vo. 2s. 6d.

Student's Edition.   Crown 8vo. 6s.

Cabinet Edition, 2 vols. Post 8vo. 12s.

Library Edition, 2 vols. 8vo. 36s.

MACDONALD (George).—UNSPOKEN SERMONS.   Three Series. Crown 8vo. 3s. 6d. each.

———— THE MIRACLES OF OUR LORD.   Crown 8vo. 3s. 6d.

———— A BOOK OF STRIFE, IN THE FORM OF THE DIARY OF AN OLD SOUL: Poems.   12mo. 6s.

MACFARREN (Sir G. A.).—LECTURES ON HARMONY.   8vo. 12s.

MACKAIL (J. W.).—SELECT EPIGRAMS FROM THE GREEK AN-THOLOGY.   With a Revised Text, Introduction, Translation, &c.   8vo. 16s.

MACLEOD (Henry D.).—THE ELEMENTS OF BANKING.   Crown 8vo. 3s. 6d.

———— THE THEORY AND PRACTICE OF BANKING.   Vol. I. 8vo. 12s., Vol. II. 14s.

———— THE THEORY OF CREDIT.   8vo. Vol. I. [New Edition in the Press]; Vol. II. Part I. 4s. 6d. ; Vol. II. Part II. 10s. 6d.

McCULLOCH (J. R.).—THE DICTIONARY OF COMMERCE and Commercial Navigation. With 11 Maps and 30 Charts. 8vo. 63s.

MACVINE (John). —SIXTY-THREE YEARS' ANGLING, from the Mountain Streamlet to the Mighty Tay. Crown 8vo. 10s. 6d.

MALMESBURY (The Earl of).—MEMOIRS OF AN EX-MINISTER. Crown 8vo. 7s. 6d.

MANUALS OF CATHOLIC PHILOSOPHY (*Stonyhurst Series*).

Logic. By Richard F. Clarke. Crown 8vo. 5s.

First Principles of Knowledge. By John Rickaby. Crown 8vo. 5s.

Moral Philosophy (Ethics and Natural Law). By Joseph Rickaby. Crown 8vo. 5s.

General Metaphysics. By John Rickaby. Crown 8vo. 5s.

Psychology. By Michael Maher. Crown 8vo. 6s. 6d.

Natural Theology. By Bernard Boedder. Crown 8vo. 6s. 6d.

A Manual of Political Economy. By C. S. Devas. 6s. 6d. [*In preparation.*

MARTINEAU (James). HOURS OF THOUGHT ON SACRED THINGS. Two Volumes of Sermons. 2 vols. Crown 8vo. 7s. 6d. each.

———— ENDEAVOURS AFTER THE CHRISTIAN LIFE. Discourses. Crown 8vo. 7s. 6d.

———— THE SEAT OF AUTHORITY IN RELIGION. 8vo. 14s.

———— ESSAYS, REVIEWS, AND ADDRESSES. 4 vols. Crown 8vo. 7s. 6d. each.

I. Personal : Political.
II. Ecclesiastical : Historical.

III. Theological : Philosophical.
IV. Academical : Religious.

[*In course of publication.*

MASON (Agnes).—THE STEPS OF THE SUN : Daily Readings of Prose. 16mo. 3s. 6d.

MAUNDER'S TREASURIES. Fcp. 8vo. 6s. each volume.

Biographical Treasury.

Treasury of Natural History. With 900 Woodcuts.

Treasury of Geography. With 7 Maps and 16 Plates.

Scientific and Literary Treasury.

Historical Treasury.

Treasury of Knowledge.

The Treasury of Bible Knowledge. By the Rev. J. Ayre. With 5 Maps, 15 Plates, and 300 Woodcuts. Fcp. 8vo. 6s.

The Treasury of Botany. Edited by J. Lindley and T. Moore. With 274 Woodcuts and 20 Steel Plates. 2 vols.

MATTHEWS (Brander).—A FAMILY TREE, and other Stories. Crown 8vo. 6s.

———— PEN AND INK—School Papers. Crown 8vo. 5s.

MAX MÜLLER (F.).—SELECTED ESSAYS ON LANGUAGE, MYTHOLOGY, AND RELIGION. 2 vols. Crown 8vo. 16s.

———— LECTURES ON THE SCIENCE OF LANGUAGE. 2 vols. Crown 8vo. 16s.

———— THREE LECTURES ON THE SCIENCE OF LANGUAGE. Cr. 8vo. 3s.

———— THE SCIENCE OF LANGUAGE, founded on Lectures delivered at the Royal Institution in 1861 and 1863. 2 vols. Crown 8vo. 21s.

———— HIBBERT LECTURES ON THE ORIGIN AND GROWTH OF RELIGION, as illustrated by the Religions of India. Crown 8vo. 7s. 6d.

MAX MÜLLER (F.)—INTRODUCTION TO THE SCIENCE OF RE-
LIGION ; Four Lectures delivered at the Royal Institution. Crown 8vo. 7s. 6d.

———— NATURAL RELIGION. The Gifford Lectures, delivered before the
University of Glasgow in 1888. Crown 8vo. 10s. 6d.

———— PHYSICAL RELIGION. The Gifford Lectures, delivered before the
University of Glasgow in 1890. Crown 8vo. 10s. 6d.

———— THE SCIENCE OF THOUGHT. 8vo. 21s.

———— THREE INTRODUCTORY LECTURES ON THE SCIENCE OF
THOUGHT. 8vo. 2s. 6d.

———— BIOGRAPHIES OF WORDS, AND THE HOME OF THE ARYAS.
Crown 8vo. 7s. 6d.

———— A SANSKRIT GRAMMAR FOR BEGINNERS. New and Abridged
Edition. By A. A. MacDonell. Crown 8vo. 6s.

MAY (Sir Thomas Erskine).—THE CONSTITUTIONAL HISTORY
OF ENGLAND since the Accession of George III. 3 vols. Crown 8vo. 18s.

MEADE (L. T.).—THE O'DONNELLS OF INCHFAWN. Crown 8vo. 6s.

———— DADDY'S BOY. With Illustrations. Crown 8vo. 5s.

———— DEB AND THE DUCHESS. Illustrated by M. E. Edwards. Cr. 8vo. 5s.

———— HOUSE OF SURPRISES. Illustrated by E. M. Scannell. Cr. 8vo. 3s. 6d.

———— THE BERESFORD PRIZE. Illustrated by M. E. Edwards. Cr. 8vo. 5s.

MEATH (The Earl of).—SOCIAL ARROWS : Reprinted Articles on
various Social Subjects. Crown 8vo. 5s.

———— PROSPERITY OR PAUPERISM ? Physical, Industrial, and Technical
Training. Edited by the Earl of Meath. 8vo. 5s.

MELVILLE (G. J. Whyte).—Novels by. Crown 8vo. 1s. each, boards ;
1s. 6d. each, cloth.

The Gladiators.	The Queen's Maries.	Digby Grand.
The Interpreter.	Holmby House.	General Bounce.
Good for Nothing.	Kate Coventry.	

MENDELSSOHN.—THE LETTERS OF FELIX MENDELSSOHN.
Translated by Lady Wallace. 2 vols. Crown 8vo. 10s.

MERIVALE (Rev. Chas.).—HISTORY OF THE ROMANS UNDER
THE EMPIRE. Cabinet Edition, 8 vols. Crown 8vo. 48s. Popular Edition,
8 vols. Crown 8vo. 3s. 6d. each.

———— THE FALL OF THE ROMAN REPUBLIC : a Short History of the
Last Century of the Commonwealth. 12mo. 7s. 6d.

———— GENERAL HISTORY OF ROME FROM B.C. 753 TO A.D. 476.
Cr. 8vo. 7s. 6d.

———— THE ROMAN TRIUMVIRATES. With Maps. Fcp. 8vo. 2s. 6d.

MILES (W. A.).—THE CORRESPONDENCE OF WILLIAM AUGUSTUS
MILES ON THE FRENCH REVOLUTION, 1789-1817. 2 vols. 8vo. 32s.

MILL (James).—ANALYSIS OF THE PHENOMENA OF THE HUMAN
MIND. 2 vols. 8vo. 28s.

MILL (John Stuart).—PRINCIPLES OF POLITICAL ECONOMY.
Library Edition, 2 vols. 8vo. 30s. | People's Edition, 1 vol. Crown 8vo. 5s.

———— A SYSTEM OF LOGIC. Crown 8vo. 5s.

———— ON LIBERTY. Crown 8vo. 1s. 4d.

MILL (J. S.).—ON REPRESENTATIVE GOVERNMENT. Crown 8vo. 2s.
———— UTILITARIANISM. 8vo. 5s.
———— EXAMINATION OF SIR WILLIAM HAMILTON'S PHILO-
SOPHY. 8vo. 16s.
———— NATURE, THE UTILITY OF RELIGION AND THEISM. Three
Essays, 8vo. 5s.

MOLESWORTH (Mrs.).—MARRYING AND GIVING IN MARRIAGE:
a Novel. Fcp. 8vo. 2s. 6d.
———— SILVERTHORNS. With Illustrations by F. Noel Paton. Cr. 8vo. 5s.
———— THE PALACE IN THE GARDEN. With Illustrations. Cr. 8vo. 5s.
———— THE THIRD MISS ST. QUENTIN. Crown 8vo. 6s.
———— NEIGHBOURS. With Illustrations by M. Ellen Edwards. Cr. 8vo. 6s.
———— THE STORY OF A SPRING MORNING. With Illustrations. Cr. 8vo. 5s.

MOON (G. Washington).—THE KING'S ENGLISH. Fcp. 8vo. 3s. 6d.

MOORE (Edward).—DANTE AND HIS EARLY BIOGRAPHERS.
Crown 8vo. 4s. 6d.

MULHALL (Michael G.).—HISTORY OF PRICES SINCE THE YEAR
1850. Crown 8vo. 6s.

MURDOCK (Henry).—THE RECONSTRUCTION OF EUROPE: a
Sketch of the Diplomatic and Military History of Continental Europe, from
the Rise to the Fall of the Second French Empire. Crown 8vo. 9s.

MURRAY (David Christie and Henry).—A DANGEROUS CATS-
PAW: a Story. Crown 8vo. 2s. 6d.

MURRAY (Christie) and HERMAN (Henry).—WILD DARRIE:
a Story. Crown 8vo. 2s. boards; 2s. 6d. cloth.

NANSEN (Dr. Fridtjof).—THE FIRST CROSSING OF GREENLAND.
With 5 Maps, 12 Plates, and 150 Illustrations in the Text. 2 vols. 8vo. 36s.

NAPIER.—THE LIFE OF SIR JOSEPH NAPIER, BART., EX-LORD
CHANCELLOR OF IRELAND. By ALEX. CHARLES EWALD. 8vo. 15s.
———— THE LECTURES, ESSAYS, AND LETTERS OF THE RIGHT
HON. SIR JOSEPH NAPIER, BART. 8vo. 12s. 6d.

NESBIT (E.).—LEAVES OF LIFE: Verses. Crown 8vo. 5s.

NEWMAN.—THE LETTERS AND CORRESPONDENCE OF JOHN
HENRY NEWMAN during his Life in the English Church. With a brief
Autobiographical Memoir. Edited by Anne Mozley. With Portraits, 2 vols.
8vo. 30s. *net.*

NEWMAN (Cardinal).—Works by:—

Sermons to Mixed Congregations.
Crown 8vo. 6s.
Sermons on Various Occasions. Cr.
8vo. 6s.
The Idea of a University defined and
Illustrated. Cabinet Edition, Cr. 8vo.
7s. Cheap Edition, Cr. 8vo. 3s. 6d.
Historical Sketches. Cabinet Edition,
3 vols. Crown 8vo. 6s. each. Cheap
Edition, 3 vols. Cr. 8vo. 3s. 6d. each.

The Arians of the Fourth Century.
Cabinet Edition, Crown 8vo. 6s.
Cheap Edition, Crown 8vo. 3s. 6d.
Select Treatises of St. Athanasius in
Controversy with the Arians. Freely
Translated. 2 vols. Cr. 8vo. 15s.
Discussions and Arguments on Various
Subjects. Cabinet Edition, Crown
8vo. 6s. Cheap Edition, Crown
8vo. 3s. 6d.

NEWMAN (Cardinal). Works by :—*(continued)*.

Apologia Pro Vitâ Sua. Cabinet Ed., Crown 8vo. 6s. Cheap Ed. 3s. 6d.

Development of Christian Doctrine. Cabinet Edition, Crown 8vo. 6s. Cheap Edition, Cr. 8vo. 3s. 6d.

Certain Difficulties felt by Anglicans in Catholic Teaching Considered. Cabinet Edition, Vol. I. Crown 8vo. 7s. 6d. ; Vol. II. Crown 8vo. 5s. 6d.

The Via Media of the Anglican Church, Illustrated in Lectures, &c. Cabinet Edition, 2 vols. Cr. 8vo. 6s. each. Cheap Edition, 2 vols. Crown 8vo. 3s. 6d.

Essays, Critical and Historical. Cabinet Edition, 2 vols. Crown 8vo. 12s. Cheap Edition, 2 vols. Cr. 8vo. 7s.

Biblical and Ecclesiastical Miracles. Cabinet Edition, Crown 8vo. 6s. Cheap Edition, Crown 8vo. 3s. 6d.

Present Position of Catholics in England. Crown 8vo. 7s. 6d.

Tracts. 1. Dissertatiunculæ. 2. On the Text of the Seven Epistles of St. Ignatius. 3. Doctrinal Causes of Arianism. 4. Apollinarianism. 5. St. Cyril's Formula. 6. Ordo de Tempore. 7. Douay Version of Scripture. Crown 8vo. 8s.

An Essay in Aid of a Grammar of **Assent.** Cabinet Edition, Crown 8vo. 7s. 6d. Cheap Edition, Crown 8vo. 3s. 6d.

Callista : a Tale of the Third Century. Cabinet Edition, Crown 8vo. 6s. Cheap Edition, Crown 8vo. 3s. 6d.

Loss and Gain: a Tale. Cabinet Edition, Crown 8vo. 6s. Cheap Edition, Crown 8vo. 3s. 6d.

The Dream of Gerontius. 16mo. 6d. sewed, 1s. cloth.

Verses on Various Occasions. Cabinet Edition, Crown 8vo. 6s. Cheap Edition, Crown 8vo. 3s. 6d.

*_*_ *For Cardinal Newman's other Works see Messrs.* Longmans *&* Co.'s *Catalogue of Theological Works.*

NORRIS (W. E.).—MRS. FENTON : a Sketch. Crown 8vo. 6s.

NORTON (Charles L.).—POLITICAL AMERICANISMS : a Glossary of Terms and Phrases Current in American Politics. Crown 8vo. 2s. 6d.

———— A HANDBOOK OF FLORIDA. 49 Maps and Plans. Fcp. 8vo. 5s.

NORTHCOTE (W. H.).—LATHES AND TURNING, Simple, Mechanical, and Ornamental. With 338 Illustrations. 8vo. 18s.

O'BRIEN (William.)—WHEN WE WERE BOYS : a Novel. Crown 8vo. 2s. 6d.

OLIPHANT (Mrs.).—MADAM. Crown 8vo. 1s. boards ; 1s. 6d. cloth.

———— IN TRUST. Crown 8vo. 1s. boards ; 1s. 6d. cloth.

———— LADY CAR : the Sequel of a Life. Crown 8vo. 2s. 6d.

OMAN (C. W. C.).—A HISTORY OF GREECE FROM THE EARLIEST TIMES TO THE MACEDONIAN CONQUEST. With Maps. Cr. 8vo. 4s. 6d.

O'REILLY (Mrs.).—HURSTLEIGH DENE : a Tale. Crown 8vo. 5s.

PAUL (Hermann).—PRINCIPLES OF THE HISTORY OF LANGUAGE. Translated by H. A. Strong. 8vo. 10s. 6d.

PAYN (James).—THE LUCK OF THE DARRELLS. Cr. 8vo. 1s. bds.; 1s. 6d. cl.

———— THICKER THAN WATER. Crown 8vo. 1s. boards ; 1s. 6d. cloth.

PERRING (Sir Philip).—HARD KNOTS IN SHAKESPEARE. 8vo. 7s. 6d.

———— THE 'WORKS AND DAYS' OF MOSES. Crown 8vo. 3s. 6d.

PHILLIPPS-WOLLEY (C.). —SNAP: a Legend of the Lone Mountain. With 13 Illustrations by H. G. Willink. Crown 8vo. 6s.

POLE (W.). —THE THEORY OF THE MODERN SCIENTIFIC GAME OF WHIST. Fcp. 8vo. 2s. 6d.

POLLOCK (W. H. and Lady). —THE SEAL OF FATE. Cr. 8vo. 6s.

POOLE (W. H. and Mrs.). —COOKERY FOR THE DIABETIC. Fcp. 8vo. 2s. 6d.

PRENDERGAST (John P.). —IRELAND, FROM THE RESTORATION TO THE REVOLUTION, 1660-1690. 8vo. 5s.

PROCTOR (R.A.). —Works by : —

Old and New Astronomy. 12 Parts, 2s. 6d. each. Supplementary Section, 1s. Complete in 1 vol. 4to. 30s. [In course of publication.

The Orbs Around Us. Crown 8vo. 5s.

Other Worlds than Ours. With 14 Illustrations. Crown 8vo. 5s.

The Moon. Crown 8vo. 5s.

Universe of Stars. 8vo. 10s. 6d.

Larger Star Atlas for the Library, in 12 Circular Maps, with Introduction and 2 Index Pages. Folio, 15s. or Maps only, 12s. 6d.

The Student's Atlas. In 12 Circular Maps. 8vo. 5s.

New Star Atlas. In 12 Circular Maps. Crown 8vo. 5s.

Light Science for Leisure Hours. 3 vols. Crown 8vo. 5s. each.

Chance and Luck. Crown 8vo. 2s. boards ; 2s. 6d. cloth.

Pleasant Ways in Science. Cr. 8vo. 5s.

How to Play Whist: with the Laws and Etiquette of Whist. Crown 8vo. 3s. 6d.

Home Whist: an Easy Guide to Correct Play. 16mo. 1s.

Studies of Venus-Transits. With 7 Diagrams and 10 Plates. 8vo. 5s.

The Stars in their Season. 12 Maps. Royal 8vo. 5s.

Star Primer. Showing the Starry Sky Week by Week, in 24 Hourly Maps. Crown 4to. 2s. 6d.

The Seasons Pictured in 48 Sun-Views of the Earth, and 24 Zodiacal Maps, &c. Demy 4to. 5s.

Strength and Happiness. With 9 Illustrations. Crown 8vo. 5s.

Strength: How to get Strong and keep Strong. Crown 8vo. 2s.

Rough Ways Made Smooth. Essays on Scientific Subjects. Crown 8vo. 5s.

Our Place among Infinities. Cr. 8vo. 5s.

The Expanse of Heaven. Cr. 8vo. 5s.

The Great Pyramid. Crown 8vo. 5s.

Myths and Marvels of Astronomy. Crown 8vo. 5s.

Nature Studies. By Grant Allen, A. Wilson, T. Foster, E. Clodd, and R. A. Proctor. Crown 8vo. 5s.

Leisure Readings. By E. Clodd, A. Wilson, T. Foster, A. C. Ranyard, and R. A. Proctor. Crown 8vo. 5s.

PRYCE (John). —THE ANCIENT BRITISH CHURCH : an Historical Essay. Crown 8vo. 6s.

RANSOME (Cyril). —THE RISE OF CONSTITUTIONAL GOVERNMENT IN ENGLAND: being a Series of Twenty Lectures. Crown 8vo. 6s.

RAWLINSON (Canon G.). —THE HISTORY OF PHŒNICIA. 8vo. 24s.

RENDLE (William) and NORMAN (Philip). —THE INNS OF OLD SOUTHWARK, and their Associations. With Illustrations. Royal 8vo. 28s.

RIBOT (Th.). —THE PSYCHOLOGY OF ATTENTION. Crown 8vo. 3s.

RICH (A.). —A DICTIONARY OF ROMAN AND GREEK ANTIQUITIES. With 2000 Woodcuts. Crown 8vo. 7s. 6d.

RICHARDSON (Dr. B. W.).—NATIONAL HEALTH. A Review of the Works of Sir Edwin Chadwick, K.C.B. Crown 4s. 6d.

RILEY (Athelstan).—ATHOS; or, The Mountain of the Monks. With Map and 29 Illustrations. 8vo. 21s.

ROBERTS (Alexander).—GREEK THE LANGUAGE OF CHRIST AND HIS APOSTLES. 8vo. 18s.

ROGET (John Lewis).—A HISTORY OF THE 'OLD WATER COLOUR' SOCIETY. 2 vols. Royal 8vo. 42s.

ROGET (Peter M.).—THESAURUS OF ENGLISH WORDS AND PHRASES. Crown 8vo. 10s. 6d.

RONALDS (Alfred).—THE FLY-FISHER'S ETYMOLOGY. With 20 Coloured Plates. 8vo. 14s.

ROSSETTI (Maria Francesca).—A SHADOW OF DANTE : being an Essay towards studying Himself, his World, and his Pilgrimage. Cr. 8vo. 10s. 6d.

RUSSELL.—A LIFE OF LORD JOHN RUSSELL. By SPENCER WALPOLE. 2 vols. 8vo. 36s. Cabinet Edition, 2 vols. Crown 8vo. 12s.

SEEBOHM (Frederick).— THE OXFORD REFORMERS — JOHN COLET, ERASMUS, AND THOMAS MORE. 8vo. 14s.

———— THE ENGLISH VILLAGE COMMUNITY Examined in its Relations to the Manorial and Tribal Systems, &c. 13 Maps and Plates. 8vo. 16s.

———— THE ERA OF THE PROTESTANT REVOLUTION. With Map. Fcp. 8vo. 2s. 6d.

SEWELL (Elizabeth M.).—STORIES AND TALES. Crown 8vo. 1s. 6d. each, cloth plain ; 2s. 6d. each, cloth extra, gilt edges :—

Amy Herbert.	Katharine Ashton.	Gertrude.
The Earl's Daughter.	Margaret Percival.	Ivors.
The Experience of Life.	Laneton Parsonage.	Home Life.
A Glimpse of the World.	Ursula.	After Life.
Cleve Hall.		

SHAKESPEARE.—BOWDLER'S FAMILY SHAKESPEARE. 1 vol. 8vo. With 36 Woodcuts. 14s., or in 6 vols. Fcp. 8vo. 21s.

——— OUTLINE OF THE LIFE OF SHAKESPEARE. By J. O. HALLIWELL-PHILLIPPS. 2 vols. Royal 8vo. £1 1s.

——— SHAKESPEARE'S TRUE LIFE. By JAMES WALTER. With 500 Illustrations. Imp. 8vo. 21s.

——— THE SHAKESPEARE BIRTHDAY BOOK. By MARY F. DUNBAR. 32mo. 1s. 6d. cloth. With Photographs, 32mo. 5s. Drawing-Room Edition, with Photographs, Fcp. 8vo. 10s. 6d.

SHORT (T. V.).—SKETCH OF THE HISTORY OF THE CHURCH OF ENGLAND to the Revolution of 1688. Crown 8vo. 7s. 6d.

SILVER LIBRARY, The.—Crown 8vo. price 3s. 6d. each volume.

She: A History of Adventure. By H. Rider Haggard. 32 Illustrations.

Allan Quatermain. By H. Rider Haggard. With 20 Illustrations.

Colonel Quaritch, V.C.: a Tale of Country Life. By H. Rider Haggard.

Cleopatra. By H. Rider Haggard. With 29 Full-page Illustrations.

Micah Clarke. A Tale of Monmouth's Rebellion. By A. Conan Doyle.

Petland Revisited. By the Rev. J. G. Wood. With 33 Illustrations.

Strange Dwellings: a Description of the Habitations of Animals. By the Rev. J. G. Wood. With 60 Illustrations.

Out of Doors. Original Articles on Practical Natural History. By the Rev. J. G. Wood. 11 Illustrations.

Familiar History of Birds. By Edward Stanley, D.D. 160 Illustrations.

Eight Years in Ceylon. By Sir S. W. Baker. With 6 Illustrations.

Rifle and Hound in Ceylon. By Sir S. W. Baker. With 6 Illustrations.

Story of Creation: a Plain Account of Evolution. By Edward Clodd. With 77 Illustrations.

Life of the Duke of Wellington. By the Rev. G. R. Gleig. With Portrait.

History of the Romans under the Empire. By the Very Rev. Charles Merivale. 8 vols.

Memoirs of Major-General Sir Henry Havelock. By J. Clark Marshman.

Short Studies on Great Subjects. By James A. Froude. 4 vols.

Cæsar: a Sketch. By James A. Froude.

Thomas Carlyle: a History of his Life. By J. A. Froude. 1795-1835. 2 vols. 1834-1881. 2 vols.

The Two Chiefs of Dunboy: an Irish Romance of the Last Century. By James A. Froude.

Visits to Remarkable Places. By William Howitt. 80 Illustrations.

Field and Hedgerow. Last Essays of Richard Jefferies. With Portrait.

The Story of My Heart: My Autobiography. By Richard Jefferies.

Apologia Pro Vita Sua. By Cardinal Newman.

Callista: a Tale of the Third Century. By Cardinal Newman.

Loss and Gain: a Tale. By Cardinal Newman.

Essays, Critical and Historical. By Cardinal Newman. 2 vols.

An Essay on the Development of Christian Doctrine. By Cardinal Newman.

The Arians of the Fourth Century. By Cardinal Newman.

Verses on Various Occasions. By Cardinal Newman.

Parochial and Plain Sermons. By Cardinal Newman. 8 vols.

Selection, adapted to the Seasons of the Ecclesiastical Year, from the 'Parochial and Plain Sermons'. By Cardinal Newman.

Certain Difficulties felt by Anglicans in Catholic Teaching Considered. By Cardinal Newman. 2 vols.

The Idea of a University defined and Illustrated. By Cardinal Newman.

Essays on Biblical and Ecclesiastical Miracles. By Cardinal Newman.

Discussions and Arguments on Various Subjects. By Cardinal Newman.

An Essay in Aid of a Grammar of Assent. By Cardinal Newman.

The Elements of Banking. By Henry D. Macleod.

A Voyage in the 'Sunbeam'. With 66 Illustrations. By Lady Brassey.

SMITH (R. Bosworth).—CARTHAGE AND THE CARTHAGINIANS. Maps, Plans, &c. Crown 8vo. 6s.

SOPHOCLES. Translated into English Verse. By ROBERT WHITELAW. Crown 8vo. 8s. 6d.

STANLEY (E.).—A FAMILIAR HISTORY OF BIRDS. With 160 Woodcuts. Crown 8vo. 3s. 6d.

STEEL (J. H.).—A TREATISE ON THE DISEASES OF THE DOG; being a Manual of Canine Pathology. 88 Illustrations. 8vo. 10s. 6d.

———— A TREATISE ON THE DISEASES OF THE OX; being a Manual of Bovine Pathology. 2 Plates and 117 Woodcuts. 8vo. 15s.

———— A TREATISE ON THE DISEASES OF THE SHEEP; being a Manual of Ovine Pathology. With Coloured Plate and 99 Woodcuts. 8vo. 12s.

STEPHEN (Sir James).— ESSAYS IN ECCLESIASTICAL BIOGRAPHY. Crown 8vo. 7s. 6d.

STEPHENS (H. Morse).—A HISTORY OF THE FRENCH REVOLUTION. 3 vols. 8vo. Vol. I. 18s. *Ready.* [*Vol. II. in the press.*

STEVENSON (Robt. Louis).—A CHILD'S GARDEN OF VERSES. Small Fcp. 8vo. 5s.

———— THE DYNAMITER. Fcp. 8vo. 1s. sewed, 1s. 6d. cloth.

———— STRANGE CASE OF DR. JEKYLL AND MR. HYDE. Fcp. 8vo. 1s. sewed, 1s. 6d. cloth.

STEVENSON (Robert Louis) and OSBOURNE (Lloyd).—THE WRONG BOX. Crown 8vo. 5s.

STOCK (St. George).—DEDUCTIVE LOGIC. Fcp. 8vo. 3s. 6d.

'STONEHENGE.'—THE DOG IN HEALTH AND DISEASE. With 84 Wood Engravings. Square Crown 8vo. 7s. 6d.

STRONG (Herbert A.), LOGEMAN (Willem S.) and WHEELER (B. I.).—INTRODUCTION TO THE STUDY OF THE HISTORY OF LANGUAGE. 8vo. 10s. 6d.

SUPERNATURAL RELIGION; an Inquiry into the Reality of Divine Revelation. 3 vols. 8vo. 36s.

REPLY (A) TO DR. LIGHTFOOT'S ESSAYS. By the Author of 'Supernatural Religion'. 8vo. 6s.

SYMES (J. E.).—PRELUDE TO MODERN HISTORY: being a Brief Sketch of the World's History from the Third to the Ninth Century. With 5 Maps. Crown 8vo. 2s. 6d.

TAYLOR (Colonel Meadows).—A STUDENT'S MANUAL OF THE HISTORY OF INDIA, from the Earliest Period to the Present Time. Crown 8vo. 7s. 6d.

THOMPSON (D. Greenleaf).—THE PROBLEM OF EVIL: an Introduction to the Practical Sciences. 8vo. 10s. 6d.

———— A SYSTEM OF PSYCHOLOGY. 2 vols. 8vo. 36s.

———— THE RELIGIOUS SENTIMENTS OF THE HUMAN MIND. 8vo. 7s. 6d.

———— SOCIAL PROGRESS : an Essay. 8vo. 7s. 6d.

———— THE PHILOSOPHY OF FICTION IN LITERATURE : an Essay. Crown 8vo. 6s.

THREE IN NORWAY. By Two of THEM. With a Map and 59 Illustrations. Crown 8vo. 2s. boards; 2s. 6d. cloth.

TOYNBEE (Arnold).—LECTURES ON THE INDUSTRIAL REVOLUTION OF THE 18th CENTURY IN ENGLAND. 8vo. 10s. 6d.

TREVELYAN (Sir G. O., Bart.).—THE LIFE AND LETTERS OF LORD MACAULAY.

Popular Edition. Crown 8vo. 2s. 6d. | Cabinet Edition, 2 vols. Cr. 8vo. 12s.
Student's Edition. Crown 8vo. 6s. | Library Edition, 2 vols. 8vo. 36s.

———— THE EARLY HISTORY OF CHARLES JAMES FOX. Library Edition, 8vo. 18s. Cabinet Edition, Crown 8vo. 6s.

TROLLOPE (Anthony).—THE WARDEN. Cr. 8vo. 1s. bds., 1s. 6d. cl.

—— BARCHESTER TOWERS. Crown 8vo. 1s. boards, 1s. 6d. cloth.

VIRGIL.— PUBLI VERGILI MARONIS BUCOLICA, GEORGICA, ÆNEIS; the Works of VIRGIL, Latin Text, with English Commentary and Index. By B. H. KENNEDY. Crown 8vo. 10s. 6d.

———— THE ÆNEID OF VIRGIL. Translated into English Verse. By John Conington. Crown 8vo. 6s.

———— THE POEMS OF VIRGIL. Translated into English Prose. By John Conington. Crown 8vo. 6s.

—— —— THE ECLOGUES AND GEORGICS OF VIRGIL. Translated from the Latin by J. W. Mackail. Printed on Dutch Hand-made Paper. 16mo. 5s.

WAKEMAN (H. O.) and HASSALL (A.).—ESSAYS INTRODUCTORY TO THE STUDY OF ENGLISH CONSTITUTIONAL HISTORY. By Resident Members of the University of Oxford. Edited by H. O. WAKEMAN and A. HASSALL. Crown 8vo. 6s.

WALKER (A. Campbell-).—THE CORRECT CARD; or, How to Play at Whist; a Whist Catechism. Fcp. 8vo. 2s. 6d.

WALPOLE (Spencer).—HISTORY OF ENGLAND FROM THE CONCLUSION OF THE GREAT WAR IN 1815 to 1858. Library Edition. 5 vols. 8vo. £4 10s. Cabinet Edition. 6 vols. Crown 8vo. 6s. each.

WELLINGTON.—LIFE OF THE DUKE OF WELLINGTON. By the Rev. G. R. GLEIG. Crown 8vo. 3s. 6d.

WELLS (David A.).—RECENT ECONOMIC CHANGES and their Effect on the Production and Distribution of Wealth and the Well-being of Society. Crown 8vo. 10s. 6d.

WENDT (Ernest Emil).—PAPERS ON MARITIME LEGISLATION, with a Translation of the German Mercantile Laws relating to Maritime Commerce. Royal 8vo. £1 11s. 6d.

WEYMAN (Stanley J.).—THE HOUSE OF THE WOLF: a Romance. Crown 8vo. 6s.

WHATELY (E. Jane).—ENGLISH SYNONYMS. Edited by Archbishop WHATELY. Fcp. 8vo. 3s.

———— LIFE AND CORRESPONDENCE OF ARCHBISHOP WHATELY. With Portrait. Crown 8vo. 10s. 6d.

WHATELY (Archbishop).—ELEMENTS OF LOGIC. Cr. 8vo. 4s. 6d.

—— —— ELEMENTS OF RHETORIC. Crown 8vo. 4s. 6d.

—— —— LESSONS ON REASONING. Fcp. 8vo. 1s. 6d.

—— —— BACON'S ESSAYS, with Annotations. 8vo. 10s. 6d.

WILCOCKS (J. C.).—THE SEA FISHERMAN. Comprising the Chief Methods of Hook and Line Fishing in the British and other Seas, and Remarks on Nets, Boats, and Boating. Profusely Illustrated. Crown 8vo. 6s.

WILLICH (Charles M.).—POPULAR TABLES for giving Information for ascertaining the value of Lifehold, Leasehold, and Church Property, the Public Funds, &c. Edited by H. BENCE JONES. Crown 8vo. 10s. 6d.

WILLOUGHBY (Captain Sir John C.).—EAST AFRICA AND ITS BIG GAME. The Narrative of a Sporting Trip from Zanzibar to the Borders of the Masai. Illustrated by G. D. Giles and Mrs. Gordon Hake. Royal 8vo. 21s.

WITT (Prof.)—Works by. Translated by Frances Younghusband

———— THE TROJAN WAR. Crown 8vo. 2s.

———— MYTHS OF HELLAS; or, Greek Tales. Crown 8vo. 3s. 6d.

———— THE WANDERINGS OF ULYSSES. Crown 8vo. 3s. 6d.

———— THE RETREAT OF THE TEN THOUSAND; being the Story of Xenophon's 'Anabasis'. With Illustrations.

WOLFF (Henry W.).—RAMBLES IN THE BLACK FOREST. Crown 8vo. 7s. 6d.

———— THE WATERING PLACES OF THE VOSGES. With Map. Crown 8vo. 4s. 6d.

WOOD (Rev. J. G.).—HOMES WITHOUT HANDS; a Description of the Habitations of Animals, classed according to the Principle of Construction. With 140 Illustrations. 8vo. 10s. 6d.

———— INSECTS AT HOME; a Popular Account of British Insects, their Structure, Habits, and Transformations. With 700 Illustrations. 8vo. 10s. 6d.

———— INSECTS ABROAD; a Popular Account of Foreign Insects, their Structure, Habits, and Transformations. With 600 Illustrations. 8vo. 10s. 6d.

———— BIBLE ANIMALS; a Description of every Living Creature mentioned in the Scriptures. With 112 Illustrations. 8vo. 10s. 6d.

———— STRANGE DWELLINGS; abridged from 'Homes without Hands'. With 60 Illustrations. Crown 8vo. 3s. 6d.

———— OUT OF DOORS; a Selection of Original Articles on Practical Natural History. With 11 Illustrations. Crown 8vo. 3s. 6d.

———— PETLAND REVISITED. With 33 Illustrations. Crown 8vo. 3s. 6d.

YOUATT (William).—THE HORSE. With numerous Woodcuts. 8vo. 7s. 6d.

———— THE DOG. With numerous Woodcuts. 8vo. 6s.

ZELLER (Dr. E.).—HISTORY OF ECLECTICISM IN GREEK PHILO-SOPHY. Translated by Sarah F. Alleyne. Crown 8vo. 10s. 6d.

———— THE STOICS, EPICUREANS, AND SCEPTICS. Translated by the Rev. O. J. Reichel. Crown 8vo. 15s.

———— SOCRATES AND THE SOCRATIC SCHOOLS. Translated by the Rev. O. J. Reichel. Crown 8vo. 10s. 6d.

———— PLATO AND THE OLDER ACADEMY. Translated by Sarah F. Alleyne and Alfred Goodwin. Crown 8vo. 18s.

———— THE PRE-SOCRATIC SCHOOLS; a History of Greek Philosophy from the Earliest Period to the time of Socrates. Translated by Sarah F. Alleyne. 2 vols. Crown 8vo. 30s.

———— OUTLINES OF THE HISTORY OF GREEK PHILOSOPHY. Translated by Sarah F. Alleyne and Evelyn Abbott. Crown 8vo. 10s. 6d.